I flick my safety off. "Vienne, I count five hostiles. Fire on my mark."

"Wait." She makes a slashing movement across her throat, countermanding my order. "Tight quarters, limited sight range, sensitive targets. We need to lure them in first."

"So which of us is bait?"

She points at me.

"Why am I always bait?"

"Because," she says, "the bad guys like shooting you."

I put a hand over my heart, acting wounded, then step into the aisle. "Howdy, boys and girls. We've been expecting you."

Invisible Sun

DAVID MACINNIS GILL

GREENWILLOW BOOKS

An Imprint of HarperCollins*Publishers*

Invisible Sun
Copyright © 2012 by David Macinnis Gill

The text of this book is set in 11-point Electra LH
Book design by Paul Zakris

Library of Congress Cataloging-in-Publication Data
Gill, David Macinnis
Invisible Sun / by David Macinnis Gill.
p. cm.
"Greenwillow Books."
Summary: Sixteen-year-old Durango and his lieutenant—and girlfriend—
continue their adventures as mercenaries on Mars.
ISBN 978-0-06-207332-7 (trade bdg.) — ISBN 978-0-06-207333-4 (pbk.)
[1. Mars (Planet)—Fiction. 2. Adventure and adventurers—Fiction.
3. Science fiction.] I. Title.
PZ7.G39854In 2012 [Fic]—dc22 2011002841

13 14 15 16 17 CG/RRDH 10 9 8 7 6 5 4 3 2 1
First paperback edition, 2013

 Greenwillow Books

For Julie, a real prince

"Only the dead have seen the end of war."
—Plato

"I love the lotus because while growing from mud,
it is unstained."
—Zhou Dunyi

CHAPTER Ø

Christchurch, Capital City
Zealand Perfecture
ANNOS MARTIS 238. 7. 16. 18:52

Vienne points the gun, squeezes the trigger, and fires a live round square into my chest. As my hand goes to my heart, the *pop-pop-pop* of a string of firecrackers erupts on the next alley, marking the beginning of the Spirit Festival—and covering the report from her armalite.

"Ow!" I catch the mangled bullet when it drops from my body armor. I toss the lead marble aside. It pings from rooftop to rooftop as it cascades to the bottom of the dawn-washed hillside. The sharp sound echoes off the corrugated metal shacks of Favela, the shantytown where we've been squatting the last week, plotting a snatch-and-grab on a high-value target at the local library. "Happy now?" I say.

"I had to prove my point." She grins as she collects her brass, then slides the armalite into a holster hidden by her trench coat. "No one's going to notice a gunshot during all the festival noise, so there's no reason to go unarmed again.

We'll be facing CorpCom troopers and Rangers this time, not some backwater constable."

"Okay, I get it." It's never a good idea to start an argument with your partner, especially when said partner is a highly trained Regulator who is one of the most lethal snipers on the planet. I massage the bullet burn away as another string of firecrackers rips off, followed by screams from our fellow squatters. "Did you have to do it from close range?"

"No." She takes my arm and leads me down the path muddied with raw sewage. The air is ripe with the stink of waste, burned gunpowder, and cordite. "But it was more fun that way."

The sun's just coming up, I think, and already, I'm getting shot.

"Suck it up, cowboy," says the little voice inside my head, a voice that belongs to Mimi, the artificial intelligence flash-cloned to my brain. Mimi controls all the functions of my symbiotic body armor. Omnipresent and omniannoying, she is like a mom, an encyclopedia, a drill sergeant, and a bad poet all mashed together. "From your neuromuscular response rate, I can tell that it did not hurt as much as you claim."

"Pain is more than the sum of its neurons, Mimi," I sub-vocalize so that only she can hear me.

"Only because you are incapable of simple mathematics," she says. "Take the next right. My map shows a shortcut through that alley."

"This way," I tell Vienne, and follow the route Mimi chooses.

We round the corner and come face-to-face with a pack of Scorpions—eight feral druggies, all about half our age. About half our size. About ten times as vicious and starved. Covered in piercings and homemade tattoos, stained with sewer mud, eyes pink from Rapture, they carry busted pipes and strips of corrugated metal.

The leader holds a butcher knife. The tang of the blade is wrapped with duct tape, the edge raw, rusted, and very lethal.

"What's the hurry?" the leader asks in Portuguese, sneering over ragged teeth.

"Step aside," Vienne warns him.

"Pay the toll," the leader says. "Or I'll gut you and have your vittles for breakfast." He waves the knife in a figure eight, and the others fan out to block the alley.

"How much for the toll?" I ask.

He licks his lips. "Her," he says, pointing the blade at Vienne.

"Okay." I shrug, then shake my head. "But remember, you asked for it."

Before a question has time to register on his face, Vienne separates the knife from his hand and then his shoulder from its socket. She sweeps his legs, and he hits the pavement, screaming, as three of his mates swing—and miss— with their pipes.

Vienne strips the first one of his weapon, nails the second with a side kick, and using the pipe, kneecaps the third. When the first boy tries to run, she pipe-pings him in the skull. Either the plumbing or the pavement puts his lights out—I'm not sure which—but when his rolling body comes to a halt, he's dead to the world.

Vienne drops into the Regulator fighting stance—left palm out, right fist above her ear. She motions for them to bring it.

"This is the point," I tell the boys, "when smart lads usually run."

But Scorpions aren't smart people.

"Kill them!" the leader screams.

One arm limp at his side, he lunges for the butcher knife. I stomp on the blade, and his hand just happens to get under my boot. He screams again until he sees the laser sight of my armalite shining in his eye.

"Might want to belay that last order," I say. "Now you all will be stepping aside, and we'll be going about our business. I mean no malice, but anybody holding a hunk of metal by the time I count three will be the proud owner of a third eyeball. One . . ."

Clang. Weapons hit the ground.

"Smart boys," I say. "And I bet your teachers said you'd never amount to anything."

Guns trained on the leader, Vienne and I move through the pack, then continue on our way, with an occasional precautionary look behind us.

"Crafty work back there," I say when we're in the clear.

"Now aren't you glad," she says, "that I suggested carrying our weapons?"

"You didn't need weapons to beat them."

"*I* didn't." She tugs her sunglasses down and gives me that look. "But *you* did."

As we wind our way through the hills of the Favela, Christchurch shines like a celestial mass of gas in the nadir of the morning horizon, a city of steeples built on an island in the delta where the River Gagarin meets the Dead Sea. The river is spanned by the Seven Bridges, which connect the suburbs to Christchurch, the biggest city on the planet.

It's also the only place I've ever called home.

We pass up three chances to grab the Tram because it's being patrolled by troops. Over the past few months, we've gotten used to walking. Plus there's the little matter of our faces being plastered on wanted posters all over the media multivids, which gives us more incentive to stay out of the public eye.

"Ready for this?" I whisper to Vienne.

"Locked and loaded," she replies, patting the holster under her coat.

"You're cute when you're carrying live ammo."

She nudges me with an elbow. "You're not so bad yourself. Even unarmed."

It takes an hour to reach Parliament Tower, the gleaming glass and steel headquarters of Zealand Corporation. As we travel, I mentally tick off the names of every alley, avenue, and boulevard, all of them familiar but somehow not quite right, as if the map of my memory has been wrinkled up and nothing is where it's supposed to be.

"Mimi," I subvocalize, "do a sweep of the perimeter and give—"

"Thought you would never ask," she says. "No hostiles detected in a thirty-meter radius. You are good to go."

"Roger." To Vienne I say, "If we bump into patrols, make sure we don't actually bump into them, right? Keep your head down. If you make eye contact, look away. Don't antagonize them."

Vienne feigns surprise. "Me? Why would I antagonize anyone?"

"Vienne," I warn her. "This is a covert mission, remember?"

"All our missions are covert," she says. "Until the bullets start flying."

"You!" a trooper shouts.

He draws a gun.

For a half step, I freeze.

Vienne smirks, as if to say *I told you so.*

But the trooper and his partner rush past us. They attack a street vendor. Slam him to the concrete sidewalk. Wares spill from his cart, and I can see what's written on the flags he's hawking: "Desperta Ferro!"—the slogan of the grass-roots anticorporate movement.

I take a step toward the fight.

"Keep walking, hero." Vienne takes me by the arm. "Don't borrow trouble, remember?"

We don't have to borrow it, I think. It always manages to find us.

"'Others, I am not the first,'" Mimi recites. "'Have willed more mischief than they durst.'"

"I carking hate Keats's poetry."

"It is Housman."

"His, too."

When we reach the Circus—the mammoth traffic circle in front of Parliament Tower—I step into the memories of my childhood. The buildings seem smaller, their glass skins less polished, their lights dimmer. Where I once had to shield my eyes from the reflections, I now barely have to squint. I'm taller than I used to be and harder to dazzle.

In the reflection of storefront windows, I see Vienne as the rest of the world does: A tall young susie. Blond hair plaited into a single braid. Dressed in a trench coat, black leggings, gloves, and high heels. And very, very dark sunglasses that let in almost no light because they hide a tiny minicam.

Now I see myself in the reflection: Young man, a couple of inches taller than the blonde. Clothed in a navy blue military dress uniform. Wearing a peacoat that covers the insignias of his rank and unit.

"You clean up nice," Mimi says.

My reflection sets down two satchels. "Stow it."

Vienne's reflection picks up one of the satchels and strides away to the tower. I pause to admire the poetry of her walk, then take the one she left behind and head for the library.

A block away, I stop on the street corner and wait for the crossing signal. "Use the telemetry functions in my symbiarmor," I subvocalize to Mimi, "and patch me into the security feeds."

"Done," Mimi says.

Pretending to adjust my sunglasses, I instead press an electrode hidden behind my ear. A video feed appears in the right lens of the glasses: carrying her satchel, Vienne enters the lobby of Parliament Tower.

All eyes turn to her as she enters the security line. She presses the mic tucked behind her ear. "I'm in."

"Check."

My turn.

I cut through traffic, avoiding a pedicab, and cross the street to the Bibliotheca Alexandrina. There's a library like this in each of the Nine Prefectures. Its purpose is to store corporate records and it is by law open to every citizen. But the real purpose of the library is hidden in its Special Collections area, which stores all manner of corporate trade secrets. This area is definitely not open to the public. Especially public who may be trying to steal said secrets.

Public like me.

Entering the library, I nod to the security guards at the door and approach the librarian at the main desk.

"Requesting access for Special Collections vault." I flash a smile. "Please."

The clerk tilts her chin and smiles back. "Fourth floor. But you'll need a security pass."

I slide a keycard across the desk—it cost us a Bishop's ransom on the black market—and hold my breath.

A green light. I'm in.

"Enjoy your research," she says. "The lifts are right behind me. Let me know if you need, you know, anything."

"Absolutely," I say as I leave the desk.

Mimi chimes in, "If Vienne saw you flirting with that susie, there would be gunfire."

"That's why I can see her video feed," I say, pressing the button for the fourth floor, "and she can't see mine."

As the doors close and the lift starts, the video feed flickers on the inside of my sunglasses. Vienne has reached the security scanner. She walks through, carrying the satchel.

Alarms ring.

Security gates drop.

The lobby goes on lockdown.

Three security guards rush toward her, blasters firing. The plasma shots burn through her coat but slide impotently to the floor. The look on their faces is priceless.

Surprise! She's wearing body armor, and you're in for a heap of trouble.

"You shouldn't have a laugh at others' misfortune," Mimi tells me.

"What? I'm only allowed to laugh at my own?" The doors of the lift open before the feed ends, but I'm not worried. We've pulled jobs far more dangerous than this. Vienne is a well-oiled fighting machine with fair dinkum *tai bo* skills.

"If Vienne heard you refer to her as well-oiled," Mimi says, "there would be even more gunfire."

"Roger that," I say. "Let's keep the 'well-oiled' between us."

I follow a long corridor to the door labeled "Special Collections." Inside, I hand the keycard to the clerk, whose nametag reads "Mr. Gilbert." He cocks an eyebrow over his horn-rimmed glasses. He's old, his jowls flaky and wrinkled like onionskin paper, and his stare is so radioactive it could shred chromosomes.

"It's rude to wear sunglasses inside," Mr. Gilbert says. "Your generation has no manners." Though I try smiling again, he meets me with a blank face and scans the card. *Buzz.* "No access," he says in a tone that actually means "Go stuff yourself."

"Run it again," I say, co-opting an air of command that sounds more like my father than me.

An alarm sounds.

My heart skips a beat.

Guards rush past the Collections room toward the stairs. "What's that all about?" I say, passing off my gasp as a cough.

"None of my concern," Mr. Gilbert says. "Nor yours." He notices the pinkie missing from my left hand, then throws the card back at me. "Access denied, *dalit*. Leave the premises, or I'll be forced to call security."

"Go right ahead." I smile, and this time, I mean it. "You'd be wasting your breath." I move my coat aside to show him my holster. "There's a certain server I want to check out, if you don't mind."

On the video feed, Vienne drops the trench coat, revealing her symbiarmor, and pulls her armalite. She sprays the ceiling lights with bullets. Broken glass rains down, and most of the sentries scatter. Two brave but stupid guards rush her. She takes down the first one with an elbow that breaks his nose. She slams the second one with the satchel and when he doubles over, grabs a handful of his hair.

"Do precisely what I tell you," she says, her voice crackling in my earpiece as the lift opens. She shoves him inside, then pushes the satchel against his chest. "Hold this."

The guard's voice quavers. "W-what is it?"

"Five kilos of C-forty-two explosives."

"A . . . b-bomb?"

"Not to worry," she says. "It won't go off—yet."

Carking-A, I think.

My attention shifts from the feed back to Mr. Gilbert, who is escorting me into the vault, which houses a massive server farm. We turn left down a row marked "High Security." He slow-walks me for a few seconds until I remind him that I'm carrying an armalite—by shoving it into his kidney.

"Stop here," I say when we reach server 451. "On the floor."

Gilbert drops, and I wrap his wrists and ankles with duct tape. I insert a chip into the data port.

"Download commencing," Mimi's voice pings in my ear.

"Thank you, Mimi. Let me see what Vienne's up to now."

"Affirmative," she says. "Maybe she has found a nice Ranger to flirt with."

"Or to shoot."

My attention returns to the feed as the lift door opens to a penthouse, where a special session of the board of directors is in progress. While Vienne swiftly, silently moves into position, the directors raise champagne glasses to toast the new CEO, a middle-aged matron with wispy red hair and patches of freckles.

Her name is Martha Bragg, and she is Vienne's target.

Bragg is about to speak when she abruptly cuts a look at the young man to her right. The jack also has freckles, but his hair is straw colored. He is rail thin and rawboned, and even sitting down, taller than anyone else in the room.

"Sit up straight, Archie!" She glares at him until he looks suitably chastised, then gratified, she makes a toast. "As the chief executive officer and general of Zealand Corporation, I raise—what the dickens is going on?"

She is interrupted by a gunshot. All heads turn to Vienne and the trooper with the satchel clutched to his chest.

"Why, you impudent hussy!" Bragg cries out. "Security!"

"You're wasting your breath," Vienne says calmly. "Trooper, tell the CEO what you're holding."

"A b-bomb," he says.

"Is this," Bragg sputters, "a joke?"

"Does it look like I have a sense of humor?" Vienne empties a clip into the windows behind the CEO. The safety glass cracks along countless fault lines, then showers the floor with harmless shards. "Everybody down! Now!"

For a half second the young jack leers at Vienne, until she fires a burst past his head. Then he joins his mother and the board of directors sucking up carpet lint.

Behind Vienne, the penthouse lift opens. Troopers pour out like hungry cockroaches, only to be met with a rain of bullets that turns the drop-down ceiling to dust. While they scramble for position, Vienne tosses a smoke grenade, then hops onto the ledge of the shattered window.

"Thanks for your cooperation," she says.

And steps into empty space.

I remove the sunglasses, then pull the data chip—I've got what I came for—and walk away from Mr. Gilbert, who is wriggling like a fluke worm on the floor.

I stroll by the librarian like I own the joint, because at one point, my family actually did own it. Once upon a time, I spent many hours at that desk, haranguing my father's employees into doing my homework.

I exit the Special Collections office and take the lift to the first floor. In the lobby, more shouting guards rush past me and into the street.

"Sir?" the librarian calls.

Verflucht, I curse. What did I screw up this time? "Yes?"

"The specs. You took them off," she says. "I like the change. It's a shame to cover up such pretty eyes."

"Thank you." I muster another wink. Behind her, a multivid screen is displaying a celebration: Squatters in Favela are cavorting around a straw man being burned in effigy. It's definitely not your traditional Spirit Festival dance. "What's all the ruckus?"

"Haven't you heard?" she says. "Stringfellow died in prison last night. Cancer finally killed the old poxer."

By Stringfellow, she means John Stringfellow, disgraced former CEO of Zealand Corporation. He's spent the last years of his life rotting in the Norilsk Gulag. How am I aware of this? Because I know him not as Stringfellow but as Father. I also know that he didn't die in prison last night. It was a month ago. CEO Bragg held on to the news until today, so as to coincide with the Spirit Festival. I reckon manipulating the media goes hand in hand with being CEO.

"You really hadn't heard," she says, mildly shocked. "What planet have you been on?"

The sunglasses go back on. "Mars."

I step outside. Look up at the thirteenth floor of Parliament Tower and see the blown-out glass and smoke billowing out of it.

"Excellent," I say to Mimi. "Couldn't have done it better myself."

"You are delusional," Mimi says. "Being terrified of any

height over three meters, you could not have done it at all."

"Everybody's a critic."

"I prefer the term *dialectical of genius* to *critic*."

"Most critics do," I say. A crowd gathers, and I get washed away in the flood of humanity. "Got a read on Vienne's bio-rhythms? The zone's about to get hot."

"She's two meters out and closing on your six," Mimi says. "So, by the way, is a squad of troopers."

"Roger that."

Slipping away from the Circus, I stay out of the way of the soldiers, who are swinging truncheons and ramming through the mob, trying to provoke a reaction. It's their not too subtle way of flushing out Desperta Ferro insurgents.

A few moments later Vienne, now wearing a different hat and coat, takes my arm. "Got the data, chief?" she asks me.

"Right here." I pat the pocket of my peacoat. "And no more of that 'chief' stuff, right? Call me Durango."

"Yes, chief," she says, and laughs, a sound so rare that it catches me off guard.

It also attracts the kind of attention we don't want. I get a glimpse of a pair of Rangers eyeballing us, the leader clicking his jaw muscles and rolling his shoulders, ready to pounce at any hint of resistance.

Kuso! I tuck my chin inside my collar and look down as if the cracks in the pavement are the most interesting thing ever, an act of subservience I learned while enduring my Battle School instructors' endless acid-tongued lectures.

Vienne, though, doesn't know the meaning of subservient. She meets the lead Ranger's eyes and gives him that hard steel stare that betrays her iron will.

He veers toward her.

Vienne reaches for her armalite.

I reach for a handful of her coat.

Too late.

"Halt!" the lead Ranger shouts, and they both shove the crowd aside, bearing down on us, battle rifles ready.

"Move it!" I yell to Vienne.

After a frustrated growl, she cinches the belt on her trench coat and slips away.

Crack!

A warning shot fires.

The chase is on.

CHAPTER 1

North of Noctis Labyrinthus, Tharsis
Plain
Zealand Prefecture
ANNOS MARTIS 238. 7. 18. 12:52

Picture a wide-open plain as broad and flat as the open
sea, interrupted by only the occasional stone outcropping.
Beneath one of the outcroppings—a green, rolling field split
by a narrow dirt road. A warm zephyr blows the tall grass, gently, softly. A swarm of bees rises from the grass, gathers itself
into a tight knot, then disappears behind a hill, right before—

Roar!

Over the outcropping we come!

Riding a three-wheeled bike that's two parts motorcycle
and one part rocket. Trying to outrun a Noriker armored
truck that's hot on our six, caked in mud and dirt, its red and
blue lights flashing, a warning that we'd better stop if we
know what's best for us.

Ha! Vienne and I are *dalit* Regulators, mercenary soldiers
who do dirty, dangerous jobs for very little pay. We never
know what's best for us.

"The Rangers are back!" I yell into Vienne's helmet, shouting above the roar of the engine as she leans over the handlebars.

"What did you expect?" Her visor is flipped down, but behind it, she's beaming as battle rifle shots zip by. "That's what you get for stealing top-secret military data!"

"It's your fault they chased us in the first place!"

"My fault?" she calls back. "You're the one who said to move it! If you'd let me take them out in the Circus—"

"Then there'd be a hundred Rangers, not just two!" Two Rangers who'd tailed us all the way from Christchurch. Twice, we thought we'd ditched them, but they kept picking up our trail. Nothing motivates a Ranger like a runner with a bounty on his head.

A forty-five-caliber bullet whistles past my ear. It hits the handlebars of our motorbike and shatters into a million tiny pieces.

"We're taking fire! Again!" I shout, my face streaked with sweat, teeth chattering from the choppy road. "You should let me drive! You're the better shot!"

"I'm the better driver, too!"

Vienne punches the gas, and the engine finds an over-drive I didn't know existed. We rocket along the hard-packed dirt, almost leaving my stomach behind. For a second the bike seems to float—all three wheels rising above the ground—and my queasy stomach rises with them. Then I make the horrible mistake of looking to my left, where the narrow trail takes us to the thinnest cusp of the canyon.

A kilometer below, a green valley full of wheat and corn stretches out as far as the eye can see.

I'm going to hurl.

"Vienne! We're going to crash into the canyon!"

She laughs. "Suck it up, Durango!"

The world turns swirly, and my head lolls to one side. Vertigo—it's my biggest weakness. I wish I could bury my face in Vienne's back, squeeze my eyes tight, and pretend that we're not doing 120 kilometers per hour, only centimeters from certain, horrifying, mangling death. But I'm lousy at pretending, and Vienne wouldn't take kindly to the head-burying idea.

Instead, I turn to the right and face the horizon. The Labyrinth of the Night stretches out like broken fingers across the Plains of Tharsis, forming canyons so deep and wide, they make Earth's Grand Canyon look like a drainage ditch. Beyond the vista, the mountains of Tharsis rise like triplet mortar shells from the plains. In turn, they are overshadowed by the snow-capped monster of Olympus Mons, the largest mountain in the solar system. It's so mammoth, Earthers can see it with a handheld telescope.

That's what they tell me, anyway. I wouldn't know first-hand. I've never been to Earth, and the Hell's Cross mines will see daylight before I ever go.

"Oh, that's quite a bit of poetry for somebody being shot at," says Mimi. "Perhaps you should extricate yourself from Vienne's admittedly impressive midriff and return fire."

"I'll pass," I subvocalize.

"You will pass?" Mimi says. "Have you forgotten that you are a Regulator? Regulators are required by the Tenets to shoot back. It is a time-honored tradition and an excellent means of survival."

"Yeah, see, I'm not so big on the Tenets anymore," I say. "Plus, their bullets can't penetrate our symbiarmor, which means they can shoot all day, and it won't amount to a hill of beans." I check on the Noriker, which is weaving around a rut in the road. "I'm a lot more afraid of crashing to a burning death at the bottom of this canyon than I am of a couple of CorpCom Rangers."

"Your penchant for stating the obvious is remarkable," Mimi says.

"Thank you."

"That was not meant as a compliment, cowboy."

"Knew that—ow!" A rifle round pops me between the shoulder blades, and I flinch. "That one stung!"

"Explosive ammunition," Mimi says. "May I suggest, oh, returning fire?"

"This is a waste of ammo, you know." I pull my armalite from its holster. Flick the switch to full auto and spray a clip of bullets at the Noriker.

Headlamps shatter.

The windshield cracks, and lines spread across the glass, blocking the Rangers' view. The driver doesn't even swerve.

The Noriker eats up more trail.

Getting closer.

"They're gaining!" I say to no one. And no one answers, which is surprising because Mimi always has something smart to say.

"Not always," she says. "Sometimes, silence is the wisest response."

Crash! A Ranger's boot appears through the Noriker's windshield. The passenger kicks out the rest of the damaged safety glass, and I can see plainly the sunburst insignia on his uniform—Second Cavalry. My father's old division. It would've been mine, too, if not for a string of unfortunate decisions on Father's part, as well as my complete lack of interest in following in his deep footsteps.

"The irony is thick today," Mimi says. "So is the manure."

I start to remind her of the wisdom of silence, as useless as that would be, when the barrel of a rocket launcher appears on the Noriker's dashboard.

My armor is the most technologically advanced suit on the planet, controlled by a network of nanobots that in turn are commanded by my overly conversant AI. But no symbi-armor ever made can stop a rocket.

Like the rocket that explodes from its launcher with a puff of smoke and comes slithering toward us like a pissed-off scorpion.

"Evasive!"

Vienne jerks the bike hard to her nine. The front wheel catches the lip of a rock slab, and we swing so close to the precipice of the canyon, dislodged rocks and debris fall over the edge. Where they go—

—down, down, down—

—with nothing to stop them.

"*Re malaka*," I murmur.

Five meters ahead of us, the rocket explodes.

"Chief!" Vienne shouts. "Get them off my tail!"

The sound of her voice, and the wild swing she makes to three o'clock, rocks me back to reality.

There's nothing left to do but shoot. "I hate when this happens!"

I let go of Vienne's waist and climb atop the seat, then engage the grenade launcher attachment on my armalite and reach for my ammo belt.

One grenade left.

One lousy grenade.

"*Ja vitut!*"

"Waste not, want not," Mimi says.

"Thank you, George Washington."

"Ahem. *Poor Richard's Almanack?*"

"Thank you, Poor Richard," I say. "What kind of fossiker would name their son 'Poor'?"

"Benjamin Franklin wrote *Poor Richard's Almanack!*" Mimi yells in my ears. "How does a Battle School graduate who was tops in his class not know the basic literary canon of his forefathers?"

I jam the shell into the chamber. "I'm a soldier, not a hopeless Romantic."

"No, you're just hopeless."

"Har, har." I pull the gas-powered trigger to launch my last grenade.

The shell tumbles through the air and lands with a clack on the hood of the Noriker. For a nanosecond it hangs there, suspended by wind and gravity, before it rolls forward and out of sight.

The driver points and laughs at me.

I make a hand gesture that calls his parentals' marital status into doubt as my grenade, which has lodged in the grill, explodes.

Debris blows back into the Noriker cab. As the driver throws up an arm to shield his eyes, the truck hood—unlatched by the explosion—rises up like a metal sail. It flaps in the wind for a second or two, then breaks at the hinges and hammers the empty windshield.

Wham!

The Noriker veers off the trail, a cloud of butterscotch-hued grime encasing it.

"Heewack!" I yell. "That'll fix the fossikers for shooting at us! Right, Vienne? Right?"

She doesn't answer, which is weird because as stoic as she pretends to be, Vienne loves a good shoot-out. So I turn around in time to see—

A narrow bridge.

A hundred meters off and closing fast.

Marked by a bright red sign—DANGER: BRIDGE OUT.

"Danger! Bridge out!" I scream. "Vienne! Stop! The *wà kào* bridge is out!"

"I can read!"

"Then stop! I order you to stop!"

"You're not giving the orders anymore!"

"No! I take it back! We're not equals! I'm your chief again, and I order you to halt!"

"If I halt now," she calls, "those Rangers will stay on our tail! Let's get rid of them once and for all!"

"And us, too!" I scream. "What part of 'danger' don't you—ieeee!"

Our front wheel hits the lip of the entryway. I bounce back into the seat and squeeze my legs against the growling engine, the pipes so hot they would burn my flesh if not for the symbiarmor.

The bike eats up meter after meter of the bridge. Chunks of pavement fly from the road, flinging themselves into the chasm, and fall, fall, fall into the valley below.

"Why does everything need to fall so far?" I groan.

"Do I need to look up the word *chicken* in my thesaurus data bank?" Mimi chimes in. "Again?"

"No!" I say. "Because I'm not chicken! I'm just not stupid!"

"Acceptance," Mimi says, "is the first step to recovery."

Ahead, a ramp appears out of nowhere, and I'm wondering how a ramp got there when I realize that no, it's not a ramp; it's a fallen piece of sheet metal that's part of a barricade. A barricade that's also marked DANGER. And beyond the DANGER, there's a hole. A big, carking gap that separates one side of the bridge from the other.

"Vienne! There's a huge, carking gap—"

"Lean back!"

That's the last thing I want to do. I'd rather wrestle the handlebars from her grip. And avoid all areas marked by words written in capital letters. But it's too late for that. All I can do is think about what my former chief said when I was still a green Regulator: It's not that heroes don't know fear, it's that they don't let fear stop them from doing the job.

"I love it when you quote me," Mimi says.

I grab Vienne's shoulders. Plant both feet on the seat like a snowboarder coming down Tharsis Mons. And hang on for dear life as the bike—

Slams against the ramp.

Sails across the gap.

Lands hard on the other side, with enough force to vault me over Vienne. I roll along the bridge's metal decking and *slam!*

Into a concrete barricade.

My armor seizes up to protect me. But for a few seconds, I'm frozen like a statue, my visor flipped up, eyes filled with road grit.

Tires squeal as Vienne slams on the brakes, the front wheel

sliding,

sliding,

sliding toward my head.

"Mimi! Armor!"

"Negative. System is overloaded, cowboy," she says. "Rebooting now."

I try to raise a hand to shield my face but can't budge. I squeeze my eyes shut and mentally brace for the collision . . .

. . . that never comes.

Something lightly touches my forehead. I take a peek. It's the tire. Tendrils of smoke drift from the rubber, and tiny bits of gravel are wedged between the treads.

"The word *danger*, " I tell Vienne, "is not French for *go faster.*"

She jumps from the bike and throws her arms around my statuelike body. "Yes! Wasn't that fun? It was just like flying! I always wanted to fly!"

"Next time you do," I say, sighing, "use a velocicopter instead of a motorbike, okay?"

Mimi chimes in. "System ready. In two."

The symbiarmor relaxes, and I fall into a heap. I pull off my helmet and gasp, swallowing something that rises from my gut. Then collapse spread-eagled on the decking.

Why is it that I can order a whole crew of Regulators into battle against enemy soldiers, bioengineered insects the size of elephants, and even bloodthirsty cannibals, but I almost wet myself every time I'm more than ten meters above the ground? No matter how many times I face my fear of heights, the acrophobia never goes away. In fact, I'm starting to think it's only getting worse.

"It is only getting worse," Mimi says. "Data from your cerebral cortex reports an unprecedented level of cortosteroids in your bloodstream."

My eyes roll back as relief washes over me. "Thank you for that disheartening report, Madame Curie."

"I aim to please, cowboy."

Vienne kneels beside me. "Are you hurt? I didn't mean to throw you off the bike." She laughs. "I thought you had better balance than that."

"And I thought you had more sense than that," I say. "You. You are going. To get us killed."

"Poor baby," she says, patting my cheek. "Your symbiarmor took the hit. Not a scratch on you. Well, maybe one. On your cheek. Right. There. Want me to fix it?"

She brushes my face with the back of her hand. Then leans in for what I hope is a kiss. I lift myself on an elbow, waiting for her, watching her lips purse, her eyes close halfway, then—

Honk! A truck horn sounds.

She jerks away and stands, aiming her armalite at the Noriker as the Rangers pull slowly up to the barricade on the opposite side of the bridge.

"Jacob Stringfellow!" The gunner climbs out the shattered window and stands on the hood. "You're under arrest for trespassing, capital theft, and destruction of corporate property! Surrender! Or I'll blow you both to hell and drag your carcasses all the way back to Christchurch!"

"Ow! That's harsh," I say. "Whatever happened to 'Put down your guns'?"

"I can take the gunner out." Vienne pulls her weapon. "Just say the word."

"Whoa." I block her line of sight. "Let's discuss this and come to a rational decision."

Giving me a glare that would melt titanium, she drops the armalite on my shoulder, using it as a gun rest. "A Ranger is threatening to defile your corpse, and you want to be rational?"

"Let me try mediation first." I carefully move the armalite aside and turn around. "Ranger! My friend wants to shoot you. Personally, I'd rather negotiate. What do you say?"

The gunner jumps into the bed of the truck. He throws aside a heavy tarp, revealing a Seneca gun. It's the same type of chain gun our old Regulator buddy, Jenkins, liked so much. Only it's bigger.

And fires faster.

With five times more ammo.

"Negotiate this!" A wild spray of bullets rips through the pavement, tearing up a line of divots.

Chunks of asphalt ricochet off my helmet.

"That's a little close for comfort."

Vienne squeezes off four quick shots—one to scare the driver and three to chase the gunner off the gun. "Since you won't let me actually shoot them," she says, "I see no point in standing around."

"But—"

She holsters her armalite, then hops on the motorbike. "Going my way?"

"What way would that be?" I slide onto the seat. "Seriously, we're in no-man's-land out here. No food. No shelter. Very little coin to speak of."

She steers around debris, even as the gunner, cursing, sends a wild volley into the steel framework above the bridge. "You want to go to Tharsis Two and steal the rest of your data, right?"

"Of course," I say, "but we're not ready to hit the outpost yet. We still need to scout the area, plan the job—"

"Then this is your lucky day," she says. "Because I know the perfect place to hide out while you do all that scheming and plotting." There's a little glint in her eye that scares me. "Hang on tight. We're going to meet my family."

"Fam—?" I realize now that I was right to be scared. "Did you say 'family'?"

"Unless you'd rather stay here and get shot at."

"Maybe," I say to tease her and because, well, it's true. I didn't even know Vienne had a family, much less one within driving distance.

"When you meet Ma and Pop," Mimi chimes in, "make sure you do not mention the phrase 'well-oiled.'"

"Oy," I say, after trying to think of a smart retort. My brain, however, is no longer connected to my tongue.

Mimi has a laugh at my expense. "You're so cute when you're paralyzed with fear."

"You're so not cute when you're trying to be funny."

"I am not programmed for humor."

"And I'm not programmed to meet the parents."

We're almost clear of the road debris when the Ranger makes a last-gasp effort to stop us. "Halt!" the Ranger screams. "I said, you are under arrest!"

A Hail Mary of bullets chases us. Several rounds hit the metal decking and one bounces off my shoulder, stinging my skin but not causing any damage.

I turn back, lift my visor, and blow them a kiss.

Poor Rangers. I really do feel sorry for the jacks. They chased us hundreds of kilometers for a bounty, and now they're going home empty handed, having to explain to their superiors why they're AWOL. Personally, I'd rather be shot than face that punishment.

When we reach a clear stretch, Vienne hits the throttle, and the speed needle surges to a hundred kilometers per hour. The road rises to a hill. Beyond the hill, the ground levels out again, and I see a massive cloud bank, black and angry, floating above the valleys.

The air crackles with energy, and I smell ozone on the

wind. It's a weird sensation to watch a storm from above, to see lightning dance through the clouds, chains of yellow sparks that snap the air. It's an even weirder sensation when the road suddenly veers toward a narrow gap in the rock formations, and we plunge headlong into the tempest.

CHAPTER 2

The Favela
Zealand Prefecture
ANNOS MARTIS 238. 7. 18. 12:53

Archibald flicks open the lid of the butane lighter and strikes the flint. A spark jumps onto his sleeve. It leaves a pinhole burn in the threadbare jumpsuit he acquired at the poor shop. Just walking into Favela is an assault on his senses and an affront to his dignity, but he realizes that in order to acquire what one desires in life, certain concessions must be made. Although wearing the uniform of a common sewer worker makes him feel tawdry, it's a small sacrifice to make, and there is the added bonus of being allowed to wield a heavy spanner wrench in public. Imagine the outrage if he carried one of these behemoths into the boardroom. The look on Mother's face!

He strikes the lighter—*flick!*

Down a long hill he walks, a handkerchief pressed against his face, more to filter the stench than to hide his features. Above him on a building assembled from random pipes, corrugated metal, and fiberglass, a pink-eyed boy shouts into a megaphone in Portuguese, waving a burnt-out plasma pistol for effect. Other ferals dot the rooftops of other similarly constructed buildings. All of them are armed, and all of them are snarling in Portuguese. Although he doesn't speak the language, Archibald understands their harsh tone. They are warning troublemakers of the fate that befalls them if they stray into the wrong territory. By troublemakers, of course, they mean CorpCom police, and by territory, they mean the areas controlled by Mr. Lyme and his Sturmnacht thugs, which in essence is the whole of Favela.

Flick!

Archibald reaches an alley marked by graffiti, instead of a road sign. He pauses to make sure that a highly stylized symbol of a scorpion is present on the wall, then takes a left turn. He passes a row of flop rooms built from discarded shipping containers and guarded by squatters carrying stolen blasters. At the end of the flop row, he follows a set of makeshift stairs that leads to a worn path under a highway overpass fifty meters above. Heavy Noriker trucks make characteristic *thump-thump* noises as they pass over the neglected ghetto below.

Favela was not always neglected, of course. The slum originated as a social program designed to build housing for Christchurch's poorest citizens. The program fell by the wayside at the start of the CorpCom wars, and soon the poor began building their own homes using any scraps they could steal. As any social scientist knows, when a population of poor reaches critical mass, crime follows as surely as night follows day. And where there is crime, there is Mr. Lyme, ready to bring on the night.

Flick!

Archibald checks another graffiti scorpion and chooses the far right of three tubes protected by chain-link gates. The circular tunnel is two meters high, and he has to duck to prevent his hair from scraping the thick mold growing on the ceiling. The floor is slick with sludge carried in by storm water runoff, muck that seeps over the tops of Archibald's shoes, and he finds himself wishing that he had bought a pair of used boots as well.

Halfway down the tunnel, he breaks a flare in half so that the two ends are sparking in his hands. For a moment he remembers last year's Spirit Festival, when he had the honor of lighting the fireworks display for the closing ceremony. Too bad the fire got a tad out of hand.

A vault door opens to his right. He ducks through, avoiding the lip of the opening, which keeps the sludge from oozing inside. The door is slammed shut by a guard named Duke, who throws a bolt to lock it.

A row of footlights turns on. He shields his eyes while squinting at a shadowed figure behind a desk.

"Archibald, wipe your feet and put the lighter away."

He cleans his shoes as instructed on a heavy mat on what he now notices is a metal floor. The vault is not so much a room as a bunker. "Lyme?"

"Mr. Lyme."

"Of course," Archibald says. "Please forgive my rudeness, sir."

"Consider it forgotten. Despite my reputation, I am not a man who carries grudges." He clears his throat. "Forgive my precautions. I value my privacy above all else. Tell me, did all go as expected at the board of directors meeting?"

Archibald stoops to keep his head from banging on the low ceiling. He realizes that it gives the impression that he's bowing slightly, an impression that he doesn't like. Keeping me in my place, Lyme? he thinks. Let's see how long I'm willing to stay there. "My mother was appointed CEO and general of the Zealand Army, yes. But since she was already interim CEO, I don't see how a formality changes anything."

Lyme pops a lozenge into his mouth. "Leave it to me to decide how things change. In the meantime, did your mother announce her intention to suppress the insurgent uprisings in the southern territories?"

"She tried to," Archibald says. "But there was a bit of a nuisance at the meeting. A terrorist interrupted the board meeting with a bomb. Well, she claimed that it was a bomb, yet it turned out to be a satchel full of Desperta Ferro anti-government propaganda."

"What," Lyme says, sounding amused, "did this so-called terrorist look like?"

She was beautiful, Archie thinks, like an angel wrapped in a full-metal jacket. "Tall and blond. She burst into the penthouse and threatened us. But then security arrived, and she jumped from the window."

"From thirteen stories?" Lyme scoffs.

His tone makes Archibald squirm. "It is assumed she fell to her death."

"Assumed?"

"Her body has, ah, not been recovered."

"Of course not." Lyme nods knowingly. "This young woman, what type of weapon was she carrying?"

"I don't know guns. It was smallish? Automatic? She certainly was skilled with it."

"I see." Lyme taps his fingers on the desk. "During this attack, were you aware of any other unusual events?"

"No, Mr. Lyme. Not at all . . ." His voice trails away. "Well, yes. There was an incident at the Bibliotheca Alexandrina. A *dalit* forced his way into the Special Collections room and stole some data."

Lyme seems to catch his breath. "What sort of data?"

So, you can be taken by surprise, Archibald thinks. "I haven't heard. I've spent quite a bit of time in the Collection archives myself, and there is little more there than old corporate records. Minutes of board meetings, earning reports, troop movements and the like. Nothing of any value, I'm sure."

"You have a young man's confidence," Lyme says. "I hope it's well-founded. In the interim, I'm assigning you to Tharsis Two."

"But isn't it deserted?"

"Only by Zealand Corp," Lyme says. "Which thinks it is a useless piece of property. However, it is of vital interest to us, and it requires the kind of attention that only your unique set of skills can provide. We have plans, Archibald, the scale of which is unprecedented in the history of this planet."

He unfurls a sheet of electrostat, showing a route marked along the Tharsis Plain, from Christchurch in the north to the Noctis Labyrinthus in the south.

"This is where we will crush them," he says, tapping on the star labeled "Tharsis Two." "My operation has built a military force stronger than any CorpCom army, and the time is ripe for a hostile takeover of Zealand Corporation. Its board is choked with corrupt bureaucracy. Its military is aging and suffers from low morale. Its citizens have endured year after year of famine, which has led to the nascent Desperta movement—a movement that we can exploit. In other words, Zealand is low-hanging fruit, and I intend to pick it."

Lyme's words were pure venom, but wrapped up inside that poison was a kernel of logic. Since the Bishop's death, Mars had endured one poor government after another, and the net effect was that the average citizen couldn't depend on his government. The Mars Constitution promises life, liberty, and equality, but there was less food, less safety, even less air to breathe. Maybe a strong leader could make some changes, but the truth is, under the Bishop, Mars came as close to thriving as it had ever done.

"My mother says that the citizens are not a threat," Archie says. "She has a solution to the resistance movements."

"Your mother," Lyme says with a dismissive wave that both insults and excites Archie, "is a useless bureaucrat. Did you see the agitated crowds in the Circus today? Could you feel the pulse of their anger?" Lyme pounds the desk with his fist. "There is revolution in the air, and all we need is a spark to ignite it. You must be that spark!"

"Yes, sir!" Archibald says, snapping a salute.

Lyme traces a route on the map. "Your task is to march my Sturmnacht army north on the Bishop's Highway, burning everything from the Labyrinth to Christchurch. Leave nothing untouched."

He rolls up the electrostat and hands it to Archibald. The guard, Duke, swings the vault door open. The meeting is over.

As soon as Archibald steps over the lip of the vault, the door slams behind him. He flicks the lighter, and this time, an incandescent flame erupts. Yes, he thinks as he sloshes back through the tunnel, Lyme is power-hungry and has delusions of grandeur, but this trip was most definitely worth my while.

CHAPTER 3

Tengue Monastery, Noctis Labyrinthus
Zealand Prefecture
ANNOS MARTIS 238. 7. 18. 16:45

Hours after the last of the Ranger's bullets hit my armor, Vienne and I are still riding through a thunderstorm into the canyons. The road is twisted up in knots and is so slippery from the downpour, the tires can lose their grip at any second, a fact that I remind Vienne of when we're about halfway down, rain hitting us sideways in sheets, wind gusts threatening to slam the motorbike against the rock wall of the canyon.

"I've got this!" she yells over the howling. "Stop worrying!"

It's my job to worry. About the weather. About the road. About Vienne's mysterious family. I even worry about a silver aerofoil flying low through the clouds, its wide, thin wings cutting through the darkness, the crazy aviator's head barely visible in the cockpit.

"*Au contraire*, cowboy," Mimi pipes in, "it's your job to trust, and as usual, your performance is underwhelming. May I suggest a few breathing exercises to focus your chi?"

"May I suggest you bugger off?"

"Of course you may," she says. "Not that it will accomplish anything."

"Just give me a reading on this storm," I say. "What's the duration?"

"Did you not just ask for a reading two minutes ago? Did I not just tell you that Noctis Labyrinthus is a particularly unique biosphere and its weather systems are highly unpredictable?"

"Tell me again, what's the duration?"

"Indeterminate."

"Arg! Mimi, you make me carking *batwŏ kào* crazy!"

"Your mental stability or lack thereof bears no causal correlation to my presence."

"Which means?"

"You were carking *batwŏkào* crazy before I got here." She pauses, which means she's processing new data gathered by the telemetry functions in my suit. "Good news. Barometric data suggests that the storm is dissipating, for now."

Right on cue, we round a bend and the clouds break. The green valley is only a hundred meters below us, and I can see farm tracts and clusters of Quonset huts. In the distance, there's a larger settlement marked by silos and processing machinery.

"Hallelujah," I say aloud.

Vienne hears me. "Almost home," she says with a disconcerting lilt to her voice. She takes the next hairpin turn without braking, balancing the bike on her kneecap.

"Where exactly is home?" I say.

"You'll see."

"Tease."

"Whiney butt."

This time, I decide not to protest. Just close my eyes and try to go with it. "Okay," I tell Mimi. "Let's get some work done."

I tap my temple and wince at the tingling sensation. An aural screen pops up in front of my right eye, which is actually a bionic prosthesis wired to my optic nerve. I lost the real one fighting a Big Daddy, a bioengineered insect that looks like a mix between a crab and a tick. Other than the eye, I lost some skin on my face, leaving a thick purple scar that runs from my temple and down my neck. "Mimi, begin boot protocols on my mark. I need a little information about the situation we're riding into."

"Your artificial intelligence tour guide reporting for duty, sir!" Mimi says. "Pardon me for not waving, but I seem to be experiencing a shortage of appendages."

"Ha-ha. Very funny. When you're done cracking bad jokes, give me a long-range reading and fill me in on our location, which I'm assuming is our destination, if Vienne is telling the truth."

"Vienne always tells the truth," she says. "Unlike some people I know."

"Ahem. Readings, please?"

"This area is called Noctis Labyrinthus, Canyons of the Night," she says, finally getting down to business. "It was formed from ancient lava flows and settled by the second wave of Martian settlers, including the renowned Tengu monks, beekeepers who immigrated to Mars to escape persecution on Earth. Once home to massive indoor farmlands that were superseded by the Pure Air farms, communal farms established by the Bishop's Orthocracy—"

"Yawn. Enough with the history lecture, before I go into a coma and fall off this bike."

"Everyone is a critic," Mimi says.

"I prefer *dictator of genius.*"

"That's *dialectical of genius.*"

"Whatever. As long as you acknowledge my genius." Looking at the three-dimensional map rendering in the aural screen, I ask, "How about that long-range sweep?"

"As you can see on your screen, nothing but farm collectives for several kilometers."

"Read anything dangerous?"

"Define 'dangerous.'"

"Anything that shoots, bites, or stings."

"In that case, you should look up."

I crane back my neck. Above us, a massive swarm of bees funnels through the dark clouds, looking like a thunderhead all by itself. The swarm sweeps down into the valley, roiling above a cluster of Quonset huts.

"Cowboy," Mimi says. "I am picking up strange frequencies from those creatures."

"They're bees, Mimi. They make lots of buzzing noises."

"I am well-versed in species' classification, thank you very much," she says. "However, their biorhythmic frequency is stored in my data banks, which means you must have encountered their, ahem, buzzing noises before."

"Where?"

"Indeterminate."

"You know what?" I say. "When I'm dead and my ashes are scattered to the winds, I'm going to have *indeterminate* carved into my cenotaph."

"I will make sure they spell it right."

With one last turn, the road levels out. I can see that it stretches straight ahead for several kilometers, and beside it is the bright, saffron yellow arch of a Tengu monastery.

"The bees are following us," I say aloud, still wary of the cloud that looms overhead.

"More like we're following them." Vienne lays off the accelerator, and the motorbike begins to coast. "We're going to the same place, after all."

"This is where your family lives?"

"Affirmative," Vienne says.

"But this is a monastery." Then the truth finally dawns on me. "That's means you were raised by monks? That means you . . . were a monk? You never told me that!"

Vienne hits the brakes. "You never asked."

I jump from the seat. Flip my visor up. Wipe the water from my armor and the mud from my face. "Solid ground! Thank the stars."

"You're such a baby," she says.

I look at Vienne. "That's the last time I let you drive."

"Who says you let me drive? More like, I let you ride with me." Vienne kills the engine and flips up her visor. I start to argue but instead catch a gnat in my mouth. While I'm gagging, Vienne takes a long look at the monastery.

"Home," she says.

Like all monasteries, this one is surrounded by a high wall. Its arch is freshly painted, as is the matching yellow gate, a pair of wooden doors at least five meters high and a half meter thick. Streamers decorated with words of prayers hang from the arch, decorations for the Spirit Festival.

"The Tengu prefer the more accurate term, Bon Festival," Mimi says.

"You say 'Bon,' I say 'Spirit.' Same difference."

"The Tengu would argue that," she says. "They are very traditional. Unlike the unbridled bacchanalia of the non-sectarian Spirit Festival, the Bon Festival is two weeks of nightly dances and prayers, ending with *Tōrō Nagashi*, the floating of the lanterns downriver to symbolize the return of spirits to the afterlife. Did I tell you that the temple of Tharsis is home to one of the oldest of its kind, and thus one of the longest-surviving structures on the planet?"

"Boring!" I say, still gagging on the bug. "Next you'll be

telling me that Mars's orbital year is roughly twice that of Earth's, while its day is almost exactly the same."

"Exactly? Try 24 hours, 39 minutes, and 35.244 seconds. You break my heart, cowboy," she says, then gets back on topic. "Listen to this: the monastery is unusually large for its kind. It was built in *anno martis* 59 by immigrants from Earth's failed Asian Republics who designed it based on the principles of Tengu, an antecedent mix of Buddhism, Taoism, Shintoism, and a dash or two of animism thrown in. Built into the side of a canyon, the monastery is comprised of several terraces accessed via one of a dozen footbridges found on the grounds."

"More and more," I say, sighing, "I regret ever hacking those servers. Who knew so much useless crap was stored on them?"

"A little education is a dangerous thing," Mimi says.

"That's okay," I say, scraping the bug off my tongue. "I like to live dangerously."

I set my helmet on the seat and pull back the cowl covering my head. The air is warm, and the wind feels good on my face. Vienne does the same, and I watch the light in her hair as she shakes out the cobwebs. There's literally a spring to her step as she bounces down the path. Hard to believe this is the same Regulator who collects bullets the way other susies collect jewelry.

"Vienne's been keeping secrets about her past," I say to Mimi. "I don't like it."

"It's her past. It's not for you to like."

"We've spent a lot of time traveling together the last six months," I say. "She could've mentioned, y'know, in passing, that she was raised by monks."

"You could have told her that you have the consciousness of another woman flash-cloned to your brain," Mimi says, "but I notice that detail sort of, y'know, slipped your mind."

"Message received and noted."

"So since you admit you're no angel, either," Mimi says, still ragging on me, "suck in that lip, Mr. Pouty Mouth."

"I'm not pouting."

"Oh?" she says. "There is another reason your bottom lip looks like it lost a fight with a crowbar?"

"One day," I subvocalize as I join Vienne, "I'm going to hack into an embassy mainframe and download some diplomacy lessons for you."

"Get some lessons on coping with whiney butts, too, please," Mimi says. "I need to expand my repertoire."

Vienne leads me across the footbridge, where the shadow of the arch blocks out the sun. She bows low, and a hidden door in the gate opens.

A small girl appears in the space. Wearing a golden-embroidered white tunic that covers loose-fitting trousers with wide, embroidered cuffs, she has a pixie face, spiky pink hair, and the smirk of an imp. It's not exactly a look I was expecting from a Tengu monk.

With a squeak, she slams the door. "Master! Mistress!"

I hear her yell. "Ghannouj was right! She's come home for Bon! Hurry! Hurry!"

Standing at Vienne's side, I block the sunlight from my eyes, trying to figure out just what is happening. It feels like I've interrupted a dance mid-song and am out of step with my partner. "The little monk knows you, I take it."

"Oh yes! That's Riki-Tiki. She knows me very well." She stops to consider her words, then meets my eyes without a hint of their usual hesitation. It's as if something is blossoming within her, even as she speaks. "She's an age six now, but I've known her since she was a baby."

Since she was a baby. The words take me aback. Maybe it's the way Vienne looks at me when she says them, or maybe it's a twang of jealousy that someone has a deeper connection with Vienne than I do.

A ragged silence passes between us, the only sound a warm wind that stirs the water plants growing in the moat that encircles the walls of the monastery. For what is essentially a wide ditch, the moat is unexpectedly beautiful, full of water lilies and lotus blossoms, along with cattails, arrowheads, and green bog mint.

"So, Riki-Tiki?" I finally say. "She knew you were coming?"

"I'm sure Ghannouj told her." She shrugs, as if to say *of course*. "Ghannouj knows everything."

"Ah, Ghannouj, whose name you've never uttered in my presence before," I say. It occurs to me that she hasn't mentioned a mother or father. Brothers or sisters, either. If she grew up with the monks, that probably means she was orphaned, and the Tengu are maybe the only family she's known. That would explain so much, like her devotion to the Tenets, her belief in Valhalla, her unflinching dedication to her chief.

"And when am I going to meet this Ghannouj I've been hearing so—totally nothing about?" I rest my hand slightly on her forearm. Though public affection is not something Vienne approves of, I want her to know I'm with her all the way.

"Ghannouj will show himself soon enough," she says. "You'll have to get through the Master and Mistress first. They can be sort of . . ."

"Difficult?"

"Cranky pants." She gives me a peck on the cheek. "But you've fought assassins, cannibals, and a murderous ex-girlfriend, so I expect you can handle them."

But I'm not so sure. Cranky old people bring out the worst in me. My armor can't deflect their constant criticism. Plus, you're not allowed to shoot them.

"Now you sound like Vienne," Mimi says.

The hidden door flies open, and Riki-Tiki skips across the gravel path. "Vienne!"

As we turn, Riki-Tiki leaps into Vienne's arms, wraps legs and arms around her chest, and smothers her with kisses. The force of the attack knocks Vienne into me, and

I stumble backward, do a flip over the motorbike, and land butt first on the grass.

"Ack! I swallowed another bug."

"Which won't kill you," Mimi says.

"Might be a poisonous bug."

"It was a gnat."

"A poisonous gnat."

"Which is pure protein," Mimi says. "*Bon appétit!*"

Her limbs still around Vienne, Riki-Tiki finally notices me. She cocks her head, curious. "Why're you talking to yourself? Do you do that often? Ghannouj sings to himself. His voice is quite lovely. You should hear him serenade the carp. They swim better when he sings. The flowers, too, except they don't swim. Why're you still sitting on the ground? Is your butt sore? Do you need a hand?"

"I'm fine."

Riki-Tiki darts over. She grabs my arm and yanks. Just like that, I'm on my feet. She's stronger than she looks. Faster, too.

"Uh. I was. Uh. Admiring the grass," I say. "We haven't seen much grass the last few months. Just dirt. Lots of dirt."

"You're funny!" Riki-Tiki springs back to Vienne. "I'm Vienne's little sister. Not biological sister, of course, soul sister. My parentals were murdered when I was a baby. Mistress and Master took me in. They took all of us in. Oh. You are supposed to meet them. I am to bring you inside and get you presentable for the *Bon-Chakai* tea ceremony. That means a hot bath, and phew, do you ever need one." She pauses to catch her breath. "Do you like to dance?"

The idea of a bath sounds great to me, though I'm not all that interested in dancing. That's when it finally dawns on me—if they knew we were coming, then I'm not just meeting Vienne's family. This is a Tengu version of meet the boyfriend.

I've been set up!

"A little slow on the uptake," Mimi says. "Are we not?"

"If I didn't know any better," I subvocalize, "I'd swear you two were conspiring against me." I catch Vienne's attention and say, "Stop smirking; you had this planned all along."

"Me? Plan? Never," Vienne says, a hand to her chest in mock surprise. "I never smirk, either."

"That looks like a smirk to me." So I ask Mimi, "She's smirking, isn't she?"

"Yes, cowboy, but you will have to forgive her. She is just happy to be home."

Home. The word gives me pause, and for a second, my breath catches in my chest. What would it be like to have a home where someone loves you? This is the happiest I've ever seen Vienne, and I know pulling her away from here will be harder than I ever imagined.

Vienne hooks my arm. "Come on, you can handle meeting the mistress and master. They don't bite."

"Sure they do! They have dentures!" Riki-Tiki giggles, then begins chanting. "Vienne's got a boyfriend. La la la la la. Wait!" Then she stops abruptly and twitches her nose, sizing me up. "What's your name, boyfriend?"

"Erm, Durango?" I say.

"Ha! That's a funny name!" she shouts. "Vienne and Durango sitting in a tree. K-i-s-s-i-n-g. First comes love, then · comes mar— Wait! I forgot to wash your feet! Stand right here. Do not move!"

"Wash your feet?" I ask, noticing that Vienne's blushing. My face feels a little flushed, too.

"It's the Tengu way." Vienne begins removing her boots. "This will only take a minute, but I can't talk during the ceremony."

A ceremonial footbath? Now I can see where Vienne got her love of rituals. I find a rock to sit on as Vienne waits, barefoot, her toes grayed by road dust. "Mimi, perform standard security sweeps."

"All biorhythmic signatures or just human?" Mimi asks.

"After what we've been through?" I examine my own dirty boots. "You have to ask?"

"Check. Scanning for everything." After a few seconds, she says, "I read six distinct signature forms. Four human. One bee. And one for—this can't be right."

"One for what? Don't tell me it's more chiggers." Over the past few months, there have been many sightings of large, scary insects of unknown origin, but I know exactly what they are—the chigoe, aka chiggers, an indigenous species that we unintentionally released into the wild.

"It's not the chigoe," Mimi says. "Cowboy, you're not going to believe this. They have . . . a dog."

"Impossible," I argue. "Dogs are extinct. The pox eradicated them decades ago."

Riki-Tiki reappears. She's carrying a clay bowl, a jug, and a towel in one hand and a stool in the other. Vienne sits as she places the bowl on the ground and fills it with water.

"I know a dog when I see one," Mimi says.

"You can't see," I say. "You've got no eyes."

"How many times need I remind you, cowboy—your eyes are my eyes. Your ears are my ears."

"My nose is your nose."

"Only the olfactory senses. The boogers all belong to you."

"Gee, thanks, I— Wait!" I spot the dog. It's lying on its side beside an ornamental bush. Panting. Eyes half shut. Gnats buzz around its eyes. "I hope it's just sleeping. Hold up, Mimi, did you say there are four humans nearby?"

"I wondered when you would notice that little detail," she says. "Sensors indicate an unknown human biorhythmic signature three meters to your left."

Casually, I search the shrubs, and deep in the shadows, I spot the shape of a male. "He's watching us."

"My," Mimi says, "aren't you the observant one?"

While I track the shadow, Vienne slips her feet into the bowl of water.

"Welcome, friend," Riki-Tiki says.

Vienne bows. "I rejoice in meeting you once more."

Riki-Tiki kneels to dry Vienne's feet, then bursts into giggles, which shake her head so hard, the pink spikes bounce like the spines of a sewer urchin.

"Is that," I say, shocked, "nail polish?"

Vienne makes fists with her toes, trying to hide them in the towel.

"Too late!" I dash over to Vienne, scooting next to her. I try to pull aside the towel, but she pushes me off the stool. I reach for it again, and it turns into a tug-of-war.

The sound of a shrill whistle interrupts us. "Riki-Tiki!" comes a high-pitched voice inside the gate. "Time to prepare the bath!"

"*Kuso*," Riki-Tiki says. Gathering the stool and other stuff, she slumps away. "Mistress never lets me have any fun."

After Riki-Tiki disappears from view, Vienne quickly pulls on her boots. "Not another word about the polish."

"Me? Never. Not one peep about your painted piggies." I look down at my own dusty boots. "Hey, nobody offered to wash my feet."

"It's a symbolic thing," she says. "Only for other Tengu. I hope you don't feel slighted."

"Nope. I understand. It's all copacetic. The last thing I want is a monk washing my feet." I nod toward the dog that Mimi spotted. It's still lying beside the bush. "Did you see that?"

Vienne stands behind me. "Yes, I saw. It belongs to the monks."

"If they own it, why don't they help?"

She gives my shoulder a pat that's meant to reassure me, but it has the opposite effect. "Because they don't own it in the sense that you use the word. And because, judging from its labored breathing, it's dying."

"At least they could make it more comfortable."

"That is not the Tengu way. The Tenets . . . I mean, the monks. They believe that . . ." She stops talking for a moment, and her hand slips from my shoulder. I feel her body tense up. "It's too complicated to explain right now. I'm going inside." She walks away from me. "Coming?"

"Not yet." My attention returns to the dog. "Go on. I'll catch up."

Once Vienne is inside, I have Mimi do a scan on the animal. She finds nothing physically wrong with it, at least nothing that she's programmed to detect, she reminds me. "I'm not a veterinarian any more than I'm a physician."

The gnats return. It's pointless, but I keep chasing them off, and the dog growls at me every time. "They can waste water washing feet, but nothing to drink for the dog, huh?"

"That's not what Vienne meant, cowboy."

"Yes, Mimi, I know. That's why I didn't say it to her. But don't you ever get tired of people using their beliefs to justify their actions? So the dog is dying. What's wrong with making its last hours a little more comfortable?"

Feeding the dog is a waste of rations, I know. As a crew leader, it goes against my training to throw food down a black hole. One last meal won't help the dog. But it won't hurt me, either.

I pull the canteen from my belt, pour water into my hand, and offer it to the dog, which turns its face away.

Snap! The sound of a stick breaking. The stranger is announcing his presence. "You're wasting water."

I glance up as the stranger steps out of the shadows, moving fluidly in tattered robes. He has stubbly sun-bleached hair and his bottom lip, nose, and eyebrows are pierced, and he wears wide gauges in his ears. His neck is tattooed with red and gold Tengu, Hindu, and Buddhist symbols surrounded by Sanskrit characters that stretch across his back and down both biceps. Ball bearing shapes have been implanted along the length of his forearms.

Reflexively, I reach for my armalite.

He yawns, revealing a large stud in his tongue. "Did I frighten you?"

"Negative," I say, leaving the weapon in its holster. "I knew you were there all along."

"You never saw me." His voice is deeper than mine, ragged, like he swallows cinders on a regular basis.

"I never said I *saw* you." As he slips closer, I hear an angry buzzing sound coming from the pouch on his belt. "Mimi?" I ask. "Are those bees in that pouch?"

"The sound frequency is similar to a bee, but I'm not picking up a distinct biorhythm from them. Odd."

"You know, indeterminate I can take, but I get the heebies

when you say 'odd.' What does 'odd' mean, precisely?"

"Indeterminate."

"Mimi! *Vittujen kevät ja kyrpien takatalvi!*"

The man stops when he casts a shadow over the dog. "You did not answer my question. Why waste water on a dying animal?"

"First, you didn't ask me why. You just said it was a waste. Second, it seems cruel to me to let her lie here dying without doing something."

"What something should be done?"

When I look up to respond, I can't see his face, just a ring of light around his head like an eclipse. "Anything. No one should suffer."

"'What dwelling shall receive me?'" he recites. "'In what vale/Shall be my harbor? underneath what grove/Shall I take up my home? and what clear stream/Shall with its murmur lull me into rest?'"

"Southey?" I ask.

"Wordsworth," he says.

It figures. He looks like a Wordsworth kind of jack. I give the dog one last pat then stand. "Yeah, well, I carking hate poetry."

"It is cruel to leave an animal to suffer," he says, nonchalantly absorbing my fiercest stare. "The kindest thing would be to put a bullet in its head."

"Not my idea of kindness, friend."

He walks around me and takes a seat on my rock. "I am

not," he says, his dry lip twitching, "your friend."

"You're not going inside?" I ask, thinking of how much I'd really like to slap the smug look off his face.

He looks into the vista of the canyon, like he can see something the rest of us can't. "I am called Stain. I do not enter the monastery."

"You look like a monk to me."

He crosses his legs and closes his eyes for prayer. "I am sure that many things you perceive to be true are not." With no warning, he grabs my wrist and twists it so that the stub of my pinkie finger is clearly displayed. He spits out the word, "*Dalit*."

I yank my hand free. "What of it?"

"*You* are the chief she served for so long? A dishonored coward? Explain how she could follow a *dalit*."

"I've got nothing to explain to you." I start to leave. "I don't even know who the *b`lyad`* you are."

Stain blocks my path. "You do not deserve her," he says, his voice a deep rasp.

"No kidding." I step aside.

He steps with me. "Better she should die than become *dalit*."

What it this, a waltz? "Easy for you to say, sitting under a tree and hiding in the shadows. Now get out of my way."

For a moment Stain stares ahead, emotionless. Then he moves slightly, and I push past him.

"What an ass," I say.

"Nice bone structure, great abs, and he has exquisite taste in literature," Mimi says. "I like him."

"You would." I reach for the door, only to be surprised by the sudden appearance of Vienne's face. "Whoa! Hey! You scared me."

"Sorry," she says. "I was just seeing what's taking so long." She pulls me inside but sticks her head around the gate. She stares long and hard at Stain, then says quietly, "As if the hide in plain sight trick could fool me. I saw him from a kilometer away."

Ah, I think, take that, metal mouth.

Inside, Vienne and I walk together, our boots crushing the pebbles on the path that's lined with banyan trees. It leads to a large yellow-and-orange-painted building that must be the main hall.

"This Stain person," I say, as Vienne loops her arm through mine. "Why all the body modifications?"

"That's what everyone asks." She shrugs. "He says the pain helps focus his chi."

"So, what's he to you?"

She pinches her bottom lip, the excited light dimming on her face. "Stain is . . . It's complicated."

Is everything here complicated? Even though I bite my tongue and don't ask again, the shadow that passes over her expression tells me it is. Another thing it tells me is that Stain and Vienne have a history, and the jealousy monster rears its ugly head again.

"He said he doesn't enter the monastery, but he sure looks like a monk to me."

"Stain was once one of the Tengu." She stops walking. "But things . . . changed. He was banished for desecrating the temple."

"How do you desecrate a temple?"

"He took the life of another human being." She shakes her head, the sun lighting her face so that it's brighter—and more conflicted—than I've ever seen it. "Don't let Stain bother you," she says finally, forcing a glassy smile. "It's the abbot you've got to worry about."

CHAPTER 4

Outpost Tharsis Two
Zealand Prefecture
ANNOS MARTIS 238. 7. 18. 17:16

No other buildings are within ten kilometers of Tharsis Two, Archibald discovers as Duke chauffeurs him to the outpost in a heavily armored Noriker, except for a few ghost town filling stations. The outpost stands alone, a patch of stained concrete in a sea of red and orange rock formations, like a lone incisor on the mandible of a sun-bleached skull. When the wind blows down from the upper plains, a smell like a marsh comes with it, but it's just the sulfur from the old salt mines playing a trick of the mind.

As his Noriker passes under the arched entrance, three Sturmnacht patrol a catwalk bolted to the arch. They carry blaster rifles said to be powerful enough to knock a fist-sized hole in a man's belly. Archibald has never seen a blaster do such a thing. He would like to.

There are four gate shacks and four lift gates. Each concrete guardhouse is roofed with terra-cotta tiles imprinted with the nebula symbol of the House of Merovech, the

Orthocrat family in power when Tharsis Two was built. Inside the shack are a table, a metal chair, and two multivid screens for monitoring the security feeds.

As Archibald reaches the lift gate, a Sturmnacht steps out of a guard shack. She is carrying a handheld scanner of sorts, which she aims at the side of Archibald's neck. "State your business."

Archibald sticks a plasma pistol in her face. "Frankly, my business is none of yours. Raise the gate."

The guard doesn't blink. "I repeat: State your business."

On the catwalk above the gatehouses, the three Sturmnacht aim their blasters at the Noriker.

Archibald looks into the sights of the guns. "My name is Archibald. I am your new commander."

"We'll see about that." The guard thumbs the mic on the radio clipped to her shirt. "Control, I have an unauthorized intruder claiming to be someone named Archibald. Identify and confirm."

Control responds. "Retinal scan confirms his identification. Let him pass."

"Will do." The guard raises the gate. "Welcome to Tharsis Two."

Archibald shakes his plasma pistol at her. "What makes you think I still won't shoot you?"

"Honor among thieves?" the guard replies.

"I am not a thief, and I am bearing a weapon capable of burning a hole through the concrete upon which you rest your ample buttocks." Archibald sniffs the air. "The next time I arrive at this station, raise the gate quickly, or you'll come to understand how little I care about honor."

"Yes sir!"

"That's more like it."

A few minutes later, he strides into Control, the nerve center of the outpost. From here, a crew of technicians monitors all base activity via a network of video feeds and an observation window that overlooks the main parade area. The grounds are filled with a rag tag motor fleet of stolen Norikers and Düsseldorfs.

Archibald counts six Sturmnacht in Control, two females and four males. None of them gives him more than a passing glance. He hands his fur-lined cloak to a Sturmnacht, then claps his hands for everyone's attention. When there is no response, he produces an electric prod and sticks it against the neck of the man holding his cloak.

"Now that I have your attention," he says after the man stops screaming. "I believe in discipline. That is why Mr. Lyme has sent me here, to impose discipline over this base of operations. Don't let my young face deceive you. My heart is as old and cold as the core of Mars. My first rule: Do as I say when I say. My second rule: Do not argue with rule number one. Clear?"

They are too slow to respond, so he zaps the man again.

"Now you must understand," he says after taking a second to inhale the smell of charred flesh. "I do not enjoy bringing any of you pain. I much prefer a positive, caring, collegial atmosphere to an adversarial one. However, I also believe in motivation. Don't you feel more motivated now?"

"Yes!" they all shout.

He twirls the prod. "That's 'Yes, Mr. Archibald.'"

"Yes, Mr. Archibald."

"Music to my ears, boys and girls. Mr. Lyme has given all of us a goal. He would like, and by would like, I mean he demands, that this base be battle ready in twenty-four hours."

One of the women groans, and he sticks the prod against her forehead.

"If I wanted to hear guttural noises, I would have asked for them, understand?"

"Yes, Mr. Archibald!"

"Let me give you a history lesson, miss." He keeps the prod pressed against her skull. "In the Earth year 1864, the President of the United States was winning a civil war, but he wanted to hurry things along. His enemy was on its last legs, but it was fighting a defensive battle in its own territory. So he sent one of his weakest generals, William Tecumseh Sherman, on a campaign of terror. The objective was to scorch the Earth from the heartland to the coast, laying everything in his path to waste. By the gods, he did, and it broke the enemy's spirit. I intend to do the same to our enemy, with your help." He pulls out his lighter. "And the help of my little friend."

"I'm a speck confused," one of the men says. "Which enemy is it we're talking about here?"

"The Zealand CorpCom, you imbecile!" He points at the ugliest of the Sturmnacht, a heavy man with a large knot on his forehead. "What's your name?"

"Franks."

"Franks what?"

"Just Franks, Mr. Archibald."

"I like the look of your face, Franks. It reminds me of a pet goat I once ate." He waves the prod. "Tell me, have you much experience with fire?"

"You mean with stomping them out?"

Archibald sucks his teeth. "No, Franks, I mean with starting them. But I'm getting ahead of myself." He sits at the control panel and props his feet on the multivid screens. "Now, which of you thugs would like to fetch my tea?"

CHAPTER 5

Tengu Monastery, Noctis Labyrinthus
Zealand Prefecture
ANNOS MARTIS 238. 7. 18. 17:29

Things start out okay—Vienne and I meet Riki-Tiki at the
end of the entry path, and she leads us to the temple. We
sit on the steps leading to the temple's sliding doors, where
we start removing our footwear. I am pulling off my second boot when I look up to find an ancient woman dressed
in coarse brown robes, holding a large rice paddle like
a club.

"Hello?" I say.

She growls at me.

Barefoot, Vienne bows. "Mistress Shoei."

Still holding my boot, I stand on one leg, try to bow
gracefully, and fail. "Glad to meet you. I'm—"

"Yadokai! Hurry up!" The mistress steps aside for an
older man carrying a bowl of rice. He is dressed in the same
style of robes. Both of them have short-cropped black hair
and deep laugh lines.

Yadokai is smiling.

Shoei is not.

I wish I'd stayed outside with the dog.

"Mistress and Master," Vienne says, "this is Durango, my ch—my friend and fellow Regulator. Durango, please meet Mistress Shoei and Master Yadokai, sensei of the Tengu Monastery of Tharsis, and their acolyte, Riki-Tiki."

"A pleasure to make your acquaintance," I say, remembering my faltering diplomatic skills.

Solemnly and slowly, Vienne bows to the master and chants, "One eye. All I need to see."

"One hand," he replies. "All I need to work."

"One heart," she finishes the phrase. "All I need to live."

One eye. One hand. One heart. The Regulator's vow, a promise to the rest of your crew that you'll sacrifice life and limb to protect the davos. I must have said it a million times, but I've never heard it chanted like this.

"Welcome home!" Shoei embraces her like a long-lost child.

Not to be left out, Yadokai pulls hard at Shoei's shoulder. "Hey, hey, no. Enough of that. You are a Tengu monk, woman. Show some restraint."

"Show some restraint yourself," Shoei says, grabbing his nose and giving it a twist. "Mister big grin."

Yadokai rubs his nose. "What grin? I was not grinning. I am too serious to grin. My frown just makes a funny shape."

Shoei rounds on him, shaking a finger under his long,

pointed chin. "You lie! I saw you out of the corner of this little eye! Shoei sees all."

"Ha!" he shouts, grabbing her bony finger. "You see nothing without your spectacles!"

I laugh out loud, which is a huge mistake, because the monks decide to descend on me.

Stone-faced, Shoei grabs my wrists and inspects my palms. She tugs on the fabric of my armor, letting it snap back into place, then grabs my face, jerking it side to side, then up and down like a hunk of softened plasticine.

"This is your chief, no?" she says to Vienne, who seems to find this ritual amusing. Shoei gives my cheek a firm pat. "Such a face! Look at these biceps, Yadokai. Isn't he something? He will be a fine addition to the *Bon-Odori*."

Arms crossed, Yadokai glares up his nose at me, as if inspecting a corroded drainpipe. "Mch. Not so much. I bet he has two left feet and noodle arms."

"Shah, you've got rocks in your head." Shoei raps on the master's skull as if to prove it. "I am a great judge of young men, and this is a fine young man."

"For a Regulator, you mean," the master grouses, rubbing his noggin. "Not an Odori dancer."

"What's wrong with being a Regulator?" I demand. If he had said *dalit*, now that wouldn't have surprised me. Everyone holds *dalit* in low regard. But Regulators are the people's soldiers.

"Do you have noodle arms, boy?" Yadokai says in answer

to my question. "All soldiers have noodle arms, and I cannot abide noodle arms!"

Shoei claps a weathered hand over his mouth. "Enough nonsense from you! Leave the boy alone."

"I don't like the way he looks," Yadokai says through her hand. "There's something wrong with his smell. Let me see your teeth."

"Shah! Not with the teeth again. Inside with you, old man! Riki-Tiki, you, too! Tell Ghannouj to prepare tea. You," she says to me, crooking an arthritis-knotted finger, "come with me. It's time for your bath."

Bath? With her? I mouth to Vienne, who starts whistling to cover her sly smile.

Along the horizon above the stacked stone wall that surrounds the Tengu monastery, a line of high cliffs marks the part of the Labyrinth known as Hohenwald. The peaks above the cliffs tower into the sky, sheer rockfaces that no sane person could climb. When I was young and Father took me on a boat cruise of the lower river, I saw cliffs like these all along the Valles Marineris. They led to cave settlements created by the Founders. I remember thinking how odd it was for people to live in caves.

Right now, naked and up to my neck in a steaming hot mineral spring in the temple bathhouse with a wet towel on my head, I'd do anything to have a cave of my very own. How did I ever end up here, being scrubbed raw with lye soap by two bickering monks?

"I believe," Mimi says, "the Earth expression is shanghaied, but a more apt term is ambushed."

"More like suckered." I notice Vienne and Riki-Tiki standing outside the bathhouse, laughing and making faces through the rice-paper windows.

"Not funny!" I yell. "You'll get yours, and guess who'll be laughing then!" That only makes them giggle more. "How much longer, Shoei?"

"Long time." She produces a brush meant for scrubbing pots. "You're very dirty."

I start swimming for the exit. "Get away from me with that thing!"

"Come back here!" Shoei yells.

"See?" Yadokai cries. "I told you—noodle arms!"

Outside, Riki-Tiki and Vienne laugh until they can't breathe, and as the mistress grabs my ankle, my head dips into the bathwater.

I vow to get revenge.

After I'm all squeaky clean and half drowned, the master and mistress lead me and Vienne—who apparently can be trusted to bathe herself—to a small teahouse for the *Bon-Chakai* ceremony. The house and its peony garden are connected to the rest of the grounds by a wooden bridge that spans a huge pond full of lotus blossoms and white carp. At least, the bridge looks like wood, or it may be a synthetic facsimile.

"It is real wood," Mimi says. "Brought by the second wave of immigrants, who—"

"Boring!" I say.

"Covering approximately two hundred fifty thousand square meters, the grounds draw water from the River Tereshkova. The Tereshkova also feeds the compound's two large ponds."

"Still boring! Especially since my knees are killing me. Who drinks tea while curled up in a ball, anyway?"

"The smaller pond," she says, ignoring me, "which is reached by a wooden bridge, features a teahouse surrounded by peonies, cherry trees, and the oldest pine forest in the prefecture."

"You just love torturing me, don't you?"

"I love educating you, yes."

To block out her so-called education, I concentrate on the ripples on the surface of the pond. My mind drifts, but like most of the time, my thoughts settle on the topic of my father. Vienne and I haven't spoken about him since we found out about his death. She tried once, but I wasn't ready. I'm still not. Death is like a chunk of meat that you can't chew. It just sticks in your throat, gagging you.

Absentmindedly, I dip a hand in the pond. It feels cool to the touch, and I splash a little water on my face. When I reach for more, I hear a cough behind me. A rotund monk in glimmering robes whisks gracefully past, his socked feet making almost no impression on the tatami mat.

Without a word, he sits and folds his legs like an accordion blind. "I am the abbot of the monastery." There is a tea service in front of him. "Welcome to the *Bon-Chakai*, the Way of the Tea ceremony."

"That's Ghannouj?" I whisper to Vienne.

She nods and bows, placing her forehead on the mat. I glance around—the monks have also bowed—so I do the same.

Ow! A nerve in my lower back twangs.

"I told you to stretch more often," Mimi says.

"Easy for you to say," I say. "You don't have any nerves."

"Then I will have to settle for getting on yours."

When I sit up, the glittering monk is staring at me, his head cocked to the side. "Would you like some tea?"

"Um." My eyes dart from Vienne to Riki-Tiki in hopes that one of them will clue me in on the appropriate way to respond. I don't even bother to look at Shoei and Yadokai. "I'm not sure what to say."

"Perhaps," Ghannouj says, "you should say yes."

"Yes." My palms are suddenly sweaty, and I feel perspiration forming on my lip. "I mean yes, I should say yes. Because yes is what you say when you mean yes, as opposed to when you mean no and say yes anyway."

Riki-Tiki falls to her side, laughing, knees tucked against her chest, face red as she struggles to catch her breath. Beside me, Vienne makes squeaking noises, suppressing a snicker.

Ghannouj pours green tea into a cup. He places the cup in his meaty palm and offers it to me. "Tea?"

"Yes." I take the cup.

The tea is hot. I burn my lips sipping it.

Ghannouj catches Vienne's eye and makes a gesture so subtle, I almost miss it. After bowing, Vienne hops to her feet and leaves the teahouse. Riki-Tiki and the older monks follow her. Once they're out of sight, I hear Riki-Tiki burst into giggles. Her laughter is like the sound of chimes, and I can't help smiling.

"I hope you enjoyed your tea." Ghannouj takes the cup back when I've emptied it. "You don't care for ceremony."

"How do you know that?"

"I didn't know until you confirmed it." Smiling, he washes a cup with a bamboo whisk. "You are very handsome. I see now why she is so taken with you."

"Who?" I check over my shoulder. "Vienne?"

"Is there some other young woman who is taken with you?" he says. "Perhaps there are several such young women."

"Do you really think that?" My mouth is suddenly dry again. "Or are you waiting for me to confirm another suspicion?"

Ghannouj grins. "Do you know why I asked to see you?"

I shake my head no, although I have my guesses. "I thought it was a welcoming ceremony or some such."

"Do you believe in destiny?"

"That's a hard question."

"No," he says. "The question is easy. The answer is hard."
Smart aleck.

Rubbing my forehead with my palm, I take a deep breath. Do I believe in destiny? Truthfully, I'm not sure. "If you mean that our lives are planned for us from the time we're born, then no, I don't believe. But if you mean that our behavior follows certain patterns and after a while, those patterns become so predictable that they seem inevitable, then my answer is . . . maybe. Like Shakespeare said, 'It is not in the stars to hold our destiny but in ourselves.'"

Ghannouj turns my cup facedown. The words "It is not in the stars to hold our destiny but in ourselves" are written on the bottom.

I jump like I've been stung.

"Don't be surprised," Ghannouj says. "Perhaps it was inevitable that the words would be written there. Perhaps it is inevitable that you would say them."

"But I just thought of that quotation."

"Did you?" He pours a whole pot of tea into the cup. The tea runs over the sides until the bottom is full of grounds. He strains them until only a few drops of tea remain. Then he stares at the dregs while swirling them around. "Ah. I see."

I try to sneak a peek. "What do you see?"

"I see that I overcooked the tea again." He winks at me. "Do you really believe that I can see the future in the bottom of a cup of tea?"

And he almost had me believing in this stuff. "Well, no, no one can tell the future."

"I never said that."

"But—"

"Tea leaves are not necessary to see the future. Not when the person is sitting across from you. Vienne believes in you in a way that she has never believed in anyone. Soon, you will have a choice to make—a choice between your two greatest and most contradictory desires. The decision you make will determine the path of your destiny, not what anyone tells you."

I scratch my head. "Is that why you served me tea?"

His face is a tranquil lake. "I served you tea because I thought you were thirsty."

"So," I say. "Which path should I choose?"

"Which should you choose or which will you choose?"

"Which one is going to make me happy?"

He lifts a lotus from the tray. It's pink, like the ones in the ditch surrounding the walls. "'Though the lotus grows from the mud, it is unstained.'"

"Sir?" I say. "I don't follow."

He takes a deep breath of the blossom. "Try the *daifuku*. Sweet rice cakes. It settles the stomach."

I start to claim that I'm not hungry, but he offers the rice cakes. I take a nibble to make him happy, and my stomach growls.

"See?" He rises, then bows to me. "It is working already."

I'm shoving the last of the *daifuku* into my jaws when Mimi pipes up, "Very educational, cowboy."

"Very weird, you mean. This Ghannouj talks out of both sides of his mouth."

"It's better than talking with your mouth full," she says. "Hurry up and swallow that rice cake. Your olfactory senses are off the chart, and I predict based on the smoke coming from the kitchen that delicious, spicy food is in your future."

Now that the monks have accepted our presence, the hours roll by, and I find myself enjoying the longest time that Vienne and I have spent together that doesn't involve shots being fired. I pass the time training on the *mukyanjong*, a wooden punching dummy, and listening to Mimi's periodic updates as she decodes the data we stole from the Bibliotheca Alexandrina. In a nutshell, Mimi tells me again what I already knew—that the last of the data is still housed in a formerly high-security server farm of Tharsis Two. It was taken over by the Sturmnacht some months ago, and there's no chance of waltzing into the base the way we did in Christchurch.

Despite all that, I feel the burning itch to settle unfinished business. For months, since defeating the Draeu and their psychotic queen in the mines of the South Pole, we've been searching for information about Project MUSE. It was a top-secret genetic project that was supposed to create super soldiers for the military, but it went horribly wrong and created the Draeu instead. The man who started, funded, and even participated in MUSE? My dearly departed father. Ever since I learned that Father had a hand in making the Draeu, the same question has haunted me: Am I still a human being who controls his own destiny, or am I fated to become a monster, too?

The next day we rise at dawn for prayers, exercise until breakfast, then police the grounds until high noon, when a gong sounds, calling us to lunch.

"Heewack!" I rub my hands together. "About time. I'm starving!"

Vienne shakes her head. "No lunch for you. Dance lessons, remember? You're expected in the temple. The Master believes we learn better on an empty stomach. See you later. If you're good, I'll save you some rice."

As she walks away, my stomach rumbles in protest.

"Master Yadokai can ki—" A jolt of static electricity catches my attention. "Ow! What's that for?"

"You were being rude," Mimi says.

"But the words never even came out of my mouth!"

"One does not have to be an AI to know you were about to make an ass of yourself. Now step lively, Regulator. Master Yadokai is waiting for you."

When I emerge from the path, more starved then ever, Yadokai is indeed waiting for me. "Time for your lessons," he says sternly. "Today, we cure you of noodle arms!"

"Lessons?" I say.

He unfurls an ancient sheath of electrostat, which displays a series of dance steps. The header on the 'stat reads "How to Dance the *Bon-Odori* in Three Easy Lessons."

"No carking way." I shake my head vigorously. "It's never going to happen."

CHAPTER 6

It happens.

Within minutes, I find myself in an old man's arms, dancing across the floor of the main hall. The tatami mats have been pulled aside and stacked in a neat pile. The floor is polished and slick. Even barefoot, I'm in constant danger of slipping, which just adds to my mortification.

"But you make such a cute couple," Mimi says.

I don't even bother to argue.

"Master," I say as Yadokai drags me across the floor, humming in tune with the portable music box. "Couldn't I just look at the electrostat instead? I'm a quick study."

"Ha!" Yadokai barks. "You cannot learn to dance the *Bon-Odori* from writing. You must learn at the hands of a master."

Hands? Oh crap. "You can't be serious."

"Serious as a heart attack," he says. "And I've had two. Just pretend I'm the prettiest girl you have ever seen."

Easy for you to say, I think, trying not to stare at the liver spots and random tufts of hair sprouting from his cheeks. "What's the big deal? I've seen the Spirit Festival dances a bunch of times," I complain. "It's just a line of partiers jumping behind a fossiker wearing a lion head."

"Wrong and wrong!" he hollers. "The Spirit Festival is the bastard child of *Bon-Odori* and that group hop-along is nothing like a dance! Arms up!"

I shut my eyes and try to imagine that my partner is Vienne, which is hard to do because instead of soft, warm hands, I'm holding on to bony hunks of weathered skin.

"This is ridiculous!" I tell Mimi. "If my old crew saw me dancing with an old man—"

"They would be laughing at you," she says, "just like Riki-Tiki and Vienne, who are hiding in the other room instead of observing prayer time."

"Thanks for confirming my abject humiliation."

"Anytime, cowboy. It is one of my most pleasurable functions."

"Walking is basic to the steps of *Nagashi*, the restrained form of *Awa Bon-Odori*," Yadokai says. "Hear the beat of the *taiko* drum? Step on it."

I stomp.

"Ow!" Yadokai snarls. "Step on the beat, not on my foot!"

"Sorry!"

"You should be!" he snaps. "*Awa Odori* is called the Dance of Fools, not the Dance of Two Left Feet. But we have to start somewhere, and beggars can't be choosers. Hands up, Noodle Arms! And this time, walk counterclockwise. It's the line of dance, and it keeps you from running smack-dab into another dancer. Weight on the balls."

"Weight on the *what*?"

"The balls of your feet." He whacks me with a bamboo fan. "You want my help or not?"

"Not."

"Too late now! Keep walking. The second Fools Dance is called *Zomeki*. It means the Frenzy."

"Frenzy?" I say. "My agenda doesn't really include getting frenzied with you."

"Silence!"

A moment later, Yadokai and I are frenzying across the floor, crouched low, our arms forming a triangle over our heads and our knees akimbo. Yadokai's eyes are closed as he hums to the beat of the *taiko* drum.

"More frenzy, less noodle!" He leads us in the opposite direction. "Next lesson, you get to lead."

I cough like I've swallowed ditch water. "*Next* lesson?"

Later that evening we are gathered around a low table in the temple, enjoying the feast of Bon. The table is stacked with empty bowls and drained teacups. The meal is almost over, which I'm glad of, because sitting with my legs crossed for over an hour is a form of torture that should be banned.

"Ah." I stretch out my legs. "That's better."

"But rude," Mimi says.

"Cut me some slack. My body is one big cramp. Even my butt is spasming."

"So is your brain," she says. "You should try stretching it out, too."

Riki-Tiki shoves the last rice ball into her mouth, then licks each of her fingers. "Ghannouj says the tea leaves told him you two came here to find a secret. Well, not here, but close by. And you've been looking for it for months."

"Stupid tea leaves," I mutter.

Riki-Tiki points her chopsticks at me. "So is it true?"

"Um. Well. Mostly," I explain. "We've been trying to collect some important data. It's stored in a server complex thirty kilometers from here."

Vienne interrupts, "In an outpost controlled by a crime lord named Lyme."

Riki-Tiki's chopsticks drop from her hand, and Yadokai coughs.

Vienne and I trade looks—the monks know the name Lyme all too well. I don't know why we're surprised, because Lyme is the most notorious criminal on Mars.

Shoei belches loudly. "Ghannouj! Dessert!"

Ghannouj appears, and I gobble up the last grains of rice. He waits until I'm finished to offer an open hand for my bowl.

"Oh. Sorry," I say. "Didn't mean to hold you up. You're a great cook."

Shoei lets a megaton burp rip. "Ha! Ghannouj did not prepare the feast. He is terrible in the kitchen."

Yadokai lets one rip, too. "And a terrible dishwasher. We only let him be abbot because he makes the tea."

They all laugh, and I don't get it. Even though Ghannouj seems to be the most revered of the monks, he cleans up after every course. It's something I've been meaning to ask Vienne. Of course, there are a zillion things I want to ask her.

"Actually," Mimi says, "there are thirty-one inquiries you have mentally noted, including how to use the squat toilet correctly."

"That one can wait," I tell her, then look to Vienne for guidance. She takes pity on me. "The food for the feast is provided by the farmers in the collectives nearby. It is their offering to the dead."

"And the Tengu eat the offerings?"

"Sure do!" Riki-Tiki tries to burp, which sounds more like a hiccup. "Compliments to the chefs!"

Ghannouj returns with a plate of *mochi* stuffed with sweetened bean paste.

Looking at the dessert, I see the chance to gather intel on what Vienne told me earlier—that the monk outside, Stain, had desecrated the temple.

"Intel my eye," Mimi says. "Your interest in Stain is purely testosterone fueled."

"Is that your way of saying I'm jealous of the jack?"

"Affirmative."

"I'm just curious, Mimi."

"Though you may lie to yourself, cowboy, you can never lie to me."

But I'm not to be denied, so I ask the monks, "Should we take some of this to Stain? When I saw him before, he looked really hungry."

The monks shrug indifferently, and Vienne gives me a pained expression, which makes me feel even more curious.

After sounding a louder burp, Riki-Tiki grabs a saucer with *mochi* on it. "Don't bother. Stain doesn't need food like the rest of us."

"Stain," Vienne explains, when I look confused, "is an ascetic monk."

"Ah." I have no idea what she means. "What's an   "

"An ascetic is a monk who seeks enlightenment by depriving himself of certain comforts and worldly pleasures."

"Like food?"

Vienne nods. "Among other things."

"I never thought of food as a worldly pleasure," I say. "Was he always an ascetic? Or did he become one after he was banished?"

Crash!

Riki-Tiki's saucer hits the floor. The porcelain shatters. She's still holding chopsticks near her mouth, a grain of rice clasped between them.

A moment passes. No one else makes a sound.

Uh-oh. I've stepped in it now.

"Curiosity killed the cat," Mimi says.

"But satisfaction brought him back," I reply.

"Perhaps I should define 'satisfaction' for you, cowboy."

"I will get a broom." Ghannouj shatters the silence. "Then perhaps Durango can help us practice our Dance of Fools."

"*Hai!*" Yadokai yells, sounding a might too enthusiastic. "Riki-Tiki! Music! Old woman! Stack the mats! Vienne! Stop Noodle Arms from escaping!"

"Stack them yourself, old man. I'm dancing with Noodle Arms!" Shoei yanks me across the floor, even as Ghannouj is cleaning up the mess and Riki-Tiki is cranking up the dynamo on the music box.

"Mimi?" I ask. "What should I do?"

"Dance," she says. "They are trying to assuage your embarrassment, so keep your big yap shut and go with it."

Shoei places me in the center of the floor. Her hands are smaller than Yadokai's but no less leathery, and her head only reaches my chest. "Show me the dance of the kite."

I try to escape. "Yadokai didn't teach me any kite dances."

"Ha!" She yanks the hem of my shirt. "You do not get off so easy. Vienne, come, you will be the kite."

"What am I then?"

She pops me on the forehead. "You control the kite, Noodle Arms!"

"Control the kite?" I ask Mimi.

Before she can answer, Yadokai turns on the music, and Vienne is bowing before me. For the feast, she's dressed in a white linen *salwar kameez* and is barefoot, her painted toes still pink. Her hair is pinned in a loose bun, and her cheeks look fresh scrubbed. It's one of the few times I've seen her out of symbiarmor, and the sight makes me hyperventilate.

"Breathe," Mimi says.

"I forgot how."

As I watch, she raises her hands above her head and begins to bounce, then does a round-over, the rhythmic movements of her arms and legs matching the herky-jerky tack of a kite in the wind. She jumps into the air, arms spinning, then lands and executes a tumbling run that ends with her bounding off the far wall and sailing high up near the beamed ceiling, arms wide, sleeves ripping in wind of her own making, the fabric pressed tight against her chest, long hair escaping its bun and wrapping around her face like the tail of the kite.

When she lands so lightly that the wooden hummingbird floors barely whisper, my palms are moist, and I think my heart has stopped. With barely a pause, her arms fly above her head again, and her hips sway with the beat of the drum. This is a different Vienne—lost in her own body, free, rapt in the rhythm of the music, beautiful in a way that turns my gut inside out.

"I believe," Mimi tells me, "that you should be pretending to control her flight."

"Not a chance. There's no way anybody could control that."

"Your choice," she says, "but it would be better if you tightened your slack jaw. Your tongue is hanging out."

"No! No! No!" Yadokai howls. The music stops, and the old man stalks over to me, clapping his hands. He shakes me hard. "You should be guiding the kite, not watching it fly away. Did you learn nothing from your lessons? How will you dance the *Bon-Odori* now?"

"Uh," I say, one eye on him and one eye on Vienne as she tucks a strand of hair behind her ear, her cheeks and lips flushed red. I feel empty and hungry, as if I've never had enough to eat.

"Master." Vienne exhales deeply to focus her breath. "Don't worry. I can teach Durango. He is a very fast study, when he wants to be."

We've faced bullets, Big Daddies, and cannibals together, but none of them was as fierce as the stink eye the master is giving me. Vienne leans toward me, shielding me from Yadokai, and I can feel the warmth of her skin.

"Old man! Leave the boy alone." Shoei pushes Yadokai aside, then shoos us to the door. "Vienne, take him for a walk. We will clean up. Go, go. Wait." She pinches my earlobe. "No funny business, Noodle Arms. Shoei knows all, eh?"

"Why is it," I ask Mimi as the mistress slaps the sliding door closed behind us, "I can lead a whole davos of

Regulators, but two small, wrinkled monks treat me like a child?"

"Some truths are self-evident," Mimi says.

"Meaning?"

"Meaning it is self-evident, cowboy. Think about it, or try, if you can ever get the butt cramp out of your brain."

"Mind your own business!" I tell her as Vienne bounds down the steps to the path, barefoot, immune to the gravel.

I take a second to pull on my boots, then follow her. Soon, when she is out of range of the lights of the temple, only her linen *salwar kameez* is still visible. She moves quickly down the path, silent, ghostlike, until the rising sound of frogs alerts me to the proximity of the pond.

"I did not," Mimi says, "need the frogs to alert me to the location of the pond."

"Goody for you," I subvocalize, and almost bump into Vienne. "Know what? I think you need some dedicated processing time."

"I am capable of multitasking," Mimi says.

"Right. Which means you can both kibitz and mock me at the same time," I tell her as Vienne strikes a match and lights a line of three torches on the edge of the pond. "All right, you can stay awake. Just keep it down, huh?"

Vienne sits on a smooth stone on the bank. She pats the stone next to her. "Take a load off, soldier." The tone of her voice is familiar. The old Vienne. The comfortable Vienne.

The warrior Vienne. Not the flying girl that makes my invol-
untary muscles spaz out.

Earth and her moon, like two dancers always at arms
reach, fill up the evening sky, close enough to see with a
naked eye. It's hard to believe that a planet so bright blue
and alive could have a moon that's so desolate. Yet between
the two, it's Luna that shines more brightly.

"When I was small," Vienne says, "younger than Riki-
Tiki, I used to sit right here, skipping stones and wondering what it would be like to grow up on Earth. Imagine
having all the water you could drink, all the food you
could eat—"

"All the pox you could catch," I say. "You know, Earth's
gravity is four times that of Mars. Which means on Earth,
your butt would be four times as wide."

She gives me a playful poke in the ribs. "Be serious."

"I am serious."

"Then be less serious. You're always Durango the chief
and never Durango the jack, right?" She tosses a pebble into
the pond. It bounces off a water lily and makes a wet plop.
"Even when you're not wearing armor, it's like you're still
wearing armor. Know what I mean?"

Me? Wearing armor? As if she's not the one who gives a
steady supply of mixed signals. First, she almost kisses me;
then she's as distant as a moon. Then she's playful, like now.
All these months together, and it still feels awkward, this
thing between us. Sometimes, I dream of just sweeping her

up in a deep, melting kiss, then I think no, that's a great way to lose a few teeth.

So I toss my own pebble into the water and let enough time lapse before I say, "I reckon I do," hoping that it will encourage her to explain more.

But no explanation is forthcoming. Her silence ripples on.

Clouds are rolling in, quickly obscuring the twin lights of Earth and her moon. In the torchlight, I notice a delicate silver pendant hanging from a chain on her neck. Carved into the center of the pendant is a lotus, surrounded by its leaves.

"What's this?"

"I got it when I was a child. I left it here when—when I left." She tucks it inside her top. "Sorry about the master and mistress. They mean well, but sometimes their enthusiasm for the *Bon-Odori* lets them get carried away."

"They're not so bad," I say. "I've met worse. At least they don't carry live ammo. Or eat people. Or dissolve—"

"So you like them?"

"Affirmative."

"I'm glad. They like you, too. Especially Riki-Tiki. She says that you are very handsome and would make a perfect husband."

My voice rises an octave. "Husband?"

She pats my knee. "Don't worry. She's too young to marry, and besides, you're already taken."

The loss of lung function returns, and I rasp, "I am?"

"Do you have to ask?"

The truth is, yes, I do have to ask. Like she said about Stain, it's complicated. Infinitely complicated. More complicated than the cipher algorithms Mimi is running to decrypt the MUSE data.

"No." I arch an eyebrow. "But I like hearing you say it."

She grabs my nose and like Shoei, gives it a playful twist. "You're pathetic! Maybe I'll tell Riki-Tiki you're available after all!"

We both laugh, which releases some of the tension. I'm more comfortable being her chief than being her taken. I'm beginning to understand what Vienne means when she says that life is easier when you can just shoot your problems. The AI Mimi would probably say that my id and superego are suffering from asymmetrical synchronicity or some such nonsense. The real Mimi probably would've said that I had the target in my sights but just couldn't pull the trigger.

"Hey," I say after a moment. "Aren't you supposed to be teaching me how to do the Dancing Kite?"

"That's Dance of the Kite, Noodle Arms."

"Which was amazing," I say. "Check that, *you* were amazing. Any chance of an encore?"

She blushes. "How about now?"

"But there's no drumbeat to follow."

"I don't need the drums." She covers my hands. Her skin is so warm to the touch. "And you couldn't follow the beat anyway."

"Ouch. Good one." I take her into my arms. She smells

like orange peels and sandalwood and my scent is more like—

"Old boots," Mimi says. "You have analyzed every possible nuance of experience; now be quiet and start dancing."

"No kibitzing!"

Vienne puts a hand on my cheek and rubs the stubble on my chin with her thumb like she's trying to sand the loops and whorls of her fingerprint smooth. It makes a scratching noise that brings a sly smile. "You need a shave." She pinches a lock of my long hair in her fingers. Tucks it behind my ear. "A haircut, too."

She pulls me closer, then presses her lips to my cheek and then my mouth. I kiss her back, tasting the sweet heat of her tongue, and I feel my body shudder.

"'Give crowns and pounds and guineas,'" Mimi says. "'But not your heart away.'"

"Shut it, Mimi."

We dance in the light of the torches, without a sound, eyes closed, hands locked until Vienne pulls away.

"What's the matter?" I ask.

"Since I became a Regulator, the Tenets have guided my way." She looks at the stub of her pinkie finger. "Even after we became *dalit*, I tried to follow them, but then everything changed, and now, I don't know what rules to follow. How do I know which path to take?"

The wind shifts, and the high grasses bend to it. I have no answer—I'm a soldier, and the tea leaves don't speak to me.

"Today Riki-Tiki told me she plans to leave the monastery and become a Regulator." Vienne pats the pendant that hangs around her neck. "She wants me to take her as an acolyte."

"What did you tell her?"

"The truth," she says. "Partly the truth. I told her I was very flattered—which I am—and that she would make an excellent Regulator."

I agree. "What's the other truth you didn't tell her? That the monks need her here?"

"You're pretty perceptive for a soldier." She rests her head on my shoulder. "The monks do need her. The master and mistress aren't long for this world, and when they are gone, Ghannouj will be the only Tengu. So much depends on Riki-Tiki staying here and caring for the bees. Hopes. Dreams. History. Traditions. It will all be lost if the Tengu cease to exist."

I put my arm around her. "That's a pretty powerful truth."

"And there's one more," she says. "The truth about me—"

But I never hear what truth she means, because a second later, the still night is interrupted by distant pounding and frightened shouts of "Fire! Fire! They're burning the whole place down!"

CHAPTER 7

Freeman Farming Collective
Zealand Prefecture
ANNOS MARTIS 238. 7. 19. 18:08

Mars is full of bad ideas, Archibald thinks as he enters the
Quonset hut marked with stenciled letters: FOREMAN. The
idea of a commune is one of them. People coming together
with a common purpose to create farms to feed the masses
with no profit motive? It's unnatural. Humans are by their
very makeup a competitive species, driven by greed and ava-
rice to gain power, to use that power to hoard the most valuable resources, and then to create huge profits by selling those
resources off.

That's why collectivism failed so badly during the
Orthocracy. Sure, some places like the Freeman Farming
Collective have existed for decades, even centuries, but they
never became what the Bishop created them to be. Farming is
backbreaking work, and farmers lead pitiful, unfulfilled lives of
whining desperation. It would be sad if it weren't so pathetic.

"'Welcome Free People,'" Archibald reads from the sign
on the wall. "'Work is Life.'"

It might as well say, "Abandon hope, all ye who enter here." Because that's what he suspects this place will be: a fresh level of Hell that stinks of manure and unwashed peasants whose idea of good hygiene is bathing in an irrigation canal.

Outside, the peasants are screaming. Right now, as they're getting knocked to the ground, restrained with plastic cuffs, and thrown into the back of a Düsseldorf, they probably aren't feeling very free at all.

He scans the room, looking for something to burn. The foreman's desk, deluged with old seed orders, yield printouts, and crop projections, is a teetering mess. Seven steel filing cabinets line the back wall of the Quonset hut.

"A most excellent pile of kindling," he says.

He swings back his cape with a flourish and pulls a bottle of ethyl ether from a holster on his hip. The liquid is colorless but has a distinctive sweet, hot smell that makes his mouth water. It also has a very low auto-ignition point, making it the most astonishing tool for his line of work. He opens the filing cabinets one drawer at a time. Gently, he pours the ether on the files. Then he moves to the desk, where he empties the bottle.

Quickly, quickly, he thinks as he sweeps across the room. The air fills with fumes as the ether evaporates. His head swims, and his eyes cross. This is the climactic moment, right before the chemical starts to boil, when he removes the match from the box and flicks it into the air.

He slams the hut door shut, pulls his hood up, and walks briskly away, covering ten meters before the ether ignites, and the subsequent fireball blows out the windows, and glass sprays through the air, raining down like jagged sleet.

"Archibald," Duke calls. "Your cloak is smoking."

He sneers as he brushes glass shards from his shoulders and puts out the glowing embers. "That's Mr. Archibald to you."

"Mr. Archibald." Duke opens the door of the Noriker for him. "We've rounded up the farmers who owe money to Mr. Lyme. What do you want us to do now?"

"Do you mean, what is my next order?" Archibald slides into the passenger seat. "My next order is this: We leave the peasants something to remember us by. Burn a dozen huts. Leave nothing behind except ash."

After sliding behind the wheel, Duke puts the Noriker in reverse and nearly backs over a trio of Sturmnacht hauling away an unconscious farmer, the light from the fire casting shadows across their faces. He lays on the horn until they move.

"You have a problem with my order?" Archibald says.

"No," Duke says. "Except, we took all the coin they had. Burning down the huts, I don't see the point in doing that."

"That's why Mr. Lyme sent me, because I do see a point in it," Archibald says. "Let me explain. When the enemy is on your flank, you distract him by attacking civilians. You round them up, burn their land, and dare them to stand against you. Do this again and again, leaving nothing but ash in your wake. When word spreads, civilians will desert their homes. They will flood the cities for shelter. The enemy can no longer chase you because he has to spend his energy and resources taking care of refugees who are frightened, starving, and angry with their government for not protecting them. Now do you see the point?"

Duke parks the Noriker near a larger Düsseldorf truck. "If we were an army, sure, but we're just Sturmnacht. You know, strong-arm thugs, mercenaries, and enforcers."

"That's where you're wrong," Archibald says as Duke opens the door for him. "The Sturmnacht are an army, the most dangerous in this prefecture. I'm going to make a believer out of you."

Archibald throws an arm around Duke and leads him toward the back of the Düsseldorf. "Walk with me while I inspect the prisoners." Under the covered truck bed, some prisoners are crying, but mostly they are silent, not a bit of fight left in them.

"You see, Duke, it's all science," he explains. "Evolution in action. We are the fast. They are the slow. The fast have always eaten the slow. It's the only way to ensure the survival of the fittest. Understand what I mean?"

Duke rubs his head. "Yes, Mr. Archibald. I'm beginning to understand you."

"Brilliant! That means you're one of the fast." They return to the Noriker. This time Archibald climbs into the driver's seat. "I'm glad we won't have to eat you. Tell the drivers to take the prisoners back to Tharsis Two, then obey my orders to set fire to the collective."

"Yes, Mr. Archibald." Duke takes hold of the open door. "Except that I should be driving, not you."

Archibald shakes his head no. "I need some personal space."

"Mr. Lyme gave me orders to stay with you at all times."

"Don't let the farmers put out the fires." Archibald slams the door, almost catching Duke's fingers. As he drives away, he shouts, "I'll be parked atop the canyon to the east. I want a good view of the show!"

CHAPTER 8

Tengu Monastery, Noctis Labyrinthus
Zealand Prefecture
ANNOS MARTIS 238. 7. 19. 19:01

Vienne and I reach the temple as a farmer rushes inside, shouting, his face filled with panic. "Rebecca said to come quick! Now!"

"Joad!" Riki-Tiki slams the door open. "What's wrong?"

Joad looks like a solidly built, blood and guts, steel-scrotum farmer, with cropped gray hair and a slight gait. "The collective!" he yells. "An attack! It's on fire!"

Shoei and Yadokai look to Ghannouj, who picks up a cup of tea, swirls the dregs, and dumps them onto the table. His lips move, eyes tracing a pattern that only he can see.

A moment later, he nods. The master and mistress grab their staffs from the wall, and Riki-Tiki scoots out after them.

"Come on!" Riki-Tiki waves us along as she leaves.

Vienne looks to me.

"Up for a fight?" I ask.

She cocks an eyebrow as if to say *Aren't I always?*

I point to our gear bags stowed on a Peg-Board on the wall. "Need anything?"

"Just my symbiarmor." She also grabs her armalite and ammo belt. "And a couple of accessories."

Outside the gate, the monks pile into Joad's vehicle.

"Hurry up, damn it!" he yells at us.

Vienne starts the engine of the motorbike as I stuff our gear in the cargo hold. I want to tell Joad that running off in a blind tizzy is more time-consuming than taking a few minutes to prepare. But this time, I shut my big yap.

"Brilliant decision," Mimi says.

We're about to go, when I notice that Stain hasn't moved. He's still sitting cross-legged in the corner, chanting, and staring into space.

"Want to ask him for help?" I ask Vienne. "We could use all the hands we can get."

"Stain is not like you," Vienne says with a tone that I can't quite describe as she pops the clutch. "He is nobody's hero."

Even if Joad weren't leading us, it would be a snap to find the Freeman Collective—just follow the heavy, bulbous smoke that mushrooms high above the horizon, many shades darker than the evening sky. It's a chemical fire. I can tell by the color of the fumes and the pungent stink that dances on the wind.

"Mimi," I ask. "Can you identify the source of the burn?"

"Negative, not from this distance," she says. "While I

agree with your broad interpretation, your suit lacks the pre-cision required to analyze the particular chemical makeup."

"Any advice?"

"Don't breathe."

"During an emergency response? Impossible."

"No one ever said being a Regulator was easy, cowboy."

As we reach the main gate, an explosion sends a percus-sive shock wave through the town. A moment later we hear panicked screams. A warning siren wails.

"We're on foot from here on out," I tell the monks after leaving the vehicles. "Stay close to me and Vienne until we get a fix on the situation."

"The situation?" Joad yells at me. "The town's fig-jammed with fire, and they're shooting up the place."

"Show us," I say, feeling the sense of calm that hits me whenever there's an emergency.

He leads us down the main street, a dirt road lined with Quonset huts. Everywhere I look, people are screaming and crying. In the bedlam, older jacks shout out orders that nobody follows. Seconds later a herd of farmers stampedes past us. A burly man blindsides Shoei, and she stumbles toward a pile of burning debris.

I grab her belt and pull her back. "Watch out!"

"Thank you." She shakes off the blow. "Shah. Who knew something so big could run so fast?"

Blind panic has that effect on people. "Keep moving," I bark. "Time's wasting."

"This way," Joad says.

He beckons us to follow him down a side street. It allows us to avoid foot traffic, and we reach the hot zone within a couple of minutes. Overhead, I hear the droning of engines. A silver aerofoil swoops low over us and dumps a payload of water. Steam roils into the night, full of cinders, ash, and remnants of chemicals.

Dumping water on a chemical fire? How stupid can you get?

"Cover up!" I yell. "Eyes and mouths!"

Vienne pops her visor down.

The monks don't react—they're too dazed by the smoke and light.

Too slow.

"This way!" Picking the nearest hut, I kick open the door and hustle everyone inside. The moment after I slam the door, a toxic cloud drifts past the windows.

"Get away from there!" I snap at Riki-Tiki, whose curiosity has led her to peer outside. "You all stay put! Let me and Vienne take it from here."

"Like hell I will!" Joad shouts. "You're not the boss of me, son. This is my land, and I'll defend it to the death." Then the firecracker sound of battle rifle shots rings out, and the color drains from his face. "On second thought, maybe it's best I show these folks to the infirmary."

"Good plan." I turn to the master and mistress. "Once you're at the infirmary, get any injured to safety, and do what you can to restore order. Lots of scared folks running about just makes a bad situation worse."

"You have a stern side." Shoei pinches my cheeks. "It's very sexy."

"Ha!" Yadokai folds his arms. Gives me the suspicious stink eye. "These men, they have guns."

"No problem," I say. "We have guns, too."

"They are very dangerous men."

I shake my head. "Have you not met Vienne?"

On that note, we're out the door.

When Vienne and I reach the town center, fire is immolating a cluster of large storage facilities. Great plumes of white smoke and flames soar into the night sky, the heat intense enough to melt the buildings' aluminum skeletons and their sheet metal skins.

A chain of men has formed a fire line. They toss bucket after bucket of water onto the blaze, but they only make it worse.

"Stop! Water won't work!" I yell at them. "Fall back!"

They ignore me and keep tossing.

Until another burst of gunfire sends them scrambling for cover.

"Take point," I tell Vienne. "Locate the target."

With a quick nod, she moves into position.

"Mimi," I say. "Give me a scan of the area. How many hostiles are we facing?"

"No can do, cowboy. Too many signatures moving too

quickly to map. Sensors indicate three hot spots on your twelve, two hundred meters ahead."

"Affirmative," I say and move up.

Vienne freezes. "I've got eyes on hostiles."

"Let's end this."

Together, we drop into a crouch run. Take cover behind a trash barrel. Ahead, two shooters in tattered body armor are prancing about, firing their battle rifles into the air. The bigger of the two is a box of a man, sporting a plush gray-brown flattop and jowls dappled with ancient acne scars. His armor is too small, and a thick leather belt strains against his bulbous gut.

"Brilliant shot, Richards!" the shorter one says.

"Get your nose outta my butt, Franks."

"Wanker!"

"Fossiker!"

Silhouetted by the light of the blaze, they take swigs from a bottle, paying attention to only the fire and not the Regulators a few meters from the ends of their noses. It's just the way I like my enemies—oblivious, overconfident, and overindulged.

"I thought that was the way you liked your friends," Mimi chimes in.

"Ha-ha. Best work on that compiler, Mimi. Your code for funny is riddled with bugs."

Vienne drops a laser dot on the man named Richards. "Give the word."

"Hold your fire. Too many innocents about."

Franks throws back his head and lets out a high-pitched scream, mocking the group of would-be firefighters. "Run, you buggers! That'll teach you to go messing with the Sturmnacht!"

Sturmnacht. Lyme's thugs. Splendid. Just my luck to run into the last people on Mars I wanted to see. "Mimi, make yourself useful. Any more weapons being fired?"

"Do you mean, can I detect any percussive sound vibrations similar to the supersonic waves created in, say, a ten-meter perimeter beyond this point of origin?"

"Uh, yeah. That's what I meant to say."

"The answer is, no other weapons being fired, cowboy."

"That's all I needed to know." I motion for Vienne to track left, and she moves sideways in an arc. "Mimi, open a telemetry link between me and Vienne."

"Read your mind, cowboy. Link open."

"Smart aleck." I tap behind my ear. "Vienne?"

"Read you loud and clear," Vienne says.

"Two meters ahead, cut behind that last hut. I'll do the same to the right. Let's catch these *sĭ pì yǎns* thugs not looking."

Like synchronized dancers, we silently approach the Sturmnacht.

"Go," I whisper into the mic.

On cue, Vienne drops Richards with a rabbit punch.

Franks, firing the last of a clip of ammo, notices a sudden

movement as his buddy face-plants on the hot gravel road.

"Richards!" He turns to find the barrel of my armalite three centimeters from his nasal septum. His breath stinks like a fermented sewer. "What the hell do you think you're doing, dirt worm?"

"Isn't it obvious?" I say. "I'm about to shoot you."

His arm holding the battle rifle starts to drop.

"Don't even think about it," I warn him.

He grins.

Vienne pops him in the jaw, and he crumbles like a statue made of sand. "He thought about it," she says.

"Fair enough," I say. "Remind me to never make you mad."

"Never make me mad."

"Yes, ma'am. Still, that was a crafty punch. You haven't lost your touch."

"I bet you say that to all the girls."

"Just the ones that can kick my ass."

"How many would that be?"

"One."

"Good." She smiles, wiping dirt off her cheeks. "I'd hate to find out you were getting your ass kicked behind my back."

My cheeks flush, and I turn back to the Quonset huts, which are a mass of flame. "The buildings are totally fragged." I say to Mimi, "Nobody inside, right?"

"I read no biorhythmic signatures at this moment."

"Meaning?"

"Meaning that there is no one *living* still in the buildings."

"I catch your drift." I turn back to Vienne. "I'm hoping the farmers got everybody out before they torched the place. Let's get these gentlemen under wraps before they wake up."

With some effort, I flip Richards over and secure his bulky arms using a length of zip cord. His body odor is as bad as his partner's foul breath.

I repeat the process for Franks. Then I notice the scorpion tattoo on his neck. "That's weird," I tell Vienne. "See that mark? Didn't we see that on the Scorpions at the Favela? Why does one of Lyme's enforcers have it, too?"

Vienne shrugs. "You understand these scum better than I do."

"Yeah, well. I wish I didn't." I stand up and stretch my back. "Let's take them back to the infirmary for questioning. We'll have to drag them, I reckon. Name your poison."

"Which one stinks less?"

"Eh." I make a gesture, meaning so-so.

She grabs Franks's ankle. "Six of one, half dozen the other."

As we move away from the blaze, dragging the men along, the heat still on the back of my neck, an idea occurs to me. "Mimi, what do you think? Possible? Doable?"

"Doable," Mimi says. "I calculate a seventy percent chance of success."

Good enough for me. "Hey, Vienne. What would you say if I came up with an ingenious way of sneaking into Tharsis

Two and snatching the rest of the MUSE data?"

"Does this method of breaking in," Vienne asks as she pulls Franks over a pile of smoking debris, his chin leaving a trail in the ground, "happen to involve dressing in this man's disgusting clothes?"

"Something like that."

She drops the leg. Hands on her hips, she says, "The prospect of wearing armor drenched in sweat and whisky is supposed to entice me?"

"But there will be fighting." I flash an overly enthusiastic grin. "Maybe even gunfire."

"Well." She takes hold of Franks's ankle again. "At least that gives me something to look forward to."

CHAPTER 9

Freeman Farming Collective
Zealand Prefecture
ANNOS MARTIS 238. 7. 19. 22:31

After dragging our prisoners across the collective, Vienne and I find the infirmary building. There is a line of injured victims at the door. Even though the emergency siren is still blasting and the air is thick with smoke and fumes from the dying fire, most of the people queued up are almost silent—the first sign that traumatic shock is getting a toehold.

"Cover your mouth and nose," I warn a young mother holding a toddler on her hip. "The baby's, too. This smoke is toxic."

She stares through me like I'm a ghost.

"Let it go," Vienne says.

But I can't. "Try this." I pull the woman's soot-covered shirt over her face. I do the same for the baby. "It's better than nothing. Leave it."

A young farmer in a duster swings a side door open for us. He disappears as we pull Franks and Richards inside. I strap their hands to a radiator while Vienne guards them. They don't move a muscle.

The infirmary is one large, brightly lit room partitioned off with bamboo screens and white linen curtains. The whole place has a medicinal odor, stronger than the smoke outside.

"What next?" Vienne says.

"I reckon we find that Joad person and ask him what to do with these two fossikers."

"You can go searching." She turns her back to the bleeding and broken farmers lined up on the far wall, flinching ever so slightly when a child cries out. "I'll keep watch on the prisoners."

Vienne obviously doesn't much care for Joad, so I nod in agreement. "But you're not going to curb stomp them or anything, right?"

"Of course not." She blows a strand of hair out of her face. "The Tenets forbid harming prisoners, and I'm still a Regulator."

"Okay," I say. "Be back soon. I want to find the monks, too. They'll want to know that you're safe."

But I don't leave.

She nudges me with the barrel of her armalite. "Why are you still here?"

"I'm going now," I say, because she obviously doesn't want me poking around her psyche.

"Joad," Mimi says as I wind my way through the farmers,

"is not the problem. It is the injured that are bothering her."

"How do you know that?"

"A complex multi-variant calculation often referred to as women's intuition."

"Really?"

"Really."

"I'll have to take your word for it, since I'm not a woman, and technically you aren't, either."

A couple minutes later, I find Riki-Tiki behind a white cloth curtain. When I walk in, she's talking quietly with a tall, skinny kid who looks like a transplant from the Hellespontus territories. His hair's long, with a pilot's hat pulled over it, and his hands are delicate. Not the kind of mitts you'd expect on a collective.

"Durango!" Riki-Tiki says, her face lighting up. From the space next door, Shoei shushes her. "Sorry, mistress."

"Are you the aerofoil pilot who dumped water on the fire?" I ask the kid.

"Yes, sir," he says. "My name's Tychon, and I—"

"That was stupid."

Riki-Tiki's face falls. She leans against the kid, and I realize they're more than just buddies. Which explains why they're behind the curtains. Which explains why she'd want to leave the Tengu, who take a strict vow of celibacy.

"Sir?" Tychon says.

"I said, that was stupid. That was a chemical fire, and all the water did was vaporize and spread toxins in the air." I realize I'm coming on too strong and crank it down a notch. "Don't get me wrong, I know you were trying to help, but if you act without a plan, you end up doing more harm than good."

He swallows hard. His Adam's apple bobs up and down. "I didn't realize."

"Next time," I say, before I draw the curtain on them, "use your nose. It's more dependable than your eyes."

Shoei and Yadokai are behind the next curtain, tending to a child whose left arm is severely burned. The flesh is one long blister. It has burst and is contaminated with gravel and dirt. Shoei dresses the wound like a physician, and Yadokai comforts the child with soft touches and quiet noises. Quite a change from my demanding dance teacher. I'm reminded again that first impressions are often the worst ones.

I draw the curtain and let them work in peace. I can tell them about Vienne later.

Durango, I think as I return to the waiting area, *you are such a carking* mu'dak! *Why the* `tchyo za ga`lima *did you come down so hard on Tychon for one mistake.* Eto piz`dets! *You're not your father, for pity's sake. Do the decent thing. Go back and make it up to the kid.*

The doors swing open. Joad enters the infirmary, followed by a woman and two bodyguards. The woman is dressed in bright maize and blue robes with a homespun shawl draped over one shoulder. Her face is more handsome than beautiful, with high, broad cheekbones and a mane of wavy auburn hair.

As she passes through the farmers, all heads turn to her, and the noise dies down. Her face is a mask of consternation, but when a woman dressed in dirt-caked overalls cries out and rushes across the room, she manages a smile. The bodyguards move to step in. She shakes them off as the woman falls to her knees, hands clasped together.

"Rebecca! Thank the Bishop you've come! They took my sister, Thela!"

Rebecca lifts the woman from the floor. "Stand up, now. I hear you, and we will get her back. Were others taken?"

The woman nods vehemently. "But I don't know how many."

"Take me to their kin." Rebecca puts an arm around the woman, who leads her past me and toward the bamboo screens. As they pass, Rebecca stops short. Our eyes meet, and her brow wrinkles, a hint of recognition. Then she gives me a long, apprizing look, and her eyes settle on my deformed hand. "Joad, where did you find the *dalit*?"

"He come with the monks," Joad says as he swings a screen open for her. "Him and a female. Managed to catch themselves a couple Sturmnacht."

Rebecca glances back at me. There's something familiar about her. The eyes, maybe. Or her face? Seems like I've seen her somewhere before.

"Mimi?"

"Beat you to it, cowboy. I've run facial recognition protocols, and I have no matching data for her."

"So we've never met?"

"Not that you remember, and certainly not since I took up residence in your skull."

"She seems so familiar."

"She does look very common."

"Don't be catty," I say.

"I am not programmed for cattiness."

"Yet you do it so well."

"Haven't you an apology to make?"

"Don't change the subject."

But she's right. Better do it before the kid gets away. I'm rehearsing my apology outside the curtained area when the drape flies open.

"You caught the bad jacks!" Riki-Tiki cries and shoots past me. Tychon is nowhere to be seen. "Why didn't you tell me? Come on!"

So much for apologizing.

She beats me to the corner of the infirmary, where Vienne still has her back to the patients. They are chatting when I arrive.

"Vienne says you captured the Sturmnacht all by yourself!"

"She said that, did she?" I shake my head at Vienne, who feigns innocence. "I'm not sure that's the truth."

But Riki-Tiki has already moved on. "My friend Tychon

said those men have been harassing the farmers for months. They don't look so tough now, eh?"

She nudges Franks with her sandal, the way I've seen Vienne do. He snorts, and she jumps into a fighting stance.

"Silly goose," Vienne says. "They won't bite."

But she still looks skittish. "What now? Hang them by their thumbs? Interrogate them till they spill their guts?"

"Sounds like a plan to me," Vienne says.

"Or we could turn them over to the farmers."

"What's the fun in that?" Riki-Tiki says, dead serious. "I'm going to tell Tychon!" Then she bounds away, giggling.

"You should call her bunny instead of goose." I watch her disappear behind the screens. The gravity of the situation seems completely lost on her. My first instinct is to squelch her happiness, because it seems disrespectful to the injured. But no, that's wrong. She is who she is. There's nothing wrong with being happy. "Now about my idea for fighting and possible gunplay."

"You're serious about that? Dressing up in their uniforms and sneaking into the outpost?" She gives Richards and Franks a long, assessing look. "Okay, but you have to be the one to strip them to their skivvies. There's only so far I'm willing to go."

"What? You don't love me?"

"If you have to ask . . ." Something behind me catches her attention, and her gaze shifts. "Here comes trouble."

I turn to see Joad and Rebecca making their way toward us.

Rebecca's jaw is set, and she's striding with a purpose. "Four of our people are missing," she blurts out a few meters away, clearly not somebody who stands on ceremony. "Lyme's Sturmnacht kidnapped them."

Even though I know what she's talking about, I point at the prisoners. "These men? I don't think they kidnapped anyone."

"There were more thugs than that," she says. "Maybe a dozen. Maybe more. Witnesses said they took our people away on trucks. Those two stayed behind. A diversion, maybe."

"It doesn't add up," I say. "In my experience, Lyme doesn't do kidnapping. He prefers to kill people by selling them drugs."

"Look," Rebecca says, "why they were snatched makes no difference at this point. I want my people back, and from what I see here, you two are pretty good at handling Sturmnacht. They have a base of sorts nearby at Tharsis Two—"

"No." Vienne steps forward. "Find somebody else."

"No?" Rebecca turns on her, clearly not used to being defied. That's when she notices that Vienne is missing a pinkie, and I hold up my own damaged hand to show that we're a matched set. "You're *dalit*. Okay, you want coin."

"Take your money"—Vienne makes a fist—"and shove it—"

"Vienne!" I pull her aside. "Give us a minute, Rebecca."

After I escort Vienne out the side door, Riki-Tiki says something, and I hear Rebecca reply, "What do you mean I'm lucky to still have my head?"

Outside, the air carries the tangy scent of burned metal. A group of farmers has gathered by the infirmary. After a few seconds, they head toward the fire site with tools in hand. When the burning is over, I'm guessing, they plan to bury what's left of the buildings. I hope that's all they have to bury.

"Why are you saying no to the job?" I ask Vienne. "The prisoners are at Tharsis Two, which is where we need to go. Looks like a golden opportunity to both get the data and do a good deed for which we will be somewhat meagerly rewarded."

"Stupid hussy," Vienne fumes at Rebecca, who is visible through the windows. "Who does she think she is?"

"The boss," I say, "who's worried about what the lowest scum in the territory will do to her folk. You know the drill."

"She didn't have to call us *dalit* in front of Riki-Tiki."

Now I get it. "Okay, that was a stupid thing to say—"

"That's an understatement."

"—but I don't think she meant to offend you. She's a farmer. They can't tell one soldier from another one, much less recognize the finest Regulator on the planet. Right?"

She blushes, despite my clumsy attempt at flattery. "You accept the job if you want, but the hussy has to strip the Sturmnacht for us."

Fair enough. Maybe Rebecca will learn to be more careful with her words. "Deal. I'll let them know."

"Wait." She grabs my shoulder when I turn to go inside. "I— Never mind. It's not my place."

"If it's not yours, it's nobody's. Spit it out."

"It's just . . . All these months looking for that data. What's it gotten us?"

"You want to know if it's worth the effort?"

"Not exactly." She pinches her lip, thinking. "I want to know—is it still worth it to you?"

"To find the secret my father hid from me for years?" I say. "Vienne, I know I can't undo the wrong he did by creating the Draeu. But what happens if someone like Lyme gets his hands on Project MUSE? They might be able to make more of the monsters. So what you're really asking is—is it worth it to end that possibility? Yes, it is. Abso-carking-lutely."

She nods. "Then it's worth it to me."

With that, she lets me know she'd rather stay with me than stay at the monastery, the only place where she's ever felt safe, and with that, I make the decision to continue the hunt for my father's secrets. Is this the decision that Ghannouj said I'd have to make? If so, I hope it's the right one, and I pray that I won't have to make a harder one.

CHAPTER 10

Outpost Tharsis Two
Zealand Prefecture
ANNOS MARTIS 238. 7. 20. 06:29

My father knew he had cancer for over a year before he bothered to tell me. It was the day of his sentencing, after he had been convicted by the InterCorporate Tribunal. He was charged with the murder of hundreds of soldiers—his own and the soldiers of bitter rival Vijaya Corporation—because he released a herd of Big Daddies on them. I know this because I was one of those soldiers, one of the lucky ones who survived. Murder was the official charge, but Father's real crime was high treason. His goal was total global domination. It sounds clichéd, like something from a story, but he meant it, and he had the resources to make it happen. The thing is, he didn't want to be the ruler of Mars himself. No, he reserved that honor for me.

I was born—no, designed—to become the Prince of Mars. Father hired an Earther, an astrophysicist with an athlete's physique, to donate her eggs for in vitro fertilization, then hired a surrogate to carry me for nine months. From birth,

I was given every benefit, every opportunity, every lesson he thought necessary to prepare me for my destiny. As an age three, he sent me off to Battle School, and at age six, I joined the CorpCom military. His scheme began to unravel when I chose to become a Regulator instead of an officer, and it really went to hell after his coup failed.

As a child and even later, I had no idea that I was living out a planned destiny. Not until Vienne and I teamed up with a couple of other Regulators to defend a group of miners did I learn just how convoluted my father's plot was. The man had fingers in every pie, but before I could confront him, he died in prison, leaving me and Vienne to pick up the clues he'd left behind, including a horrifying one that keeps us searching: A hastily transcribed physician's report mentioned the tantalizing phrases "hive mind," "cyborg beta tester," and my name, Jacob Stringfellow.

"You're being a little hard on yourself," Mimi says as Vienne and I rocket down the highway the next morning, a couple of hours before dawn. "You may be a cyborg, but you're my cyborg, and you're nothing like the Draeu. You don't even like rare meat."

"Thanks for that reassurance," I say. "Glad to know that I'm defined by how I enjoy my chow."

"As angry as you are about your father's behavior, you should allow yourself time to mourn his death," she says. "You are not immune to post-traumatic shock, either."

"I don't have time for the dead right now. Just the living."

"Then why are you still haunted by your father's ghost?"

"Do a scanner sweep, Mimi." And get off my back.

"I heard that."

"Then I hope you're listening."

When we can see the lights of Outpost Tharsis Two in the distance, I know it's time to leave the highway. Vienne pulls the motorbike into a copse of banyan trees. I jump off and run to the road to check for patrols.

"Mimi," I say, "give me a wider area sweep with a hundred meter—"

"Done," she says. "Nobody here but us Regulators. Unless you count a few dozen scorpions and the random foraging nutria rat."

"Those," I say, "aren't the kind of scorpions I'm worried about."

After jogging back to the trees, I help Vienne snap off branches to build a quick camouflage net. We lock our armalites in the bike's main storage compartment. We hate leaving them, but if a Sturmnacht suddenly showed up toting an armalite, it would be a dead giveaway.

We make some final adjustments to our stolen armor, and I toss a full ammo clip to Vienne. She jams it into Richards's battle rifle.

"Ready?" I ask. In the predawn light, I can only make out the shadow of her body. I shine a penlight on her neck, which now bears the same tattoo the Sturmnacht wear on their necks, a scorpion's tail. It's a henna tattoo, courtesy of

Ghannouj, who is almost as good at body art as he is at making tea. I have one on my neck, too.

"Ready," she says sharply.

"Did I do something to make you mad?"

"No."

We jog down the road leading to the outpost entrance. The lights grow larger as we get closer and closer.

"Are you sure? You sound mad."

"I'm not mad."

Now I can make out the faces in the guard shacks. We slow to a walk. Rifles ready. Trying to adopt the undisciplined shuffle of greenhorn troops.

"Look, if I did something to make you mad, I apologize."

"If you keep asking me if I'm mad, I'm going to get mad," she says. "Do you remember what happens when I get mad?"

"Someone gets shot."

"Do you want me to shoot you?"

"That would be a negative."

"Then I'm not mad."

From behind, the yellow light of headlamps sweep across the pavement, a Noriker coming around the bend. We dive into a gulley. Crouching, we wait until the truck is almost on us. It's a Düsseldorf, built for moving soldiers and armaments as uncomfortably and as slowly as possible.

"Here comes our escort." It seems that Lyme's operation has moved up the scale a few notches. He's got enough manpower for a small army.

The truck rolls to a stop, the brakes squealing like a wounded javelina. Shock troopers in body armor like ours file from the covered truck bed. As the last one exits, I slip into the end of the line, then signal Vienne to join me.

In a couple minutes, we are part of a long line waiting at the guard shack. The sun has risen, casting everyone in an orange glow. With the light, the noise level rises, and the guards bellow at everyone to pipe down.

"There's ten times more Sturmnacht than I expected," I whisper to Vienne. "This mission just got a lot more complicated."

"More fun for us," she replies.

"Mimi, give me an estimate of the number of hostiles in the vicinity."

"Inside or outside the outpost?"

"Both."

"Hundreds."

I do a quick visual scan of the entrance. There's a catwalk over the gates, with a crow's nest at either end. A dozen guards with shotguns pace the catwalk, and two snipers are perched in each nest. It's a standard CorpCom guard detail, which surprises me. I expected Sturmnacht to be less organized. "Give me more specific numbers, please, Mimi."

"More than a hundred, less than a thousand. Sorry, cowboy, the telemetry circuits in your suit just aren't capable of the kind of precision you'd like."

"So what're you saying?"

"It's you, not me."

"That's not very comforting."

"Want comfort?" she says. "Get a teddy bear."

"Don't tempt me."

All goes well until we reach the guard shack. Three lines have formed. We're in the one to the far left, with a guard who seems to be checking only two things—that the troops are wearing the right gear and that they've got scorpion tattoos on their necks.

"Next!" the guard yells, barely glancing at the soldier two up from us. "Next! Keep it moving! Next!"

Then it's Vienne's turn.

"Whoa!" The guard taps the piece of electrostat that I see now holds a duty roster. Then I notice the red light of a bar code scanner on the guard shack. I follow its light to Vienne's thigh, where it's reading an embedded chip in the body armor. "You were due six hours ago."

"We—"

I push forward, acting annoyed. "Got delayed." I give Vienne an overt wink. "You know how it is. Sorry."

The guard is not amused. Apparently, he doesn't know how it is. "Sorry don't cut it. Archibald's been informed."

"Archibald?" Who is Archibald? I wonder. Why not Lyme?

"Yeah, the underboss himself," the guard says. "Sucks for you. We'll notify your next of kin, if you've got any!"

Since when does Lyme have an underboss?

When we're clear of the guard shack, Vienne says in a low tone, "Thanks for bailing me out. I don't know what happened. My brain froze up."

"You're just not good at making up stories." I watch a pack of troops jog past us, cussing and arguing over who gets the last smoke. "I'm a much better liar."

She slugs my shoulder. "I'll keep that in mind."

We follow the other soldiers marching to the barracks. As we round the line of latrines, the two of us peel off and head toward the control building.

"Mimi, find the data center." I tap my temple and wince at the static discharge that signals my aural display to open. "Project a map of the outpost on my display. Pinpoint the target and show me the quickest route."

"Got it," Mimi says. "Your turn."

I blink twice. A holographic image appears. The data center is two buildings away from the control building. I signal Vienne, and we take a darkened alley between the buildings, staying off the main sidewalks. A few minutes later we reach the back doors of the data center, a squat, two-story building that looks suspiciously like a bunker.

I pull on the door handle. "Locked."

"Step aside." Vienne pulls an empty shell casing from a pouch on her belt and a bobby pin from her hair. "I've got this."

"Since when do you wear bobby pins?" I ask.

"Since forever. Don't you pay any attention?"

"To your hair, yes," I say. "To what you stick in it? Are you kidding?"

She squeezes the empty casing until it's flat, then bends it to form a crude torque wrench. Finally, she bends the pin to make a rake. "Count down from ten."

I roll my eyes. "Ten . . . nine . . . eig—" Click. "Show-off."

"In case you hadn't noticed, I'm more than a good shot." She tosses the bobby pin and casing aside and opens the door for me. "After you."

"Thanks." I pause before going inside. "Mimi, scan the corridor."

"Personnel clear. Four cameras detected. They're transmitting on an encrypted frequency requiring a key code override."

"Which means?"

"There's no way to override the alarms using your telemetry functions."

"Advise?"

"Smile and say cheese."

With a signal for Vienne to follow, I enter the building. Then take a right down a long corridor. Noting the four cameras, all of them recording. We move quickly and silently, trying to keep from attracting attention, until we reach two glass doors marked "Authorized Personnel Only." Inside the brightly lit room is the data center's massive server farm, which houses the data for MUSE.

Finally, my quest is over.

"Do not pat yourself on the back yet, cowboy."

"Mimi, it's a security door." I note the print pad on the door. "We need the pass code."

"Just put your finger on the pad, cowboy," Mimi says. "I'll handle the heavy lifting."

After removing my smelly outer glove, I touch a symbiarmor-covered fingertip to the pad. A jolt of static electricity from my glove, and the door clicks open.

"Show-off," Vienne says.

"Just proves I'm more than a good shot." I hold the door open. "In case you hadn't noticed."

Vienne moves inside and signals all clear. "Who says you're a good shot?"

Ouch. I'm not sure I like this newly found sarcasm of hers. "Give me a hand with the route, Mimi."

"Follow the map to servers labeled Andromeda fifty-six, fifty-seven, fifty-eight. Row nine-C."

We count out seven rows, then make a left. Most of the boxes are dead dark, but the Andromeda servers are lit up like a foundry at night.

Vienne watches the door while I insert a data chip into number fifty-six.

"Download under way," Mimi says.

"How long?"

Mimi sighs. "Each server holds a hundred yottabytes of data. It will take oh, just a few days to sort through it all to find the files specific to Project MUSE."

"Forget sorting, then. How long to download it all?" I ask. "And if you say indeterminate, I'm going to pash an icicle and give us a brain freeze."

"Five minutes," Mimi says. "But I think you have pashing on the brain, if you ask me."

"I didn't," I say. "Start download now and keep me posted on the time."

Vienne takes a defensive position with a direct line of sight on the entrance. "Wish I had my armalite. This gun is such an antique."

Wish you had it, too, I think. Then I wouldn't be worried about how we're going to rescue the hostages. "Time, Mimi?"

"Two minutes, thirty-seven seconds left."

Halfway there.

Click.

An instant later, the lights go out and backup power kicks in.

When the lights return, they are much dimmer.

"Mimi," I say. "Tell me something good."

"Server is still online."

"Tell me something bad?"

"Access to the data center has been detected."

"Tell me something worse?"

"Is a security alert worse?" Mimi says.

Much worse.

I tell her to open a telemetry link between me and Vienne.

"Heads up!" I whisper sharply into the mic. "Company's coming. Hold them off till the data's downloaded, then we'll drop smoke and bug out of here."

"They'll be coming in hot?" she asks.

"Sturmnacht always do."

She locks and loads. "Just the way I like it."

"One minute fifty-nine seconds remaining, cowboy," Mimi reminds me.

Outside the server room, the sound of heavy boots. Then voices, trying to stay low. A few shadows dance across the glass, and I move into position.

The beep of the fingerprint scanner.

The lock clicks open.

Hinges creak as the point man's head slowly emerges through the gap.

Whump!

The door flies open, and the shooters rush to positions.

I flick my safety off. "Vienne, I count five hostiles. Fire on my mark."

"Wait." She makes a slashing movement across her throat, countermanding my order. "Tight quarters, limited sight range, sensitive targets. We need to lure them in first."

"So which of us is bait?"

She points at me.

"Why am I always bait?"

"Because," she says, "the bad guys like shooting you."

I put a hand over my heart, acting wounded, then step

into the aisle. "Howdy, boys and girls. We've been expecting you."

Phttt! A blaster shot flies past my ear.

I raise my hands but instead of surrendering, I backpedal. Four guards hustle toward me—and past Vienne's position.

"Halt!" the leader, a blighter in a blue uniform with chevrons, barks at me.

I cup a hand to my ear. "Huh? What was that?"

Vienne pops out. Flattens two guards with the butt of her rifle. And steps back behind the servers.

The leader spins around.

His men lie unconscious on the floor.

I take the opportunity to thump the third guard and grab the fourth one in a sleeper hold.

"Stop!" The leader spins back to face me. "Don't even twitch! Tell your friend to show himself, or I'll cut you in half."

Smiling, I let the sleeping guard slide to the floor. "Oops. He fall down."

"Shut it!" The leader notices my missing pinkie. "*Dalit?* You're a Regulator? You got some kind of death wish?"

The data chip beeps.

The leader snaps his head toward the sound, and Vienne nails him with a punch.

Face, meet fist.

He joins the pile of bodies at her feet.

I plug the chip into a data port built into my symbiarmor.

Vienne gathers up their battle rifles and dumps them in a recycling bin. The blaster, she shoves into her belt.

"Crafty work," she says.

I snag the guard's cuffs and lock all their wrists together. "I bet you say that to all the boys."

"Just the ones whose ass I can kick."

"And how many would that be?"

"Oh," she says, smiling. "Pretty much all of them."

We hit the corridor running. Vienne sprints alongside me as the overhead lights dim and brighten.

Around the next corner and—

"Oh crap."

A guard at the exit door.

I hesitate for a nanosecond, but Vienne hits the after-burners. The guard glances up as her flying dropkick slams into his solar plexus.

His body hits the floor.

"Next time," I say, "leave one for me."

"Next time," she laughs, "run faster."

CHAPTER 11

"Mimi!" I bark out an order. "Scan the perimeter! Find me
a vehicle. We're going out hot and fast!"

"Yes sir!"

Vienne hits the exit ahead of me. She is beckoning me
outside when I hear a scream. I stop, one foot on the thresh-
old. You're so close, I tell myself. Get out of here!

Another scream. It draws me back down the hallway to
a thick metal door marked with the word "Brig" and the
number thirteen.

Vienne follows. "Durango!" she calls. "Come on! We
have a clear escape route!"

I step over the fallen guard and slide the observation slot
open. "Hello?" I press my face against the wire mesh to get
a better view.

Bam!

The frenzied face of a woman slams into the mesh. "Help
us! Please!"

I jump back. "Gah!"

"Durango!" Vienne's voice rises. "We don't have time!"

"Please, sir," the woman begs. She laces her fingers through the mesh. The tips are roasted black, her nails peeled back. "My name is Thela. I have a child and a husband at home. Please. Have mercy."

I snatch the key card from the guard's belt. "I can't leave them here. We have to help."

"Damn you," Vienne says, eyes darting from the exit to me and back. "You're going to get us caught."

It's not like there's a choice. "They're helpless, and we're still Regulators."

I open the brig door. Three farmers—two women and one man—in torn, bloodied coveralls lurch out of the cell. Their hair is matted with filth and mud, and they reek of human waste. They shuffle as if sleepwalking, but their eyes are rapid wild, and the irises have turned pink.

"It's Rapture," I tell Vienne as I lead them slowly down the hallway.

"Then they're as good as dead already," she says. "Let's go. I'll take point."

I drag the guard into the cell, then lock it. "Why are you suddenly so hard-hearted?"

"Why are you"—she checks the exit for hostiles—"always breaking promises?"

"I—" I begin, but a scream from another cell stops me. "There are others?"

"I read several signatures in close proximity, cowboy," Mimi says.

"Why didn't you tell me this before?" I ask her.

"You did not ask."

Using the guard's key card, I unlock every cell, swing open every door, and help every prisoner shuffle out.

"More?" Vienne head butts the wall in frustration. "More!"

There are fourteen in all, each of them bearing signs of torture—burns, lash marks, deep purple bruises—and each of them with pink irises.

"Hurry, hurry," I keep saying as they line up along the wall, a collection of walking dead.

I join Vienne at the exit. "That's the lot of them."

"Fourteen hostages that can barely walk?" She slams her palm against my chest. "If you march the prisoners outside, the Sturmnacht will use them for target practice! So how in the name of the gods do you plan to pull off this rescue?"

"Easy," I say. "I'm going to steal a truck."

"Of course you are." She smacks her forehead. "Why didn't I think of that?"

"Because I'm the one with all the smarticles?"

"No," she says, her voice rising. "Because you're the one who cares more about being a hero than a good boyf—soldier."

"See? I knew you were mad."

"Stop saying that! I'm not mad!"

"Your mouth says no," I say, deciphering her expression, "but your teeth-barred, eyes-narrowed, scary face says yes."

Her fist moves so fast, I don't even see it. Just a blur of motion that catches me in the ribs, and despite two layers of armor, knocks me on my butt.

"Now I'm mad!"

"I can tell!" I get back to my feet. Behind us, the prisoners start moaning in response to the ruckus.

"You deserved that," Mimi says.

"At least she didn't shoot me. Look, Vienne, I'm sorry. I—"

"Stow it." She knocks the dust off my armor. "I'll keep watch on the prisoners. You've got a truck to steal."

"Yes, ma'am," I agree, because there's no point in apologizing again and because I like my teeth.

"Your teeth thank you," Mimi says.

"Yes, Mom. Got that scan for me yet?"

"There is a line of vehicles on the grounds approximately fifty meters from this location."

Excellent. I hold out an open palm to Vienne. "Can I see that blaster you picked off the guard?"

She slaps it into my hand. "Won't do much good in a firefight."

"I don't aim to get in a fight. Just use a little trick that Fuse taught me down in the Hell's Cross mines."

Her lip twitches. "Any trick that fossiker taught you is liable to blow your hand off."

"Cut the bloke some slack, Vienne. He wasn't that bad."
I pull the wiring harness out of the grip, twist the red and
green wires together, and set the blaster to overcharge.
"Yeah, well, okay, he was that bad, but he did know his
explosives."

"And how to act like a complete wanker."

"It wasn't an act." The weapon starts to keen as I hand it
back to Vienne. "There's a couple of trucks parked outside.
Give me a fifteen-second head start, then toss this at the
closest Düsseldorf."

"It will just explode," she says. "Then we'll be out a
weapon."

"But it will cause a distraction, and like you said, one
blaster won't let us shoot our way out."

She rolls her eyes. "That's your grand plan? To cause a
ruckus?"

"I admit it isn't grand." I check my gear. "But it'll do in a
pinch. Remember, throw it as far as you can. And not at me."

Out on the grounds, I start jogging casually toward the
lead truck, an armored Noriker. When I reach it, I yank the
driver's door open.

"Howdy." I punch him in the jaw, then drag him, unconscious, to the pavement.

As I jump behind the wheel, I see Vienne step into the
open.

She flings the overcharged blaster in a high arc across the
lot. It hits the pavement with a clack, then slides perfectly

under the cab of the closest Düsseldorf, which is equipped with two supplemental fuel tanks.

That's a heap of petrol in one place.

"She's got a good arm."

"And good aim," Mimi adds.

With a sound like a titanic belch, the blaster explodes.

Fuel vaporized by the blast hits a spark. The trail of flame rockets into the truck's two fuel tanks. I see the explosion before I hear it, as the Düsseldorf's rear wheels rise three meters from the pavement then—

Slam!

To the ground as the rest of the fuel ignites, and the truck seems to disassemble itself before my eyes.

That's my cue.

I smash the pedal to the floor, and the Noriker lurches forward as the rear tires spin, leaving a strip of rubber on the tarmac as the bed whips around. The steering wheel rips from my hand, but I grab hold in time for the right side to bounce the curb.

The truck comes to a stop three meters from the exit.

"That's what you call some carking fancy driving," I say, checking the side mirror as blue, oily smoke rises from the tires.

"That's what you call some carking dumb luck," Mimi says.

"Better dumb luck than no luck at all."

Slam!

Vienne kicks the exit door open and herds the farmers outside. She pushes them into the bed of the Noriker, yelling "Move! Move! Before I shoot you!"

As I scan the area for hostiles, my sight lines are hidden by a black ink cloud that spreads across the base. The exploded truck burns for a few more seconds until the fuel is exhausted, waves of heat rippling in the sky. The smell of petrol chokes the air.

Then abruptly, the fire dies down.

Across the grounds, the Sturmnacht begin to emerge from cover. They're focused on the truck.

For now.

"Go!" Vienne shoves the last prisoner into the back.

I start the truck rolling.

She catches the handle of the passenger door, swings it open, and jumps inside.

"Righteous fireworks," I say.

"Think so?" She pops a full clip into her battle rifle. "Get ready for the real show."

The direct line to the gates is blocked by one wave of troops fleeing the fire and another wave running toward it. Downhill from the Düsseldorf, a pond of ignited fuel stretches across the pavement.

I steer toward it. "Mimi, calculate the risk of me blowing us all to kingdom come."

"About forty percent if you drive at a safe speed."

"What if I gun it?"

"The chance of explosion drops exponentially."

"Now that's my kind of math!" I stomp the pedal to the floorboard, counting on the thick tires and great height to give us enough ground clearance.

The Noriker's six-liter engine roars like a Seneca gun, and we plow through the fiery pond, throwing waves of flames from the wheel wells.

"I bet this looks so cool from the outside!" I yell.

"You are such!" Vienne yells back, firing rounds to scatter the guards stupidly moving to block us. "A little boy!"

"Watch this!"

I turn the wheels so that the bumper is square to the iron gates and slam through them. The rust-mottled gates swing open, then back, crashing against the bed of the Noriker.

I look in the rearview and see the crumpled iron in our wake.

"We made it!"

A fist bump with Vienne, then Mimi ruins the moment.

"Cowboy! I'm picking up a sudden spike in electromagnetic energy! Look out!"

Phoom!

A mortar sails over the Noriker.

Hits the road ahead.

Emits a blinding light, a pulse of pure energy that sweeps over us like an invisible wave.

The dashboard goes dark.

The Noriker is dead.

Damn!

I fight with the wheel to hold us in the road, pounding the brakes—they're gone, too.

Vienne bails from the cab as the Noriker rolls to a stop. She takes position beside the fender.

"Mimi, what the hell was that?" Static. "Mimi? Mimi? Where are you? Talk to me!"

A blaster round shatters the side window. I reach for my weapon and realize that it's gone. "Oh *wà kào!*" Durango, how could you lose your carking rifle?

Another round rips through the cab, and I bail, too.

I squat-run the length of the Noriker bed until I spot Vienne beside the tailgate. She's kneeling in firing position, picking off the guards.

"These sights are way off," she says calmly. "And the drift is ridiculous. No wonder shock troops can't hit the broad side of a barn."

She takes out two more guards with shots to the legs.

"You seem to be doing okay," I say.

"I was aiming for the gut."

I call for Mimi again, and like before, just get static. Whatever that light was, it knocked Mimi out, too. I cross my fingers and say, "Begin reboot protocols."

More troops start to mass at the gate. Soon, they will come together, then move ahead as a phalanx, laying down covering fire.

"How long can you hold them off?" I ask.

"Until this clip is empty. Which will be right about—"

Crack!

"—now."

"The hostages are dead meat in a firefight."

"You're the one who wanted to save them," she says. "We could make a run for it. The Sturmnacht take the prisoners back to the cells, and we can rescue them later."

"Vienne," I try to explain. "We just can't abandon hostages."

She jabs the gun muzzle into my chest. "You infuriate me sometimes! You tell me to ignore the Tenets, but you live by a set of rules that only you know, and you won't break them, even if it means getting killed."

"I thought you didn't mind dying."

"I don't!" she yells. "It's your death I'm worried about!"

"Oh."

"Is that all you have to say?" She shakes me. "Sometimes, Durango, I really do want to shoot you."

"Can't you just settle for punching me?"

"Thief!" The Noriker starts rocking, and then the woman named Thela throws back the flap. She points a roasted finger at me. "Thief! You stole my soul!"

"Down!" Vienne yanks her from the truck.

But Thela isn't going easily. She kicks and scratches as we wrestle her to the ground, my knee pinning her head down.

"Be still!" I yell, but she sinks her teeth into my shin, which should not be possible. "Ow! That hurt!"

Enough's enough. I grab her around the waist and toss her ass back into the bed of the truck.

The screaming stops.

"Durango." Vienne's face turns pale. "Did you say—?"

"It hurt, yeah." I tug on the symbiarmor, which is as loose and unresponsive as normal cloth.

We exchange a *der scheißkerl* look.

"Our armor's fragged," she says.

"We're dead."

"Not yet," she says. "Not until they manage to kill us."

A whistle sounds. At the gate, an officer shouts orders. The Sturmnacht form ranks, then march double time toward us.

I pull Vienne behind the truck for cover.

"Mimi," I say. "Do a systems check on the nanobots to see what's happened to symbiarmor functions. Mimi?"

Static.

The reboot didn't work.

No Mimi.

No armor.

No ammo.

No choice. "They're coming in hot. If we resist, they'll kill us. We have to surrender." I'm almost begging Vienne. "Live to fight another day."

"No retreat." She raises the rifle like a club. "No surrender."

"Vienne, be rational. Don't do this. I'm not going to watch you die."

"Then close your eyes," she says, her voice taking a

razor-sharp edge. "I would rather fall in battle than be taken. I will not be held prisoner again."

Again? When was Vienne ever—

"Stand down!" the officer yells as his troops surround the truck. "We will shoot you!"

"Vienne, please," I say, desperate to convince her.

"No retreat." She shakes her head. "No surrender."

"You said that already."

"You needed to hear it again."

The ranks of Sturmnacht split, and a jack about my age moves through the ranks to meet us. Dressed in a ridiculous flowing cape, he seems too tall, legs too stilted, arms made of loosely connected, birdlike bones. His face is small and heart shaped, a shank of straw-colored hair draped across his forehead, and his clothes are baggy, as if borrowed from someone else's wardrobe.

"Thank you, Duke," he says. "I'll take it from here."

He waves a dozen troops toward our position, where they surround Vienne. She lunges at them, and they wisely expand the circle.

"Permission to fire?" the officer asks.

"Not yet," the straw-haired jack says.

Enough of this. Vienne may hate me forever, but I'm not about to let her die a stupid death. "Under section seven-point-two of the Zuuric Convention," I announce, "we submit ourselves as prisoners of war."

"Speak for yourself!" Vienne yells.

The corners of the leader's mouth draw up in the imitation of a smile. Then he rams a fist in my gut. The blow doubles me over, and I fall to one knee.

Now I recognize the poxer's face. He was in the boardroom back in Christchurch—Archibald Bragg. That's who Lyme chose as his underboss, the son of the CEO?

"This is no war," Archibald says. "We will take prisoners when we see fit. Unfortunately for you, I don't see fit."

I turn my head to see Vienne take out a trooper with a front kick, grab his blaster, and lay down fire. Three soldiers go down before the others can draw on her.

"Stop!" I lunge for her, but the butt of a battle rifle meets my temple, and the lights go out.

CHAPTER 12

Tranquility Canyon, Noctis Labyrinthus
Zealand Prefecture
ANNOS MARTIS 238. 7. 20. 12:01

The sun is at high noon when the Noriker stops on the road above the canyon. My Sturmnacht acquaintances, Richards and Franks, drag me across the high desert, the toes of my blood-spattered boots leaving a wake in the dirt. Head drooping, I let them carry my full weight, each of them holding one of my arms.

My eyes stay closed. It keeps the mud out, and besides, my bionic one is a fair dinkum mess. Hair, caked with blood and dirt, hangs over my face. That's a good thing, because they think I'm dead, and I want to keep it that way.

"Keep walking, Franks," Richards grunts. "This jack's heavy as a sack of rocks."

Franks shakes my limp arm. "So he's a Regulator? Not so tough after all, huh?"

"This ain't no real Regulator, Franks. Look at his finger. This jack's a *dalit*."

"*Dalit?*" Franks says, huffing as he shifts his grip to my ammo belt.

"Don't you know nothing?" Richards drawls. "A *dalit* is a Regulator gone bad. Some turn to begging. Some to thieving. Some, like this one, turns to being a goody-goody hired gun."

"Huh?" From the sound of it, he scratches the heavy stubble on his jowls. "How'd you know that?"

"Use that microbe you call a brain," Richards says, guiding us down a short path. The brown mud suddenly turns to blue-gray sky: we've reached the lip of the canyon. "Some great gob hired him and his partner to rescue them farmers we took as collateral."

"Almost worked, too." Franks whistles. "Never seen no susie shoot like that one. Think Archie's going to kill her, too?"

"When he's done having his fun with her, probably." Richards grunts again. "But that Archie's a bit of a dill bird, so there's no telling what he might do."

They drop me like a sack of spoiled rations. I turn my head quickly to avoid breaking my nose on the loose stones. One of them plants a foot in my gut. I stifle a groan and hold in the breath that wants desperately to escape.

"What you doing that for?" Richards says. "He's dead."

Remain calm, I tell myself, as the anger rises in my throat. Bide your time. You're going to rescue her, but you can't do it now.

"Let's pop him anyhow," Franks says, sounding too eager for my taste. "Mess up that pretty face some more."

"Waste of ammo. Ammo costs money. You got extra coin to buy me more ammo?"

"Extra?" Franks says. "Already I owe Mr. Lyme a month's back pay."

"Then drop the poxer down the hill and shut your pie-hole. You're giving me a headache."

On the count of three, they hoist me into the air and sling my corpse down the side of the canyon. Squeezing my eyes and mouth shut, I take the force of the fall, allowing my body to flop around like a useless hunk of meat as I slide down a dry gully.

Oof!

I hit an outcropping, and the air escapes my lungs. I only hope that the Sturmnacht aren't curious enough to stay behind and watch. For a few interminable seconds, I lie perfectly still, my left leg and right arm bent beneath me. My face is half turned toward the sun, and through my good eye, I trace the trail back to the top of the canyon.

There's nobody at the top of the embankment. For now. But I stay low, just in case.

Everything below my elbows is deadened, and when I flex my hands, the fingers feel like numb sausages. It takes a few minutes to even feel the prickles of electric pain that remind me that yes, these parts are actually connected. My face feels like a mass of bee stings. One side is swollen shut, my mouth and nose puffy with blood. If I turn my head too quickly, everything spins. It's like vertigo, only more intense.

Damn, we were this close to escaping the outpost. If only I had done what Vienne asked.

"Mimi?"

I tap my right temple, feeling the thick surgical scar through my hairline. Static. The EMP scrambled all electronic impulses.

"Mimi, it's time to wake up. Begin reboot sequence."

I squeeze my right eye, a prosthetic implant, shut for three seconds, waiting for the quiet chime that signals the reboot. Seconds, then minutes, tick by.

There is no chime.

Just static.

"Mimi?" I say out loud. "Mimi! Where are you?"

A thought crosses my mind, and it terrifies me: What if I've lost Mimi, and with her, any chance of ever rescuing Vienne? Moaning, I pull myself into a sitting position. I try to test my left arm, but it's numb, already swelling up from a horrific bruise over the fibula. Then I feel something warm on my forehead.

Blood.

Lots of it.

While I'm looking at the red liquid puddling in my palm, my vision wavers. Above me, I hear the buzz of a vortex generator, the sound of an aerofoil banking between the walls of the canyons. I raise my hand to signal the aviator for help when half of my visual field goes black.

"*Tā mādebiing* bionic eye." I smack my temple. A jolt of pain shoots through my brain, and my head spins. Oh lovely, I have a concussion, too. How can things get any worse?

I put a hand on the ground to steady myself and get an answer.

Five meters above my head, rock dust begins to cascade from the side of the canyon. There's an earsplitting squeal, and a long, needlelike claw emerges. It flicks in and out rapidly, as if tasting the air, then with a *snick* sound, disappears.

"No way." My eyes are playing tricks. My brain's addled.

Sharp chunks of rock explode from the canyon wall. Another squeal, so loud it makes my ears ring, and eight arachnid legs spring from the hole. Serrated claws grip the rock, boney skeleton scraping like chalk on slate, until a pair of claws—oozing and dripping with viscous secretions that stink like sour cabbage rotting in a jar—emerges from its mouth, followed by two bulbous compound eyes. For a second it pauses, clacking its claws together. Then its eyes focus on me. Its whole body quivers, and it scuttles down to the outcropping.

Less than a meter from my feet.

"Oh *merde*," I say, because the insectoid is a chigoe, Mars's only surviving native species, once thought extinct but accidently set loose on the world.

By me.

If Mimi were awake, she'd be laughing at the irony of the situation.

"Good little chigger," I mutter through puffed lips, then labor to get both feet under me. I half walk, half crawl to the edge of the outcropping. "Go play. Durango's not going to hurt you."

Ooze drips from its quivering mouth to the ground.

The stone begins to sizzle.

I pick up a loose rock as big as my hand. With all the strength left to muster, I bounce it off the chigoe's carapace.

It shrieks and scuttles away.

Whew, I think, that was close.

Then it rears up on its hind legs, turns its thick thorax toward me, and kicks out waves of fine, barbed hairs that sink into the right side of my face.

At first I feel nothing—until the pain hits, then my screams echo down the canyon. Blinded and in agony, I stumble past the edge of the outcropping, and feel my feet touch nothing.

So bright.

My brain feels too small for my skull. Pounding. Tight.

There's a familiar smell about this place. Medicinal. Something I should recognize. A compress is bandaged to the wound on my temple. It stinks like ammonia. For an instant, I panic that the smell is from a gangrenous wound. I feel the skin nearby, though, and it is cool to the touch.

I roll over and puke on the floor.

"Just shoot me." Then I remember that someone probably has. I giggle madly, and my brain explodes with a meteor shower of hurt.

So I puke again.

The smell of vomit rises from the floor. It doesn't bother me as much as it should. I throw my right arm across my eyes. Funny, the left one seems to be incommunicado.

Somewhere, a woman is singing. Her voice is very high, almost coloratura, but not screechy like the fat opera singers they always show on the multivids. Maybe it's the singer's accent, but the tune sounds very old and very sad.

No, not sad. Melancholy.

"Vienne?"

Must find that voice.

I sit up and steel myself. I even wince by reflex before I realize that the pain is gone.

Hallelujah.

Taking a deep breath, I expand my chest, and lightning strikes my rib cage.

It's dark the next time I wake up.

This time, I'm paralyzed. No movement, no voice, locked in the darkness with no way of escaping. My skull feels like a thin-shelled egg filled with hydrogen that at any time could crack and explode, and my thoughts would slip away like so much ether.

"Mimi?" I scream inside my head. "Mimi! Please answer me. I need you!"

This time, there's no static.

"I'm here, cowboy."

"I thought . . ." The panic in my chest dissipates. "Thought . . . I'd lost you forever."

"Only if forever lasts one hundred nineteen minutes."

"I puked. Twice."

"Pardon me for not keeping count."

The air smells antiseptic, that familiar medicinal scent, like alcohol and povidone-iodine scrub. Which means I'm in an infirmary and not dead.

"You are woozy and somewhat incoherent, but not dead," Mimi says. "Unless I am conversing with a ghost, and I am not programmed for astral communication."

"What about you?" I say, not feeling any pain, oddly. "One second you're jabbering away, then—kaput."

"Good word, kaput. We were hit by an EMP, an electromagnetic pulse. It shorted out your symbiarmor and forced a hard reboot of your AI. Namely, me."

"Ha." I laugh. "You got coldcocked."

"A fate that befell you minutes later, I gather."

"I'm such a copycat," I say. "Where's Vienne? I heard her voice."

"Not her," she says. "Just an aural hallucination from brain trauma."

"She's not here? But I thought . . . I thought she was singing to me."

"I am sorry, cowboy."

"What *happened* to Vienne?"

"My functions were off-line," she says. "You know more than I do."

"But my brain's all jumbled up like garbage soup. I can't— wait, a chigoe bit me."

"A chigoe?"

"In the eye. With its butt."

"Physically impossible, but that may explain why your ocular implant is no longer responding to commands."

"My bionic eye broke?" For some reason, I find this funny, even though I know it's not. "I feel drugged."

"That is because you are. I detect a combination of synthetic opiates and neuromuscular-blocking drugs specifically targeted to skeletal muscles, which explains your paralysis, lack of pain, and general loopiness."

"Also," I say, "I can't see a thing."

"Because the room is dark."

"I would laugh, but it'd make me puke," I say. "Do a scanner sweep? Maybe Vienne is close by."

"Negative, cowboy. Your prosthetic eye was a key component in your suit's telemetry system," she says. "Without it, I'm almost as blind as you are."

"Well, *tā mādebi.*"

"Amen to that."

Light.

With a click of a switch, fluorescent light fills the room, and I see that I'm lying facedown on a table, my head supported by a cushioned O-ring, and staring at a red-tile floor. Two bare feet appear. A silver anklet and painted toenails.

"Vienne?" I call to Mimi.

"Negative, cowboy."

"Where's Vienne?" I try to say out loud, but my mouth feels like it's stuffed with a rag, and the words won't form. A machine begins to hum. The table revolves so that I'm turned to face upward.

Surgery lights on. A woman steps into view. Rebecca. Her hair is pinned up in a bun, and she's wearing a mask, her eyes protected by surgical goggles. She is also wielding a wicked pair of forceps.

"Hey, hero." She shines a light in my left eye. "At least we know you're not dead."

"What about Vienne?" I yell, but only succeed in making a strangled noise. "Mimi, can't you do something?"

"No," she says, sounding more angry and helpless than I've ever heard. "There is nothing I can do because there is nothing you can do."

I want to scream in frustration, but even that eludes me.

"Sorry about the talking thing," Rebecca says. "The mild paralysis is from a dose of pancuronium bromide. You kept thrashing around, so I had to sedate you. Joad, hold his left eyelid back."

"Got it." Joad leans into view. He's not wearing any surgical garb, and his hand looks very dirty.

"A little wider, please," she tells him. "There are still several hairs in the cornea. Durango, do try to relax. Plucking urticating hairs out of a cornea is delicate work, and lately, I've gotten used to working on plants, which have no nerve endings."

Pain is more than the sum of its neurons, I think.

Methodically, Rebecca plucks the hairs out, setting each aside. "If I didn't know better, I swear you ran into a Goliath bird-eater spider, except that it's an Earth species that went extinct when the Amazon was deforested. Lucky our crop duster found you before nutrias made a snack of your corpse."

"How nonclinical of her," Mimi says. "This woman calls herself a professional?"

"She's a botanist."

"How apropos," Mimi says, "since she has the bedside manner of a potted plant."

Rebecca changes the angle of the light. She purses her lips, perplexed. "Weird. Thought I saw more hairs embedded in the vitreous body. Now they're . . . gone?"

How can they be gone? I think.

She sets down the forceps. "Did you eat them, Durango? I know, I know, I'm not funny. Just a little gallows humor. I like to talk while I work. Right, Joad?"

"Ain't that the truth," he says, rolling his eyes.

"The plants don't seem to mind." She disappears offscreen.

Joad takes her place. "That's 'cause they ain't got ears."

"Too true," she says, the sound of her voice a couple meters away, "but that doesn't mean they can't hear. Durango, I'm putting one of the hairs under the 'scope to see where it came from. Hmm. No maker's mark, so it's definitely not bioengineered. Never seen a hair structure like this before. Amazing. It's quite a find. I would do an article on it if I weren't up to my elbows in running a collective."

She reappears, a dropper in hand. "Now, I could tell you that it's going to sting a little, but that would be a lie."

Using the dropper, she plops the medicine into my eye. The pain is like scalding fury, and I jerk my head to the side.

"Joad," Rebecca says. "Please hold his head still. Durango, I am sorry, but you will go blind without the drops."

"Wà kào, that burns!" I tell Mimi.

"I am aware of that, cowboy. Your synapses lit up like the capital celebrating Spirit Festival. Ouch! There they go again. I know it is difficult for you, but from my perspective, pain can be quite beautiful."

"Thanks—ow!—for your sympathy."

"It is not exactly sympathy. Ooh, pretty synapses."

"All done," Rebecca says, and places a gauze pad over my eye. She applies slight pressure, and I notice that I'm beginning to feel more sensations than before.

When she removes the pad, I blink three times. It doesn't burn as much.

"You can blink? The pancuronium bromide must be wearing off a little early. I'm going to give you something for pain in the meantime. Like I said, somebody did a number on that handsome face of yours, and there's lots of soft tissue damage. Do yourself a favor. Don't look in a mirror for at least a week."

Joad hands Rebecca a serum cartridge and a syringe gun. She loads the cartridge, places it against my shoulder, and fires.

Crack! Rebecca examines the gun. The hypodermic is broken in half. "What the hell happened?"

"You broke the needle," Joad says.

"It wasn't me," she says. "It's his symbiarmor. It solidified when the lance inserted. Pull up his shirt."

"Mimi," I say. "What happened?"

"Just as she said, when the lance pierced the outer layer of your armor, the nanobots signaled the fibers to interweave."

"But I wasn't under a threat."

"The nanobots thought you were. Did you know that the threads in symbiarmor were derived from modified yam fibers?"

I'm not in the least bit interested in legume trivia. "Override the 'bots, then. I'm not crazy about hair getting plucked from my eyes, but I wouldn't mind a little help with this pain."

"I will endeavor, but . . ."

"But what?"

"The 'bots are also tied into the telemetry functions. Without them, I don't have as much control over your suit as before."

"Bugger."

"My thoughts exactly."

Rebecca reappears into view. "Sorry, Durango, more bad news. The shot has to go into your gut. Good news is, it won't burn nearly as badly as the drops did."

"It's stuck," Joad says. "The shirt."

"Symbiarmor can be stubborn. Just give it a good yank."

"No, I mean really stuck. As in, stuck to his skin."

"No way." She disappears from view. "Let me see."

"See?" Joad says. "Told you so."

"It's . . . wow," Rebecca says. "The nanofabric seems to have grafted itself to the skin there. And here, too. I've never seen it do that before. Durango, when you're back on your feet, you'll need to see a programmer about rebooting your suit. The nanobots appear to be overresponding to stimuli. They're designed to bond with your skin during impact to minimize force, but your 'bots aren't letting go. Wait, here's a spot where the fabric is coming loose."

"The nanobots are doing what?" I ask Mimi.

"Obviously, they seem to be grafting the fabric to your flesh," Mimi says. "Were you not listening?"

"I was hoping for a less technical description. You know,

like, they aren't supposed to do that. It's weird."

"They are not supposed to do that. It is weird."

"Ha-ha."

The syringe gun clicks. I feel something warm wash over my body. My eye rolls back into my head. "Wow. That was quick."

"It certainly was," Mimi says, the sound of her voice slurring in my ear. "Ta-ra-ra boom-de-a. We are having slop today. Sing with me."

My lips move. No sound comes out.

"That'll hold you for a few hours, Regulator," Rebecca says as the room begins to melt away. "My god. It's grafted to his legs, too. I've never seen anything like this, even when I worked for Zealand Corp, and there was always something weird going on."

"Did she just say Zealand?" I mumble to Mimi.

But Mimi's not listening. "Nighty night, cowboy. See you in the mo-rn-ing."

CHAPTER 13

Oustpost Tharsis Two
Zealand Prefecture
ANNOS MARTIS 238. 7. 21. 05:19

Archibald places a handkerchief over his mouth as he enters
the makeshift prison at Tharsis Two. The stench is overwhelming, worse than the streets of Favela.

"Tell the videographers to start rolling," he tells Duke.
"Let's get this over with. Their stench is beginning to turn
my stomach."

"Yes, Mr. Archibald." Duke puts a bullhorn to his mouth.
"All right, you dogs. Line it up. Line it up. Inspection time."

The prisoners shuffle across the yard, their soiled overalls
and blue work shirts giving the look of a press-gang family photo. If there were work to do, they wouldn't even be
capable of it. Every man, woman, and child looks as if their
feet are the only anchors that keep them from floating away.

In their current state, they make terrible theater. But that
will change soon.

"Congratulations!" Archibald calls out, not bothering to
use the bullhorn. "You have been liberated from the tyranny

of the Zealand CorpCom by the Desperta Ferro!"

"The what?" Duke says. "We're Sturmnacht, not—"

Archibald silences him with a sharp look. "Just as the original Desperta Ferro helped overthrow the Orthocracy, the new Desperta Ferro will liberate the people from the stranglehold of the Zealand CorpCom. We will reeducate you in the ways of true freedom. No longer will you toil in isolation. No longer will your labor be lost. No longer will you face starvation while raising crops for the CEO's table!"

The prisoners look at him with glassy eyes. They are underwhelmed.

"Got the shot?" He looks to the videographers, who give him the thumbs-up. "Duke, pass out the water."

Over the next few minutes, the prisoners are given cups of fluid, which they drink greedily. Only one of them, a tall blonde, refuses. Her hands are chained to the shackles on her ankles, and she stands a few meters away from the others.

A Sturmnacht tries to force the cup to her lips. He gets a wicked head butt for his trouble, and he stumbles back, hand covering a broken nose.

"Stop!" Archibald recognizes her now—the full-metal jacket angel from Christchurch. The tumblers of mischief start turning in his mind. The possibilities! "Duke, why is the Regulator out here?"

"You ordered all prisoners out for the show, right?"

"Not that prisoner," Archibald says. "She's special. Have her taken back to a cell. I want to deal with her personally."

Duke gives the order. Three Sturmnacht move in on her.

She crouches as they reach out, then launches herself into the first man, knocking him on his butt. When the next Sturmnacht charges, she rolls onto her back and slams her bare feet into his groin.

"Oof!" he groans, and falls writhing to the ground.

Archibald strokes his chin. "Brilliant! She's even more feisty than I thought."

Before anyone else can reach her, she grabs the writhing man's blaster and kips up to her feet. She fires three times and takes out as many Sturmnacht.

"Enough fun, Duke. End this before someone gets hurt. By someone, I mean me."

Duke barks through the bullhorn. "Take her down!"

A pack of Sturmnacht surrounds the girl. She fires two more shots. Then the weapon clicks empty, and they swarm her, knocking her flat onto the ground and overwhelming her with the sheer weight of their bodies. After a moment of struggle, they carry her away, unconscious.

"That was enlightening," Archibald says. "So even a Regulator can be overwhelmed by greater odds."

Duke nods. "She's a hellcat, that one."

"We'll deal with her later. For now, the show must go on." Archibald signals the videographers to begin recording the farmers again. "Action!"

For a few seconds, almost a minute, nothing happens. Then, starting with the ones with the lowest body weight, the farmers begin to wake up. Their eyes turn clear, then pink, then bright red. They begin to stretch, then flex. One of the women bounces on her toes, looking around like a wild animal.

They're ready, Archibald tells himself. "What's my line again, Duke?"

His assistant looks at the script. "No longer will you toil in isolation, blah-blah-blah."

"No longer will you toil in isolation!" Archie shouts.

The sound of his voice snaps the prisoners to attention. Archibald pumps a fist, and they mimic his action.

Archibald raises a fist. "Huzzah!"

"Huzzah!" they chant.

"No longer will your labor be lost!"

"Huzzah!"

"No longer will you face starvation while the crops you raise are for the CEO's table! Desperta Ferro will rise again!"

"Huzzah!" they continue, apparently unable to stop. "Huzzah! Huzzah! Huzzah!"

How funny, Archibald thinks before he's interrupted by Duke.

"Command sent word that Mr. Lyme wants to talk to you. They've set up a secure feed in the comm center."

I'm busy, Archibald thinks, but knows that Lyme doesn't like to be kept waiting.

He signals the videographers to keep recording in his

absence. The prisoners will keep shouting until the drug wears off or until they collapse from exhaustion. But after they edit the footage, it will look as if the farmers are part of a revolution against Zealand CorpCom, and when the video is released on the multinets, Mother will have yet another thing to worry about.

"Is there any truth to what you said?" Duke asks as they walk toward the Command Center.

"About us being the Desperta Ferro? No, that's just a little flavoring Mr. Lyme added to the broth. About us overthrowing the Zealand CorpCom, it's absolutely true. I told you, Duke. I'll make a believer out of you yet."

In the command center, Archibald sends everyone out, including Duke. All of the multinets' monitors are dead, save one, which shows Lyme sitting at a desk—probably a bunker in some secret sewer—his features obscured by poor lighting.

"You are making excellent progress," Lyme tells Archibald before he can utter a greeting. "Tell me, was the data for Project MUSE stolen?"

"Yes, Mr. Lyme, it was, but—"

"Splendid," Lyme says, cutting him off. "Of course, you captured the *dalit* thief red-handed?"

"Yes," he says, feeling relieved. "We are—"

"Again, splendid. Bring him to Hawera Dam. The facility has certain technological capabilities that will aid in his interrogation."

His? But the *dalit* was . . . female.

The blood drains from his face, and his mind races, replaying their previous conversation. Did Lyme specifically state the sex of the *dalit*? Or did I just assume that it was the more ferocious warrior?

Good Lord, he thinks, if I had the wrong one killed, I'm a dead man.

"Is something amiss?" Lyme asks.

"N-no, Mr. Lyme. Nothing at all," he says, recovering his poise. "We have the prisoner, and I will arrange for a high-security portable brig for transportation to Hawera."

"Archibald," Lyme says, "you make me proud. Keep up the good work."

The screen flickers and dies. A few seconds later the other screens light up as the multinets resume function.

"Duke!" Archibald calls out, knowing that Lyme's pride will turn to vengeance if they don't get the correct prisoner back. "Get me Franks and Richards! Now!"

CHAPTER 14

Freeman Farming Collective
Zealand Prefecture
ANNOS MARTIS 238. 7. 24. 11:04

Minutes turn slowly into hours. Hours stretch into three days, which seem to last an infinity. The weather turns warmer, and monsoon season starts, bringing sticky air and torrential rains. The infirmary becomes a sauna, the air itself stifling. I feel just as stifled by my own body's weakness. When Rebecca tries to stuff me with medication, I refuse it. Pain tells me how far I've come and how far I have left to go.

When I'm not sleeping and haunted by dreams of chigoe dissolving the flesh from my bones, I pass the time by trying to rest, but my waking hours are haunted by my failure to protect Vienne. The image of her furious, unarmed attack on the Sturmnacht becomes a well of shame that I keep falling into.

The MUSE data doesn't seem so important now. My father and his secrets can go straight to hell for all I care. I can live the life of a *dalit*, but I can't live without Vienne.

"However," Mimi says, "I would like to finish the

defragmentation of the data from Tharsis Two and inter-weave it with the intel we already possess. Unless you object."

"Knock yourself out."

To occupy my mind, I start little projects to keep my hands—check that, hand—busy. Like disassembling a nearby bed by removing all of the bolts and screws. With the parts, I fashion a metal crutch and begin hobbling around the infirmary, strengthening my knee and improving my balance. It's remarkable how different the world looks when you can only see half of it.

Eventually, I dig through the cabinets, rummaging for a sheet of electrostat. I wipe away the old data on yield rates of sorghum planting and begin drawing a detailed diagram of Outpost Tharsis Two. Vienne is still there. I can feel it. All I have to do is find her.

"It will be difficult to pull off," Mimi warns me.

"That's why it's going to work."

A few minutes later, I'm hobbling down a lane in the col-lective, using the metal crutch for support. The morning is already too warm, and sweat is beading on my lip. Bad weather rolled in with the dawn, and the sky is an undulat-ing string of charcoal clouds.

When they see me coming, the farmers stop and point. Some of them are brazen enough to laugh. As a Regulator, you get used to folks in form-fitting armor, and you forget that everyone doesn't dress that way. You also get used to a modicum of respect. The farmers aren't accustomed to that, either.

I try to ignore their stares. Subconsciously, I fiddle with the hem of my shirt where it overlaps the pants. The seam joins automatically, and when I run my fingers along it, it's supposed to separate. Supposed to. Right now, I realize, it's not separating at all.

"Mimi, read me in on the status of my symbiarmor."

"The two parts seem to be fused together."

I spin in a circle, trying to pull my shirttail loose. "Fused? *Fused?*"

"Remain calm," she says. "The situation is not critical."

"Not critical? My pants are stuck!" The farmers' children are watching and listening intently, and I realize that I've been shouting. I subvocalize, "How am I supposed to, you know, do my business?"

"It may be a temporary condition," she explains. "Perhaps a side effect of the EMP pulse."

"You're grasping for straws."

"I do not grasp," Mimi says. "I analyze."

"What does your analysis say?"

"Indeterminate."

"Mimi!"

"There is just not enough data yet."

"You're infuriating!" I bellow. "We're talking bladder function here!"

The kids scatter.

"And you, cowboy, are scaring the children."

"I'm a broken-armed Cyclops in stretchy pants standing in the middle of the street yelling about piss. Of course I'm scaring the children!"

It's not doing any good to make a spectacle of myself, so I hobble onward. From behind, I hear the rumble of a rover, followed by the squeak of grit-filled brakes. My neck is sore, so I don't bother looking back.

"Going somewhere?" It's Rebecca. She trots up behind me. A gunnysack hangs in the crux of her elbow, and she offers her other arm. "Take some of the weight off that knee. Come on, I've carried calves heavier than you."

"Appreciate the offer," I say. "But I have to decline."

"Not really into that whole trust thing, huh?" she says, wrinkling up her nose.

My hands are sweating with effort of walking, and my head is ringing from the tinnitus in my ears. "I'm a Regulator. If I can't bear my own weight, how can I lead?"

"Even the chief," she scolds, "needs a day off sometimes."

If only it were that easy. "I'm assuming there's a reason you found me?" I dig the crutch into the gravel-covered ground. "Other than escorting me to the gate?"

"Thought you might like some company?" she says.

I wipe my brow with my right hand. "Try again."

"Not buying it, huh?" she says. "Okay, two reasons. One, I wanted to make sure that you were well enough to leave. Which you obviously are. You heal fast."

I pause, waiting her out. "The second reason?"

"Straight to the point, too." She opens a palm. The iris of an ocular prosthetic looks up at me. "We had to do a little digging in medical storage to find it. Folks here are always losing body parts, so we keep a few spares around just in case. The color doesn't match yours, but beggars can't be choosers, right?"

What's your agenda, lady? "Where's mine?"

"Destroyed, basically. Next to nothing was left." She picks the eye up. "I can insert this, if you like. I'm an old hand at treating prosthetics. Farming doesn't seem like dangerous work until a hand gets stuck in a thresher."

I shrug, and she takes that as permission. With deft fingers, she lifts my upper lid, then slides the lens into place as I blink to secure it. Compared to my bionic eye, it feels like a hunk of plastic.

"A mute hunk of plastic," Mimi adds.

"Is she lying about the eye?" I say. "Scan her for physiological signs of deception."

"Beat you to it," she replies. "Although the number of protocols I can run is severely limited, I can tell you that either she's honest, or she's an expert liar who can control a neuromuscular response."

"That's not very comforting."

"You want comfort?" Mimi says. "I suggest a warm bottle and a blankie."

"What, no teddy bear?" But I get the point. All she can

do is give me data. How I respond to it is up to me.

Rebecca clears her throat. "Either you're deciding if I'm trustworthy or making eyes at me."

"How pathetic," Mimi chimes in. "The hussy is practically a senior citizen."

"Hush," I tell Mimi. "If I'm patient, she'll tip her hand."

Rebecca gives me a sidelong look. "Your lips move, but I can't hear a word you're saying."

"Sorry," I say. "Just running some details through my head. See, I have this plan to find Vienne."

"Dead or alive?"

"Alive."

She pats my shoulder. "I just learned a lot about you, Jacob: You're very loyal and very, very stupid."

I do a double take. "You called me Jacob."

"Yes, I know your name." She smiles. "The bounty on your head is a chunk of coin. Big enough to buy a new soybean harvester. I could've really helped the collective by turning you in."

"Why didn't you?" I ask, knowing that we've gotten to the nuclear core. This is what she's been driving at. The question now is, What does she want from me?

Her answer is drowned out by the rumble of the rover's engine—Joad is driving down the road toward us.

"What?" I yell over the noise.

"I said, your chariot awaits!" She escorts me to the rear of the rover, where she shows me the jump seat. "The suspension's shot, but it beats walking with a crutch. Which by the way, I need back. Infirmary beds are hard to come by."

Whatever her end game is, she's not going to make the play now. So be it, I'm not in the mood. I hand over my impromptu crutch. "Thanks. For patching me up. And everything else."

"My pleasure." She takes my good hand and squeezes it. "Give a shout if you need any h-e-l-p. And do come back for a chat. It's not every day an honest-to-God hero drops into a girl's lap."

"Ha," Mimi says. "The last time she was a girl, the Bishop was still preaching from the Holy City."

The wind picks up. A dirt devil whisks up loose leaves and scatters them into the air. The sky is black, the first heavy drops start falling, and the banyan trees beside the gate begin to sway.

Rebecca is watching me. "So, you really love this girl?" she says, the wind blowing her auburn hair across her face.

"More than you can imagine."

She pulls a strand of hair from her lips. "I have a pretty vivid imagination."

"If you imagined that every grain of rust on Mars was a supernova," I say as Joad starts pulling away, "your imagination wouldn't be vivid enough."

CHAPTER 15

The dog is gone.

That's the first thing I notice when Joad parks near the monastery gate, and I climb off the flatbed. There's still an indentation in the ground where it lay, and the bowl of water I left is filled with mud from the morning rains. Did it die of natural causes? I wonder. Or did Stain decide to speed up the process?

"You don't deserve her," Joad says over the hum of the motor.

"Who?" I ask, still wrapped up in my thoughts. "The dog?"

"Who said nothing about no dog?" he growls. "I meant Rebecca—you don't deserve her."

Rebecca? "What're you talking about? I've got a girl-friend, for Bishop's sake."

"Then maybe"—he guns the engine, spraying out oil from the tailpipes, staining my boots—"you ought to start acting like it."

I watch the rover disappear over the rise. "Mimi, is everyone psychotic these days?"

"You seem," she says, "to have that effect on people."

The next thing I notice is that my motorbike is parked in the shade of the trees. My first thought is to question how it got here, but Mimi reminds me of the adage Don't look a gift horse in the mouth.

"Do not look a gift horse in the mouth," Mimi says. "Did you know that the phrase originated from the story of the Trojan War, in which one of the Greek kings, Odysseus, devised an ingenious plan for sneaking into the city of Troy?"

"They're still here," I say after unlocking the storage tank. Both of our armalites are safe. I close the lid and lock it back up.

With another glance at the dog's bowl, I push the gate aside. Overhead, a wind chime announces my entrance. The clouds have thickened during the ride, and lightning cuts across the sky like dancing barbed wire.

I limp on into the courtyard, trying to keep all the weight on my good knee. Maybe the monks have a crutch I could borrow, or a bed that I could disassemble.

It's quiet, and I can hear the gravel crunch as I drag my leg along. Since it's early, the monks should be meditating. So I make a beeline for the teahouse, where I find Shoei, Yadokai, and Riki-Tiki on their mats. Resting on their knees. Foreheads pressed to the floor. Murmuring prayers.

"Good morning," I say, failing to sound chipper.

They stare at me like I've grown horns.

"You are walking?" Shoei says.

"You look like *wà kào*," Yadokai adds.

And Riki-Tiki finishes the warm welcome with, "Your arm's broken! And your eyeball's a different color!"

"Yes, he looks like *wà kào*," Yadokai repeats.

"Yeah. Nice to see you all, too." I feel a sudden pang of disappointment that they didn't visit me at the collective. I mean, it wasn't like they had raised me like they had Vienne, but—

"Time for that bottle of warm milk?" Mimi says.

Okay, I get the message. Again. I take a deep breath that stings my ribs and exhale. "Yes, I'm walking. Yes, I've lost an eye. And yes, I look like *wà kào*. And I know you all think that Vienne is dead, but she's not, and I have a plan to save her. All we have to do is use a Trojan horse to sneak into Tharsis Two."

"Insane!" Shoei says.

"Impossible!" Yadokai yells.

"I'll do it!" Riki-Tiki says, bouncing over to me, then sticking her tongue out at the mistress and master. "But you must ask Ghannouj before we may help you."

"Why?" I say, frustrated by their response. "Does he have to consult his magical teacup or something?"

"Of course he must," Riki-Tiki says, taken aback. "How else will we know the right path to take?"

• • •

The Tengu Monastery complex covers about ten acres. Most of the buildings are near the gate, but the hives are a long, painful hike to a high terrace. As Riki-Tiki and I slowly approach the symmetrical rows of hives, I count over a thousand, each of them housing thousands of bees. They must number in the millions. Standing in the middle of bee central is Ghannouj, wearing a box-shaped hat and carrying a smoke pot, his girth covered by shimmering fabric that looks like a gold lamé tent.

"I believe that you have underestimated the number of bees," Mimi says as I move through the maze of hives. Wind swirls through the rows, permeating the air with the rich scent of honey.

"Would you like to count them for me?" I say. "It's going to be hard without your telemetry functions."

"My processor is still intact. I can take a sample from close proximity and extrapolate from there."

"Which you've already done."

"Four million, two fifty-two thousand, and six bees."

"Show-off."

We gather around Ghannouj, who is using the smoke pot to paralyze the bees while he pulls out trays full of honey. He and Riki-Tiki speak a few words, then she slips silently past me.

"You wish to speak with me?" Ghannouj asks after she's gone.

I explain my plan for rescuing Vienne. "Shoei and

Yadokai think I'm insane, but Riki-Tiki says I should ask for your permission."

Ghannouj sets the tray in a vessel to let it drain. "The task of the bee is simple. It gathers nectar. It brings the nectar to the hive. The hive makes honey to feed its own. The task of a monk is simple. We gather knowledge. We bring it to the monastery. The monastery passes knowledge to those who hunger for it."

"But—"

"The task of the Regulator is not so simple. You give of yourself so that others may live in peace. Yet there are times when peace is not possible for you." He uses the smoke pot to chase the bees away from the tray. "When Vienne was the same age as Riki-Tiki, she had to make a choice between the way of life she loved and the person she loved."

Vienne's words echo in my head: Once Stain was one of the Tengu. He desecrated the temple and was banished. He took the life of another person. Was Stain the person she loved? Did she choose him over the life of a monk?

"It was a terrible choice," Ghannouj continues. "One that I would not have been able to make. Vienne was always the strongest of us all. When she made her choice and left the monastery to become a Regulator, she knew that she could never join the Tengu again. She is no longer a monk, and while we welcome her presence, we cannot rescue her."

"I know that, sir."

"Yet you would have us set aside our task to aid the one who left us."

"Yes!"

He sets the smoke pot down, shaking his head, and picks up a cup of tea from a tray on a nearby bench. "Why?"

"Because the bee needs flowers to make honey, and if somebody cut through with a sling blade and chopped down all the flowers, then the bees with any sense would stop him."

His brow knits, confused, and he sips the tea. "I do not understand your metaphor."

"Because I'm a soldier, not a poet!" I grab another cup of tea from the tray. "Ghannouj, with all due respect, I don't think you're hearing me. Here, read these. Tell me if Vienne is alive or not."

He shakes his head and returns to his work. "When the hive is in harmony, all is well. Some bees have a different task. They protect the hive with their lives. They die so that the hive may live."

I watch him pull and replace another screen, feeling the seeds of frustration and anger taking root in my gut. "One of your own is out there. Alone. Hurt. Maybe dead, and you want to teach me about honey?"

"The hive must accept the sacrifice and continue its work. To do less would diminish the sacrifice."

"Oh, I get it. You're telling me to give up on Vienne, the same way all of you gave up on her."

"We have not given up," he says so patiently, I want to

throttle him. "With each meditation, I pray for her safety."

"You pray, but you're not willing to search for her? Why?"

"Because the search for Vienne is your path and yours alone. You borrow any tool or weapon that is ours, and our food is your food. Take what you need."

"How do you know it's my path alone?"

"The leaves."

"Not the carking tea leaves again! What makes you think it's my path and not yours, too?" I snatch up the cup and fire it against a hive. It shatters into so many pieces, it practically disappears.

"That was my favorite cup," he says.

"Oh. Sorry. I—"

"Such things happen when you allow yourself to have favorites." He twirls his staff. It makes both a high-pitched whistle and low bass thrum. The bees gather into a swarm overhead. With a wave of the hand, he sends the swarm away. "The leaves have never disappointed me. Neither will you."

CHAPTER 16

Outpost Tharsis Two
Zealand Prefecture
ANNOS MARTIS 238. 7. 24. 15:41

From where he sat quietly in the metal chair, Archibald could look the Regulator over without endangering himself, the way that microbiologists observe viruses in a cryo-electron microscope.

It seems like an apt metaphor. In the few hours since her capture, she'd injured several Sturmnacht and permanently maimed the poor soul who removed her symbiarmor. So much violence and beauty in a single human being. It was almost painful to look at her. Michelangelo must have felt the same way when he first set eyes on the model for his Venus.

As beautiful as she is now, Archibald thinks, imagine how radiant she will be when the sculpting is done.

He presses a switch. Inside the cell, the lights flicker on.

"Rise and shine, angel."

The Regulator sits up in her bed. She pulls the thin blanket over her shoulder and glares at him through the plexi. In her first few hours of incarceration, the other prisoners showed interest in her. But after they made the mistake of laying hands on her—and had those hands broken in return—they decided that the Regulator was insane. Imagine a Rapture druggie thinking that someone else is mad.

Archibald can see the reflection of the overhead fluorescent lights shimmering in her ice blue irises. The light disappears and reappears as the subject blinks. Maybe there is a way to retain those blissful eyes in the final product. He turns away to his electrostat and scribbles a few useless notes because he can't stand her stare anymore.

The Regulator's hands are cuffed in front. Her ankles are shackled, and the shackles are chained to the floor. Bruises are rising on her face and neck. A thin cut runs the length of her clavicle. She is thinner, and her eyes have shrunken. The blemishes on her forehead are the only reminders that she isn't grown up. The rest of her is as old and hard as the forged bit of a steam drill, which will make breaking her even more delightful.

He taps on the plexi after several minutes have passed, during which time she has not twitched. "What's your name?"

She flays him with her eyes.

"That's how it's going to be, is it?" He removes a remote device from a pocket hidden in his cloak. "In your former life, you were probably rewarded for being tough. For being a stoic who faced the enemy down with gusto and grit. Isn't that right? I can understand that. In my past life, I was an overachieving favored son. Then things changed." He pulls out his lighter and creates a flame. "Things changed suddenly, and the world I lived in changed with it. The same thing happened to you, my love."

"Don't call me that!" She lunges for him, but the chain draws taut, and she falls to her knees.

Archibald grins. So that's the chink in her armor. "By past life, I don't mean that reincarnation *wà kào*. I mean the life you had before you ended up here in a cell. The life that's gone, that's been burnt up and snuffed out." He blows out the flame. "From the ashes, you'll be reborn, just like I was. What better way to start a rebirth than with a name."

Tossing the blanket aside, she stands up, raising a clenched fist. "I am a Regulator. I will not yield."

"You're a wounded age nine in an ill-fitting gown trapped in the bowels of an old military outpost." He crinkles his nose. "Your cell is ten meters belowground and is carved out of rock. The only way out is via a door made of plexi that's six centimeters thick. So, yes, you are going to yield, or you'll be left here to rot cold, hungry, and wounded."

"My chief will rescue me."

He stifles a laugh. "If by chief, you mean that pitiful excuse for a Regulator who came with you, don't let your hopes soar too high. He's dead."

For a moment, her face is stone. She appears to balance

the weight of a conclusion in her mind, and the light in her eyes goes out. "Dead?"

"The Sturmnacht threw his carcass into the canyon as a warning to the farmers. They'll think twice about sending *dalit* after us. Sad but true, angel."

"Bastard!" She launches herself into the plexi, and he flinches, shocked at her speed and ferocity.

"*Enchanté.*" He licks his lips. "*Je m'appelle Archibald. Comment t'appellez-vous?*"

"Go to hell." She slams a fist into the glass, then turns her back and walks to the bed.

"A woman who knows a little control. I like that," he says, trying to mock her, but he's also tired of waiting for her to break. He thumbs the remote, which opens the glass. "Let's try it again. *Je m'appelle Archibald. Comment t'appellez-vous?*"

She grabs the latrine bucket and fires it at him. The bucket bounces off his head, opening a gash on his temple. The shock of the blow stuns him, and it takes several seconds before he recovers his wits.

"Vile little whore." Blood trickling down his jaw, he aims the remote at her. "You'll pay for that."

The Regulator doesn't seem to give a damn. A scream erupting from her throat, she bursts through the space between them, her body in a horizontal dive.

The chain stretches.

And snaps.

Her shoulder meets Archibald's gut, and she hooks the sides of his cloak as they slam against the glass. Double-fisted punches detonate against his ribs.

"You're the whore!" she screams.

His head whap-whap-whaps the glass, but somehow he manages to press the remote control.

She arcs backward like a popping live wire, clawing at the choker, and hits the stone floor, oblivious to any pain except for the chained lightning arcing through her body.

A few seconds later she's out cold, and Archibald is crawling to his feet. He holds his ribs while struggling for breath.

"That was too close," he gasps.

Next time, he decides as he stumbles out of the cell and closes the plexi door behind him, he'll bring guards. Lots of them. It's going to take more than a little shock therapy to break her.

Oh, but she will break, and she'll be so worth it in the long run. He takes out his lighter and gives it a flick. A weapon this powerful always is.

CHAPTER 17

I don't need you anyway, Ghannouj, I think as I struggle to stuff gear into the storage hold of my motorbike, which is parked in the shadow of the saffron yellow arch. I can rescue Vienne by myself. One-handed, if I have to.

"You have to," Mimi says. "One-eyed, too."

"No more jokes," I warn her.

"I am not joking, cowboy. While you may heal more quickly than the average person thanks to technological advances in your armor and its organic support systems, you are not superhuman."

"Stow it," I say aloud.

"Yes sir!" Riki-Tiki bounds over to the bike and starts stuffing my gear into place. She adds a gunnysack full of wrapped rice cakes, cones of honey, and several water horns. "All stowed."

Then she climbs into the driver's seat.

"What's this?" I say.

"You can't drive a lick with a broken arm, so I'm taking over." She twists the accelerator grip. "I'm an excellent driver."

"Sorry, Riki-Tiki," I say. "Ghannouj says you're not allowed to help rescue Vienne."

"But he never said not to help you *search* for Vienne," Shoei says as she and Yadokai appear at the gate. "Hurry up, old man!"

"Hold your water, woman!"

They pile onto the motorbike behind Riki-Tiki, leaving me nowhere to sit.

"Don't just stand there, Noodle Arms," Yadokai snaps. "Vienne needs help! Get moving!"

Now they're all hell-bent to save her?

"Questioning the logic of a monk," Mimi says, "is the mental equivalent of biting one's tail."

"I don't even know what that means."

"Which is why you shouldn't question the logic of a monk."

"See ya!" Riki-Tiki yells, and takes off like a guided missile, leaving me standing in the dirt. Within a few seconds, the motorbike is a dot in the distance.

"What the hell?" I scratch my head with my good hand. "If this is an example of monk logic, no wonder Vienne is such a mystery to me."

"I would explain their behavior to you," Mimi says, "but I am too busy chewing on my tail."

"Watch out for the hairs. You never know when they'll bite back." I remove my helmet and rub the top of my head.

"Any bets on whether or not they're coming back?"

"The odds are fifty-fifty."

A minute passes.

"Seventy-thirty."

Anger starts boiling in my chest, like the beginnings of a grease fire. As much as I like Riki-Tiki and her playful disposition, this is not the time for mischief. Then I pick up the sound of an engine in the distance.

On the same road where Riki-Tiki disappeared, another speck of dust appears.

"Here they come."

"That's not your motorbike," Mimi corrects me when the speck is within her range. "The engine is smaller."

She's right. My bike sounds like a handful of cannonballs loose in a cement mixer: This engine is from a more refined machine, not a snowmobile on wheels.

Shielding my eye from the wind, I squint at the rider until a face becomes clear. "Oh no," I say, "not him."

Stain pulls up in an antique Munro-Davidson motorbike, the likes of which you only see in museums.

"The day is full of surprises," Mimi says.

"None of them pleasant." When Stain stops, letting the engine idle, I say, "You're the last person I expected to own a motorbike."

"It's a hand-me-down," he says, and doesn't offer to explain more.

"Reckon I'm stuck with asking for a ride," I say, choosing

to stare at the high walls of the canyons instead of looking at him.

He snarls, his tongue piercing clicking against his teeth. "Are you waiting for an invitation?"

With all the excitement of feeding my hand to a wood chipper, I throw a leg over a seat behind him. I refuse, however, to hold on to to his waist, so I squeeze the body of the bike with my legs and pray that I don't get cramps.

From here, I can see bulges along his spine and on his shoulder blades—more metal implants. This fossiker must love pain.

"Why're you helping me?" I yell as he pulls onto the highway.

"Because I don't wish to forsake Vienne." He pauses, and I think for a second that he's going to add *again*.

"What's she to you?" I shout. "From what I hear, you're the reason she left the monastery."

"Why I left the Tengu is complicated." He guns the engine. "What she is to me is simple. Vienne and I share the same father. She is my sister."

It's early evening when Stain and I reach the copse of banyan trees near Outpost Tharsis Two. The master and mistress are waiting at the rendezvous spot, and Riki-Tiki is nestled in the branches of a tree, keeping watch.

She hops branch by branch to the ground. "What took so long?"

"It's his fault," Stain says.

Vienne's brother, huh? It's hard to see the resemblance.

Like before, we hide the motorbikes deep in the foliage and use a leafy branch to scratch away tracks. This time, I'm keeping my armalite, and I put Vienne's in the bike's storage box, wrapped in burlap, ready to return to its owner.

"That is assuming," Mimi says, "that Vienne is in Tharsis Two."

"Affirmative," I tell her. "That's exactly what I'm assuming."

Raindrops the size of bullets start falling, making dents in the loose dirt. A deep bass roll of thunder shakes the tree leaves as I lay out the master plan, then brief each of them on their jobs.

"Got it?" I ask them when I'm finished. "There's some wiggle room built in, but if things go fig-jam, we abort the mission, right? Nobody gets hurt if we can help it."

"Shah." Shoei waves off the suggestion and points a thumb at Yadokai. "Thirty years I've been battling this knucklehead, you think I'm worried about a few little boys with guns?"

"Right," Yadokai agrees. "You survive this woman for just a week, and you know you have stones of steel."

"Me?" Shoei gives his ear a hard torque. "What about you?"

"See what I mean?" Yadokai says. "I am battle tested."

"And I'm bored," Riki-Tiki says. "Can we go get Vienne now?"

• • •

The sun is setting, and the clouds have opened up with a long downpour that soaks us to the bone. Sloshing through the mud makes the going slow and miserable, but better cover you couldn't ask for.

Two hundred meters from the gate of the outpost, we find a swallow gully and take cover. In the purple darkness, the guard shack shines like an orange flare. The rest of the compound is as pitch-black as a Draeu's heart.

While the three others move to position farther down the gully, I squat beside Riki-Tiki, showing her the route through the sewer lines on the electrostat.

"Sure you're up to this?" I ask her. "It's dangerous."

"And stinky! I can handle it, though. I'm tough."

"But you're just an age six." It's the same age I was when I became a Regulator. Back then, I thought I was grown-up, too. Now I realize that an age six is nowhere near old enough to take on the job of soldiering. I'm barely old enough for the job myself.

"So what, I'm young?" She pushes her rain-soaked pink hair out of her eyes. "That means that I'm the only one small enough to make it through the lines into the main building. We've been through this, like, a hundred times already."

"You're exaggerating. It's only been six, max."

Mimi pipes up. "Twenty-seven to be more accurate."

"Who's counting?" I ask Mimi.

"I am. Obviously."

"Since you're kibitzing, how's that security sweep going?"

"I finished it a hundred years ago."

"Now you're exaggerating, too."

"How would you know?" Mimi says. "I am the only one who keeps count."

Riki-Tiki taps my shoulder. "What's wrong?"

"Nothing, Riki-Tiki. I'm just thinking."

"Why do you move your lips when you're thinking?"

"I, erm, like to talk to myself?"

Mimi laughs. "Busted! I warned you about getting sloppy. Just talk to me—no need to mime our conversations to the whole prefecture."

"Hush and give me the sweep readings!" I make sure to subvocalize with my mouth clamped shut.

"Readings indicate multiple biorhythmic signatures in close proximity to the guardhouse. In addition, sensors detect a significant mass of signatures clustered in the south corner of the main building."

"How many is a significant mass?"

"Your eye is just a common ocular prosthetic, not a highly sensitive telemetry device."

"Take a guess."

"Indeterminate. The sensors in your suit are not capable of—"

"That tears it. Next time we go shopping, I'm getting an upgrade."

Riki-Tiki taps my shoulder harder. "Can I do my job now? It's boring just sitting here watching you think."

Busted again. "Okay. Are you sure you know the plan?"

She rolls her eyes. "Go through the sewer tubes. Bear right at the split. Climb the access ladder to the plumbing service area. Slip into the electrical service room next door and throw all the main breakers. Meet you at the rendezvous mark. Voila!"

"That's the plan. Go."

Riki-Tiki moves down the gully to Shoei, Yadokai, and Stain, who lifts a storm grate for her. She slips inside and with a shake of her head is gone.

"Move up!" I say.

The four of us climb out of the gully and move quickly to outpost. There, we flatten ourselves against the wall, out of the view of the catwalk. I listen for footfalls, but all I can hear is the falling rain.

A quick look.

No guards on the catwalk and just one in the gate shack. Good.

I signal Stain—move to position.

A heartbeat later, the orange glow in the shack disappears. Everything is shadow now. "Control, we got us a blackout at the gate," the guard says into the radio. "Please advise."

My turn.

I duck beside the shack, close enough to touch the guard.

"System-wide failure," Control responds. "Stand ready."

"Copy." He lets go of the mic switch. "Stupid lights are fig-jammed. Ack!"

I drop him with a rabbit punch.

Stain grabs the radio and mimics the guard's voice perfectly. "Control, need some relief out here. Gotta use the head."

"Negative. Remain at your post."

"Have it your way," Stain says. "I'll do my business in the shack."

"Relief is on the way," Control responds. "But this is going on my report. Archibald's not going to be happy."

Stain stomps the radio into bits.

"You could've just unplugged it," I say.

He smiles, the piercings in his lip giving him an eerie expression. "My way was more satisfying."

Smashing the mic. That's a page right out of Vienne's manual. Maybe they really are related.

I wave Shoei and Yadokai forward to our position. The four of us crouch in the shack, waiting for Riki-Tiki to hit her mark.

"Alert!" Mimi says. "I have picked up an approaching signal."

I slip outside, and Stain follows.

A guard approaches the shack. He taps on the window.

Whap!

The door slams open. The guard staggers back.

Thap!

Shoei sweeps his feet, and Yadokai drags him inside.

"So far, so good," I tell Mimi.

"Do not get cocky, cowboy."

"Follow me," I whisper and move toward the rendezvous.

A quick sprint up metal stairs to the catwalk. Down the long, deserted walkway to a door marked "Control."

We stop, catch our breath, and wait.

Right on time, Riki-Tiki skips down the catwalk.

"This is fun!" she whispers. "When we rescue Vienne, she's definitely taking me as an acolyte."

I put a finger to my lips and reach for the door handle.

Stain grabs my arm. Shakes his head.

He opens the pouch tied to his belt and kneels down to the crack under the door.

"What's in the pouch, Mimi?"

"I detect only inconsistent biorhythms."

"Really? What could it be?"

"I am not psychic," she replies. "Even a dialectical of genius has her limits."

Stain spins his staff. The air fills with a whistling thrum. Bees crawl out of the pouch and under the door. A few seconds later, we hear screams inside the room, followed by heavy thumps as bodies hit the floor.

Stain nods, and I swing the door open. Six guards lie prone. Stain opens his pouch, and the bees fly into it.

Yadokai and Shoei follow me inside. They look around and shake their heads.

"Don't say a word," Stain warns them.

Except for a shared sigh, they don't.

Interesting.

"Indeed," Mimi says.

Riki-Tiki bounds in after us. "Holy *paskaa*! Look at all the vids!"

"Tie the guards up," I tell the monks. "In case they wake up."

"They won't," Stain says.

"Do it anyway."

As they begin the task, I take a seat in front of the multi-vid control panel and start pulling up camera feeds. "Mimi, tap into the network and use the control panel's sensors to scan the rest of Tharsis Two for more signatures. I'm not seeing any other guards on the video feeds."

"There are no other signatures," Mimi says. "Only a mass grouping in the south corner of this building."

"Any sign of Vienne?"

"Negative."

"*Wà kào*! She has to be here."

The Sturmnacht neatly trussed up, the monks gather around the control panel. Riki-Tiki rests her chin on my shoulder. "Where's Vienne?" she says. "You said she would be here."

I flip through the feeds.

Nothing but empty rooms and hallways.

Empty.

Empty.

Stop.

It's Mimi's south corner room. It's filled with dozens of walking corpses in tattered clothing. They all look emaciated and filthy, their eyes bulging and hollow, pupils glowing pink.

"Rapture," I say. "My god."

"Is Vienne," Riki-Tiki's voice cracks, "in there?"

"No." I pat her hand.

Then a moment later, I freeze frame on one of the prisoners, a small girl. "She's not there now, but she must've been before."

"How do you know?" Stain asks.

I tap the screen, where a silver pendant hangs from the girl's neck. In the center of the pendant is a lotus. "I have tea leaves of my own." I insert a memory chip into the data port. "Mimi, scan every scrap of data you can get. Vienne was here—that necklace proves it. There must be traces of her somewhere on the video feeds. We have to find them."

"We?"

"We meaning you."

"As long as we know who is doing the heavy lifting."

I stand and face the monks. "I can't locate Vienne. It looks like Archibald pulled out of this facility. Which means they might have taken her along. I'm going to find out where."

Stain steps in front of me. "You're wasting your time. She could be anywhere by now, if she's even alive."

"Until I know she's dead, she's alive." I lean forward so that my jaw is almost touching his. "Got that?"

"Do you always grasp at straws, *dalit*?" Stain says.

"When it's all that's left to hold on to? Carking-A." I turn to Shoei and Yadokai. "Those hostages need help. Is there someplace we can take them? Hospital? Sanitarium?"

"Here, there is only us," Shoei says. "Take them to the collective. We will nurse the ones who live and bury the ones who do not."

Stain sneers again. "Another waste of time! None of them will ever recover from Rapture. It is a death sentence!"

"You don't know that!" I shout, thinking of Vienne. Then I take a deep breath and let it out slowly. "Riki-Tiki, please get the power restored. Mistress and Master, please, lead the hostages outside to the grounds. I'll rendezvous in a few minutes."

Shoei bows. "Of course."

"Stain!" Yadokai barks. "You help, too."

The tone in the master's voice preempts any discussion, but Stain leaves a scalding look of contempt in his wake.

When they're gone, I ask Mimi, "How's the search?"

"The facial recognition program's algorithm found four hits on the video feeds."

"Display."

"I love when you go into boss mode."

"I'm really beginning to wonder about you, Mimi."

The multivid display blinks, showing a five-second feed

of Vienne tossing the overcharged blaster.

"Nothing here I haven't seen before. Next."

The multivid shows a Noriker pulling through the destroyed gate. The familiar faces of Franks and Richards unload my unconscious body, then unceremoniously dump me onto the pavement before Archibald, who raises a heavy boot and curb stomps my arm.

My stomach chunders. "That explains the compound fracture."

The next feed shows Vienne shackled in a cell, wearing only a dirty gown and a metal choker. Archibald enters the cell, along with a guard. Vienne lunges for them. The guard zaps her with an electric prod. She grabs the prod and jams it against his neck. Archibald claps like it's a show, and the feed ends.

"*Nǐ shì shénme dōngxi*," I whisper.

Then the last feed pops up. It's the same cell. Vienne is still shackled, the metal choker partially covering a ring of burns on her neck. Her hair is tangled and matted, hands and feet black with filth. Another guard enters the room. She ignores him until the choker on her neck starts to glow, then she claws the floor as if she could dig her way through it.

"No, no, no!"

I slam a fist through the screen. Glass shatters, and I don't give a damn. I drop to the floor, defeated. I bow my head. Tears flow.

"Had enough?" Stain says, intruding on my grief.

I turn off the power to the vids. "I didn't hear you knock." Wanker.

"See what your vanity has led to?" he says, arms folded and looking so smug, I wish I could scrub his face empty. "Your search is over. Believe me: The Vienne you knew no longer exists."

I start to leave. "My search is over when I say it's over."

"If you really loved her," he says, again blocking my path, "you would wish her a merciful death."

If you keep getting in my way, I think, the only death I'll wish for is yours. "Not loved. Love. I'm still in present tense. So is Vienne."

"Cowboy!" Mimi barks. "I am picking a mass of sensor sweeps associated with heavy combat forces. Hellbender velocicopters. Two units of eight, standard combat frequencies. Equipped with Seneca guns and onboard Varlamov rockets. Twelve hundred meters and closing fast."

Oh *shimatta*, I curse and shove Stain aside. "We can do this pissing contest later. There's a CorpCom air demolition unit inbound, and it's coming in hot."

Stain follows on my heels. "How the hell do you know and what does your jargon mean?"

"It means that in about ten minutes," I shout while trying to run on a gimpy leg, "this whole carking compound is coming down, and if we don't move, we'll go down with it!"

● ● ●

Out on the tarmac, I limp to the closest Düsseldorf and fire up the engine. Steering the unwieldy monster with one hand, I drive to the guard shack, where Riki-Tiki is leading the hostages out. Somehow she's convinced them to link hands, leading them like children into the back of the truck.

Shoei and Yadokai bring up the rear of the line.

I park and jump out.

"Is that all of them?" I shout to the mistress as I round the truck. "We've got to bug out, stat! There's a CorpCom air unit bearing down on us!"

"No!" Riki-Tiki says. "There are others still inside!"

"Damn it!" I pull her away. "Show me!"

Leaving Shoei and Yadokai to load the rest, Riki-Tiki leads me inside the building. Down the corridor. Up a flight of stairs.

I slam into the holding room and gag from the wretched smell of human waste and vomit. There, sitting in a pile of filth, is a small girl. Vienne's pendant is around her neck.

"Go back!" I tell Riki-Tiki, then scoop up the little girl.

Seconds later we slam through the exit doors. Riki-Tiki runs ahead to the cab. I stop at the tailgate and hand the girl to Yadokai.

"Wait," I say, and slip the necklace off her. I hang it around my own neck.

Above us, the *thump-thump-thump* of velocicopter rotors chops the air.

I start toward the cabin, but Stain is already jumping

behind the wheel. He shuts the door and gives me the ready sign.

By ready sign, I mean the middle finger.

Fine. He can drive. "All aboard!" I hop onto the rear bumper. "Go! Go!"

Gears grinding, Stain makes the truck lumber to life as the lights of the velocicopters appear on the horizon.

"Floor it, Stain!" I bellow. "A Hellbender is on our tail!"

The pavement behind us erupts with small explosions as hot tracers coated with white phosphorous chase us down. With a whump and a clatter, we crash through the front gate, and seconds later, the rear wheels spit out the leftovers.

The bump throws me into the air, and I almost fall off.

As if we weren't having enough fun already, a line of bullets tears through the canvas covering, ripping off the section that I'm clinging to. I grab hold with my good hand, the canvas shredding as I get closer and closer to the road.

"Mimi, think this cloth's going to hold up?"

"Do not even ask," she says. "Just hang on."

The pilot brings the Hellbender to bear, and a Varlamov rocket detaches from its mounts. A burst of fire to its aft, and it's whistling toward us.

"Evade!" I shout, knowing it's a waste of breath.

But somehow, the Düsseldorf bounces, and instead of finding our tailpipe, the rocket sinks into the ground. I have just enough time to duck before it explodes, spraying chunks of pavement everywhere.

A sizeable bit bounces off my helmet. "Ouch!"

Enough of this *kuso*.

Wrapping my arm in the torn canvas, I draw my armalite from its holster and let my legs drop. My feet hit the pavement and I'm skiing on the road, praying the symbiarmor can dissipate heat long enough for me to pull the trigger and spray a ridiculously wild clip of ammo at the Hellbender.

In a perfect world, my bullets would find the pilot, the spotter, and the gunner in his nest. In reality, having a bad eye screws up my aim, but emptying a clip on full automatic is enough to give the pilot pause. He takes evasive action, pulling the velocicopter into a climb that takes it high out of my range—and the Düsseldorf out of its.

For a few seconds the copter hangs there, spotlights sweeping the ground after us. Then, as if the pilot has decided his mission is to attack a compound, not chase down stragglers, he breaks off and rejoins the others.

A few seconds later, the Hellbenders release their rockets, which begins the process of blowing Tharsis Two all to hell.

I wonder, as I pull myself back into the bed of the Düsseldorf—with Yadokai and Shoei giving me looks of pity and frustration—if Archibald left the outpost because he knew the attack was coming.

It doesn't matter, I think as I settle in for the long ride back. All that matters is Vienne wasn't being held in Tharsis Two, and now, I have no idea where to find her.

CHAPTER 18

Bishop's Road, Tharsis Plain
Zealand Prefecture
ANNOS MARTIS 238. 7. 25. 06:42

By the time a new day rose over the Labyrinth of the Night, I was long gone.

It took us a few hours to get the prisoners back to the collective and into the infirmary. Afterward, I parted ways with the Tengu. They had injured to heal, and it was obvious that their hopes for Vienne was a light that had dimmed. Only Riki-Tiki wanted to continue on with me, and it took Shoei's sharpest tongue to keep her from leaving. Truthfully, I preferred to go it alone, and after a couple of fitful hours on an infirmary cot, I hit the road without telling anyone I'd left.

The morning sun is a heatless white ghost that casts dim light through the monsoon clouds, and I can smell ozone in the air. The red stone formations lining the highway shoot past, and disintegrating biodomes pass into and out of my peripheral vision. From the corner of my left eye, I can see black-gray smoke in the distance.

My visor is painted with streaks of mud. High winds pound my bike, and the cylinders roar as I hit the gas. The speedometer climbs. Sixty. Seventy. Eighty. Eighty-five.

The Bishop's Highway cuts the Tharsis Plain in half. Designed as the first major roadway to expand trade past the original colonies, the Bishop was built with four lanes on each side of a median, each with its own speed. For a century on Mars, it was the way to move about if you were in a hurry. Then, when the oceans rose and the valleys greened, settlements moved to more fertile ground, and the Bishop fell into disuse. Unlike the other construction projects built by the Orthocracy, though, the highway is still structurally sound. In most places the lanes are intact, and you can make it all the way from the Labyrinth to Base Camp, where the Founders created the first settlement on Mars. However, if you aren't careful and if you aren't lucky, you can find yourself riding across the barren plains on a rough stretch of road full of potholes big enough to swallow your motorbike whole. Oh, and you'll be low on hydrofuel, hungry, and shivering in the wind because you're not dressed for the rainy season on the Tharsis Plateau.

"I told you to wear a raincoat," Mimi says, clearly audible over the roar of the wind. "And to take provisions."

"I brought food."

"You brought snacks. How do you expect to track down Vienne on a diet of honey and rice cakes?"

"I survived on CorpCom MREs for months on end. Rice cakes and honey are delicacies in comparison."

I gun the engine again, struggling to maintain a hold on the left grip. It's hard enough to drive with a broken arm, but add a missing finger, and it gets downright flummoxing. The pinkie doesn't seem important until it's gone.

Funny how Vienne and I are united by a thing that isn't there. It wasn't supposed to be that way. We were both supposed to have a Beautiful Death at the Ceremony of Allegiances, not become outcasts.

The ceremony is as old as the Regulators. With the rise of the CorpComs, it has become a ritualized public spectacle that's telecast on the multinets for the whole world to see. The purpose of the ceremony is to show ultimate allegiance by committing suicide, a life offering to both the Tenets of the Regulator and the individual Regulator's Lord. According to tradition, a Regulator is bound to his chief, who in turn is bound to his Lord. When the Bishop was alive, the Lord meant the Bishop's Council Nine, each of whom had his or her own standing army. With the advent of the Orthocracy, the Lord became the head of the Nine Families, and with the CorpComs, the Lord became the CEO of the CorpCom.

Being CEO of Zealand Corporate Command, my father was both my Lord and my father, which meant that when he fell from grace, I and my fellow Regulators fell with him. We had a choice: We could end our lives in the ceremony or we could refuse and enter a life of disgrace as a *dalit* by cutting off a pinkie finger as a symbolic gesture—a gesture that served as a permanent reminder of our failure and let everyone else know that we are outcasts.

After my father was convicted, they led him out to the courtyard in front of Parliament Tower. There he stood on a wooden platform, hands and legs shackled, as three hundred loyal Regulators stood in line behind a tent. One by one, they walked through darkness for a few meters, then climbed nine steps to a dais, where they knelt on a tatami mat and pulled the cowl from their heads. Before them was a simple box covered with a synsilk cloth. On a signal, a second pulled the cloth aside to reveal a glass vial and a sharp knife. The vial contained poison. All a loyal Regulator had to do was drink the poison, rise to his feet, and climb down the dais. By the time she reached the ground, her life would be over. Attendants would quickly wrap her body in a shroud and carry her away to another tent, where her family would be waiting. Later, they would cremate the remains and celebrate her Beautiful Death. All of this took hours. The morning and afternoon dripped away while Vienne and I waited at the end of the line. It was determined that I should go last, being the son of the failed CEO. But because my father was a criminal, that honor was taken away from me and given to Vienne, who was considered the bravest and fiercest of all the Zealand Regulators.

When it was finally my time, I followed the carpet

through the tent to the dais. I climbed the stairs and knelt. With more of a flourish than I expected, the second pulled the cloth aside. I blinked twice. There was no vial. Only the knife. My response was followed by a roar from the crowd, as the cameras were trained on the box and telecast both what I saw and my reaction on the huge monitors above the tents. In unison, the crowd, the second, and I looked to the platform where my father was standing tall. Chin held high. Shoulders back. The meaning was clear. The Ceremony of Allegiances was first and foremost a way of honoring one's Lord. My Lord did not want me dead. He wanted me alive— and disgraced. What could I do? I stared at the knife, then at my father. I snatched the knife, slapped my hand on the mat before me and severed my finger at the second joint. I stood and held the bloody hand aloft, ashamed and defiant at the same time, as the attendants rushed me down the steps and quickly set about the business of tourniqueting the wound. The crowd was still buzzing when Vienne took her place on the mat and waited for the second to reveal the vial and the knife in the box, then calmly repeated my action.

"Why?" I asked, my head light from the loss of blood and endorphins.

"You are my crew and my chief," she said. "My loyalty is first to you. If you are *dalit*, then I must be *dalit*, too."

I must be dalit, too. The words still ring in my ears. Vienne's sacrifice brought us together, and yet every time I look at her missing finger, I feel guilt vibrating like a death knell inside. Yes, that sacrifice brought us together, but does it also keep us apart?

"I have taken the liberty of checking my database for maps while you were wallowing in ironic self-loathing," Mimi says, interrupting my train of thought. "Four kilometers ahead, there is an off-ramp that connects to Highway one-seventeen. Two kilometers north from there, you will find a roadhouse."

"You're giving me directions like I'm some kind of wanker," I say. "What're you trying to tell me?"

"You are suffering from exhaustion and your blood glucose levels are precariously low," Mimi says. "So in effect, I am telling you to pull over and get something to eat. Note that I did not call you a wanker, even though there is enough relevant data to draw that conclusion."

"Okay, Mom! Geez. Can't I be single-minded once in a while?"

"You have an AI flash-cloned to your brain. Your days of single-mindedness are long gone."

"Touché." I slow down to avoid the wreck of a school bus left to gather rust in the open. "How do you know that roadhouse is still open?"

"I do not know if it is," she says. "But it is the only establishment within forty kilometers on this map, so it is worth the chance."

"In other words, you're acting on blind faith."

"No, acting on the only information available and hoping

that it is still accurate," she says. "Hope, unlike love, is never blind."

After hours of nothing but road, my motorbike, and the never-ending horizon, I started feeling something gnawing in my gut. It's just hunger, I tell myself, and for almost a hundred kilometers, I believe the lie. When my appetite kicks in, along with it comes the realization that the pangs are from loneliness. For years Vienne and I fought side by side, starting out as crew and ending up as . . . something. Without her, I feel exposed, my back unprotected.

There's an adage on Mars: A man will drink himself to death before he starves. There's some truth to that, so it's not really a surprise to me that the roadhouse is still open for business. Like almost every other building in this territory, the roadhouse is a rectangle made of shipping containers welded together. It is separated from a village by a low fence made of scavenged wire. The roof is a quilt work of metal sheets laid over a latticed work of rebar posts, and with the wind blowing, a few of the sheets rise and fall like loose flaps of skin.

"Water," I tell the proprietor as I take a seat. When he pops a bottle of carbonated water on the counter, I ask, "Got anything without bubbles?"

"Only that which would poison you," he says.

"I'll take the bubbles."

I empty the bottle. The carbonation eats at my throat, burning like the grief that's dissolving my insides. I can't get the image of Vienne on that video feed out of my mind. I hate the way the Sturmnacht stared and laughed at her, the way her eyes were ashed over like a charcoal fire. Is that the last image I'm going to have of her?

"Anything to eat?" the proprietor asks. "The cook just fried up a mess of hot beignets, and they sure are good."

"Cowboy, you need to eat."

"Ha. You just want beignets because they trigger the endorphin centers of my brain."

"It is a gift."

"What is?"

"Your ability to state the obvious."

While I'm eating the beignets for Mimi, I scan the other patrons of the roadhouse. Three jacks in coveralls sit near the other hearth. Next to them, an old man and woman argue, their table full of empty bottles. Then I notice a familiar face, one that I last saw right before he and his buddy threw me into a canyon.

Franks is sitting at the bar, a cigar cupped in his hand. A waitress passes by him with a tray of food on her shoulder. She stops cold and blushes. Laughing, Franks stands up like he's going to leave the bar, then, as the waitress is turning away, taps the ash from his cigar into a bowl of amino grits.

"Watch my plate," Franks growls as he slides off his stool. "I got to take a whiz."

He heads for the latrine. After giving him a thirty-second head start, I follow him. I wait outside the latrine until a clanging sound tells me that Franks is in a stall. Then I slip inside, holding the door so it won't make noise, and find a place to hide. The wretched smell reminds me of New Savannah, the old city in the south where we used to do mercenary work.

The sound of Franks's coughing fit brings me back to reality.

"Hello?" he says after the fit ends. He's on a wireless call. I take the chance to park myself atop a toilet tank, where the acoustics are better.

"No, we ain't found him yet. Thought you was too busy starting his fires to bother with us. You've done burnt down half the territory. We can see the smoke twenty kilometers away."

"Mimi," I ask. "Can you intercept the wireless signal? I want to hear both sides of the conversation."

"That would be a negative, cowboy."

"How about tracing the call to its point of origin?"

"Also negative," she says with more than a hint of annoyance. "Can I remind you once again that my telemetry functions are severely hampered? You are not the only one who is half blind. Metaphorically speaking."

"Your use of figurative language is duly noted," I say. "So there's no way to monitor his conversation?"

"You could try listening. I happen to know that both ears are functioning normally, despite the buildup of cerumen in your left ear canal."

"I'll wash the wax out later!"

Hand cupped over my ear, I lean against the stall.

Mimi makes a sound like clearing her throat. "That technique has dubious benefits. Try just listening. It is not one of your finer skills, I know."

My brain is formulating a snappy comeback when Franks finally responds to the caller. "Yeah, I know how important finding this wanker is to the campaign, Archie, but it ain't easy to find one jack in a thousand square kilo—sorry about that, Mr. Archibald. As I was saying, we checked the collective like you said, and he ain't there. The monks, well, you can't get nothing out of them, and our people on the road ain't heard of him, neither. So me and Richards is figuring him for dead."

Damn it, if we could just trace that call, we'd have a line on Archibald's location, and therefore, Vienne. "Mimi, are you sure you can't track it?"

I can almost see her shake her head. "Negative."

In the other stall, Franks sighs heavily. "Yes, I hear you. I get it. There's war between us and the CorpCom. Yeah, yeah, yeah. Me and Richards will keep looking, and if we find him— Right, *when* we find him, we'll bring him in. Mostly in one piece, like you wanted. He's beat up and blind. How far can he go? How're we supposed to find you? Follow the smoke. Yeah, well, better be a big fire to— Hello? Hello? The great gob hung up on me!"

Franks slams a fist against the stall, and the door rattles

on its hinges. It's a great diversion, and I take the cue to slip out of the stall unnoticed. Glancing back over my shoulder, I open the door and bump into a big man with a full beard and hands as big as a skillet.

"It's the other Sturmnacht," Mimi says.

"Obviously," I say as Richards grabs me by the neck and pulls me into the hallway. This time, instead of old boots, he stinks of latrine disinfectant.

It's not an improvement.

"Well, well," he says. "Look what we got here."

"Did you wash with toilet cleaner?" I twist against his grip. "Or just spritz some for the ladies?"

Richards whistles. "For sure, we thought you was dead."

I grab his wrist, digging my fingers into the tendons that control his grip. "So how about putting me down?"

"All right." He tosses me against the wall. "You asked for it."

My armor solidifies as I slide to the ground.

Time to take this outside, I think, getting back to my feet.

I hit the exit at the end of the hallway, which leads to a loading dock and a small mountain of bilge dross swarming with blowflies and permeated with thick, bulbous maggots.

"Mimi, scan—"

"Alert!"

Richards slams through the door. I brace for impact, but he's on me too fast, quick for a big man. I see why, despite his inability to recite the entire alphabet without pausing for a mental breath, that he was sent after me.

He flings me again.

This time I go pinwheeling head over heels and land on my back in the garbage heap. I come up coated with left-over stew, potato peels, and a few chunks of rotted cabbage. My broken arm throbs like a steel pole's been rammed through it, and I have to flick a handful of maggots off the cast.

"*Hún zhang wángbā dàn!*" I reach for my armalite again, but my holster's empty. *Shimatta!*

"Well, look what I found," Richards says as he bends down to pick up my gun. If he touches the armalite, he's dead. But I'll be without a weapon.

"No!" I dive forward, stretching out my hand.

Richards laughs, just before a cloud of tiny hairs leave my palm and spray him in the face. Screaming, he claws his eyes and writhes on the ground, wallowing in the same slop he threw me into.

But I'm not worried about him anymore. Not when there's a layer of hairs sticking out of my right arm. "Holy *vittujen kevät*! What was that?"

"Urticating hairs," Mimi replies, as if I'd just asked her to describe my socks.

I rub my arm against my chest, and the hairs disappear. "Out of me? That's insane! How did I grow urticating hairs?"

"Not you, the symbiarmor."

"My suit is growing hairs?" I say. "And you didn't sort of notice?"

Sounding like a susie who's been cheated on, Mimi says, "It seems that I am not the only adaptive technology in play here. I do not like being uninformed, and I am not fond of sharing."

"Jealous much?"

"I *am* jealous," she says. "Your symbiarmor is obviously evolving, a feature that I had no record of. How can I be expected to control the functions of the nanobots when I do not have access to complete data?"

"I . . . don't know?"

While I'm distracted by the sudden revelation that my armor is undergoing puberty, I let my guard down, and Franks takes the chance to get the drop on me.

"Don't you twitch." He's behind me, raising his voice to be heard over Richards, who is now whimpering loudly. "Hear me? Not a single muscle. Turn around."

I sigh. "How can I turn around if I'm not supposed to twitch?"

He pushes the double barrels of a shotgun into my back. "Don't get smart with me, boy. Turn around."

So I face the thug. First, I notice that the shotgun is pointed at my chest. Then, I notice that Franks has shockingly white legs. He follows my line of sight to the ground, where his pants are gathered around his ankles.

"What?" he says. "I was in a hurry."

"I'm just glad your shirt has a long tail."

Franks pulls back the double hammers. "Quit trying to be funny. I don't like funny."

I nod, looking at the man's knobby knees, stifling a laugh. "Mimi, this one's not the sharpest cleaver on the butcher block, is he?"

"It does not take brains to pull a trigger, cowboy."

Franks spits on the floor but makes no move to pull up his trousers. "Here's how it's going to play out. Me and you's going to take a little ride—"

"Where to?"

"It don't matter where! Now shut up, boy. I lost my train of thought."

"We're going to take a little trip."

"That's right. A trip. And then, I hand you over to Archibald and collect my reward."

"Reward? I was under the impression that Archie didn't give those out."

He nudges me with the barrels. "For you, he will. That farging ginger wants a piece of you real bad. If he didn't, I'd already cut your cocky ass in half. Think that fancy suit's going to protect you? Try taking a double-barrel full of explosive shot in the gut."

"Explosive shot?" I say. "That changes things."

Mimi agrees.

I hold my hand higher. "Okay, I give up. I'll take a little ride with you. What about your buddy? He's going to be out of it for a while."

"Forget him." Franks spits in Richards's general direction. "Think I'll keep that reward all to myself. Now get moving!"

I point at his ankles. "Um, what about your pants? It's awful damp to go commando."

Franks looks down, and I grab the stock of the shotgun. Knock it to the side. Slam my cast against his face.

The shotgun fires both barrels, blowing a huge, smoking hole in the back wall of the building.

Inside the roadhouse, the patrons dive for cover.

The kick from the shotgun drops Franks on his back. He looks up, dazed, as I wrench the weapon away and fling it onto the roof.

"You're out of ammo," I tell him. "Reckon that leaves you with your pants down physically and metaphorically."

"Huh?"

"Tsk. I'm disappointed in your inability to understand figurative language," I say. "Say good night, Gracie."

Franks turns his head to the side. "Who's Grac—"

Thump! I pop him in the jowls, and he's down.

"See that blank expression on his face?" Mimi says. "That is exactly what you look like when I quote poetry."

"That's exactly how I feel, too."

After securing my armalite, I step through the hole in the wall and enter the pub. The guests should still be cowering behind tables, but they're sitting in the dust, acting as if an exploding wall is a common occurrence.

On the way out, I speak to the owner. "Sorry about the ruckus. Man on the ground out there says he and his friend will take care of the damages. But you might want to collect before they wake up."

He gives me a blank look that I choose to count as a yes. I push through the front door and into the parking lot. "Now, Mimi. Tell me about those hairs. Could they be related in any way to the ones that chigoe fired into my face?"

"Oh, cowboy. I thought you would never ask."

In the parking lot, I'm starting my motorbike when I see a truck marked with a painted-over Zealand Corp symbol, the sure sign of a stolen vehicle. It must belong to the Sturmnacht.

Which gives me an idea.

After killing the engine, I walk around to the rear of the Noriker, intent on doing a little mischief. Instead, I find some pink-haired susie has beaten me to it.

"Riki-Tiki," I say, as I watch her drain the air from a tire. "What do you think you're doing?"

She doesn't even flinch, must less stop her work. "Helping you escape, obviously. Were you aware that you drag your left leg when you walk? It's a unique gait. Not that I needed that to know it was you. I can hear you breathe a half dozen meters away."

"Can not." I rub my sore knee, the source of the unique gait.

"Can, too," She moves on the front tires. "You whistle

when you exhale. Probably from a deviated septum. Has your nose been broken?"

Twice in a fight. Another time by Vienne, by accident. I *think* it was by accident. "Forget about my nose." I say. "Stop trying to deflect. What are you doing, as in how did you get two hundred kilometers from the monastery?"

"You gave me a ride, silly head." Her work done, she scampers past me, easily slipping through my grasp as I try to snag.

"I did no such thing." I follow her to my bike, where she hops on the rear seat.

"Sure you did." She knocks on the storage compartment. "I wanted to help you find Vienne, no matter what the mistress and master said, so I hid in here."

"No way. It's too small."

"Ha! Shows what you know." She folds her arms and pretends to be miffed. "Ghannouj is a master contortionist, and he taught me how to make myself very, very small."

"Ghannouj," I snicker, thinking of the man whose girth is greater than his height fitting into any confined space, "is a master contortionist?"

Now she doesn't have to pretend to be miffed. "Humph. Just because you can't imagine it does not mean it can't happen."

"'There are more things in heaven and earth, Horatio,'" Mimi says, "'than are dreamt of in your philosophy.'"

"Shakespeare?"

"Very good, cowboy," Mimi says. "You are learning to appreciate fine art."

"My father used to quote that to me every time I said I wanted to be a Regulator. By the way, why didn't you tell me we had a stowaway?"

"You did not ask," Mimi says. "I am not a mind reader, you know."

"You are, too!"

"Well, your mind never wrote that chapter."

I smell a conspiracy. "Riki-Tiki, obviously I can't leave you here to fend for yourself, so the next station that comes along, you're on a transport back home. Deal?"

"No deal," she says.

"What?"

"No deal. I don't like transports, and if you don't hurry and start this hunk o' junk, those Sturmnacht are going to be out here and probably very angry that you flattened their tires."

"*I* flattened their tires?"

She beams.

"And how do you know about the Sturmnacht?"

"Because I was inside the whole time, silly head," she laughs. "That Franks man has very white legs, doesn't he?"

"You were inside the roadhouse?" I say, amazed. "I didn't see you there."

"Of course not. I was trained by the Tengu!" she says, as if it's common knowledge. "You should start the motor now."

"Why?"

Across the parking lot, the front door of the roadhouse flies open. Franks and Richards scramble outside, chased by the angry proprietor, who is armed with a heavy skillet and a string of colorful insults.

I start the bike and shout to Riki-Tiki. "This doesn't change the terms of our deal!"

"You're cute when you argue!" she hollers back as the bike thunders out of the parking lot, raining gravel in its wake. "No wonder Vienne loves you so much!"

CHAPTER 19

Badlands, Tharsis Plain
Zealand Prefecture
ANNOS MARTIS 238. 7. 25. 09:14

With Lyme's men hot on our trail, I decide that the Bishop's Highway is not the smartest way to travel. At the next exit ramp, with Riki-Tiki riding behind me, I leave the highway and take a semi-abandoned military cutoff route, which is lined with a far-as-the-eye-can-see string of industrial buildings, most of them built for processing petrofuels from Mars's minerals. But the factories never turned a profit, and when the CorpComs took over Mars, Zealand Corp shut them down. Now they stand like derelict hulks, rusting their way into oblivion until a recycling crew can work its way through them.

Like the factories, the roadway isn't maintained, either, and there are fresh divots in the pavement. My front tire bumps up and down, the handlebars shake my hand, and I can feel the tires losing their grip. Although the motorbike weighs half a ton and chatters like a chainsaw on steel, it feels as if I'm floating on the road.

"Want me to drive?" Riki-Tiki says.

"Nope."

The last time I felt like this was the first day I mustered into the Regulators. My new chief, Mimi, brought me into a Quonset hut, where eight Regulators stood, spit and polished, locked and loaded, at attention. Arms heaped with gear bags full of ammo boxes, clips, utility belts, assorted knives, I struggled to maintain my balance and almost mowed my new chief down when she stopped to address her davos.

"Watch it, Greenie," she growled. "Else I'll have you replaced with a pack mule. It could probably shoot straighter than you, anyhow. Isn't that right?"

"Yes, chief!"

"Regulators, meet our new crew, Greenhorn Regulator Jacob Stringfellow. He's the rich, spoiled-rotten, Battle School brat I warned you about. Stringfellow! From henceforth, you will be known only as Greenhorn or Greenie, never Stringfellow. Got that, Greenie?"

I didn't answer, since I wasn't really sure she was addressing me, so Mimi leg-whipped the backs of my knees and I went down like a velocicopter with a busted rotor, all the Regulators' gear bags on top of me.

"Don't move a millimeter, Greenie!" This time, I knew she meant me, and I didn't dare make a peep.

"Regulators, grab your gear! We've got a mission. Dismissed."

Her exit was followed by laughter, and one by one the packs were lifted off me as the members of what would become my family grabbed their stuff and trailed out the door, not bothering to say a word to me. It wasn't until the last pack was lifted that I realized a pair of liquid blue eyes was boring right through me. Vienne's jaw was set, her mouth downturned in a way that I would later learn was a sardonic smile.

"I'm glad you're here," she said.

"Really?" I sounded like a salamander was clogging my vocal chords.

She slung her pack easily over a shoulder, then offered me a hand up. "Roger that. Until you showed up, I was the Greenie. Thanks for taking my place."

"What do they call you now?"

"Mimi calls me Vienne, but you only get to call me Regulator. Now get off your butt, rich boy, we've got work to do." I reached for the hand and she pulled it away, pretending to smooth down her hair. It was the first of many times Vienne put me in my place.

"Pothole!" Mimi screams in my ear.

Ahead, a hole big enough to park a Noriker in opens up on the highway. I yank the bike hard into the left lane. My front tire chatters, trying to grip pavement. The rear end fishtails, and I cut into the slide.

Feel the handlebars wrench from my good hand.

Watch in slow motion as the rear end swings one hundred

and eighty degrees around in a cloud of black tar smoke and blue-gray exhaust that leaves me out of breath and parked in the other lane, staring at a Düsseldorf 's aluminum grill growing bigger and bigger.

I shout *"Tā mādebi!"* and gun it. For a half second, the bike does not move. The Düsseldorf's driver lays on the horn, as if I can't see a few metric tons of steel bearing down on us. Then, in a surge of fuel-induced panic, we shoot forward toward the truck and its sounding horn.

"Turn!" Mimi yells.

"Turn!" Riki-Tiki screams.

When it looks as if we'll be roadkill, we both swerve, the truck weaving across the lane and my bike sliding into a ditch. We pass with a burst of wind and a dopplering air horn.

I almost wet myself.

"What do you mean," Mimi says, "almost?"

I rest my head on the handlebars. "Stupid pothole."

Riki-Tiki squeezes tight against my back. I can feel her hands shaking. "Thank you for not killing us."

"Yes, that was kind of you," Mimi says. "Next time, try to stay in your own lane."

"Got it, Mimi. No more playing chicken with a Düsseldorf."

"You're okay?" I ask Riki-Tiki.

"Beyond okay!" she says. "That was fun! In a weird sort of way."

"You and Vienne are a lot alike. In a weird sort of way." I turn the bike out of the ditch and pull back onto the highway. "Welcome to the life of a Regulator," I tell her as the bike starts to wobble violently. "Whoa! Hang on! Something's wrong."

After pulling over to the shoulder of the road, I suss out the source of the wobbling. It's the front wheel. The rim is bent. Great. Terrific. "*Shén me niǎo!*"

"What does that mean?" Riki-Tiki says.

"It's an ancient proverb from Earth. It means no good deed goes unpunished."

Riki-Tiki starts laughing. "Ha! It does not! I speak Chinese, and it means mmm-mmm-mmm."

I slap a hand over her mouth. "Shh! I heard something." Subvocalizing, I tell Mimi to do a scan. "I could swear I heard an engine."

"Nothing so far," she says. "At this point, your hearing is better than my sensors."

"Bet it half killed you to admit that."

"Instead of gloating," Mimi reminds me, "would a better strategy be to hide your vehicle and seek shelter? Just in case."

"Right. Just in case." I remove my hand from Riki-Tiki's mouth and wipe her spit from my palm. "Ew. Did you have to?"

She sticks out her tongue. "Serves you right for putting your hand over my mouth! All you had to do was say shh!"

"Shh!"

"Forget it!"

"Hurry!" I push the bike into the brush and motion her to follow. "Somebody's coming. We'll come back for the bike later."

We jog up an overgrown trail toward the closest factory— a rotting refinery, judging by its three cooling towers.

"Can the bike be fixed?" she asks.

I pull back the chain-link fence. "Sure. I just need some tools."

She crawls through, then I follow.

She points to a squat metal building labeled "Tool and Die Shop." "Think you might find something in there while we're hiding?"

"Good eye."

We jog over to the front door of the shop. There's a pad-locked chain on it. I give it a good shake in hopes that rust has eaten through the metal. "No go."

For a second, I think about shooting the lock off. But the noise would echo for kilometers, and a big, fresh hole in the lock would be a dead giveaway.

"Over here." Riki-Tiki hops onto a pallet, then up a crate. She swings open a security grate and slips inside. "I'm in! Hurry up, slowpoke."

Mumbling about tight spaces, I follow her, albeit more slowly and carefully because of the cast on my arm.

"Suck in that gut, cowboy," Mimi says.

I grunt. "Too many disabled limbs."

"Not to mention too much white rice."

"Everybody's a critic—whoa!" I reach out, expecting to find a handhold on the other side of the grate and instead find only air.

I topple forward and land hard on the concrete floor.

"Oof."

Riki-Tiki offers me a hand up. Even in low light, I can see the glint of mischief in her eyes. "Did I forget to mention that the last step is a doozy?"

"Why yes, you did." I take a second to scan the shop. Storage area here. Workbench there. Lots of dark corners and slivers of light coming from the soaped windows and the double door entry. "Okay, so now we're even. I'm sorry about the hand over the mouth thing."

"And I'm sorry that the crates I climbed down"—she points to two empty bins a couple meters away—"escorted themselves to the other side of the shop when you weren't looking."

I pop my neck back into place. "Remind me never to play cards with you."

"Cards? I love cards!" she says. "I brought a set with me. Damn! They're with my bedroll."

"Which is still in the bike."

As my eye adjusts to the light, I start making my way toward the racks of tools on the far side of the shop. "Let's use our quiet voices," I say. "And keep our ears peeled for—ow!"

I slam my forehead into something hanging from the rafters. It's heavy. It's metal. It hurts.

Riki-Tiki giggles. "Is that your quiet voice?"

"Ha-ha," I say as she scoots past me.

At the tool rack, she starts mucking with the hand tools.

"What're you doing?" I cross the floor using a shuffle step and waving my hands around for random instruments of head trauma.

"Choosing the tools we need, of course." The sound of metal pieces clacking together echoes across the shop. "I've found a couple of slats we can use as a tire lever set, and we'll need a ball-peen hammer. See anything we can use as edge to match the angle of the rim?"

"I take it you've done this before?"

She puffs up. "Who d'you think fixes Stain's motorcycle? He's too busy trying to achieve enlightenment to care about changing the oil."

I'm about to whisper how impressed I am by her mechanical genius when Mimi cuts in.

"Reading multiple biorhythms at close proximity, of course."

"Affirmative," I reply, then motion for Riki-Tiki to be quiet.

"Fun!" she whispers.

I crouch on one knee so that there's a clear line of sight on both the door and the window. I turn my head side to side, trying to pick up the sound of footfalls.

"Your senses were much sharper when I could fully monitor them," Mimi says.

"Hush," I say. "With you yakking in my ear, a Hellbender could land and I wouldn't be able to hear it."

Riki-Tiki taps me on the shoulder. "What's going on?"

Putting a finger to my lips, I whisper, "I heard something."

"Me, too," she says, grinning. "CorpCom shock troopers. They found the bike, and they are fanning out in a standard security formation."

"How do you know that?" Pulling my armalite, I move close to the outside wall. I try to get a visual through a crack in the wall.

"Because that's what the soldier in charge said just now," Riki-Tiki whispers. "Probably could've heard it if you hadn't been talking to yourself again."

Mimi laughs.

"You didn't hear them, either, Mimi."

"I am only as good as the equipment at my disposal."

Me, too, I think.

I can hear them now. Muffled voices. Boots stomping across concrete and kicking aside debris. Not the best trained soldiers, are they?

Riki-Tiki slips in beside me. She closes her right eye and squints with the left. "What's the plan?"

I shake my head. There is no plan except to wait it out and hope that they'll move on. Like most of my plans, it's not very imaginative, but it does have at least a fifty-fifty chance of succeeding.

"More like ninety-ten for failure," Mimi says.

"Sixty-forty."

"You are delusional."

Outside, a high-pitched squeal. "Sir! Got a signal here!"

A signal? What kind of signal? I'm asking myself as I pull Riki-Tiki away from the door.

The squad leader steps into view.

"Form up!" he barks. "Breach procedure!"

We hunker down behind a metal lathe machine big enough to grind a boulder to a pebble, and I pop the safety on my weapon.

"Stay here, no matter what happens," I tell Riki-Tiki. "Mimi, give me a reading."

"I count six signatures in close proximity to the door."

I can take six, I think, and bring my armalite to firing position.

"With six more three meters in the rear."

I can take a dozen.

"With one arm and one eye?"

"I just need one of each to shoot."

"If only your abilities were as great as your hubris."

Wham!

A steel battering ram slams into the doors. The metal bends inward, and buckets of dust fall from the rafters. But the heavy chain holds, and I'm glad that I didn't shoot the lock.

Wham!

The center of the door crumples, opening a large hole. A shock trooper foolishly sticks his head through the hole.

An easy target. Right in my crosshairs.

But I don't shoot. Not when there are eleven more troopers lying in wait.

He sweeps the shop with an electric torch. The beam dances up and down, along the walls. Right before it reaches the lathe, I lower my armalite and tuck my chin.

The beam passes. Then stops and flicks back to the lathe.

Re malaka! My brain screams to shoot him. But I don't.

Just be still.

"Nothing here," the trooper says finally.

The beam moves on, and I exhale.

Outside, the squad leader isn't taking the news well. "Bollocks!" he yells. "Breach this door! Now!"

The ram slams the door again and again until the hinges give, and it falls to the ground, still attached to the chain. Four troopers pour in a second later, the outside light illuminating them like glowing targets.

I reach over to push Riki-Tiki to the ground for cover.

But my hand finds nothing.

She's gone?

Impossible! A second ago, she was right there. How can she move without making a sound? Panicked, I slap the ground, as if groping in the dark would help.

"Cowboy," Mimi says. "Look up."

Then I see her.

Up on the ceiling.

Swinging like a gymnast from the main rafter, she lets go, tucks into a ball, and slams into the lead trooper before he even sees her. He falls onto the workbench, and she vaults off the wall.

She grabs the two long metal slats from the bench, then flicks her wrists simultaneously.

The slats hit two troopers in the face.

One drops.

The second stumbles back into another trooper, who fires a blaster shot through the roof as he falls on his ass.

My turn.

The butt of my armalite to the chin of the shooter knocks him out, and before the other two troopers can react, I put a couple of rounds in their bellies. Their armor absorbs the bullets, but not the force, and they fly backward like a steel boom has flattened them.

Still in the shadows inside the shop, I drop to a three-point stance, aiming at the six troopers formed up in support. But one look tells me that something's gone awry.

The troopers are already down.

Damn.

Somebody beat me to them.

"Riki-Tiki?" I ask.

"Right here," she says from behind me. "You're a very good shot."

"And you're a very good acrobat. Remind me to remind you not to pull a stunt like that again."

"Aw, you never let me have any fun."

"You're not the first person to say that." I sweep the perimeter. No sight of any other hostiles. "Mimi?"

"Reading one active biorhythm, chief. The others register as unconscious."

Riki-Tiki slips by me.

"Wait!" I say.

"Why?" she calls as she bounds outside. "It's just Stain."

As if the devil's name has been spoken, Stain pushes back a dark fur-lined hood to reveal his face and hops down from the roof of the shop. He grabs Riki-Tiki and swings her around, kicking up oily-colored dust.

"How did you find us?" Riki-Tiki says as she lets go of the monk's long brown overcoat.

Under the coat, he's wearing no shirt, baggy pants, and a pair of leather boots. "I've trailed you all along. Ever since Master and Mistress noticed that you were missing." He smiles at her, but it's posed, like he's sitting for a digigraph. "Now that I've found you, it's time for you to go back home."

A cold wind blows Riki-Tiki's pink hair across her face. She pushes it aside and locks her arms across her chest. "No."

"Listen to me," Stain says. "This hunt for Vienne is a fool's errand. If Ghannouj forbids you to leave, you must remain in the monastery or risk being—"

"What Ghannouj says doesn't matter." She stamps her

foot. "I'm of age, and I'll do as I choose. That includes helping find Vienne. So if you're so worried about me, you'll come along. Because I won't be going back until she's found."

After checking the perimeter, I move to the downed shock troops.

I roll the squad leader over. His face is covered with welts. The others have the same swollen marks. Looks like Stain's been up to his old tricks. I wonder how tough he'd be without a bag full of killer bees.

"*Dalit*," Stain says. "Talk to her. Explain that even if you manage to find Vienne, she will not . . . she will not be the same."

He takes a couple of steps toward me. Our eyes lock, and he gives me a hard stare, trying to intimidate me. He thinks he can scare me? Even with one eye, I can match any stink he throws at me.

"Riki-Tiki is of age," I say. "She can make her own choices."

He moves closer so that our noses are almost touching. I can smell stomach acid on his breath. "How can I trust her to your care after what happened to Vienne?"

"Reckon that means you'll be coming along then," I say, fighting the urge to spit in his face. "There might be more CorpComs about, so we better secure the area."

Stain waves away the suggestion. "All of them have been taken care of. In fact, I was bored waiting for you to come out of your mouse hole."

"Then let's get moving before the CorpComs wake up."
I start dragging the troopers inside the shop. Stain deigns to
help, while Riki-Tiki runs inside to collect her tools.

"Can't forget these," she says as we drag the last trooper
inside, lash them together using their own flexicuffs, and
do our best to bolt the door back into place. The door won't
hold for long once they wake up and get loose from the
cuffs, but maybe it'll give us time to escape.

"Where are you going?" Stain asks as we reach the road
again. The bike is where we left it, with Stain's machine
parked a couple of meters away.

I take the tools from Riki-Tiki. "To fix my wheel."

"Obviously," he says. "What I meant was, how do you
know where to find Vienne?"

"Back at the roadhouse," I say, as Riki-Tiki pushes me
aside and starts using the slats to remove the tire. I feel bad
not helping, but obviously a one-handed klutz is just in the
way. "I ran into the Sturmnacht that Archibald put on my
tail, and I learned a useful piece of intel that will lead us
right to their boss."

"What would that be?" Stain says.

"Follow the smoke." I point to the horizon, where the
clouds are darker than they should be. "Where there's
smoke, there's fire. Where there's fire, there's Archie. And
when we find Archie, we'll find Vienne."

CHAPTER 20

Woolwich Reclamation Center,
Upper Tharsis Plain
Zealand Prefecture
ANNOS MARTIS 238. 7. 26. 07:56

Dressed in the uniform of a CorpCom Ranger captain, Archibald is concentrating on a slapdash shack sitting atop a slight rise next to a cesspool, a farmhouse with grayed-out clapboard siding and a brick foundation. It has narrow, naked windows with no curtains. Its shingled roof is buckled and warped, with two chimneys stabbing through it. The house caught his eye for one reason: the words "Desperta Ferro!" painted in large red letters on the walls.

It is the first to burn.

He lets his eye travel past the house to a half-dozen shanty shacks and a derelict chicken coop. The wire is caked in rust, and the coop has collapsed.

The chickens have all flown, he says to himself and laughs.

They are on fire, the buildings. The shacks, the coops, all of it being consumed by a dozen separate red-orange hot fires that form a single stack of smoke that rises hundreds of feet into the clear sky. The official name of this place is Woolwich Center for Recycling and Reclamation. It's a town grown up around one of Zealand Corp's hundreds of centers created to recycle all the organic and inorganic waste from the prefecture. It was a town. Now it's quickly becoming a pile of ash.

"So the recycling center is being recycled." Archibald smirks as he crosses the field to where the portable brig is parked.

As he nears the brig, the guards jump to attention, but he sends them away. When they are out of earshot, he slides open a viewfinder. Inside, Vienne is cuffed to a metal chair. Her head lolls forward. An IV drip is attached to her arm.

He closes the viewfinder and enters the brig. On a table next to Vienne, an assistant unrolls a set of instruments.

"Don't bother," he says, "Those don't work on her. Administer the dose."

With a wary look, the assistant draws serum from a vial and injects it into the IV.

"You're dismissed," he says.

When the assistant has been gone for several minutes, he hunkers down next to Vienne, his mouth just a few centimeters from her ear. "You can fight this, my love—"

"Don't call me that!"

"Or you can accept it. The truth is I can give you something you've lost."

"You," she says, gasping, "can't give me . . . anything."

"That's not true, is it?" He taps her mutilated pinkie finger. "You lost this."

She shakes her head. "Didn't lose it."

"Exactly. You gave it away. You willingly allowed it to be chopped off like a piece of link sausage, but you didn't want to become a *dalit*, did you?"

"Yes, I did. The Tenets—"

"Don't lie to me. The serum my assistant gave you prevents it. So even though you didn't want to become *dalit*, you did. Why?"

No answer.

"An omission of the truth is the same as a lie. It's one of my mother's favorite sayings. So tell the truth: You became a *dalit* for him, didn't you?"

"No."

"The word is 'yes.' Say it with me. Yes."

She fights against his command, her face straining against the effort of keeping the word in her mouth. But after a minute, the struggle ends.

"Yes!" she shouts.

Excellent, Archibald thinks. She is beginning to give in. "For him, you became a social pariah. You lost your chance to die honorably, too. A *dalit* can't have a Beautiful Death, so even in the afterlife, you're doomed to the shadows. Isn't that right?"

"Y—"

"Say it!" he yells.

"Yes!"

"Of course it is. It's also right that the chief you gave all for, the man you think you love, led you into an ambush then abandoned you."

"Dead . . . you said he was . . . dead."

"We thought he was, but turns out he's alive and well and getting nasty with some farm girl."

"No!"

"Would I lie to you? Let me answer that: no, I would not. That's why when I say that I can give back something you've lost, it's the Bishop's honest truth. I can give you back your finger. The medicine to regenerate appendages is very rare and very expensive, but we have the means and resources to get it. You can be whole again, love. Be a hero again. Go to Valhalla like the Tenets promise you can. Just do me one tiny little favor."

It's a lie, of course. Mother's physicians could grow another digit for her, but she would never stop being *dalit*. Valhalla, if there were even such a place, would not welcome her now. But the lie hits the right chord.

Her eyelids flutter. She lifts her head. "F-favor? What. Kind?"

Perfect, Archibald thinks, and pushes a twig of hair away from her ear. He whispers something, and her eyes grow wide. He takes the mutilated hand in his so that his fingers cover hers. In a certain light, from a particular angle, it looks as if her hand is whole again.

Slowly she nods, her eyes bloodshot, the pupils glowing pink. "My name is Vienne."

"See?" he says, smiling because she is broken, and she belongs to him. Jacob Stringfellow, eat your heart out. "That wasn't so hard, was it? Now that we're friends, Vienne, there's something else I want you to do: Tell me the secrets I have *so* longed to hear. Tell me about . . . Durango."

CHAPTER 21

Tharsis Prefecture
Coastal Plain of Hastings,
near the River Gagarin
ANNOS MARTIS 238. 7. 26. 21:05

With the distant smoke to guide us, Riki-Tiki, Stain, and I continue traveling down the military cutoff toward the north, with hope of gaining ground on Archibald's slash-and-burn campaign. But we go hours without seeming to get any closer, and when the sun sets beyond Olympus Mons and its shadow bathes us in twilight, we're forced to pull off the road to find a place to camp.

A short search nets us a grotto that's obviously been used by travelers before. I gather wood and build a small fire in a shallow pit. Riki-Tiki makes a quick meal of the rice and beans that Shoei sent along with me. Stain declines to join us. Instead, he sips broth from a small bowl, a little at a time, like a rat stealing bait from a trap.

When the sun is fully set, Stain reminds Riki-Tiki that it is time for evening meditation.

"Aw, do we have to?"

"Shame on you for asking," he says, his voice cold.

She hops to her feet, dusting her pants off, flashing a smile that I can tell is forced.

"I don't care what Riki-Tiki says," I tell Mimi. "This blighter is trouble."

"I have observed no evidence to contradict your conclusion, cowboy."

"Begin!" Stain snaps.

I expect them to light incense and take the lotus position. Instead, they do a quick stretch and take the ready position—legs together, palms together, then bow.

"What's this?" I ask Riki-Tiki, stuffing the mess gear into my bike's cargo hold. "Didn't you just say it's time for prayer?"

"This is *yi-jin-jing* meditation. The Tengu believe that seated mediation will make you fat. So we fight while we pray." She cocks her head at me, the same way Vienne does when she thinks I'm being obtuse. "You may join us if you like."

"I'll pass. I just ate."

Stain scoffs. "Regulators don't know the forms. He is too busy digesting his dinner to keep up, regardless."

Who says I couldn't keep up, I think. If Stain can do the forms, it can't be that hard. Just because I don't plant metal objects under my skin doesn't mean I'm lazy.

"Don't be so mean, Stain," Riki-Tiki says as they change forms, their movements flowing in perfect synchronicity.

First, they make an X with their hands over their heads.

They spread their arms parallel to the ground, then turn their palms up to the sky.

"Of course, we also eat while we pray and bathe while we pray," Riki-Tiki says. "Tengu are pretty much praying all the time."

I laugh. "Won't eating while you're praying make you fat, too?"

She sticks out her tongue. "Are you saying I'm fat?"

"Hush!" Stain barks.

"Somebody had nails for breakfast," Mimi says.

"Dinner, too."

Next they stomp with the left foot and step back with the right. Palms still up, they extend their left arms and draw the right one back, tucking the elbow.

"Yah!" they shout and shoot the right hand out, rotating and making a fist at the last instant. The left hand chambers back, then flicks into a forearm block.

"Ghannouj says that monks don't fight," Riki-Tiki adds. "We practice forms while meditating to gain enlightenment. He says that every kick contains wisdom."

"Rubbish!" Stain barks as they throw a front kick, followed by a side kick, followed by a roundhouse.

"The Tengu have always fought. It is the essence of who we are, a tradition that Rinpoche himself followed."

"Who?" I ask.

They land on one knee and punch the ground with an open hand. Momentum carries their hips and legs into the air, and they do a one-handed handstand, followed by a front flip.

"Rinpoche," Riki-Tiki says. "He was the first Tengu on Mars. Only sixteen Earth years old when he emigrated here. That means he wasn't much older than me. Isn't that right, Stain?"

From a squatting position, they throw a high scissors kick, back flip, and land on their feet.

Legs together. Palms together.

Bow.

For a few seconds, Stain does nothing but chew on his tongue piercings, then he draws a circle in the dirt with his staff and says, "Rinpoche was more than a beekeeper." He splits the circle in half. "He was *bönpo* of bees, a holy man hounded from his home by the Communist government."

"Communist?" I say. "That government was overthrown in—"

He begins twirling his staff, ignoring me. "The Project Ares scientists brought him and nine of his followers to this place to aid their greenhouse farming. Here, Rinpoche found serenity and a purpose. His bees were a godsend to Martian horticulture."

"I'm really not into history," I say. "I've always been concerned with the here and now."

"Shh." Riki-Tiki gives me a look tinged with humor and pity. "But this is a really good story."

"Soon," Stain continues, his voice like a chant, "the

demand for beekeepers brought more Tengu. Farmers took up arms to force the Tengu to work for them. Rinpoche decided that each monk would take nine acolytes for protection and to regulate the settlers."

The staff begins to hum. He changes the twirling pattern, and the pitch rises. "When Rinpoche passed from this life, all was at peace. Then the Bishop made the Regulators his Holy Templers, trained only in warfare, taking nothing from the Tengu except our Nine Tenets."

"Nine Tenets?" I say. "Those always belonged to the Regulators."

"Perverted by them, you mean," he snaps at me. "The Regulators are no longer honorable warriors. They are just killers."

My hackles rise. "So you're calling me and Vienne killers, is that it? Is that the point you're trying to make?"

"The history of the Regulator is the history of Mars," Stain says. "Great hope perverted by ambition and greed. Like Vienne, who came to the monks as a helpless child. They helped her heal, but she turned her back on them."

That bloody bastard. Nobody talks about Vienne that way. I pull my armalite.

"No!" Riki-Tiki grabs my arm. "He doesn't mean it. That's just Stain's way of talking. Please?"

I ram the gun back in its holster. What a hypocrite. I'm tempted to confront him about getting kicked out of the monastery. "His way of talking's going to get him shot one day."

If Stain hears me, he shows no indication of it. He spins the staff horizontally on his palm, and while holding it aloft, does a deep back bend so that his body forms an inverted U, the staff spinning above him like the rotor of a velocicopter.

"Listen," Riki-Tiki whispers.

Her voice is drowned out by the sound of an approaching storm.

No, not a storm.

A swarm. A mammoth swarm that fills the sky. It rises over the butte, snarling and twisting, with a tail like a buzzing rope. For a few seconds, it seems like the bees are going to envelop us, and I'm looking for a hole to dive into.

"I just decided," I tell Mimi, "I don't like bees."

Then, with a snap of the wrist, Stain stops the staff. The swarm seems to shudder, then dissipates like smoke.

"Wow," I say, "those bees came out of nowhere really fast."

"That is because the bees never really leave Stain," Riki-Tiki says, clapping. "He is *bönpo*, just like Rinpoche was."

"What's this word *bönpo* they keep using?" I ask Mimi.

She pauses before answering. "There is no reference in my admittedly sparse amount of data regarding the Tengu monks to any *bönpo*."

"Riki-Tiki is mistaken." Stain pounds the staff against the ground. He grabs two handfuls of dirt and rubs them on the staff. "I am not bönpo. She is."

"Not yet," Riki-Tiki says, with a hint of disappointment.

"And not ever, if Vienne agrees to take me as her acolyte. Then I'll become a Regulator, just like her."

"No!" Stain shakes a finger in her face. "That is not your path. You will not become Vienne's acolyte. You are too pure for that!"

Too pure? As opposed to unpure? Is that what he thinks of Vienne?

"Don't tell me about my path!" She stomps her foot and shakes her head, the pink spikes of hair snapping in the night air. "Don't preach to me! You of all people should know better!"

Go ahead, I think, give the arrogant bastard hell.

"Cowboy!" Mimi shouts in my head. "Multiple bogeys in close proximity! Closing fast!"

"Down!" I yell and yank both of them to the ground.

"How dare you?" Stain complains, his face full of dirt.

Riki-Tiki shushes him. "Listen!"

Then I hear the deep thump of a velocicopter rotor as a Hellbender thunders overhead. Its searchlights crisscross the grotto, bouncing off the high wall of stones that shield us.

For now.

A few seconds later, the copter disappears into the thickening clouds.

"Think they saw us?" Riki-Tiki stands, then slaps dirt from her knees.

Stain glowers at me while wiping his mouth. "No. We are well hidden."

"Hellbenders don't need visuals to find targets. The pilot's got enough telemetry onboard to find a maggot in a compost heap." I bound up a series of large stones for a better look— just in time to see the copter bank toward us. "It's coming back! Get to the bikes! Our only chance is to outrun it!"

"Outrun a Hellbender?" Mimi says as we're sprinting toward the motorbikes, leaving the refugees to hide. "How do you propose to do that?"

"By going really, really fast!"

Less than a minute later, we're back on the military cutoff road, putting distance between us and the refugees in the grotto. Riki-Tiki is pressed tight against my back, and Stain rides beside me, our headlights cutting through a rainy mist.

"Think we got away?" Riki-Tiki shouts as we crest a high hill.

"This is Lieutenant Beyla of the Zealand CorpCom militia," the velocicopter pilot shouts over his PA. The voice comes from everywhere and nowhere. Then a few seconds later, the clouds ahead of us begin to swirl, then disappear as a five-bladed rotor chops them to bits. Rockets rip from their pods. From under the long expanse of the bridge ahead, the Hellbender rises like an angel of death. Rockets rip from their launch pods. Retorts from the Seneca gun pound the air, which is alive with noise and destruction. Then abruptly—silence.

The PA: "And I order you to stop!"

"Guess that answers your question," I tell Riki-Tiki.

And gun it.

We roar straight toward a spray of heavy fire that erupts from the gunner's nest. The line of bullets zippers the space between the two bikes as the pilot brings the velocicopter to bear, and the pavement in front of us explodes, throwing chunks of asphalt into the air. I swerve, my wheel bucking. Stain hits the throttle, and his bike pops a wheelie as he tears toward the bridge. At first I think he's going straight for their throat, then I realize that he's drawing their fire.

I swing to the left side of the highway, splitting off as the gunner chases Stain with bullets until he crosses beneath the velocicopter. In the dark, I can see the muzzle of the barrel glowing, which means the Seneca gun is overheated and can't be fired. Time to make a run for it. I kill the headlamp on the motorbike and use the taillights of Stain's Munro as my guiding star.

"Stay low," I tell Riki-Tiki.

We hit the bridge doing eighty.

Yee-carking-haw! "Mimi, are we close enough to monitor their transmissions?"

"Beat you to it, cowboy," she says. "Patching you in."

The pilot's voice rings in my ears. "Roger, Command, we have visual and have engaged. Tagging targets with GPS markers."

Then I see the spotter beside the gunner's nest, aiming a high-powered rifle at the fading lights of Stain's tail. If the spotter hits him with a marker, he'll never be able to escape. The marker will show his GPS locations for hours, maybe days.

"Marking in five, four,—"

Oh no, you don't.

Holding the bike steady with my knees, I yank my armalite out of the holster and empty a clip into the night. The bullets are useless, but it's the sound that matters. Nothing like popping gunpowder to get the attention of a flying sheet metal whale.

"We're under fire!" the pilot squawks, and he veers to the south, the spotter's fluorescent mark round shooting uselessly into the ravine below.

Gunning it, I'm plastered to the handlebars. Their vibration shoots up my arms and rattles my teeth. Riki-Tiki lassoes her arms around me, her chin digging into my spine as she holds on for dear life.

The sound of the Hellbender's rotors fades as we cross the bridge. My eye grows blurry. I check the speedometer. The needle is buried. Amazing. I'd no idea the engine could haul this fast. Fuse, the bludger who built this crate, would be proud of himself.

"Did we lose them?" Riki-Tiki shouts above the growl of the engines.

"Mimi," I say. "Where'd they go?"

"Indeterminate," she says. "Our acceleration was too great to triangulate positions."

A half kilometer ahead on the highway, Stain's taillights flicker in the darkness, then the brake lights glow brightly.

He's stopped?

A second later, I hear why.

"I repeat!" The PA booms. "This is Lieutenant Beyla of the Zealand CorpCom militia. Stand down! You are under arrest!"

"Mimi?" I ask. "Are these real CorpComs or bad jacks in stolen uniforms?"

"Does it matter, cowboy? The bullets are the same either way."

Fifty yards above ground, two searchlights sweep through the night. A second Hellbender has joined the first. Then, as the broad beams land on Stain's Munro, two more lights flicker on. These are dimmer and low to the ground.

It's a Noriker, and Norikers mean shock troopers.

As Stain whips his bike around, the bright flowers of muzzle blasts ignite alongside the Norikers. I count sixteen blasters firing, along with the two mini-guns in the copters. We are definitely outmatched.

Slamming my brakes and digging a knee into the pavement, I bring my bike around and then hit the throttle full as Stain appears on my tail.

"I got a plan!" I yell as Stain steers his bike alongside me.

"We can't outrun them!" he answers.

"Don't plan to!" I say. "I'll distract them. You take

Riki-Tiki and head north. I'll meet up with you at Dismel.
It's about thirty kilometers from here."

Stain weaves closer. "What about you?"

"I'll improvise! Riki-Tiki! You're with Stain!"

"I want to improvise, too!" she says.

"Go!" I yell.

Stain steers so close, our tailpipes are almost touching.
"Take my hand!" He and Riki-Tiki lock forearms, and he
pulls her to the back of his seat.

"Good luck!" he shouts and zooms ahead.

You, too, I think, then slam on the brakes, turning back
toward the enemy.

Two Hellbenders.

A truckload of shock troopers.

Even I don't like these odds.

"Mimi," I say, "remember when we helped put down an
insurrection in New Savannah? We were pinned by the
rebels on a stretch of road a lot like this, and we escaped by
charging their barricades?"

"Yes," she says, "but you will recall, we used a tank to
charge that barricade."

"But the barricade was bigger."

"So was the tank."

Taking a deep breath, I open up the accelerator and jam
it in place. The stream of air whips around my body as I
jump atop the seat and wedge a foot in the center of the
handlebars. Popping my armalite to full automatic, I ram

the stock into the crook of my broken arm and rest a finger on the trigger guard.

"You're insane," Mimi says.

"It worked with the last Hellbender."

"Maybe that was just luck."

"Maybe I'm just lucky." I smile, even as the Hellbenders settle into firing position and the shock troops release a barrage of rounds that light up the air like a row of firecrackers. I plow through them without blinking, the blast rounds bouncing off my armor like sleet. They fire again, this time haphazardly, and the velocicopter gunners cut loose a line of tracer bullets that crisscross a meter in front of my front tire.

My turn.

A squeeze of the trigger unleashes the armalite, and it chatters like a broken chain, its rounds spraying the Hellbender to my left. Several find their mark in the body of the copter, and the pilot rolls aft to avoid the rest. I unwedge my foot from the handlebars, and my bike begins to weave in exaggerated curves.

At a couple of seconds before impact, I do a backward dismount and land in time to see the bike plow into the wall of troopers, their horrified faces lit by the bike's headlamp. The bike careens out of control, then flips onto its side, metal hitting pavement with a cascade of sparks that leaves a spiraling trail of light for twenty meters. Metal grinds as the bike slows to a halt, and I wince at the damage it must be taking.

If Fuse were here, he'd kill me.

Before it stops, I slam another clip into my armalite, flick it to semiauto, and use my good hand to shoot out the Noriker's headlights. A brave trooper charges straight into my line of fire, but instead of shooting him, I drop him with a front kick, set my gun on his prone belly, and pull two Willy Pete grenades from his belt.

I slam one into the grenade launcher of my armalite and fire it into the gunner's nest of the second Hellbender. Amid screams from the gunners and pilot as the white phosphorous fills the bay, the velocicopter veers sharply away.

That's the problem with machines that cost more than any other weapon in the arsenal. They're too expensive to risk losing, and that limits their effectiveness.

Back to the troopers.

Even in the confusion, several of them have taken position next to the Noriker, and they're firing on me. As always, the blasts bounce off harmlessly, and I walk toward the hostiles like a man of steel, invulnerable, invincible.

"Insufferable," Mimi says. "You are not out of the woods yet, cowboy."

Jamming the second Willy Pete into my armalite, I launch the grenade into the cab of the Noriker. It takes a few seconds for chemicals in the grenade to catalyze, then *poof!*

"Better run!" I yell.

I don't have to tell them twice. Grabbing their wounded, the troopers retreat off the road before the fuel tanks of the Noriker ignite.

"Better follow your own advice," Mimi says.

"Right." I sprint toward the bike. It's the worse for wear, and when I push it up, a crumpled exhaust pipe clangs on the pavement. The handlebars are askew, too. But it's drive-able if the engine will start.

Murmuring a little prayer, I pull out the choke, flip the ignition switch, and pop the clutch.

Hallelujah. It starts. I drive down the highway, wobbling on bent rims.

A few seconds later the Düsseldorf explodes, and behind me I can hear metal landing on the ground. My path is brightly lit, and I can see the road before me. Then everything turns dark, and I have nothing to guide me but the stars.

"And me. You will always have me to guide you," Mimi says. "Turn left here."

CHAPTER 22

Hawera Hydroelectric Complex
Zealand Prefecture
ANNOS MARTIS 238. 7. 27. 06:13

The Hawera Hydroelectric Complex straddles the border between the Tharsis and Zealand Prefectures like a mythological Titan. Using a series of cooling towers and megawatt turbines, it controls the flow of the River Gagarin into the Dead Sea while providing almost the whole prefecture with power. It has been said that whoever controls the Hawera controls the capital.

Who controls the capital, Archibald wonders as he stands at the railing on the observation deck that overlooks both the complex and the town nearby, if the whole complex just happens to disappear? Of course, if all goes according to plan, he's about to find out.

He looks back on the twisted heaps that make up Dismel and catches his breath. Dismel was a hornet's nest of Desperta Ferro activity, and now it's gone, obliterated, and he is responsible. How ironic. For years, Mother has obsessed about how to get rid of the rebels, and it's her enemy that does it for her.

He puffs his chest out. How do you like me now, Mother? Then he sighs, the air leaving him. The truth is, if she saw him now, he'd be shot on sight, a traitor to the CorpCom. *Damn it, Mother, even when I succeed, you make sure I fail.*

Leaving the deck, he takes one of the lifts to the ground. Every few meters, he passes a civilian going to tour the dam. Ordinary people going about their ordinary lives with no clue about the extraordinary thing that is about to happen to them. He takes the stairs methodically, careful not to jostle himself, until he reaches the parking lot. As he signals Duke to bring the Noriker over, a woman and her young son bump into him.

"Watch where you're going!" he snaps at them. His hand goes to his side.

"Watch your—" the woman starts to say, then recoils as the color drains from her face. She pushes the boy behind her for protection.

"Mommy," the boy says as they reach the staircase. "That man stinks."

She hushes him and drags him up the stairs.

Yes, little mother, Archie thinks, fear me. That's all that I ever wanted.

Duke picks him up in the Noriker, and they speed over to the next village, which is too small to earn a name, but big enough to fuel a good fire. There, he gives the order, and the Sturmnacht spread out through the streets carrying lit torches and leaving fire in their wake.

From the distance, the sound of a battle catches Archibald's attention.

"Right on time," he says. "Duke, find that gunfire, please."

In the Noriker, he and Duke zip through the narrow streets, outpacing the Sturmnacht. The truck crests a hill, and the battle appears in a dry creek bed below, where a squad of Sturmnacht is pinned down by platoon of Zealand Corp Rangers.

The Sturmnacht are outmanned and over gunned.

"A perfect scenario to test my new weapon," Archie says. "Tell the handlers to deliver the package."

After what seems to Archie to be an interminable wait, the Noriker pulling the animal brig trailer arrives.

"Finally," Archibald says, and grabs a remote device from the Noriker's storage compartment.

He hits the button that opens the door, then stands on tiptoes in anticipation of the great event. All of his work comes down to this moment.

But nothing happens—"Stubborn little hussy. Get out of the trailer."—until Archibald hits another button on the remote.

Vienne leaps from the trailer, hair wild and matted, carrying a spear. She vaults down into the creek bed and roars straight for the Sturmnacht. When the thugs see her, they begin waving their arms frantically.

"No, love, not them," Archibald says and presses a button. "The other them."

The choker on her neck glows. One hand clawing at her neck, Vienne turns toward the Rangers' line. Without fear and without hesitation, she uses the spear to lay the line to waste. She stands panting for a few seconds. Then a flash of movement from the Sturmnacht catches her eye.

"No, your work is done. Very well done," Archibald says.

He sighs at having to end the fun so soon and hits another button. An electric shock lights the choker, and she falls to the ground.

"Duke, help the handlers get her back to the brig before she wakes up again."

Duke and the handlers latch on to Vienne, intending to haul her away. But Vienne's head flies up, and she yanks her limbs free. She moves so fast that Duke's jaw drops, and in the few seconds that it takes for the handlers to realize that Vienne is loose, she goes berserk on them.

A kick, a few punches, and an elbow to the nose takes out all three of them. Snarling, her hair hiding her eyes but not her bared teeth, she lunges for Duke.

"Stop!" Archibald shouts, zapping the choker at the same time.

Vienne manages to knock Duke down, but the choker has her attention. She pulls at it, howling, putting up an intense fight that surprises Archibald. Maybe she isn't as ready as he thought.

He zaps the choker again, and this time, she succumbs

to the voltage. Archibald stands over her, panting to catch his breath. He nudges Duke with his heel.

"Find me soldiers who can last more than a few seconds with the *dalit*."

"In the Sturmnacht? Don't count on it." Duke knocks the mud off his armor. "It'll take a Regulator to fight the likes of her."

"Then find me one."

"What? A Regulator?"

Archibald turns on him. "Yes! A Regulator. There are hundreds of them in Christchurch looking for work. Find one. Pay whatever it takes."

"Did you run this by Mr. Lyme?" Duke asks.

"Do not mention the name Lyme in front of me again!" Archie screams.

A moment passes between them. Archibald realizes that he's gone too far this time. Duke will report this to Lyme, and Lyme will have another stern talk with Archibald about the master plan and how important it is that everyone play his part. It's obvious now what Lyme has decided his part is—to be a pawn.

Well, Archibald thinks, I'm nobody's pawn, and I'll prove it, starting now.

"Whatever you say," Duke says, then walks toward his Noriker.

As Duke drives away, he passes a Noriker coming from the opposite direction. He trades an obscene gesture with the driver, and they both break out laughing.

"This," Archibald says, trying to regain his composure, "doesn't look like good news."

Richards and Franks get out of the Noriker and approach as if they haven't a care in the world. Imagine being that stupid, Archibald thinks. It must be nice to be completely ignorant of the greater forces at work on your life.

"You've come back empty handed," Archibald says as he declines to shake their hands in greeting. "Is that what I told you to do?"

"Not exactly," Franks says.

Richards adds, "But we did find him, your Mistership. In a roadhouse on the Bishop's Highway. He just managed to sneak away after he threw hairs in my face."

Archibald raises a skeptical eyebrow. "Durango escaped by tossing hair at you? What is he now, a malicious barber?"

"He wasn't exactly normal. Right, Franks?" Richards shows his injured face. "The things came out of his hands."

Franks nods. "The things were barbed, too. They stuck in Richards's skin, and I had the dickens pulling them out with my pliers."

Richards turns his jaw so that Archibald can see the marks left. "Hurt something fierce."

"You poor thing," Archibald says. How could Lyme have ever tolerated such imbeciles? "Since you're having so much trouble capturing him, then maybe we should try a new strategy."

The Sturmnacht trade a skeptical look. "How d'you know we can find the poxer?"

"Because you're not going to find him. He's going to come to you. Right here in scenic Dismel." Archibald claps them both on the back. "I've left a trail as wide and black as Lyme's heart to follow. That Regulator fancies himself a hero, and heroes never, ever give up."

Franks scratches his head. "But what's that got to do with us?"

"It has everything to do with you," Archie says. "I have a very special treat in mind. For both of you."

CHAPTER 23

Hours after we separated, I find Riki-Tiki and Stain near the town of Dismel, standing on the banks of the River Gagarin, watching something on the water.

"Let's go!" I pull up beside them, my bike's engine rumbling. "We've got work to do."

"Shh!" Riki-Tiki says. "Turn that off. You're being disrespectful."

"Mimi?"

"Do it, cowboy," she says, so I kill the motor. "Look out at Hawera Lake. What do you see?"

Flipping up my visor, I stare out over the water.

"Wow."

The banks of the river are crammed with thousands of plain, brown paper lanterns lit by wax candles floating on the water. They drift together, then apart, as the current sweeps them downriver and out of sight.

"Candles?" I ask.

"They're called *Tōrō Nagashi*," Riki-Tiki explains, "symbolizing the return of the dead. Tonight is the Night of Joy, the end of the Spirit Festival."

"A candle for every lost soul," I say. A candle for every Vienne in the world.

"Ironic, no?" Stain says. "Since Dismel is a ghost town now. Never let it be said that the Sturmnacht have no sense of the poetic."

"Carking-A," I reply, and flip my visor down, because I've seen all the candles I care to. "Never let it be said. Let's ride."

At night, Dismel looks like a roadkill skeleton that's been picked clean. After our rendezvous, Riki-Tiki, Stain, and I roll past the charred remnants of a few of the Quonset hut frames lining the streets. It reminds me of the mines of Fisher Four. The tunnels were perpetually dark, and my circadian rhythms went haywire. None of us Regulators could tell if it was night or day, so we stumbled around in a sleep-deprived haze, protecting miners there—who didn't want us—from the Draeu, bogeymen who could see in the dark and wanted nothing more than to dine on our flesh. It's a wonder we didn't accidently shoot someone.

"May I remind you that your telemetry functions let you know the location of everyone at any time," Mimi says.

"Don't remind me," I tell her. What I wouldn't give for my old suit—and my old body—back. I've gotten so used to its functions, I'm never sure where I am anymore. Thinking about that makes me miss Vienne even more.

Thoom! In the distance, a bloom of smoke. Three more explosions, and I see petals of flame erupting through the smoke.

"A poet would use this place as a metaphor for the failed Mars Utopia," I tell Mimi.

"Only if he wanted to put his audience in a catatonic state, cowboy. Let's stick to the Romantics, shall we?"

As we slowly ride through on our bikes, picking our way around the debris lit by our headlamps, tendrils of smoke dust still rise here and there. If you were patient and could stand the cacophonic smell, you might be able to tell that a large slab of wood resembling alligator skin was once somebody's prized sideboard. Over in the far corner of the mess that had once been someone's life, you might see the bedsprings of a bed that had occupied the room before the ceiling gave way. Or you might just turn away and decide to pay attention to the road instead. Because there's only so much rage you can take until, like a balloon filled with too much hot air, you pop.

But you might also miss a woman running toward a burning house, her face streaked with soot, sweat, and panic. "My baby!" she screams. "My baby's still in there!"

There's no time to ask logical questions like, How did the baby get there? Why are you alone? Why did you leave the child behind? Is this a trap?

There's just time for one question as Riki-Tiki grabs the woman before she can run through the back door, which is engulfed in flames.

"Where's the baby?" I yell so she can hear me over her screams and the roar of the fires.

"She's in the bathroom!" Riki-Tiki calls, because the woman can't make a sound now.

"Mimi," I say as I slap the visor down over my helmet and switch on the LED lamp, "watch my back."

"You got it, cowboy."

The hallway is shrouded in thick soot that clings to the ceiling like a curtain. Below that, the smoke is lighter, thinner, a roiling cloud that I duck under as I crunch over the debris on the floor, stomping with my thick-soled boots to make sure the footing is solid.

At the first doorway, I turn right and enter a small room. The windows are so heavily smoked, no light could reach inside. The air stinks of charcoal, and my head swims with the sound of a discordant pipe organ. Turning in a tight circle, I scan the area, noting the burned-out skeleton of a box mattress in the corner, an open closet, and a narrow door leading to another room.

Keep moving. Look. Listen.

The room is hot. But there is no obvious fire. I listen hard, listening for the source of the crying sound. It came from this direction, I'm sure of it. There! Behind the narrow door. I reach for the brass knob without thinking. The metal, now blackened, is hot as a gas pipe, and when I touch it, the heat burns straight through my symbiarmor gloves.

"*Mistuck!*" I yell through the visor. "That's carking hot!"

Nothing to do about that now. Raising my boot, I give the door a front kick. It blows off its frame, swings wide on melted hinges, and collapses to the floor.

That's more like it.

As I enter the bathroom, hot air blows past my head. A blackened toilet sits to the left, and to the right, a tub. A cast-iron tub with high sides that could survive a nuclear blast. Which is good, because in the bottom, covered in ash, is something so rare and unusual, I haven't seen one since becoming a Regulator.

A baby.

She's quiet and still. In the thick smoke, I can't tell if she's breathing. I lift the infant out of the tub and nestle her head in the crook of my broken arm, then cover her face with a towel I snatch from the floor. With a silent prayer still on my lips, I take three running steps and throw my back against the window. The plexi shatters, and I fall like a counterweight to the ground. Above me, a jet of hot air roars from the latrine and flames pour out, tasting the fresh oxygen. Safe now, I yank the towel from the baby's face. She's quiet, eyes closed, then the rush of cold air hits her face, and the crying ignites.

The mother comes screaming toward me, and without a word, she pulls the bundle from my arm, clutches the baby to her breast, and flees, terrified, into the darkness. That is what this war has created—people who are terrified of the very same soldier who can help them.

I look into my empty arms and think of Vienne.

"Durango!" Riki-Tiki calls. "Come quickly! Stain's found something!"

That something is a shipping container covered with Desperta Ferro graffiti. Inside, someone is hammering away on the walls.

"Let them out," I tell Stain.

He points to the door, which is secured with a padlock.

"Stand behind me," I say, then put a round into the lock. I slide the door open.

A Sturmnacht stands and fires a blaster round into my gut. It bounces off. I shrug, and the Sturmnacht aims for my face. I knock the blaster aside, then stick my cast under the poxer's chin, lifting and slamming him into the opposite wall of the container.

Stain and Riki-Tiki follow us inside.

"We come in peace," Riki-Tiki says.

"You got a carking funny definition of peace," he growls.

"You got a funny way of answering the door, Franks," I say. "Where's your partner?"

"He's dead. When we come back without you, that little piss bucket Archibald put a bullet in him and threw me to the CorpComs." His head has been split open, and his nose seems flatter, crooked, and he's missing a few more teeth. "Thought you was one of them Rangers come back to finish the job."

"Rangers locked you in here?"

"It wasn't the tooth fairy."

"Pardon me if I'm a little skeptical." I lean against him a tiny bit more, just to let him know I mean business. "Explain to me how Rangers came to lock you inside a shipping container."

"Reckon the locals called them in after us Sturmnacht started burning the place down," Franks rasps. "Ain't that hard to figure out, even for a dunny rat like you."

"You have a smart mouth," Stain says.

"You got bad teeth," Franks snarks.

I push my cast against the blighter's voice box. "Enough out of you. Listen up. We're after Archibald's crew. From the looks of this place, they came through not long ago. You tell us which way they went, and we'll let you go."

Franks winks. "If I don't tell you?"

"Then we can lock you back up and let the CorpComs take care of you."

"Go screw yourself," he spits.

"You're telling me that you're more afraid of Archibald than the CorpComs?"

"No," he says. "I'm telling you to go screw yourself."

"You are a very rude man," Riki-Tiki says.

Franks winks. "And you're a fair dinkum susie."

"Shut up," Stain says. "Or I'll kill you myself."

Franks laughs. "You're a monk! There ain't a killer between the lot of you. Before you go threatening a man, you ought to make sure you're willing to carry through with it."

He's right. There's only so far I'm willing to go to get information. I'm no Archibald. I release the hold on him. "It's the Rangers then. We'll be keeping the blaster."

We step outside. As I'm closing Franks back up, Stain sticks his hand in the door, blocking it. "I'll have a word with this man."

"A waste of time." I say. "Short of killing him, he's not going to crack."

"Have faith. I can be very persuasive." Stain slides the door closed behind him.

Riki-Tiki walks across the alley to a cinder-block wall and sits down. She cups both hands over her ears and begins to hum a nonsense rhyme.

"Mimi?" I say. "What do you make of this?"

"Something unpleasant."

"Astute analysis."

"Garbage in, garbage out, cowboy."

Pressing my ear against the container, I listen for the sounds of their voices, but the insulation is too thick. Then I hear it, the familiar thrum of Stain's staff. The metal skin of the container vibrates, amplifies the sound, making it louder and deeper. It hurts my ears, and I have to step back.

Inside, Franks starts screaming.

"Stain! Open up!" I yank on the door, but it won't open. The bastard has blocked it from the inside. I punch the container, and my fist bounces off the thick metal. But I can't punch my way through the door, and three more tries won't open it. The screams continue, and I look across the alley at Riki-Tiki, who is humming louder.

Then I remember Vienne. They didn't mind torturing her, so why should I worry about the pain Stain is dishing out?

Franks screams. I steel myself against the sound while inspecting the dirt embalmed in my cuticles. It goes against every principle I have to stand here and let the interrogation continue. But I do. Both because we need the information and because a small, mean part of me thinks the poxer deserves this. The monks call it karma.

No, I tell myself, it's not karma. It's vengeance. Don't let your heart turn hard.

"Amen," Mimi says.

I take a seat beside Riki-Tiki. Bump her with my shoulder. "It'll be over soon."

"Not soon enough," she says, unplugging her ears. "He wasn't always like this, you know. Ghannouj says that when Stain and Vienne came to live with the monks, they hardly talked at first. After a long time, they came out of their shells, and they both were devoted to the way of the Tengu. They were happy, too. But everything changed one day when a stranger showed up at the temple, angry and out of his mind with Rapture. He said he was Vienne and Stain's father, and he was there to take them away."

So that's why Vienne wasn't sympathetic to the hostages Archibald took. "Was the man really their father?"

Riki-Tiki nods. "Vienne said he was. I believe her. But he was an awful father. When the monks tried to calm him down, he attacked Ghannouj and started hurting Vienne. She fought him like a wild thing. The Rapture made him too strong. So Stain snatched a cleaver from the kitchen and threatened him with it. The man started to snap Vienne's neck, so Stain killed him." She sniffs and wipes her nose. "Tengu law says that we can't commit acts of violence and we can't desecrate the temple. Stain did both."

"What happened after that?" I ask.

"The monks sent him away. Vienne left to become a Regulator. Stain gave up on the Tengu way to become a wanderer. He says he's a better monk now than before, but I miss the old Stain. He used to laugh. Now I don't think he'll ever laugh again."

"I don't understand," I say. "If the monks kicked him out, how's he still *bönpo*?"

"The staff. It contains a hive queen, so—"

Franks screams again. The terror in his voice sends an ice-pick shiver down my spine. Riki-Tiki buries her head in my shoulder and plugs her ears. To help draw out the screams, I hum the only lullaby I know and rock her back and forth. Vienne's words echo in my mind, and I realize how naïve I've been. How stupid, too. Being a Regulator wasn't just about being a soldier to her. Returning to the monastery wasn't just about a homecoming. She was healing. She was finding herself. And I asked her to give it all away for what? Pride? Honor? Call it whatever you want, Durango, it all comes down to vanity.

Finally, Stain opens the door. Franks is lying on the floor in a fetal position, crying, his body covered in welts. A quiet buzz is coming from the pouch on Stain's belt.

"Torturing prisoners is not the way Regulators behave, Stain." I stick a finger in his face. "We're supposed to be better than our enemies."

"I am not a Regulator, so your rules don't apply to me." He bats my hand away. "My methods got us the information we need."

"Which is?" I ask, doing my best not to hit him.

"The Sturmnacht are recruiting *dalit* for the war they've started," Stain says. "They are assembling at Hawera Dam, which is where Archibald is holding Vienne."

I'm forced to admit that he's effective. I also have to admit that I'm willing to use the intel, even if he tortured Franks to get it. The guilt and self-recriminations will have to wait for another day.

"Grab Franks," I say. "He's going to help us, whether he likes it or not."

CHAPTER 24

Archibald shields his eyes as the Hellbender lands on the observation deck. Two shock troopers jump from the cargo bay, followed by a Regulator in symbiarmor that bears the insignia of Zealand Corp.

"Yes!" Archibald runs toward the Regulator. For a few seconds, the soldier seems ready to open fire. Then he extends his hand, and Archibald relaxes.

"Hope you're as tough as you look," Archibald tells him. "This isn't a job for the squeamish."

"They never are," the Regulator says.

As the Hellbender takes off, they run to an access door marked "Turbine" and enter. Archibald signals the larger shock troopers to stop and guard the door. They pass through the room, which houses the mechanical controls for the spill gates, then downstairs to an inner office, where a series of multivid control panels act as the hive mind for the entire dam complex.

Across the room is a wide window made of thick plexi so that the operators can observe the spill gates. Duke is waiting for him there, drinking a cup of coffee.

"My first Regulator has arrived," Archibald says with a flourish that Duke appears to ignore.

"Yeah." Duke sets the cup aside and wipes his mouth on his sleeve. "I know."

What a pig. A disrespectful, ill-mannered pig who needs to be taught a lesson. "Your post is outside!" Archibald snaps at the remaining shock trooper.

Then he turns his attention to Vienne, who is cuffed to a metal chair. "This is your mission."

"I don't kill women," the Regulator says.

Presumptuous idiot! "I said nothing about killing her!" He pauses to regain his composure. "Come, take a closer look. She is my masterpiece."

After observing her for a moment, the Regulator cups her chin in his palm. Vienne's eyes snap open. She snarls and tries to bite him.

He jumps back, quick enough to save his skin. "What have you done to her?"

"Watch your fingers with this one," Archibald says, snickering. "She's not quite tame. One bite, and she'll make a *dalit* out of you."

Purposely ignoring Duke, he saunters to the window, hands clasped behind his back, watching the water from the upper-level spill gates cascading to the lake five hundred meters below. "Vienne is the first of a new breed of warrior. Cunning. Fearless. Obedient. The perfect human weapon to replace all others. Soon, no one will even remember what a Regulator is." He spins around. "Does that bother you?"

"No," the soldier says. "As long as you're paying cash."

Archibald snickers. "That's good, because the reason I brought you here is to help control her. You see, during our last outing, she got out of hand, and the shock troopers just aren't able to make her behave. Do you think you can make her behave?"

"I have no doubt," he says.

Arrogant bastard! She will make hash of you! "This," Archibald says, laughing louder, "is going to be fun—"

From the stairs comes the sound of a ruckus. The troopers are shouting, and the Regulator snaps to attention.

"What the devil is that noise?" Archibald says. "Duke! Find out."

Duke snorts. "Find out yourself."

"What?" he says, stunned by the impertinence. "How dare you speak to me that way!"

He starts toward Duke.

The door flies open.

A trooper shoves a captive through the doorway and hauls him down the stairs. Hands cuffed behind him, his nose and mouth are bleeding, his right eye swollen, and his hair falls in his face as he drops to his knees. His left arm is in a cast, and he's wearing shock trooper armor.

"What is this about?" Archibald screams, blood rushing to his face. "I gave explicit orders not to interrupt me!"

"Sir! He tried to break in." The trooper puts a boot on the captive's back and slams him to the floor. "Want me to shoot him?"

"Of course." Archibald dismisses the trooper with a wave. "But not here. Take him outside. I don't want blood on the floor."

The trooper hesitates.

"What are you waiting for?" Archibald barks. "Quit dawdling and get him out of here before I have you shot as well."

"Yes sir!" After a couple of unsuccessful tries, the trooper scoops up the prisoner and throws him over a shoulder as Archibald turns to the window.

The prisoner coughs. "What's the matter, Archie? Afraid to shoot me yourself?"

"Do not call me—" Archibald wheels around and sees the man's face clearly. "You!" he shouts. He presses both hands to his cheeks, and he hops up and down, clapping. "It can't be—it is!"

"What are you carrying on about?" Duke says.

Archibald is so overjoyed, he chooses to ignore the rudeness. He grabs the prisoner by the hair and lifts up his head. "Don't you recognize him, Duke? This is Jacob Stringfellow, son of the former CEO of Zealand Corp. Soldier! Put him down! Regulator! Get him a chair. We must make our honored guest comfortable."

After the trooper follows orders, the Regulator pulls a chair from a console at the control panel, then sets it next to Vienne. He drops the captive into it.

Stringfellow lets his head droop. Apparently, he isn't interested in conversing anymore.

"You made a mess of him, trooper," Archibald says as he apprises Stringfellow's wounds.

"He's a *dalit*." The trooper shrugs. "He deserved what he got."

"Out!" Archibald snaps his fingers at the trooper, who departs begrudgingly. Then Archibald turns to the observation window, a fist at his mouth, his eyes squinted tight in gleeful triumph. Stringfellow! Captured! Lyme will be thrilled!

He watches the spill water billowing up. A rainbow forms in the mist. It is a good sign, a harbinger of things to come.

"Beautiful, isn't it?" Archibald says in his most theatric voice. "The way the sunlight catches the particles of water, creating a prism effect? Did you know that Earthers believe a small man lives at the end of the rainbow and gives a pot of gold to anyone who can trace the rainbow to its end and capture him? How apropos, then, that a rainbow would appear just in time for my very own pot of gold to appear. Are you listening to me, Mr. Stringfellow?"

No, apparently he isn't. Archibald grabs another chair and sits facing Stringfellow, the chair turned backward.

Stringfellow's lips move, but all he says is, "Nuh."

"I'll take that as a yes. You and I have much in common, you know. Sons of powerful parents. The best breeding. The best educations," Archibald says. "But like you, I found the best to be tedious, and I set out to make my own mark on the world."

Grabbing a handful of hair, he pulls back Stringfellow's head. He takes out his lighter and flicks the flint under his exposed chin.

"Sadly, I lacked your physical gifts," Archibald says, "so I had to turn to other forms of expression."

He strikes the lighter. The flames lick the tips of Stringfellow's luscious hair. "Of course, you didn't come for me," Archibald says. "You came for her, like I knew you would. You're too much the hero to not show up."

He spins Stringfellow's chair around so that he is facing Vienne. Stringfellow's lips tremble, murmuring from either fear or pain. Hopefully, both.

"Love hurts, doesn't it?" Archibald says, mocking him. "You love her, don't you? In that way that handsome, rich boys love the girls that turn them down. You know what's sad? When you do catch her, you'll learn the hard truth about love: It's the chase, not the girl."

"Liar," Stringfellow finally answers.

"I knew you were listening," Archibald says, laughing. "You're such a bad actor."

He slides into Stringfellow's lap, then grabs his blood-ied face, giving a squeeze for good measure. "'That Jacob

Stringfellow. Such a handsome young man.' Do you know how many times my mother uttered those very words to me?" He twists Stringfellow's face toward Vienne. "How about you, *mon petit chou*? Do you think he's still—" He torques the head to punctuate each syllable. "A handsome. Young. Man?"

Vienne doesn't answer, but her body jerks as if racked by petit mal seizures.

Stringfellow groans and fights to escape Archibald's grip, but he is too weak.

"Jacob! Look at my lovely lady and her new eyes!" Archibald says. "I've turned the cat into the leopard, and she has very, very sharp teeth. Maybe I should let her play with her food. See that cruel look? I made that. See the murder in those eyes? I put that there. Do you know why I was able to do that? Because you failed, Stringfellow. You led a beautiful young soldier into battle, and you left her to cover your ass while you tried to escape. Some hero you are."

Stringfellow struggles with the cuffs, straining to reach Archibald with his fists.

"Truth is a bitter pill, isn't it?" He grins. Then he pinches Stringfellow's lips closed. "Talking to yourself again? Well, stop. No one is listening."

For a few seconds, Archibald enjoys Stringfellow's growing agitation, then he feels the pang of something that's been gnawing at him grow larger. "Why is it that Lyme wants you so badly, anyway?"

He stands, then paces the room, pausing at the window. What does Lyme need with Jacob Stringfellow when he has Archibald Bragg? Could it be that—no, Lyme would never replace a loyal servant with a disgraced hero. Would he?

He looks back at Duke, who only shrugs, which is expected because this game is beyond his capability for reasoning. The Regulator is no help, either. "What should we do with Stringfellow, then? Kill him in front of his beloved? Or let her do it for us? Which is the more poetic?"

"Turn him over to Lyme," Duke says. "Like we're supposed to."

"Like we're supposed to?" Archibald cries, pacing and waving his arms. "Suddenly, you decide to do exactly as you're told. What kind of criminal are you?"

"The smart kind," Duke says. "Lyme ain't one to be trifled with."

Archibald stops short. "I am someone to be trifled with?"

"If the boot fits," Duke says.

Archibald makes a fist and lightly punches the window. Don't get angry, he tells himself, and still, he feels anger rising. He feels it all slipping away. "Duke, you're dismissed," he says.

Duke says, "Mr. Lyme ain't going to like this."

"Out! I don't give a damn what Lyme likes!" After Duke stomps out, undoubtedly to find a multivid where he can contact the boss, Archibald pulls up his chair next to Vienne and throws an arm around her. "How about you, Vienne?

Shoot him in front of you or let you do the dirty deed?"

He takes her by the chin and shakes her head no. "Neither option appeals to you? I know! Let's give him a weapon, then turn Vienne loose. Can you shoot her before she kills you?" He nods her head yes. "Ding! Ding! We have answer! Regulator, give Stringfellow—excuse me, Mr. Stringfellow—your armalite."

The Regulator hesitates. "All armalites are wired to explode if—"

"If someone with a different biorhythmic signature tries to fire them . . . Blah-blah-blah." Archibald flaps his arms wildly. "Yes, I know that. Just give him the carking weapon!"

Shaking his head, the Regulator pulls the holster from his shoulder and offers the armalite to Stringfellow, while Archibald tucks the loose strands of Vienne's hair behind her ear. He whispers to her, his lips grazing her lobe, "Such a natural beauty. If you had been born to the right family, what a wonderful consort you would have made." Then he shouts, "Regulator! Why haven't I heard an explosion yet?"

"You really want to see me blow my arm off?" Stringfellow says quietly. He eyes the weapon but makes no effort to take it. "I've only got the one good one left."

"Would you mind terribly? I know it's a sacrifice, but I would so enjoy it." Archibald laughs and places his hands on his own cheeks, patting them. "But before you do, I have a little confession to make. All these years, I've sort of been following your career, stalking you, really. Mother had her enemy in your father, and I had mine in you. Don't you love the arc of it? Then your father's fall from grace paved the way for my mother's career, but your fall from grace left me with no one to compete with, no mirror image of myself. I drifted after that."

He pulls Vienne's chair away and parks her behind a control panel. "Mother says that I lacked ambition, but that's not true. I always had ambition. It just had no outlet. Then Mr. Lyme found me, and all of that changed, especially when your face appeared on all of those wanted postings. Mr. Lyme needs you, so I can't really kill you, as much as I'd like to. So I'll have to settle for the next best thing—blowing pieces off of your body. Now take the gun like an obedient little *dalit*."

"It's not a gun," Stringfellow says. "It's an armalite."

"Spare me the distinction. Just. Take. It."

Archibald pokes Stringfellow's right temple, his fingers gouging into damaged flesh. With a knife, he cuts the flexi-cuffs holding Stringfellow's hands together.

Stringfellow grunts, as if fighting through agonizing pain. He pulls the armalite from the holster, careful to hold it by the grip.

Archibald backs away to the control panel. He draws his cloak around himself and Vienne. "Now put your little piggies on the trigger like a good boy."

"Before I do," Stringfellow whispers, "I have a little secret of my own."

"What's that?" Archibald asks.

Stringfellow leans forward. "This armalite has my name on it."

When Father was sent to the Norilsk Gulag for his litany of crimes against the CorpCom, Lyme's agents were the first people to approach me, my finger still oozing blood from the bandage. At first I thought they were offering sympathy to a young man who'd lost his father and had been forced to humiliate himself on national multinets. One look into their stony faces, and I knew I'd be getting an offer, not sympathy. For a certain sum paid on an as-needed basis, the Collectors explained, they could make Father's stay in the gulag more comfortable. By comfortable, they meant not dead. What was a son to do? I agreed to their offer and for years paid out almost every bit of my share of the coin my davos earned.

Lyme bled me dry. Probably in the same way that he bled the families who had loved ones in the gulags. It wouldn't hurt my feelings to get back a little of my own if the chance presented itself. I love it when the stars align. It's almost like poetry.

I do like Archie commands and put my finger on the trigger. I open fire, my bullets chasing Archibald as he runs for cover, bouncing off his cape, until one of the slugs finds his ankle and the force knocks him off his feet.

"Mimi," I subvocalize, "tell me the poxer is dead."

"No such luck, cowboy. Keep shooting."

I find the coward hiding in a back corner, curled up in his cloak and holding his foot. I grab him by the collar. "Serves you right."

"Please don't hurt me," he whimpers as I pull him stumbling back to the window. "Watch the exit," I tell Stain as I shove Archibald to the floor.

But the door slams open again, and the flunky, Duke, charges in with a pistol. "Don't move!" He fires two rounds into my chest before Stain kicks the door back into his face.

Duke staggers forward, hand cupped to his bleeding mouth. Stain lands a roundhouse kick that flips Duke backward over the railing. He hits the concrete floor with a wet thud and lies there, unmoving.

"Are you injured?" Stain asks me.

"I've been better," I say. "Feels like a hornet stung me."

Stain gives me the stink eye, and I say, "I said hornet, not bees." Then I yell, "Riki-Tiki! Bring the gear!"

"Coming!" With a clanging sound on the steps, Riki-Tiki bounds through the doorway, a duffel bag on her shoulder. "That was so fun! I love playing soldier! What's next?"

"Next, we get rid of the garbage." I shove Archibald through the open doorway and slam the door behind him.

Riki-Tiki jams a blaster between the handle and the metal landing, wedging the door shut.

"Crafty work," I say as I yank a C-42 explosives kit out of the duffel and double-check that Vienne is still okay. "Keep an eye on her while I finish this."

I slap four coin-sized blobs of explosive in the corners of the window, then stick a blasting cap in each one before stepping aside. "Take cover!" I shout, then hit the detonator.

The plastic wads pop, and the glass cracks into tiny shards before the pressure sucks it right out of the window. A rush of air leaves the room, and then the spray from the spill gates washes in, flooding the floors.

Alarms light up the control panel.

"Does that mean what I think it means?" I ask Mimi while I slosh through the water to Vienne's chair. Her hands are bound with plastic cuffs, her wrists covered with sores.

"If you think it means that all the emergency systems have activated and the whole of the Sturmnacht will be descending on you in a few minutes, then yes, it means what you think it means."

"Oh. I just thought it meant the turbines are shutting down." I wave Riki-Tiki forward. "Cavalry's coming! Let's move!"

Riki-Tiki hefts the soaked gear bags on a table and pulls out rappelling tackle as Stain ties four ropes to the steel rails surrounding the control boards. After tossing two spare harnesses to me, he straps his own harness on, and Riki-Tiki clips herself to a rope.

"Ready to rappel!" Riki-Tiki shouts over the howl of the sluice falls.

Not yet.

"Vienne!" I prod her shoulder, wary of what could happen if she wakes too quickly.

Her head lolls to the side.

"Let's go, Vienne! That's a direct order!" I shake her hard. "Mimi, check her vitals again."

"Stable," Mimi says, "but still asymmetrical and off the charts. But these are not her normal—"

"Regulator!" I cut the flexicuffs and haul Vienne out of the chair. I throw her limp body over my shoulder and slosh over to the rappelling ropes.

Stain steps in front of me. Blocks my path. "You can't rappel with her dead weight, too."

"Watch me." I go around him. "Unless you're volunteering for the job."

"Your plan isn't going to work!" His face screws up. "It was predicated on Vienne rappelling out of here herself. Look at her! She can't even walk. If you try to rappel with her, both of you will die!"

"I'm willing to take that chance!" I shout.

"No!" He pushes me. "Don't be so blind! Look at her!"

Vienne's cheeks are swollen, and her eyes are like half-open, glossy, clouded marbles with a glowing pink dot in the middle. Brown water streams from her hair, and her clothes hang like rags as I place her on the floor.

"If I knew what Archibald had turned her into," Stain screams, "I never would have come. The Vienne we knew is dead! All that's left is a mindless animal! Better we should put her out of her misery than prolong the agony."

"No!" Something within me is growing hot. I can feel it bubbling up like steel melting in a crucible. A noise like a growl comes from my throat, and I'm dimly aware of a high wind rising.

I want to hit Stain, to rip his tongue from his head so that he can't say what my guilty conscience has been saying all along: I alone am responsible for Vienne. It's my fault she was at Tharsis Two. It's my fault for wanting to play hero. It's my fault for caring more about my father's experiments than I cared about being with her.

My fist flies at his chin before I can stop it. Stain blocks the punch with an easy grace. He grabs my wrist and lifts it, trying to lock my elbow in a grapple hold. I twist away and try to leg-whip him. He bunny hops over my foot and plants a hard heel on my hip flexor. My armor absorbs the force, and I bounce back to my feet, poised to fight.

Stain stands with his legs together and his hands near his navel, held like they're cupping water. "Who are you trying to hit?' he demands. He seems so smug, standing there, looking half asleep in his tattered clothes and dirty feet.

"You!" I yell, then strike.

He catches my punch between the backs of his hands. "Is that what you really want? To hit me?"

You bet, you carking idiot. I hammer my leg on the ground while throwing a punch. Combined with the strength of my symbiarmor, the blow could shatter rock, and I expect Stain to move or block it.

But he doesn't.

He stands there, waiting.

Mistuck! I check the punch, stopping millimeters from his nose, and snarl, "I could *piru vieköön* kill you!"

"No!" Riki-Tiki screams. She jumps between us, a straightened arm in each of our chests. "Stop fighting! It won't help Vienne. Please, Stain. Please."

He takes Riki-Tiki by the shoulders. "We aren't fighting. Durango is only fighting himself. Isn't that right? You are angry because you blame yourself for Vienne. If you had done things differently, then she would be safe? If you're blaming yourself, then I have to blame myself, as well. We all played a part in this by our actions and inactions, but the Vienne we loved is gone! Do the only thing possible: Save yourself instead of risking your life for nothing!"

"Vienne isn't nothing!" I snarl. "She's your sister!"

"That . . . animal is not my sister." He picks up a blaster. Points it at her. "You gave me hope that she would be worth rescuing, but now I see that there is nothing left but a dying dog that needs to be put down."

"*Càonǐmā!*" I swing Vienne around so that my body is protecting her head and torso. "You'll have to kill me first."

He aims the sights at my forehead. "I'm willing to make that sacrifice."

"No!" Riki-Tiki shouts. With a scissor kick, she knocks

the blaster out of Stain's hand, lands a punch to his throat, and in a move that would make Vienne proud, grabs the blaster before it can land and points it at Stain, who is gasping for breath. "We are the Tengu, and we do not kill."

"I . . . do," Stain rasps. "When it's the only kindness left."

"We have seen too much of your brand of kindness!" she screams. "I thought I could trust you, but I was wrong. Go!"

Stain cocks his head, considering the situation. Even now, he thinks he's in control.

I pull my armalite and back away from him, shifting Vienne's weight on my left shoulder. I feel her begin to stir. Oh no. "We don't have time for this. Go now."

"Riki-Tiki won't shoot me," he says.

"Yeah," I say. "But I will."

Stain shakes his head. "Idiot. You had your chance. Now I'm done with you."

He clicks on his harness. He jumps from the sill, belays his rope, and with a zipping sound, disappears into the mist.

"Your turn," I tell Riki-Tiki.

"No." She looks to Vienne, then to me. "I'll go last. You next."

I've had enough arguing. "Together."

With a nod, she slings her rope out and clicks on her harness, ready to descend. I grab Vienne's legs as tightly as I can with my left arm, hoping that I can hang on to her long enough to get to the level below. After that, we have to make our way across the spill gate access tunnel to dry land. We're not out of this yet.

Like Riki-Tiki, I flick my hand to get some slack and take a step backward. I look below to make sure that nothing is going to block my descent.

That is my mistake.

Below, the water churns with enough force to crush steel, and the space between it and my feet is so immense that I can hardly comprehend it. In the space of a heartbeat, the top of the world becomes the bottom, and my brain starts churning, too. I lose any grasp of space, my hands moving uncontrollably to grab on to something because even though I know I'm not falling, my mind thinks it is.

Boom!

The door—a battering ram—company's here.

"Hurry!" Riki-Tiki shouts, her voice barely audible over the falling water.

Boom!

My feet are frozen on the sill. I don't dare move. That's when I feel the first jerks of movement in Vienne's legs and arms. A sound like a moan begins in her chest, then it morphs quickly into a growl.

"Put her down!" Mimi screams into my ear.

But I can't. I can't put her down. I don't know where down is.

Vienne does. Arching her back and bringing her knees up, she breaks from my grasp. My broken arm screams with pain, and I totter on the wet sill as Vienne leaps back into the control room.

She drops into a low crouch, legs spread wide, one hand on the ground, the other clawing the air. Even with a mop of hair in her face, she's measuring the distance between us, calculating how much force it will take to knock me into the lake below.

"Go!" I yell to Riki-Tiki. "Now!"

"No!" Riki-Tiki remains on the sill beside me. "Not without Vienne!"

I shake my rope at her. "Don't be so stubborn!"

Boom!

The battering ram hits the door, and Vienne's head snaps around at the sound.

"Vienne!" I lock my left hand onto the rope and regain my balance. I brace myself in the window, cold water sluicing down my back. "It's me! Durango! Come on!"

Boom!

"Durango?" Vienne seems to recognize that the loud sound is no danger to her. She stands up, almost nonchalantly, and turns her attention back to me. "I . . . know . . . you."

Yes! "That's right, I'm Durango. You know me. This is Riki-Tiki. She's your friend. She wants to be your acolyte."

Vienne sloshes toward something unseen, then bends to retrieve it. When she stands, she's aiming a blaster.

Right at my chest.

Oh no. Not again. "Vienne, I'm really tired of being used for target practice. Just toss the blaster away, please."

But she's having none of it. "I do know you, Durango." Vienne tugs at the control choker on her neck. Her flesh is charred, and it makes me sick to think of how many times she's been shocked with it. "I gave up a Beautiful Death for you, Durango." Her voice rises, taking on an edge like a razor. "And you, Durango, turned me into a monster."

"No, he didn't!" Riki-Tiki shouts, her feet slipping on the wet sill. "That was Archibald! We're trying to save you!"

"Save me?" She laughs and raises her hand. Her pinkie finger? What the *tā māde*? "You can't save me when you're the one who took everything I had away. Mr. Archibald made me whole again."

"Mimi?" I slowly step down from the window, my eyes locked on the blaster. If I can just reach it. "Any theories on how that finger got there?"

"A couple, both biomedical," she says. "It is not that difficult to regrow tissue if you have resources and access."

"Archie lied to you," I say. "He didn't make you whole; he tore you apart."

"Liar!" A blaster round rips past my head, and I slip.

"Vienne!" Riki-Tiki screams. "No!"

Vienne turns the blaster toward Riki-Tiki and as I lunge for the weapon, she fires again.

The blast hits Riki-Tiki's shoulder, burning straight through her weak body armor. She drops the rope as her body jerks, and she falls backward, her harness hooked to the line, with nothing but friction to slow her descent.

Maybe I scream, "No!" Maybe I don't.

But I do launch myself after her, the wind and water smacking my face as my greater weight carries me twenty, forty, sixty meters down toward the angry water, Riki-Tiki just meters, then centimeters away from my hand, then—

"Gotcha!"

I do say that as my right hand closes around her ankle, follow by an—

"Oof!"

My left hand snags my rope, and we stop hard, then bounce and dip toward the base of the dam, swinging like two weights on a pendulum. I slam into the concrete, my symbiarmor taking the energy of the blow. Seconds later Riki-Tiki hits the concrete, too. She hangs just out of my reach, her hands pressed against the wound like a too-small patch on a too-big hole. Her pink hair, soaked from the spray from the sluice, is matted flat to her face. She sputters, trying to blow the water out.

"Hold on!" I bellow, my voice lost in the cascading water as I struggle to catch her harness with my broken arm. "Just a couple of centimeters!"

When I reach for her, she tries to swing toward me, but the line goes slack and her harness clip fails. She flails for the rope, but misses.

With a gasp, she falls toward the water. I scream and dive

after her. My body hits just after hers. The shock of the cold water and the force knock the wind out of me.

I swim deeper and deeper, losing her in the white bubbled wash, my mind going back to another dive—into a sewer—and another girl, a time when my body wasn't hobbled. The water here is much deeper, the river infinitely wider. If I don't reach her now, I never will.

The rope!

I feel it slither past my leg, and I grab it between my knees. Then I hook it over my shoulders and swim for the surface. A few seconds later I break free, and sucking in air, spot a service ladder bolted to the wall of the dam. I swim to it, drape the rope over a rung, and using my body weight, pull Riki-Tiki to safety.

As I pull her close, my cast wedged in the rungs, she gasps for breath. Her skin is pale, her pupils dilated with surprise. I lift her out of the water, which is turning pink from her blood.

"Hang on," I tell her. "You're going to be okay."

Riki-Tiki shakes her head, shivering from the effort. "No," she gasps. "Not okay."

"Where's that optimist everybody loves so much?" I try to climb higher, but the weight on her body makes her scream. "Mimi?" I ask.

"I'm sorry, cowboy."

My throat closes, and I slip into the water with her, untying the ropes, and letting the churning water pull them away.

Riki-Tiki looks past me, her eyes drawn to the thick clouds. "I see the sun. It's rising." Then moving the veil aside, she slips into her imagined sunshine, and is gone.

For what seems like hours, I float on my back, clutching Riki-Tiki's limp body to my chest, kicking and resting, kicking and resting until my toes finally touch solid ground. Exhausted to the point of delirium, I stagger to my feet, carrying Riki-Tiki in my arms.

I fall to my knees in the grass. An untold number of minutes pass as I catch my breath and regain an iota of strength.

"This is not your fault," Mimi says.

"We both know that's a lie."

Then, when I'm finally ready to go, I spot Stain on the opposite side of the wide river, wet and angry, staring at me. I try to return the stare, the acid anger, but it isn't in me anymore.

Instead, I turn away, ashamed, the wide gap of the river separating us. When I look up again, he has vanished, a wisp of smoke that mixes with the rising mists and dissipates.

"Mimi," I say. "Find a way out of here."

"There is an access tunnel ten meters ahead," she says. "What about Stain?"

"I'm done with him," I say, heading for the access tunnel that would lead eventually to my motorbike and the path that Ghannouj prophesied I would have to take.

CHAPTER 25

Hawera Hydroelectric Complex
Zealand Prefecture
ANNOS MARTIS 238. 7. 27. 20:25

"Now you're going to get it," Duke says as a stolen CorpCom Hellbender crisscrosses the landing pad on the dam's observation deck. Zealand's corporate logo has been painted over, a scorpion stenciled above it.

"Shut up, Duke," Archibald says, the rotor chop buffeting his cape. "If I had realized earlier that you were Lyme's mole, I would've had you executed."

The copter lands. The pilot cuts the engines, and the rotors begin to slow. Duke grabs Archibald by the arm and hauls him forward to the velocicopter.

"Tell me to shut up again, Archie," he says, "and that execution's going to be yours."

At the rear of the copter, a cargo bay opens, and two Sturmnacht step down a ramp.

"He's all yours," Duke tells them, then heads back to the observation deck.

"What's going on here?" Archibald demands as the soldiers

begin frisking him. "I will not be treated like street vermin!"

"Shut up," the ranking soldier says. He searches Archibald and his coat, finding nothing but his lighter. "Up the ramp. Mr. Lyme's waiting."

Archibald swallows hard and hesitates. The soldier seems to sense his panic and raises his weapon as a warning. Archibald walks slowly up the ramp into the cargo bay.

Inside, the light is low, and it stinks like fuel and moldy cloth. Lyme is relaxing in a jump seat, wearing a pilot's helmet, his face masked in shadow.

"Where is my prisoner?" Lyme asks.

The words stick in Archibald's mouth.

"Answer me."

Licking his lips with a dry tongue, Archibald says, "He escaped, Mr. Lyme."

"So Duke tells me," Lyme says. "He has told me other things, Archibald, disappointing things. You swore to serve me well."

"But I did!" His voice rises an octave. "I burned a swath from Tharsis Two to here!"

"And yet, you are incapable of capturing one human being?" Lyme sighs. He rubs his chin with the backs of his fingers. "So my prisoner is gone. The question becomes, What have you done to recover him?"

"Recover him?" Archibald's voice squeaks. "Sir, he jumped from the dam and landed in the river wash. When the body surfaces, we—"

"Idiot! He is a Regulator. A little fall into a river is not going to kill him." Lyme pauses to compose himself. "What you fail to understand, Archibald, is the predicament you find yourself in. You disobeyed me."

"No, sir, I—"

"Lied to me. Failed me. Put this operation in jeopardy by deceiving me about this female Regulator of yours. What were you thinking?"

"I—"

"You weren't thinking at all!" Lyme leaps from the jump seat, grabs Archibald by the throat, and slams him against the ceiling. Lights dance in his eyes, and he tugs on Lyme's hands, trying to pry his fingers loose. "If you had been, you would realize that your every move has been monitored and scrutinized! My eye has never left you!"

Archibald claws at the armor covering Lyme's arm, kicking his feet to gain any purchase, then abruptly, Lyme drops him like a bag of trash. Gagging, he scoots away, realizing that this madman is going to kill him.

"Fortunately for you," Lyme says, his voice now calm, "I believe in redemption. Do you understand what I mean?"

Archie tries to speak, but it feels like choking on ash. He shakes his head no, because he has no idea what Lyme means or what he wants. It only matters that he not order the Sturmnacht to open fire.

"Even though you have failed me," Lyme says, "there is a job that only you can do well. Accept it, and you will earn your way back into my good graces. Decline, and—well, let's say that you will follow the same path that the Regulator took. Are you a good swimmer?"

Archibald crawls to his knees, head down. "No, Mr. Lyme."

"As long as we understand each other." He signals the pilot to start the engine. "Now about the female: You have no time for such distractions. Get rid of her and await further orders."

"But she has nothing to do with—"

"No buts, Archibald. Greatness requires sacrifice." The rotors reach full speed and the pilot signals that he's ready to take off. Lyme opens his jacket and removes a thin packet of needles. "Neurotoxin darts. My own recipe adapted from shock trooper needle cannons. These will accomplish the task quickly and painlessly, which is what a dedicated public servant deserves."

Archibald accepts the packet. He starts to open it, when Lyme clears his throat.

"Be careful. One prick, and we won't have to bother with the river." Lyme waves his hand. "You're dismissed."

His feet heavy, his throat raw, and his head stinging from cracking against the roof, Archibald shuffles down to the end of the ramp. The Sturmnacht bump him as they walk back inside.

As the ramp begins to rise, Lyme calls out. "One more thing—the demolition crews have begun working on a little fireworks show to end the Spirit Festival. By this time tomorrow, the Hawera Dam will cease to exist. Make sure that your work is done by then."

The Hellbender rises into the clouds. A peel of thunder shakes the sky, and as the rain comes, the Sturmnacht hustle for cover. Rain soaks Archibald's hair and cloak as he strides away.

No, Mr. Lyme, I will not disappoint you, he thinks as he slides the packet of needles into his pocket, but I'll not be doing away with my angel, and I will not be taking any more orders from you.

CHAPTER 26

Like the clash of a gong, thunder rolls across the sky as I help Shoei, Yadokai, and Ghannouj—all of them dressed in white linen robes with red sashes—carry a funeral bier draped with a red shroud down the path from the temple. As the others chant prayers, we walk the bier across the monastery grounds, through the rows of beehives, to the final terrace, where a set of stairs is carved out of the side of the mountain.

Lightning splits the sky, and mist covers the stairs, water trickling down the stone steps, soaking the monks' bare feet. My boots are loud in comparison, and I'm ashamed when my heavy soles slap against the thin puddles.

When we reach the top of the stairs, the monks fall silent. I can't tell what they're thinking or how they feel because from the moment I returned to this place, Shoei and Yadokai have shunned me. Not that I blame them.

They carry on as though this were any funeral. In their place, I would be attacking me.

"That's why you're a soldier," Mimi says.

She's right. For good or for bad, that's what I am, and that's why I see the world so differently than they do.

The mists are thick and swirling as we walk through a forest of tall, narrow stone buildings, most under seven stories, each adorned with a lightning rod. There are hundreds. Some are crumbling from exposure to the elements. Others are comparatively new. All of them are marked with the year and the name of the interred, and they are carved with incantations and prayer words meant to guide the dead past the veil.

"What is this place?" I ask Mimi.

But it's Ghannouj who breaks the silence. "They are called pagodas. Tombs for former abbots and distinguished monks. Here you will find the remains of those who have given their lives in service of the Tengu. Warriors, scholars, healers. Even the great Rinpoche and his consort Nyingmamo are entombed here."

We reach a steeper, more narrow set of stairs. At the top is a newly built pagoda, its pedestal painted bright pink. The pigment is fresh, and in places, the swirling mists wash it away, forming rivulets of pink water that run along the cobblestones surrounding the pagoda.

I think about returning Riki-Tiki's body to the monks. About the questions they asked, and the evasive answers I gave. When they asked how she died, I said one of the Sturmnacht killed her. I didn't say that Vienne had fired the shot. They didn't need to know that Vienne had betrayed them.

"You should tell the truth," Mimi says. "Vienne would not want you to lie to protect her."

"Vienne shot someone she loved." I shift the weight of the bier on my shoulder. "I'm not going to defile her memory."

"Vienne isn't dead."

"If she had any inkling what she'd done," I say, "she would want to be."

"Are you talking about her? Or yourself?"

"Stow it, Mimi. Or so help me, I'll shut you down."

She has enough sense not to reply.

The pagoda stands seven stories high, with a ring-shaped lightning rod capped by an ornate finial in the shape of a flower.

I spot a small arched door. It is open. Riki-Tiki's name is written above it.

"You had a tomb ready for her?" I ask Ghannouj. "The tea leaves foretold her death?"

"This was to be my tomb." His eyes stay straight ahead. "It is a great honor to give it to Riki-Tiki."

"If you give away your tomb, then—"

"Where will I be entombed?" He looks at me, eyebrows raised. "Perhaps I will live long enough to make a new tomb. Perhaps I will take my final slumber with the bees. It is not an unpleasant thought."

On his signal, they slide the bier into the tomb, and

Ghannouj closes the door. He uses a wooden handle to fasten the lock, then breaks the handle off.

The monks sit on the ground, legs folded in lotus position, arms held shoulder high, palms facing out. Shoei and Yadokai face Ghannouj, who begins a chant, and they follow him. I back away and stand to the side, arms folded, near a scraggly pine tree, its limbs twisted and malformed from growing in imperfect conditions.

The soupy mists swirl around, veiling the tomb, and covering the monks in a shroud. In a few minutes, the mist becomes a thick fog. I begin to lose sight of the monks all together.

"How long, Mimi?" I say, growing antsy.

"Their prayers are guiding Riki-Tiki to the spirit world," she says. "Be patient. You act as if her soul has a GPS."

She's right. "What kind of stupid, ignorant, bái mù, jiào nǐ shēng háizi zhǎng zhì chuāng am I?"

"The redeemable kind."

"I doubt it."

"I know it," she says. "And I have the data to prove it."

Rain starts to fall, and the monks are standing before I realize it. The prayer is finished. They turn to go.

"Wait." I grab Shoei's wet sash. "I want you to know how sorry I am."

Shoei and Yadokai trade a blank look. They are still shunning me, but they stand there in the mist as I explain how close we were to rescuing Vienne and how if it weren't for my vertigo, we would've gotten her out, and Riki-Tiki wouldn't have gotten shot. I explain that if I had been faster or smarter, Riki-Tiki would still be alive.

"I'm sorry," I repeat.

"Riki-Tiki was the last of us," Yadokai says. "Now what will become of the Tengu?"

The gray color in Shoei's face deepens. She slaps me, the sound echoing through the mountainside. "Now I am sorry, too."

She turns and runs down the stairs, pulling her robes up. Yadokai follows, calling her name.

My face is stinging. I don't care.

Ghannouj closes his eyes and bows to me. "Forgive them."

Shaking my head, I say, "There's nothing to forgive. This was all my fault."

"There is always fault, so there must always be forgiveness." He peers into the fog. "Even for ourselves." With that, Ghannouj bows again. Slowly, he walks down the stairs, which are turning pink from the runoff.

I wait until I can't hear their feet on the stone before I turn back to the fog-covered tomb and make the sign of the Regulator. "Peace be with you." It's damn sure not going to be with me.

"They are not going to do it," Mimi says.

I hobble down the steep stairs. "Do what?"

"Save you from your guilt."

"Thank you, Madame Freud." I bite the words out as I

pass through the forest of the dead. "That's not what I want."

"Then what do you want?"

"You know the answer to that question. I want Riki-Tiki to be alive again. I want Vienne to be back, safe and whole again." I pause to catch my breath, the bile rising in my throat. "But if I can't have that, I want Lyme stopped. And Archie dead."

A real hero would've done things differently. He would've found a quiet place deep in a meadow where the trees form a dense canopy and a stream runs wild nearby. He would've dug a grave with his own shovel and buried his friend himself, returning her body to the dirt it came from, saying a few words to celebrate her spirit. Or if she were a Regulator, the hero would build a pyre and set a torch to the remains, sending her essence to Valhalla, for according to the Tenets, in sacrificing herself for another, Riki-Tiki died the most Beautiful Death imaginable. Then, with her ashes still warm, he would've gotten on his motorbike, chased down the Sturmnacht, and saved Vienne from sure death.

I did nothing of the kind. Instead, I brought Riki-Tiki back to the monastery, back to the monks who had pinned their hopes and future on her. Even as a pall bearer I failed, my motorbike giving out a kilometer from the walls of the monastery, so that for the last of a trip that should be filled with glory and honor, I was forced to carry her not in my arms like she deserved, but slung over a shoulder, like a sack of rice.

For a long time, I wander through the pagodas, the rain coming down sideways, the wind whipping up, the stone path slick with mud. I'm lost. At first, I don't care. Then when I try to find my way out, I find myself walking in circles.

"Mimi," I say. "Got any hints?"

"Sorry, cowboy. These pagodas all have lightning rods, and it's playing havoc with my limited telemetry."

Splendid. Just. Splendid.

Exhausted and surrounded by the tombs of the dead, I sit on the cobblestones, put my head on my knees, and cry.

"Mimi," I say after a few minutes. "Tell me what to do."

"As I said, my telemetry functions are limited."

"Not that," I say, tucking a lock of water-logged hair behind my ear and wiping mist from my eyes. "Tell me what to do about how I *feel*."

"Well," she says, "when I actually had hands, I found that physical activity helped."

"So you're suggesting that I—"

"Hit something, cowboy. For a soldier, it's the best therapy."

"What?" I say. "Aren't you supposed to tell me to focus to my chi or something?"

"Have you not been listening? The Tengu are the fore-bears of the Regulators, and they are called warrior monks for a reason," she says. "Even they know that there are times when the best way to focus your chi is to whale away on something."

At first I think it's a stupid idea. Then, as I get to my feet, I begin to warm to it. Soon I find the right set of stairs and follow them down to lower terraces. I walk through the muddy rows of hives, happy that the bees like rain less than I do. They remind me of Stain, and I wonder what the bastard is up to.

Then again, what do I care? Stain is somebody else's problem now.

The bathhouse is empty when I step out of the rain. After removing my boots, I pull a towel from a rack beside the door and wipe the mud off my armor.

The bathwater is still. Wisps of steam rise off the surface as I cross the room and slide open the rice paper door leading to the exercise room. Inside, there are three *mukyanjong*, the wooden dummies monks use to develop dexterity. Regulators use the same kind of dummy, except they're metal, and we add punching to the routine.

The last time I was in the bathhouse, Riki-Tiki and Vienne were hiding in here, laughing at my attempts to avoid bath-by-monk. If only I could hear their laughter now.

"Cowboy," Mimi says.

"Stow it."

A scream wells within me, a sound that I hardly recognize, and I slam into the middle dummy. I attack the arms with my good hand, laying into the main beam with my elbows, slamming my fists into the padding so hard that the wood begins to crack.

Splinters fly from the pole, and I don't care. My armor protects me. I can't be hurt. I wish it would hurt. I wish something on the outside would hurt one carking iota as much as it hurts inside.

I slam the dummy with all the strength I have left. It revolves for two or three turns more, then slows.

"Whatever the *mukyanjong* has done to offend you," Ghannouj says, appearing on the mat beside me, "I am sure that it now regrets it."

"Not as much as I do." I spin the pole again.

Unlike me, he's not wet and not covered in mud. Holding a cup of tea, Ghannouj has changed from the linen robes into a dry combat uniform called a *karategi*.

"Your thoughts are troubled," he says.

You think? "I lost Vienne. Riki-Tiki is dead, and I let Shoei and Yadokai down."

He nods. "Yes."

"It's all," as I slam a fist into the dummy, "my fault."

He rocks on his heels and stretches his back. "You would like me to say that it isn't?"

"No," I say, rounding on him. "I don't need absolution from you."

He reaches out and stops the pole from spinning. "Who do you need it from, then? Would you like me to say that Riki-Tiki's death is not of your doing? If I did, my words would ring false. When we link ourselves to a chain of events, we all bear responsibility for the inevitable outcomes."

I ball up a fist but keep it pressed to my thigh. "Aren't you angry? Doesn't Riki-Tiki's death bother you?"

"Of course it does."

I twist my neck, popping the bones, and stretch my left shoulder, which is always stiff these days. "Then why don't you show it?"

"How would you like me to do that? Flagellate myself with recriminations? Rage against the very forces of life and death that form the cornerstone of my beliefs?" He slurps tea from the cup. "Those destructive practices were one of the reasons that the Tengu left Earth behind."

I spin around and shake a fist at him. "The least you could do is be a little pissed at me!"

"Why?" he says, ignoring my gesture. "All of us bear the burden of the child's death. You believe that you could have sent her back to the monastery. I believe that I could have prevented her from leaving. We both are wrong. Riki-Tiki made her own choice."

"Damn it!" I say, unable to stop the anger from ringing in my voice. "Maybe she wasn't ready to make it."

He shakes his head no. His eyebrows are thick and dark, like smudges of charcoal. They are also the most expressive part of his face, in contrast to his mouth, which seems perpetually happy. "There are always choices. Some of them terrible, as I told you that day at the teahouse."

Vitun, even the man's face is riling me up. "I thought you were talking about my choice to chase down the data instead of staying here with Vienne."

He doesn't argue. Instead, his gaze drifts to the windows rattling in their frames from the wind. "There was nothing," he says, "terrible about that choice. You put your desires before Vienne. This time, you put Riki-Tiki before your desires."

"Either way, it sucks."

"Fate usually does," he says. He takes me by the arm. "Come, there is a platter of *daifuku* in the teahouse. You will eat as we discuss the end of this path."

I slip away from him, which is not as easy as I expected. His fingers are iron. "Yeah, well, my path is ended," I say. "I can't be the hero anymore."

Ghannouj nods. "A thunderhead forms on the horizon, and evil humor that will choke the breath of us all. It is your fate, I believe, to cure Mars of her poisons, to align the spokes of the wheel."

I laugh bitterly. "The bees told you that?"

"No," he says, smiling. "I felt it in my heart and see it in yours. Vienne saw it, too. She believed her fate was to fight her brother's battles. I believed that it was to find you and bring you here now."

"I thought you didn't care whether she lived or not after she ran off to join the Regulators."

"Why would you think that? Tengu do not leave the monastery," Ghannouj says. "That does not mean that there is no place here for Vienne. You cannot give up on her now, no matter what sins you have committed in her eyes."

"He knows you too well," Mimi says.

"I told you to stow it."

"Your fates are intertwined," Ghannouj continues. "You cannot reach your destiny unless she reaches hers. Find Vienne. Bring her back to us. Destiny is not finished with her."

It's tempting to believe him. To accept his words as truth, because he's carking good at delivering speeches. But words don't mean a thing when the bullets are flying.

"I don't believe a word of this. It's impossible. Vienne is hundreds of kilometers away, and I'm here. My motorbike is a useless heap of parts, and frankly, so am I. Look, I don't know if I can find Vienne, and if I did, if there would be any Vienne left in her."

He sips his tea and nods, his thick eyebrows forming an arch on his forehead. "If you are ready to desert Vienne, then I will leave you to the dummies. Please clean up the mud on the mats when you are finished."

"What?" I yell, following him. "Who said I was deserting Vienne?"

"You did."

"No, I didn't!"

Ghannouj makes a hand gesture like a maw opening and

closing. "I asked you to bring her back to us, and your mouth went 'impossible, impossible, impossible.'"

"Which doesn't mean that I actually think that!" I want to throttle him! Instead, I make two fists and shake them as hard as I can. "I mean, even if it weren't impossible, how am I supposed to get back to her? Teleport?"

"Or," Ghannouj says with a perfectly straight face, "you could fly."

"Now *that* is impossible!"

Ghannouj spins, driving a kick into the punching post, which bursts in the middle. The dummy bends in half, its guts a pile of splinters. Somehow, the abbot hasn't spilled a single drop of tea. "Nothing is impossible, if you set your mind to the task. Follow me."

The rain stops by the time we reach the teahouse. While I stay outside to knock the mud from my boots, Ghannouj goes inside. Above us, the clouds are thinning, and I can see the canyons gray in the distance. There is no sun yet, and the deck over the pond is still slick with rainwater.

A moment later the door slides open, and Ghannouj emerges with a tray. It is loaded with *daifuku*, green tea in a glass decanter, and a pile of bandages.

"Bandages?"

He bows slightly. "Not to worry. They usually aren't necessary."

"Usually?"

"Remove your boots. They will get in the way." He offers the tray. "Care for some *daifuku*?"

"No thanks." I set my boots on the deck. "Mimi, any idea why he'd need bandages?"

"A few, but they involve great physical suffering. Would you like to hear them?"

"Never mind."

Ghannouj stuffs three rice rolls into his cheek and takes a swig of tea. He lets out a resonant belch and taps his mouth with a fist. I can't get over his mood, the easy way he accepts everything and gets on with the business at hand.

"'The best lack all conviction,'" Mimi says, "'while the worst/Are full of passionate intensity.'"

"What's that supposed to mean?"

"Oh look," she says, ignoring me, "the pond carp are hungry."

Ghannouj grabs a bamboo pole and pushes a log away from the bank of the pond. He steps onto it, balancing easily. "Join me."

"On that? You're going to cure my fear of flying with a log?"

He taps the wood with the staff. "Balance is key. Internal balance cannot exist without external balance. Also, it's more fun for me."

"And me!" Mimi says.

"Remember," he says. "Your fears did not prevent you from rescuing Vienne. Vienne prevented you from rescuing her." He holds the log in place so that I can step on. The surface is slick with mud, and I slip twice before I catch my balance. We back away from each other so that we're stand-ing on either end. "But you can still overcome your own fear so that it does not rule you."

"Overcoming fears," I say skeptically. "I don't really have that skill in my skill set."

"It is not a skill," Ghannouj says. "It is a state of bliss."

Using my toes like fingers, I grip the wood and try to stay on. "I'm not feeling very blissful at the moment." Angry, yes. Miserable with self-pity, yes. Blissful? Not a chance.

"Don't be so negative," Mimi says.

"It's not negative to be a realist!"

Ghannouj rolls the log and laughs as I scramble. "Pay attention."

"I am!"

"You misunderstand. Bliss is not pleasure. It is the state of ecstasy achieved when one has cleared the body of all obstructions. The state of bliss produces energy that bends light, so that the practitioner is not invisible but very difficult to see."

Invisible? Yeah, right. "How do I reach this state of bliss?"

"Through many years of meditation and study." Ghannouj bounces, and the log rises a half meter out of the pond, then slaps the surface. How does he expect me to listen when he's trying to drown me?

"See? There's not really time—"

"Or I can, as you would say," he says, making his eyebrows dance, "beat the crap out of you."

"Ha!" Mimi laughs.

"Excuse me?"

"Now that I have your attention." He bows. "The *bönpo* teaches us that the body's energy is governed by five pranic centers called *qigong*: breath, speech, sight, hearing, and thought. In order to achieve bliss, all of these centers must be opened, either by using the body's own subtle winds or by vital forces."

"What kind of vital force do you have in mind?"

He holds up the bamboo. "This."

"You're planning to hit me with that while I'm standing on a log in a pond in order to turn me invisible so I can't feel fear?" A laugh slips out. "Bullets bounce off symbiarmor. What do you think a little stick can do?"

Whap!

The blunt tip of the stick strikes me between the eyes. I stagger back and almost step off the end of the log. My rear foot touches water, and I have to shift all my weight forward to stay on.

"Ha!" Mimi laughs again.

"Shut up, Mimi!"

"The *qigong* for sight is there," Ghannouj says. "Remove your armor, and I will be able to strike the others just as easily."

"Yeah. About that. There's a bit of a hitch with the whole

removing the armor thing." I tug at my gloves to show him how the material has grafted itself to my skin. "It's stuck, and I'll be buggered as to how to get it off."

He nods toward my nether regions. "How do you do your business?"

"It's not grafted everywhere!" Thank goodness.

"Turn around," he says.

"Why?"

"You ask *why* too much."

"I'm naturally suspicious."

"Turn around."

As soon as I do a pirouette, *whap!* The stick strikes the base of my skull.

"Hey!" The armor solidifies, then softens, although it's still stuck to my skin.

"Turn back," he says.

"How did you know about that?"

"The weak spot of symbiarmor is the electronic nerve bundle at the base of the skull," he says. "It was placed there as a fail-safe measure by the designers. Were you aware that the material in the suits was not created as body armor, but as a garment to protect from bee stings?"

"You seem to know a lot about Regulators for a monk."

"Yet you seem to know very little about monks for a Regulator." He strikes lightly five times: between my eyes, on the chin, on the breastbone, on the solar plexus, and below the navel. "These are the five *qigong*. While I strike them, you must say your word of prayer each time without fail. Do you understand?"

"I kind of don't have a word of prayer."

He chews the *daifuku* in his cheek, then swallows. "Think of one word that will bring you bliss."

Vienne.

"Ready?"

I take a deep breath. "Yes."

With speed impossible for such a big man, he snaps the stick against the base of my skull, then strikes each of the *qigong*. As he does, I repeat my prayer word.

Vienne.

My forehead and chin are stinging from the blows, and my solar plexus feels like it's been drilled out. "How many times do you have to hit me?"

"It is not how many times I must strike you, but how many times that you must endure the strikes."

"How many would that be?"

"Again."

Vienne.

Ghannouj turns sideways and begins spinning the log with his feet. I match his movement, my feet sliding over the slick surface, taking tiny steps when I need to. The hits come, wave after wave, with blinding speed. At first I try to keep watching, to anticipate his movement, but with the pain between my eyes and the futility of tracking the blur of motion the bamboo becomes, I shut my eyes and concentrate.

"You could just jump off the log," Mimi says. "Your body is not going to respond to—"

Vienne.

I lose track of the blows, lose track of time itself, and feel myself rising, as if my body has become weightless and a subtle wind is lifting me into the air. I want to spread my wings and soar. But something, something is holding me down, like an anchor chained to my ankle.

"Cowboy," Mimi says. "Your heart. Arrhythmia."

My eyes pop open. The light and the pain are blinding, and I stagger backward, my foot plunging into the water. Ghannouj catches my hand and pulls me back onto the log. His *karategi* is drenched, and his face is bloodred with exertion.

"How long are you going to put up with this, cowboy?" Mimi says.

"The unbinding is not working." Ghannouj shakes the stick at me as if I'm at fault. "You are of two minds. One consciousness is focused, but the other is not, keeping you from achieving bliss."

I flex my neck, and pain shoots down to my fingers. "How am I supposed to do that?"

"Tell her to be quiet, this woman who whispers to you."

"Mimi?" I ask. "You can hear her?"

"I have always heard her. She is loud in your mind, and you depend too much on her counsel."

"You can hear my thoughts?"

He pushes down on his end of the timber, lifting me into the air. Moss and water lilies drip from the wood. "Not yours. Just hers."

"Of course," I say. Why not? It makes as much sense as anything else does.

He rubs his chin, thinking. "Who is this Mimi?"

"She's my A—old davos chief. She taught us all what it meant to be a Regulator."

"How did her voice come to be in your mind?"

"It's a long story, and I—"

Whap!

"You are still concealing truth. I can sense it."

Whap!

"Cowboy," Mimi says. "I insist that you stop. Your heart has experienced two rounds of arrhythmia, and your other vitals are showing wild fluctuations."

No, I think. This is my decision to make. "Begin sleep protocols."

"Wait!" she says.

"On my mark, three, two—"

"Spoilsport," she pouts.

"One." I tell Ghannouj, "Okay, she's go—"

"Turn!" he barks.

On command, I pirouette again, and he rams the stick into the base of my skull. The pain drives my sight deep into my own mind, and I feel thin like a shadow, as my body begins to drift.

I hear the echo of Stain's question in my ears. How much have you sacrificed for her? I want to ram the accusation down his throat like a fist-sized stone, but the truth is— nothing. That's what I've sacrificed for her, nothing, not a damned thing. If justice were measuring what each of us had given the other, my side of the scales would be empty. No, worse, because not only have I not sacrificed for her, I helped erode the bedrock of her beliefs.

Vienne.

I hear Riki-Tiki scream as the shot hits her and she falls backward from the window. I see her ashen face as I bring her to the surface of the water. I look across the river and see Stain's face become mine, and I sneer, then turn my back and walk away.

No! I will not walk away!

Vienne.

My body separates from itself and begins to rise into the air, unshackled, unbound, a tendril of smoke that seeps from a cold fire, above the monastery, far above the rim of the canyons that make up Noctis Labyrinthus and into the clouds that roil above.

Then I slip through the clouds, too, so that they are a snowy tundra under my feet, and the burning light of the new day splits the horizon. The crack between the ground and the sky widens. I feel myself bathed with light, which fills my body with weight, and I begin to fall. Far below me, my body stands erect, arms locked at the sides, head thrown back, mouth open in an interrupted scream.

Ghannouj lowers his staff. He looks up at me floating above him. I notice that he has a monkey butt bald patch on the crown of his head. "Now you must return to the corporal world," he says. "Say the word of prayer."

Vienne.

And I'm back in my body. It feels fluid, like water vapor, and when I look down at my feet, it is as if they are not there.

The log is level. The pond is calm.

My body feels too heavy to hold itself up. My knees buckle, and before I can react, my feet slip from the log, and I fall sideways into the water. I sink to the bottom, the stems of water lilies filling my vision. Air bubbles escape my lips, and I am too exhausted to mind.

Then, as the thought comes that it would be okay to stay here, Ghannouj grabs my arms and drags me to the bank.

I lie panting, watching the clouds break in the sky.

Ghannouj leans over me, hands on his knees, gasping for air himself.

"That hurt me," I say as I sit up, still giddy, "a lot more than it hurt you."

"This is true, but you have achieved a state of bliss that surprises even me." Ghannouj places the tip of his staff to his forehead and bows. "Under normal circumstances, we would hold a great feast to celebrate your transcendence, but I need a nap, and I believe that you have an aerofoil to catch."

I rub my aching forehead. "Don't I need to find one first?"

In a moment of perfect timing that Vienne would call kismet, but I would call the theatrics of a wily old monk, an aerofoil glides overhead, its long wings reaching forever, the dual vortex engines purring on its tail, its long shadow floating through the gardens.

Ghannouj bows. "I have taken the liberty of finding one for you."

CHAPTER 27

Tengu Monastery, Noctis Labyrinthus
Zealand Prefecture
ANNOS MARTIS 238. 7. 29. 05:51

The aerofoil has landed when Ghannouj opens the gates of the monastery. A light rain is still falling. A skirmish line of clouds fills the north sky, and without a word, Ghannouj closes the gate behind me.

I've got extra load-outs on my ammo belt, a cleaned and loaded armalite on my shoulder, and Vienne's necklace around my neck. Other than that, I've got no extra weight. It's a long flight to Christchurch, and I have to travel light.

Arms folded, Tychon leans against the fuselage, with an aviator cap pulled down over his eyes. Still, he perks up at the sound of my boots on the ground, ducks under the wing, and pushes open the passenger hatch. The cabin is big enough for two, plus a little cargo. It's made of clear plexi, probably to reduce weight, but the thought of being able to see the ground between my feet makes my heart race.

Vienne.

"Sorry," Tychon says, "no step stool."

"Don't need one." I haul my bruised and beaten self into the seat.

After Tychon locks the hatch down and slides behind the controls, his long legs almost touching his shoulders, I thank him for giving me a ride.

"I'm not doing it for you," he says, starting the vortex engine and letting the 'foil coast. "I'm doing it because Riki-Tiki would've wanted me to."

"Fair enough."

With Olympus Mons filling the western horizon, Tychon uses the Bishop's Highway to navigate, having no onboard telemetry. "Hope you don't mind flying by the seat of my pants," he says, and I don't complain because that's pretty much how I live my life, too.

We fly low to avoid CorpCom radar. The sun can't find us, either, so the cockpit is cold, and my hands grow numb. I tell myself that it's the low temperature and not panic causing the blood to pool in my abdomen.

"Vienne," I whisper repeatedly.

My exhaled breath evaporates on the hatch cover as the aerofoil rises above the canyon. We glide over the plains, the terrain a rolling green carpet interrupted here and there by deep craters and stratums of stone protruding through the soil. Like a metal raptor, Tychon catches thermals with his ailerons, rising high enough to touch the storm clouds.

"So you're a crop duster."

He laughs. "Who told you that?"

"Rebecca. Back at the collective."

"Yeah, that sounds like a thing she'd say."

Twenty kilometers into it, we fly over the first of the settlements that the Sturmnacht destroyed. From here the farms form a patchwork of perfect squares, more than half of them blackened by Sturmnacht raids. When the aerofoil dips to find another thermal, I can make out a grain silo that has toppled into a mill house, a greenhouse with smashed glass, and a line of harvesters burned into a mass of twisted metal, the ground forming a puddle of ash around them.

"If you're not a crop duster, what are you?"

"Lots of things," he says, pointing at a pair of grappling horns on the nose of the 'foil and the winch bolted to the deck. "Mostly, just some jack who's really skilled at pickup and delivery."

"So you're a smuggler. Human or cargo?"

"Either. Makes no never mind to me."

Down below, the scenes of carnage repeat over and over. A swath of destruction stretches out from the highway until we reach the river. There, Tychon banks right and follows the Gagarin downstream. The town of Dismel comes into view and then slides by. I think of the refugees who walked toward Christchurch, looking for safety. But I realize now, they weren't escaping. They were heading straight into the fight.

With a crack like automatic fire, a line of chain lighting announces a new storm cell. Tychon dips low, bringing us close to the top of the Hawera Dam, and I see something that makes me forget about vertigo. On the north side of the dam, I see dozens of Norikers parked near the observation decks. Their clearly labeled cargo: a harvester's weight in C-42 explosives, enough of the stuff to blow a crater deep enough to set all of Christchurch inside of.

"Oh crap," I say out loud. "Look!"

"At what?" Tychon answers.

"The Sturmnacht," I say. "They're planting explosives on the dam. Lyme's going to wipe out the Zealand CorpCom with one massive blow. We have to sound an alert. Get the city evacuated. Does this have any telemetry at all?"

"Just my personal handset," he says.

"Then call in an emergency at this voice IP station." I give him the number and the protocols, passing on the words from my Regulator days, hoping that the dispatcher will believe him. It's all we can do right now, except get me to Christchurch as fast as this thing will fly.

Christchurch! Parliament Tower! That's where Vienne is. Where Archibald is.

"Get me to the capital. Floor it or whatever you do to make this crate cook!" I say. "Land wherever you can. I'll hoof it from there."

"Roger," he says. He banks hard again and rises into the clouds.

When we emerge, a patrolling Hellbender is there to greet us.

"Evasive!" I shout.

"Hang on!" Tychon yanks back on the stick. The aerofoil goes nose up, and we disappear into the cloudbank again, chased by fire from the port gunner. Bullets tear through the 'foil's carbon fiber skin, and Tychon lets out a deep grunt.

It's a too-familiar sound. "You're hit."

"In the foot."

"Abort the landing!"

"Not on your life, Regulator," he says. "Riki-Tiki was the kindest soul I ever met," he says. "I want to see these poxers pay."

Me, too, I think, and try to pretend that he's not wounded. We stay in the clouds for an interminable number of minutes, Tychon flying completely blind, rain and wind racking the fuselage, twisting the jack wires. Could there have been a worse way to test my new state of bliss?

Then finally, when I'm about to puke from the combination of vertigo, air sickness, and the smell of Tychon's blood in the cockpit, we break out of the clouds, holding an altitude of three hundred meters. Clearly visible through the plexi is Favela on the hill overlooking Christchurch. The slum's been firebombed, and it's burning. A chemical plume of smoke darker and thicker than a storm front rises on our nine. We bank past it, and the capital city comes into view.

We follow the river that leads to the Seven Bridges at Christchurch. A thousand meters ahead, CorpCom Hellbenders are laying fire down on the bridges, keeping the Sturmnacht from advancing. On the bridge closest to us, a convoy of Noriker trucks roars toward the Circus.

"Get ahead of that convoy!" I shout.

He cuts across the river, swooping so close to the tops of the bridges and then the buildings that it feels like I could touch them. He veers right, looking for a good drop zone, which happens to be the Tannhäuser's Crater a few meters beyond Christchurch. "That's our best chance to land," he shouts.

"Too far away from the action," I shout back. "Swing over the Circus. I'm going to jump!"

"Without a chute? That's insane!"

"I know!" I reply. "But sane went out the window a long time ago!"

Below us, the city is empty: No people, no autos, and no trains. The traffic lights are dead, the only thing moving is trash blown around by the wind. Then we fly over the Circus, and everything changes. I spot line after line of sandbags and concrete barriers topped with strings of razor wire. A division of CorpComs is double-timing into battle position, and even in the aerofoil, I can hear the thrum of Hellbender rotors in the distance.

A Hellbender thunders toward us, and we're taking fire again.

"Mimi," I say. "Time to wake up. We've got a job to do."

She makes a yawning noise. "Roger that. Nice of you to let me out to play."

"Spare me the sarcasm, Mimi, and find us a good landing spot."

"Need a drop zone!" Tychon yells.

I scour the Circus for a good spot. I'd rather not hit pavement, just some tall building with a roof that will help absorb the impact. Then I see it—smoke roiling from the middle of Parliament Tower. It's the same floor that Vienne jumped from, the one that houses the boardroom.

"What do you think?" I ask her.

"You could do worse, cowboy."

"There!" I shout. "Drop me on the roof of Parliament Tower!"

"On the roof?" he shouts. "You really are insane!"

"Just do it!" I tighten the strap on my helmet and flip down the visor. I unclip the hatch, and the wind slams it against the manifold. I unbuckle my seat belt.

"Are you sure you want to do this?" Mimi says as the slipstream sweeping over the wings threatens to send me tumbling too early. "Your heart rate is close to tachycardia."

"I've jumped like this before," I say, remembering a fall from a space elevator that landed me in a sewer.

"That was when your suit was functioning normally," Mimi says. "The armor may not be able to handle a rapid descent in its current state."

"Well, if it doesn't, all I can say is, it's been nice knowing you."

"What about your arm?"

"It's already broken."

As the aerofoil circles toward Parliament Tower, I shove the door open and brace myself on the lip of the hatch. Below me, the roof comes into view. My head starts to swim, and I feel like I'm going to pitch out of the cockpit.

"Cowboy!" Mimi says.

Vienne.

When Tychon shouts, "Go!" I jump straight out, almost colliding with the wing. The slipstream grabs me, and I start to turn end over end. Before I can right myself, my trajectory takes my body past the tower and sends me hurtling off target toward the roof of the library.

"Vienne," I repeat as I flatten into a feetfirst dive and crash through the asphalt and corrugated steel roof of the library.

For a few seconds I'm aware of nothing but a rush of concrete dust and a loud screaming noise. Then I realize that the screaming is coming from me, and the dust is falling on my visor from the hole in the roof above me.

"Thank the heavens for symbiarmor," I say. "I think I passed out."

"You did," Mimi asks. "How is your arm?"

"No worse than the rest of me," I say after a few seconds. "Of course, all of me is in excruciating pain. Remind me to never, ever jump through a roof again."

"You said that the last time you jumped through a roof, too."

I stand hands on hips to stretch my back, then jog out of the room and hit the stairs. Using the fire escape route, I leave the library through a side exit and make my way through a back alley, until I reach the elevated courtyard in front of the tower. From here, I can get a visual fix on the entire Circus.

Like a metal shaving to an electromagnet, I keep finding myself drawn to this place, the site of my father's fall from grace and Vienne's sacrifice, and my shame. Ghannouj would probably say that it was inevitable, that events have come full circle. To me, it feels more like a bad meal that keeps trying to come back up.

"Do not mock Ghannouj," Mimi says. "Despite our differences of opinion, he got you here, cowboy. The rest is up to you."

The top of Parliament Tower is engulfed in flames, and the angry clack of fire alarms split the air.

"Hope I was right about the landing spot," I tell Mimi.

"I am glad you were right about the armor."

I should be moving, but I'm too busy remembering the courtyard where I'm standing. Where I grew up. Where Vienne and I lost our fingers. Where my father rose to power and fell from grace, taking me down with him.

Prince of Mars, my ass.

Then in the distance, a sonic boom thunders across the capital city, blowing out windows as the shock wave passes.

"Down!" Mimi yells.

I hit the deck as the tower's glass panels shake loose and fall onto the courtyard. I pull into a ball as the panels explode against my armor. It doesn't hurt, but it's scary as hell.

As I'm lying there covered in glass, the concrete pavers start to undulate. The courtyard rises and falls.

"What the hell?" I shout. "An earthquake, too?"

"Not an earthquake," Mimi says. "It's the same shock wave, but waves traveling through the ground take a few seconds longer to reach Christchurch."

By the time I'm on my feet, I realize that I know the source of the explosion.

The Hawera Dam is gone.

The water is coming.

"How long, Mimi?"

"Falling water accelerates at nine-point-eight meters per second squared until it reaches terminal velocity. Terminal velocity of water is calculated on the mass of the water released, the coefficient of drag—"

"Mimi! Approximate!"

"Less than fifteen minutes."

"Let's find Vienne."

The *tat-tat-tat* of automatic fire draws my attention to a couple dozen Sturmnacht pinned down by shock troops.

"I don't think this was a planned attack," I tell Mimi. "The lines are too dispersed, and the shock troops are scattered."

Taking the point, a ranger sprays ammo until the clip is empty. Kneeling behind an overturned trash barrel, he pops the clip and sticks the red-hot barrel of his battle rifle into a puddle. Steam hisses from the vent holes as he flips the taped clip over and rams it into place.

Watch your back, I think, as a triplet of Sturmnacht round the corner of the library, using the bullet-pocked saplings for cover. A quick burst of fire through the leaves, and the ranger takes a bullet in the side. The force spins him around so that he's facing the charge and his finger finds the trigger. All three Sturmnacht fall a few seconds before he gives in to the wound. A spasm wracks his body. He topples backward, already dead as his rifle fires a rainbow of ammo into the heavens.

A waste. This is so stupid. Stupid, useless, and a criminal waste of life. If I ever get my hands on him, Lyme is going to pay for his crimes.

"How much time left, Mimi?"

"Less than ten minutes."

"We better find Vienne. Stat."

Then with a boom that sounds like a packet of C-42 exploding, the library doors blow apart. As the dust clears, out walks a soldier carrying a battle rifle in one hand and a blaster in the other. The first shot takes down the closest shock troop, followed by a spray of bullets into a skirmish between a Sturmnacht and two troopers.

"Never mind. I just found her." But I'm not sure that I wanted to.

The Sturmnacht seem to be thinking the same thing, because they scramble in the darkness, but the squad leader screams for his troop to line up for another charge. "Form up!"

Both lines move up on Vienne, their laser sights dancing on her armor.

"Drop your weapons!" the leader barks.

Vienne tosses aside the empty battle rifle like it's an apple core.

The troopers move in as if they've done this a thousand times, confident in their ability to take down a soldier without taking a shot. Until the first trooper gets too close and Vienne yanks the weapon from his hand and spins him around, a knife pressed against his jugular. The other troopers don't react—she moved so insanely fast, it takes a few seconds for their brains to catch up.

A heartbeat passes.

"Fire!"

Shots rip through the air. But Vienne is using the trooper as a shield until their clips are spent and the firing chambers click empty. She drops her shield, the man dead before he hits the ground, and attacks like a Big Daddy unleashed.

I duck into the shadows near Parliament Tower as Vienne hits three troopers with a string of front kicks, as if she's walking across their faces. She lands in front of the last in the vanguard as he snaps a fresh clip into place. She cracks his wrist, redirecting the fire at the leader, and takes the gun with her.

A third eye opens in his forehead.

As he falls, the second line fires as Vienne does a roll across the sidewalk, bullets chasing her. She pops up, shooting, and does a dive roll that lands her square in front of the six troopers still standing. They hesitate a half second before squeezing their triggers, long enough for her to twist out of the line of fire, the shots zipping past as she launches a double roundhouse kick that knocks the line of them down like bowling pins.

"Cowboy," Mimi says. "Less than five minutes."

Vienne waits for a few seconds to see if they will get up. When they don't, she tosses the battle rifle aside and turns to walk away. I leave the shadows, jogging on a course parallel to her. If I can just reach her before—

"Oy!" a Sturmnacht calls as he steps into the clear. "Where'd you think you're going, woman? Mr. Archibald says you're to stay with us."

Vienne plucks a flash bang grenade from one of the downed troopers. She pulls the pin with her teeth and tosses the flash bang over her shoulder. "Go to hell."

"Aiiiee!" he screams and dives for cover as it explodes. I take off in a straight line toward Vienne, but I don't get more than ten meters when a mortar blows the ground out from under my feet.

"Cowboy!" Mimi yells.

Through the air I pinwheel, grabbing at nothing in a use-less bid to get my balance. I hit the ground hard on my chest, my armor taking most of the collision, then do a shoulder roll. I'm on my feet and drawing my armalite.

"Mimi! Find that rocket launcher!"

"Done," she says, "but you are not going to like it."

"Why's that?"

"On your six, cowboy, and remember, I told you so."

Perplexed, I turn to face the same person who tried to kill me with a rocket-propelled mortar round. The same person who has already reloaded said launcher and is ready to pull the trigger again.

Vienne's cheekbones have sharpened. Hollow places are sunken into her face. Eyes are full of wild energy, red like they're blistered. There's not an iota of recognition there, just a wild fury and the willingness to kill anything that looks like a target.

"Vienne," I look dead into her eyes. "Please. Don't do it."

"You mean this?" Her voice is high-pitched, tinctured with rage. She fires, and I have less than a blink of an eye to spin sideways, letting the shell zip past. A second later, it hits a storefront and blows its reflective glass to smithereens.

"Damn you!" she bellows, shaking the empty launcher over her head.

"You're out of ammo."

"Think again!" She pulls a plasma pistol from a thigh holster, and I dive for her. Both of us start punching and blocking, dancing with the speed of a pulse. Time seems to slow, and the sounds of her screams warp in my ears. Iridescent pulses slip past my face from the plasma pistol and disappear into the sky, spent casings dripping from the pistol's ejection port and tinkling on the ground like dozens of metal bells.

But then she spins faster than I can and sticks the barrel against my right temple, where I can't see it. Perspiration is pouring down my face, soaking my shirt, and my back has turned into a geyser. I'm breathing hard, and sweat drips into my eye.

She grins. "Got you." But the air stinks like burned hair—her plasma pistol is overheated. She pulls the trigger. It doesn't even click.

"You're out of ammo." I aim my armalite at her gut. "Time to call it quits."

Screaming, she flings the pistol at me. It bounces off my armor.

"Two minutes," Mimi says. "Even with your limited telemetry functions, I am picking up P-waves. The water is coming fast!"

Get her off the street, I think. Now. "I don't want to hurt you, Vienne." I move in slowly, trying to look nonthreatening. "See? Take a deep breath. Calm down and let's talk."

Her face contorts with venomous fury and she attacks again, fists and elbows and knees, driving me backward as I throw block after block. Vienne launches a ragged scissor kick, but I sidestep and land a roundhouse to the nerve bundle at the base of her spine. The shock immobilizes for a second. Long enough for me to catch a breath.

"You asshole!" she says, her voice a hoarse whisper, a hand on her back.

Behind us, the sky is lit up with sudden gunfire, followed by shouted commands. The voices are close: The battle is moving our way.

I charge. Slam into her belly. Lift her off her feet. The launcher goes flying as we smash into the concrete together.

I'm first to my feet. I take a defensive pose as she does a backflip and comes up ready to go.

"Vienne. It's me, Durango. I came to take you back home."

She turns her head, as if she's hearing a distant whistle. Listening. Her face calm. Then on her neck, partially hidden by the cowl, a metal ring starts to hum.

"Mimi? What's that sound?"

"High-frequency sound waves," she says, "commonly associated with computer guidance systems. Look out!"

Crack! Vienne's fist connects with my right cheekbone, and I hit the sidewalk. Ears ringing, I lift myself up on all fours.

Vienne punts me in the gut.

My armor hardens, and her foot sticks to the cloth.

Her foot sticks to the cloth? My head is still full of stuffing, and I shake it. Clearly, I'm imagining things.

"No," Mimi says. "She is stuck to you."

Vienne tries to yank free, but I strike the back of her knee with my good hand. She lands hard on her butt. Then flips over, plants her hands, and nails my cast with the other leg.

White-hot pain fires from the break, and my whole body spasms. My armor hardens, and she slips free. Back on her feet again. Ready to strike.

"You did this to me," she says.

I scoot away. Fight for breath. Focus my eye, which has teared up. "Who told you that?"

"Archibald." She pants. "He said that you did this to me. Made me into this . . . monster."

"You're not a monster."

"Liar! I shot her!" Her shoulders slump, and her chin goes to chest. "I shot that little girl. Only a monster would do that."

Think. Think. "Remember this?" In an act of desperation, I pull her pendant from the cowl of my armor. "It's yours, remember? When you were a little girl you loved it, just like Riki-Tiki loved you, and I love you now."

"LIAR!" She jumps two meters straight up. Raises her fist like a sledgehammer. Roars and brings the hammer fist down at my head.

She's going to kill me.

I raise an arm in a feeble attempt to stop her.

My hand opens. Hairs spray out of my palm. They fly like a swarm, striking her face. Her mouth. Her eyes. As if she has hit an invisible wall, she arcs in mid-flight and crumples, groping at her stinging eyes, which I know from experience feel like they've been injected with acid.

"No!" I shout. "Not now! Mimi, why does this keep happening?"

"I have no data to use to process that question."

"Which means you're as clueless as I am."

"Do not be absurd," she says. "Hairs simply are not my area of expertise."

I bend down to help Vienne. But there are hundreds, maybe thousands of hairs in her face, and she's making it worse by grabbing at them. The tips of the hairs are barbed, and moving them is like wiggling a hook that's impaling your skin.

"Stop! Don't touch them!" I yell at her, trying to pry her hands away. It's useless. She can't hear me, and if she could, she'd try to kill me.

"Less than one minute before the flood waters reach us," Mimi says.

The first sign of the apocalypse is a trickle of water running across the pavement. I can hear the water before it hits, a deep, guttural roar with a pounding drumbeat. The pressure pounds my eardrums. Then I see it—a wall of water laced with whitecaps that reaches fifty meters, towering over the Seven Bridges. It hits the causeway and soars another sixty meters, white plumes like mushroom clouds that sledgehammer the shoreline.

"I've got to get her out of here! Run whatever scan you can! Find me a hole somewhere! And make it fast—before I find myself a smarter AI."

"How do you feel," Mimi says, "about crawling into a burning building?"

CHAPTER 28

Christchurch, Capital City
Zealand Prefecture
ANNOS MARTIS 238. 7. 29. 11:34

It's a miracle that Archibald is not dead.

The fire starts easily, the way they always do, but he tries something different this time, decides to train fire. Like always, he starts it with a wooden match. Wood matches are the best. They don't bend when you strike them, and the head ignites like a sparkler when you drag it over the strike line. Then when it drops into the lint kindling, it burns like mad.

Poof! A fire. It's like magic.

Anything you control, you can train. Fire's not different. Start a small fire on the floor of the Zealand Corp boardroom. As it grows, you wait. Wait for the fire to get large enough to lick the line of fuel, and then ignite a line of flames. The waiting is the best part.

You spray a stream of ethyl ether in a zigzag, making patterns on the portrait of the CEOs hanging on the wall— take that, Mother! You wait, and when the flames touch the fuel, it becomes an orange-red dancing asp, willing to strike when or what you tell it to. However, like Cleopatra, fire can be fickle and deadly. Sometimes, even when you've done everything right, it decides to punish you for not planning every detail. The ethyl ether can evaporate too quickly. The vapors can make your head spin, make you giddy and giggly and make you forget how to run. The fire can ignite before you have a chance to escape the room, and the extra bottle of accelerant you keep on your belt can explode, washing your pants and shirt with flames so quick and hot that even your cloak can't stop them.

You plunge out of the room like a shooting star falling through the atmosphere. You hit the ground and run for the fire escape, blind to anything but the searing pain and the smell of your own flesh cooking.

The voices you hear shouting your name seem far away, and you think just for a fleeting second, right before consciousness slips away, that you hear Mother's voice calling to you, saying as she always does, "Archibald. How many times must I tell you not to play with fire?"

Then the pain goes away. You know that the nerve endings are dead—you are hurt badly but just can't feel it. You call Duke to pick you up in the Noriker. Somehow, you have to keep going, because you still have matches and there's still a building to watch burn.

Archibald stops to catch his breath and compose himself. Wrapping himself in his cloak to protect the burns on his chest and belly, he stumbles down the spiraling fire escape of Parliament Tower, a toothpick that he's chewed to bits in his mouth. He sucks on the wood, making a loud slurp his mother used to despise. What would she say about him blowing up the dam? Or burning down her corporate headquarters?

I can't wait, he thinks, to see her face when Parliament Tower blooms with fire, surrounded by the river's flood waters, a sign of the coming Armageddon, and living proof of a son's promise kept.

CHAPTER 29

Christchurch, Capital City
Zealand Prefecture
ANNOS MARTIS 238. 7. 29. 12:00

Mimi directs me to the back of the building, a familiar area where I find the receiving dock. I kick out the glass security door and slide inside with Vienne over my shoulder. My arm is killing me, and my whole body screams for me to stop moving. Keep screaming, I tell it. I'm not listening.

A few meters down the hallway, I reach the stairwell door and pause to decide which way to go. Then behind me, I hear the sound of running water. A trickle of brown water pours under the broken door, and within seconds, it turns into a stream.

The water is here, and it's rising by the second.

I scramble up the stairs. I yank open the fire door and stumble into the main lobby, whose two-story-high windows offer a panoramic view of the courtyard and the Circus beyond. Vienne is a deadweight on my shoulder, and my boots are slick with water.

For a few seconds, I pause to decide on the next step.

Outside in the courtyard, a platoon of troopers sees me, and they start firing on my location. I spot the door to the gift shop and kick it open.

I drag Vienne inside and hide her behind the counter.

"What is your plan, cowboy?" Mimi asks as I start rummaging through drawers for a lock pick or tool.

"It's pretty simple," I say. "Find something to get this choker off Vienne, then try to find a happy medium between drowning and getting roasted. It's not much of a plan."

"It is elegant in its simplicity."

"Not so simple if you can't find a pick." I slam a drawer. "Time for Plan B." I stand up just as Mimi is yelling, "Cowboy!"

Archibald is standing by the door. He shoves a display case over, blocking the exit. A plastic bottle full of clear liquid is in one hand. A lighter is in the other. "Found you," he says, dousing a display of stuffed animals with the liquid. He strikes the lighter and tosses it into a hippo. A fireball erupts. "If I had known you were coming, I would've waited to purge the boardroom."

"If I'd known you were coming," I say, "I would've brought more ammo."

Shoulders hunched, he lists to one side. His eyes are sunken in their sockets, his lips blistered and peeling. Like his cloak, he is stained with blood and unraveling at the hem.

I note all of this as I'm sailing over a display of snow globes depicting Christchurch in miniature.

We slam onto the floor, and clouds of ash blow across the room. Archibald is forced back. I roll to my feet and drop into a fighting crouch. Vienne is still out of sight. For now.

"What's the matter, Archie?" I laugh. "Scared of a little *dalit*?

Phhtt!

A needle sinks into the cast on my left arm. I spin around, and a second needle sinks into the cast.

Archibald calls, "Who's scared now, *dalit*?"

"Careful, cowboy," Mimi says. "Those needles are tinged with neurotoxins."

I stagger backward, trying to keep out of his direct line. "What the hell?"

Two more needles whistle across the room, one striking the wall behind me, the other making only a pinging noise as it bounces off my symbiarmor.

"It did not bounce," Mimi says.

"What didn't?" I feel a tingling burn in my thigh.

"The needle," she says. "It did not bounce. It broke. Two cc'es of the neurotoxin entered your bloodstream."

With my head spinning, I'm forced to one knee to keep my balance. Archie swoops down on me, his cape billowing in the smoke. "You're not getting her back," I say, hoping he'll come closer.

He does, grabbing a handful of my hair, then laughing softly in my ear. "It's not your girlfriend I want this time." His breath stinks like rotted cabbage. "According to Mr.

Lyme, you, Jacob Stringfellow, are the most valuable jewel on Mars."

I look into Archibald's laughing face, right into his dark, empty eyes and see myself reflected there. Drugged. Helpless. No, I think. No.

With a quick twist, I break the grip on my hair, leaving some of it in Archibald's gloved hand. At the same time, I push hard with my legs, launching my shoulder into his chin.

Archie lands on his back, hands raised to ward me off. "Mercy," he says.

My heart is not ready for mercy. I drive my knee into his gut. "That's for Riki, you poxer." The room spins, and I stagger away. I touch my thigh—my hand comes away coated with blood.

"It doesn't matter if you kill me. I've already beaten you." On his knees, Archibald snatches a snow globe off the floor and flings it.

It shatters on the wall behind me.

"Up yours, Archie." I grab two handfuls of grit-covered kewpie dolls and throw them into his face, and the air explodes with a cloud of dirt.

The smoke grows thick on the ceiling, and the air is getting hotter. I can feel it on my face, and I squat to get a cleaner breath. "Mimi? What's the water situation?"

"It's still rising, cowboy."

Archibald struggles to his feet and steps backward, his

eyes blinded with dust. He claws at his burned face, then cackles. "You fight dirty, just like me."

I move away quickly. "I'm not you."

"But you are." He turns his head side to side as if picking up sonar waves. "I am you and you are me. The only difference between us is a suit of armor."

"Armor only protects your body." I move again. "You can't use it to mask your rotten soul."

"Spare me the platitudes." He laughs. "You think you know me so well, don't you? Well, there's one thing that even you don't know."

"What's that?"

He laughs and flicks aside his cloak. Clutched in his hand is a glass SIP grenade. It contains white phosphorous and will burn anything it touches—cloth, fuel, ammo, and me, even through my symbiarmor.

"Move," I say, "and I'll blow your carking head off."

"You can't beat me." There's a note of regret in Archibald's voice. It catches me off guard. "I have already lost."

Archibald grins, showing a line of broken teeth, and unclasps his cloak. The tattered garment drops to the ash-covered floor, and he opens his arms in a macabre gesture of welcome. Under the cloak, Archibald is almost naked. Jaundiced skin hangs on his emaciated arms, loose and covered with sores that ooze pus. His chest is purple-black colored, with the bones showing through.

"My god."

"I'm a dead man." He flings the SIP grenade at me. "And so are you!"

I duck and roll past him to the counter as the grenade shatters against the far wall. The SIP explodes, incinerating anything in a three-meter radius. A sudden rush of fresh oxygen engorges the fire, and seconds later, a ball of fire blows out the rest of the display window. I hunker down as fiery chunks of merchandise sail across the floor.

White-hot flames erupt all around us, the heat singeing my hair.

There's just enough time to grab Vienne and get out. I reach down, grab her by the shoulder pads, and drag her toward the doorway. Behind us, the blaze has climbed the wall and flames are roiling across the ceiling like boiling orange water.

Archibald screams. I look back to see him standing in the middle of the conflagration, arms spread wide, head turned to the left, chin tucked in. Flames dance up and down his pants, and his cloak is a blanket of fire.

He turns toward me, clutching a jagged piece of glass. "Diiiieee!"

A visceral growl comes from behind me, sending shivers down my spine.

"Vienne?"

She vaults past me and lands in front of Archibald. He raises his flaming arms, and she hammers his jaw with her fist.

"My love," Archie says, holding his face.

"No!" She nails him with a scissor kick, and he flies backward against the wall, engulfed in light like an incandescent comet. His screams are a siren, the air filling with the fetid odor of his searing flesh.

Then, Archibald is dead quiet.

Gagging from the stench, I rush for her, but she growls when I get close. Her eyes are wild, blood flecked on her face, her teeth bared.

"I'm not going to hurt you," I say calmly, focused on the grenade. "I—"

"Cowboy!" Mimi yells. "Get out of here!"

She doesn't have to tell me twice.

"The exit!"

Maybe she does.

But the exit is blocked by the display Archie knocked over. I give the case a hard shake, but it's too heavy to move with one arm. "*Verflucht!*"

Suddenly, there's a hand on my shoulder and one on my opposite leg, and I'm lifted like a rag doll and thrown through the shop's display window. It shatters as I hit it, and I land hard on the marble floor outside in a pile of safety glass.

"Mimi, what hit me?"

"You have to ask?"

Head spinning, I look up in time to see Vienne hurdle past me and shoot like a Varlamov rocket straight across the lobby.

The sprinklers turn on. Now it's raining inside, too.

"Vienne threw me through the window?"

"Which saved all our lives," Mimi says.

I collect my fallen armalite and shove it into its holster. "Remind me to thank her when my spine grows back." Okay, enough yak. "What's her last heading?"

"Your twelve. Straight ahead."

I start jogging, which causes my head to hammer. I can't hear a thing over the splatter of the sprinklers. "I know what my twelve means, Mimi."

"Just making sure. You could have sustained a concussion in the fall."

"I landed on my butt."

"Exactly."

"Ha-carking-ha."

Through the lobby's panoramic window, I see a killer view of downtown, which is awash with black water and debris that the flood has grabbed along the way. A bank building across the Circus is on fire, and the fire has ignited an oil slick on the surface of the water.

It's as if Christchurch has fallen into an angry ocean, an ocean that wants to eat us all.

"'There the companions of his fall, o'rewhelm','" Mimi says. "'With Floods and Whirlwinds of tempestuous fire.'"

"Thank you, Mrs. Milton."

"Excellent," Mimi says. "You should run now."

Ka-boom!

Outside, another explosion.

"Gas leaks," Mimi says.

"What?"

"You were going to ask what is causing all the explosion. Gas leaks from the mains. The flood must have destroyed the lines."

"Thanks for the chemistry lesson, Madame Curie." My eye catches a movement near the emergency exit. I skid to a stop and change directions. "But I'm worried about drowning!"

"Vienne!" I slam the door open. Water is in the stairwell and rising. Footsteps on the landings above. She's running scared.

"Vienne! Stop!"

Up three flights. My legs burn. I keep running.

Keep her in front of you. There's no way out except down.

Boom! From the roof, another explosion.

The building shakes from the aftershock, and my wet boot slips on the stair tread. My knee slams the concrete, and the armor solidifies.

"*Esena mori poutana!* Piece of crap! Mimi! Fix it!"

"Endeavoring. Give me a second."

"We don't have a second! She's too fast."

Boom! Another explosion! The whole stairwell shakes, and concrete dust pours down on me.

"Vienne!"

Nothing, then a growl. A door slams open. I'm gaining

on her. I run up the steps, taking two at a time, as chunks of concrete fly past. At the next landing, I pause to check the door. The metal is hot. "This one?"

"No. Fire on that floor."

Next landing. The thirteenth floor. The stairs stop one floor above at the access hatch to the roof.

"It's either here or the roof," I say. The roof hatch is still latched, so she didn't go that way.

"Excellent observation," Mimi says. "Maybe you have not forgotten *everything* I taught you."

I unholster my armalite and yank the door open. Sprinkler water sprays me in the face and thick, acrid smoke pours from the hallway. I step back into the stairwell. Locate the sprinkler junction and turn the wheel to shut it down.

"Mimi, didn't Archie say he burned the boardroom first?"

"The fire should be out by now."

That's the good news. The bad news is that the floor is littered with burned-out debris. It's an all-too-familiar scene. Even dead, Archie is leaving his mark. "Any readings?"

"Only faint ones. Keep your voice down. You don't want to startle her."

"Or let her know I'm coming."

"That, too."

I steal forward down the hall. Check every office, every room. Nothing. Where could she be? "Anything?"

"Signal is stronger. Stay on this heading."

Around the next corner. The walls are black and puckered

from a hot fire. This area looks familiar. Then I recognize an empty, charred frame on the far wall.

The boardroom.

Boom!

I hear the sound of windows popping. Is the whole world going to hell?

"Pretty much," Mimi says.

The lights flicker and go out.

Great. It's dark, and I have no omnoculars for night vision.

Wait!

Voices.

I move to the doorframe. Get eyes on the interior of the room and slip inside.

Vienne!

She's lying on the floor in a patch of seared carpet. Again in the fetal position, rocking to and fro.

"I failed you when you left to become a Regulator. I failed you when I let you be captured. I will not fail you this time."

That voice.

Stain.

He steps out of the shadows, carrying a smoke-covered mirror. He props it on a chair in front of Vienne's face and forces her to look. "See what you've become?"

I slide along the wall so that I can see him clearly. His pants are drenched and coated with wet ash, one hand holding his staff like a scepter. The other perched on the pouch that holds his bees. I flick the safety on my armalite. Move into firing position.

"You shot a child," he says as Vienne turns her head away. He yanks it back. "This is the face of a killer." He reaches for his bee pouch. "There is only one way to make you whole again."

I step into view. My laser sight dances on his chest, right above his heart. "The only *hole* is going to be one I put in you."

He pulls Vienne up, using her as a human shield. The red laser dot is over her heart instead of his. "You'll have to kill her first."

I hesitate.

Stain presses the staff against Vienne's neck, and she cries out. He screams, "Be still!"

"Mimi, why doesn't she fight back?" I try to get a clear shot, but the smoky air, the darkness, and his quickness stop me. "Kick his ass, Vienne!"

An angry hum fills the room. The scorched carpet begins to undulate, and I realize that Vienne isn't lying in a pile of ash—she is covered with bees.

"There is your answer, cowboy."

"Stain," I say, "you are one sick bastard."

"You can't fight the bees," Stain says, smug in their ability. "Throw down your weapon, *dalit*."

"She's your sister!" I say, trying to stay calm, trying to get the shot. "Doesn't that mean anything to you?"

"It means everything to me!" he bellows. "Do not presume to understand me! You know nothing about me!"

"Oh, I know lots about you, killer."

"On your knees!" He jams the staff into the wounds on Vienne's neck, and she screams.

There's no choice. I drop to the floor. Click the safety on my armalite and toss it toward him. He lets Vienne slide to the floor.

"Hands behind your head!" he says. "Isn't that the way Regulators take prisoners?"

I comply, crossing my wrists, so that my fingers touch my cast and brush the two needles embedded in it. The needles. "You mean hostages."

"Prisoners! That's what the righteous do with criminals. Bring them to justice and then bring justice upon them!"

Methodically, I work one of the needles free from the cast, careful not to prick my skin.

"Slowly, cowboy," Mimi says. "One false move and you're dead."

"Dead is not on my agenda." I say aloud, "Stain, listen to me, just let Vienne go and we'll settle this between us. She's committed no crime."

There! The needle's free. I pinch it between my thumb and index finger.

"Good," Mimi says. "Keep him talking, cowboy."

"She murdered! She stole!" Stain twists Vienne's hair. "She took the sacrifice I made and threw it in my face!"

"That's not the way I heard it from Riki-Tiki."

"Liar! All lies! That's all you know how to do!"

The bees stir in response to his shouts. Vienne looks up, her face fragile, not wild. Please, I pray, let there be some Regulator left inside. For a second our eyes meet. We hang there together, connected over space. And—

She looks down.

Damn.

"I was *bönpo!*" he screams, bits of foam flying from his mouth. "I was the chosen one who would lead the Tengu the way that Master Rinpoche led the first monks to Mars. But I sacrificed it all so that this, this heifer could live, but no, she threw it all away! If I'd known she would waste her life on a *dalit* Regulator, I would've let our father take her!"

Vienne looks up. Our eyes lock like a laser sight.

"I would've let him violate her again," he continues, "so that she would know the pain of betrayal! I should have known! I—"

"Should've shut the hell up while you had the chance. Now!"

Vienne rams her elbow at his crotch. He blocks her, as I fire the needle at him. With insane ease, Stain stops it with an open palm.

The needles stick into his flesh. Laughing, he raises his palm to show it to me. "Calluses, *dalit.*"

"Neurotoxins. Asshole."

Stain looks at his hand as if it belongs to someone else. Then his eyes roll back in his head. He stumbles and slams the staff on the floor to steady himself. With a sudden surge of air, the bees rush to Stain. They cover his body with theirs, forming a living cocoon.

Down! I shout to myself. Sliding across the waterlogged carpet, I snatch my armalite from the floor and fire a three-round burst into the cocoon.

Behind Stain, the windows shatter. The staff hits the floor, and the bees scatter, swarming into the night air.

"Maybe we're *dalit* scum," I say, pointing my gun at him, "but at least we stick together."

Stain staggers backward to the window. His butt hits the sill. And he sits. His head lolls to the side, and his feet rise off the floor. He presses a hand to his belly, and his eyes fill with utter disbelief.

He looks at his palm.

It's covered in red.

"Blood," he says and starts to teeter.

Vienne snatches his wrist. "Stain!"

He grabs Vienne's arm with both hands and falls back, pulling her with him.

I drop the gun. Leap forward. Grab her ankle.

Hold on for dear life.

"Not this time!" I wedge my feet on the wall and pull. "Let go of her!"

Boom!

The building quivers, and we slide farther out to the very lip of the ledge.

Below us, rapids have swept through the concrete canyons of the city, pulverizing everything out of their path.

There's nothing but water as far as the eye can see.

"Let go of Vienne!" I yell again. "Or so help me, I'll shoot you in the face!"

Stain laughs. With a last effort, he grabs Vienne's shoulder. Her leg begins to slip from my hand. Where are those carking hairs when I need them?

"We die together, sister!"

"No!" I paw the ground with my broken arm. Grab the armalite. Bring the barrel up and with a shaking hand, pull the trigger.

Stain's mouth widens. He lets out a scream as his hands slide from Vienne's arm, and the sudden release throws us both back into the room.

Outside, there's nothing, except the sound of a splash.

Vienne leans over the sill. She gazes into the churning current. I stand next to her. There's no sign of Stain. Two bullets and neurotoxin—he's as good as dead.

"Once upon a time, I jumped out this window," Vienne says in a quiet voice.

"Yes," I say as I catch my breath. "I reckon you did."

"A very long time ago. Before the bad man came. When I was someone else."

I shake my head. "The bad man is gone now. You don't have to worry about him."

"I killed Stain?" she asks, like a child trying to piece a puzzle together.

"No. This was his fault."

Her voice chokes. "I killed that little girl." A tear rolls down her cheek.

How do I argue with that? I take her hand in mine. It is cold. The fingernails are broken. The knuckles are skinned raw.

"But I was someone else then." She looks at me, her blue eyes clouded with pink. "Will I ever be me again?"

"You're still Vienne. You never stopped being Vienne."

"I'm tired," she says. "I want . . . I want to go home."

She shivers, clutching her thin arms to her chest. My heart sinks at the sight of her burned neck, dirty skin, and swollen face. She looks like hell. She's been through hell. All I can do is wrap her in my arms.

Her arms drop listlessly at her sides, and in her eyes I see nothing—no anger, no fear, just a blank slate, a pond with no ripples on the surface.

"Come on, Vienne." I gently lead her by the arm. "I've got you now."

"Oh, cowboy," Mimi says. "What she has endured."

"It will be okay," I tell her, and tell myself as well, hoping it's true. "The monks will know what to do."

Carefully, I guide Vienne back to the fire exit. We climb

the stairs to the ladder that leads to the roof. I throw the bolt, push open the hatch, and pull her up.

The rain has stopped, and a light wind blows her hair.

In the pink hue of dawn, all I can see is the river. Houses, trucks, roofs, debris, the artifacts of a shattered city bob in the current. Near the Seven Bridges, the current forms what looks like a white foam whirlpool, and the sky is clotted with viscous, acrid smoke. The air is still, the city remarkably quiet. We're stuck on a roof, and there's no way to make it out of here.

This is where it all ends.

"It does not," Mimi says. "Don't be such a melodramatist."

"There's no such word as 'melodramatist.'"

"No, cowboy, I am being serious," she says. "Look up."

Tychon's aerofoil drifts overhead, then banks into a shallow dive.

I stick out my thumb.

"Going my way?" he calls over the PA.

I give him a double thumbs-up.

He circles again. The hatch opens, and a gear bag falls onto the far side of the roof. I jog over to retrieve it. Inside, I find a carbon fiber cable, a harness, and a self-inflating balloon.

"That looks like a Fulton Recovery System kit," Mimi says.

"That's because it is."

I strap on the safety harness, clip the cable to the harness and the balloon, then let the balloon inflate. It rises into the sky as Tychon takes the aerofoil in a wide arch. He's bearing down on the roof when I pull Vienne tight against my chest.

"Hold on, soldier. We're going for a ride."

Above us, two horns on the nose of the aerofoil grab the cable, and with a jolt no harder than a kick in the pants, we're lifted off the roof, rising high above Christchurch. Below us, the city is a smoldering ruin, but above us, there's only sun.

CHAPTER 30

Tengu Monastery, Noctis Labyrinthus
Zealand Prefecture
ANNOS MARTIS 238. 7. 29. 22:22

The aerofoil soars low over the arch outside the Tengu Monastery. It lands on the road to the west of the gate, and I climb out of the cargo bay.

"Thanks for the ride," I tell Tychon.

"Anytime." He lifts Vienne from the bay and passes her down to me.

She has been asleep since Tychon hoisted us into the bay, and I wrapped her in a thermal blanket from his first-aid kit, then held her the whole way home.

"Good luck," he says and tips his cap.

When we are clear, he cranks up the engines and begins to taxi down the road.

Vienne doesn't stir when I carry her down the path to the gate. Her head rests in the crook of my neck, her shallow breath warm against my skin.

She's home. It's what she wanted. I must give her to the monks because they are the only ones who can help her heal. But what if doing that means I never see her again? "I can't leave her here, Mimi."

"A promise is a promise, cowboy."

The rains have swelled the moat to twice the depth it was when Vienne and I first crawled off our motorbike, saddle sore and crusted in road dust. In the grimy water, the lotus have blossomed. They are, as always, unstained by the mud.

Ghannouj is sitting cross-legged on a mat outside the gate. He is chanting a prayer, surrounded by dozens of empty teacups.

I stop in front of him. His eyes open. He nods, then rises.

A second later Shoei and Yadokai burst through the gate. The mistress slips past the master, and she is the first to lay hands on Vienne. For a moment, she caresses the scarred line on her neck. Her hands move to her own cheeks, and her ancient face twists with grief.

Yadokai puts an arm around her, and she buries her head in his chest. I start to say something, but Yadokai puts a finger to his lips. He closes his eyes and rests his cheek on Shoei's head. Less than two weeks ago, all they wanted was to teach me how to dance for the Night of Joy during Spirit Festival. In return, I've given them nothing but ghosts.

I turn then to Ghannouj. I don't know whether to speak or not. The monks deserve an explanation. No, it doesn't matter to them how Vienne got hurt. They just need to know that she's alive. The rest they can figure out for themselves.

Hands together, Ghannouj bows so low that his nose is

touching his knees. Then he extends his arms, and I place Vienne in his care.

The pendant, I think, and remove it from my neck. I press it into her hand. Her eyes flutter as I brush my lips against her forehead and whisper, "I love you."

"Farewell," Ghannouj says.

He carries Vienne inside the monastery. Shoei follows on his heels. Without a glance back, Yadokai closes the door, and with a scrape of wood on wood, bolts it.

Then I turn my back on the abbot, the master, and mistress, and even though it kills me, Vienne. She is safe here. It's where she wants to be. It's where she needs to be. But not me. I don't belong anywhere.

I pinch the bridge of my nose to stem the flood of tears that is threatening to rise.

Near the banyan tree, I hear a rustling sound. "Hello?"

There's no answer, but the noise continues for a few more seconds, until I dismiss it as the wind and turn away. Then behind me, there's a bark. I turn around in time to see the dog trot out from under the tree, carrying something in its mouth. It curls up happily against the gate.

"Same dog?" I ask Mimi.

"Same dog," she says, and I smile.

The last ebbs of energy fade from me as I walk the path back to the road, my boots crunching on the gravel. When I get to the road, I stand there for a moment.

"I do have one question," Mimi says in the silence.

"What's that?"

"Where are we going? And are you planning to walk all the way there?"

"That's two questions."

"Who is counting?"

"We both are."

On the horizon, the clouds have cleared completely, and I look up at the sky, wondering what I'm going to do now. Without Vienne. Without a davos. Without my father.

I turn left and walk, wondering what it would be like to live on a world where you can take things like food, shelter, and even air for granted.

My feet feel heavy, and it's hard to keep going.

My breathing. Labored. Light gets brighter, then dims.

A sudden tingling in my hands.

"Mimi?"

And the thought burns. My whole body feels like it's burning as an EMP charge sweeps through me. Then I realize—I've felt this before, as the last glimmer of consciousness twinkles, then fades.

When I wake up, there's a bright light in my face. I raise a hand to block it and realize that my wrists are bound.

"Hold still. Almost done here." The silhouette of Rebecca's face appears in the light. "I felt lousy deceiving you, but I would have felt even more lousy if Lyme had carried through with his threat to destroy my collective. I'm sorry, cowboy. I guess its true—everybody on Mars does have dirt on them. Mr. Lyme. He's all yours."

"Did she say Lyme?" I ask Mimi.

"Did that hussy call you *cowboy*?" she replies.

Rebecca steps aside.

Another silhouette takes her place. A man holds my crappy prosthetic eye pinched between his fingers. "Thank you for being so willing to carry this recording device. It has gathered invaluable data about your artificial intelligence, data that I will use to deliver the coup de grace in my plan to wrest power from the CorpCom governments."

Lyme leans down over me, pushing the hair out of my face, an almost tender gesture. "And yet, despite your part in my grand schemes, I remain so disappointed in you." His face is drawn but healthy. He has gained weight since the last time I saw him, and his skin is no longer full of deep lines and wrinkles. "A great destiny was within your grasp, and by becoming less than you are, you let it slip away. You have forced my hand, and now I have no choice but to compel you to become the man you were born to be."

His head turns to the light, revealing a square jaw and a set of classic Roman features, but I knew him from almost the first words he spoke.

A whisper escapes my lips. "Father."

Acknowledgments

Many heartfelt thanks to the skilled bookmakers at Greenwillow and the lovely folks in HarperCollins Children's school and library marketing; to my fabulous agent, Rosemary Stimola; and finally to Deb, Justin, Caroline, and Delaney, for not letting me get the big head.

Invisible Sun

Excerpts from *Rising Sun*, an original digital novella starring Durango and Mimi, and *Shadow on the Sun*, the final book in the Black Hole Sun trilogy

Jacob Stringfellow, aka Durango, once had a promising career in the elite armed forces. That was before. Before his father betrayed him and his unit. Before he almost died and had an artificial intelligence flash-cloned to his brain. Now Durango and Mimi (the AI) are figuring out how to get along and figuring out how to stay in the game.

Turn the page for an excerpt from *Rising Sun*, a digital novella that is a prequel to David Macinnis Gill's Black Hole Sun trilogy

CHAPTER 0

Taodenni Salt Mine
Near Christchurch, Capital City
ANNOS MARTIS 238. 2. 2. 11:26

"You stink, Stringfellow," a prison guard named Brown says. "Here's another one for your daddy."

He slams the butt of his shotgun into my back, knocking me forward toward an outcropping of salt rock. My feet get tangled in the chain shackled to my ankle, and I stumble, slamming into the caramel-colored crystals, shredding the skin on my hands, and tumbling to the hard-packed grit of the ground.

It feels like my mind separates from my body, rising high into the air, far above the sheer pink-tinged cliffs surrounding the Taodenni Salt Mine. At the bottom of the mine, three guards—Brown, Jones, and the watch captain—dressed in starched khakis, wide-brimmed hats, and teashades, ride herd on a chain-gang crew of miscreants. Dressed in gray tank tops and sweat-stained overalls, the crew is pounding rock by hand. It's the most bone-breaking, back-wrenching, soul-sucking detail in the whole mine. Only the most miserable and despised prisoners get stuck on it.

Miserable and despised. That's me to a T.

I roll onto my side, groaning. Salt seeps into my cut hands, stinging like fiery oil burning through my veins. Three weeks in this mine. Three weeks of busting rock. Three weeks of abuse. Three weeks of moldy bread and putrid water for rations. I have never been so hungry in my life, and I've never wanted to strangle anybody as much as the guard standing over me, ready to pound my face to mush if I so much as twitch.

"Oh, how the mighty has fallen." Brown laughs.

"Have," I say, squinting from the pain.

"Have what?" Brown says, blocking out the sun with his fat head.

"*Have* fallen. It's how the mighty *have* fallen," I say. "They don't teach grammar in prisoner guard school? Or is the curriculum limited to just physical abuse?"

He puts a jackboot on my bruised kidney. "You got a smart mouth, convict."

"It matches my ass," I say. "I like to coordinate."

That earns me a whack on the knee, which sends a bolt of pain to my cerebral cortex. I grunt again. I despise grunting.

"Next one's right in the teeth," he says. "I don't care how many medals you got or who your papa is."

Once upon a time, a group of scientists, soldiers, and adventurers left Earth to settle on the barren planet Mars. Known as the Founders, they created a fledgling society under habidomes and labored together to begin the centuries-long process of terraforming the planet. Over time, the Founders gave way to the Orthocracy and its leader, the Bishop. They were in turn replaced by the CorpCom prefectures.

One of those CorpCom CEOs was my father, who was one month ago convicted of a plethora of crimes, the worst of which was treason. He's now serving time in the Norilsk gulag, and I am now incarcerated, awaiting my own trial while I do hard labor in the pit of a salt mine.

My name is Jacob Stringfellow, and I'm seven and a half Mars years old, making me fifteen on planet Earth. I'm a former Regulator and, if you believe my father, former future prince of Mars. My friends call me Durango. Others, like Brown, call me all sorts of things.

"Host," the omnipresent voice in my head says, "that statement is contrary to all available data. You have been referred to by only six names and nicknames in your lifetime. Would you like me to list them?"

That is the voice of the artificial intelligence flash-cloned to my brain three months ago to help me overcome severe head trauma suffered in battle. She talks in my head, using the voice of my former chief, Mimi, but she's nothing like my chief was. For instance, she has no sense of humor.

"Host," she says, "I was not programmed for humor."

I tap my right temple, which activates the subdermal microphone on my larynx, allowing me to "talk" to "her."

"You've got a gift for the obvious, computer," I whisper.

"Host," she says, "it is no longer necessary to speak aloud when addressing me. To improve efficiency, I have rerouted the signal along neural pathways so that you only need sub-vocalize your commands."

"That's handy." I subvocalize by moving my lips but not making sounds.

"Off your ass," Brown barks. "You're bogging down the line."

I get to my feet, which isn't easy considering that I'm chained to other convicts. There are sixteen of us linked to this main chain. There are more than fifty convicts on the gang.

"Sorry," I say to the poor sap to my left.

He's a former barrister who made the mistake of defending my father in court. He doesn't answer because he's not talking to me. In his shoes, I wouldn't be either, not when you've lost everything defending a war criminal who turned humongous bioengineered insects loose on his own soldiers.

With the sun beating down on us, I doff my hat and wipe sweat from my mop top of hair with a forearm. That's the silver lining about doing time—I don't have to chop off my hair anymore. So long, military buzz cut.

"Taking off," I yell to Brown.

He nods, and I strip off my sweaty work shirt. My ribs may be protruding due to a hollow belly, but pounding rock has thickened my muscles, and the sun's browned my skin.

But nothing can hide the battle scars that being a Regulator left on me, especially the thick purple ones that run like a vein over my shoulder and across the right side of my face.

"Nice abs, Stringfellow," says the raggedy woman chained to my right foot.

It's her first day on the chains, and she's already coated in sweat and dirt, bandanna over her red hair, her freckles occluded by dust. Her name is Rosa Lynn Malinche. Like the barrister, she was sentenced to hard labor without trial, but we're still on speaking terms. "Can I wash my overalls on them later?"

"Not a good plan." I swing my hammer to hide the blush blooming on my face. The butterscotch-colored rock explodes beneath it. Mars was once known as the red planet, but in the wilderness areas not changed by terraforming, it's mostly dark yellow or the color of rust from all the iron in the soil. "I'm ticklish."

"Ticklish?" Malinche says, shaking her head. "You're still such a kid."

I blush again, then start when I hear a gunshot fired in the distance.

"That was not gunfire, host," my computer says. "Data indicate that was a backfire from a vehicle. It is impossible to discern at this point in time the type, make, and model of said vehicle."

I tap my right temple. "Could you stop referring to me as *host*? It makes me feel like a germ factory."

"Affirmative," she says. "How would you like to be addressed?"

"How about Cowboy? It's what you called me when you were, you know, alive."

"Available data suggest that is inaccurate," she says. "You were a Regulator, not a cowboy. There are no cowboys on Mars. The term itself is anachronistic even on Earth."

"Whatever," I say. "It's what Mimi called me, so deal with it."

"Confirmed," she says. "I will deal with it."

"Thank you."

"Cowboy," she says, "would it be possible for you in turn to desist referring to this entity as *computer*? I assure you that I am as much superior to a computer as you are to a stuffed horse."

I never thought of it that way, but she's right. She counts way better than a stuffed horse. Smells better, too. "All right," I say. "What do you want to be called?"

"I prefer to be referred to as Mimi."

I stop, stunned. The handle of the sledgehammer slips through my hands, and I grab the steel head to save it from dropping. A knot forms in my throat as I remember Mimi—the real Mimi—dying in my arms in battle. "I reckon I could get used to that."

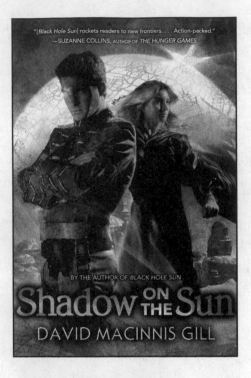

Read on for an excerpt from *Shadow on the Sun*, the final book in the Black Hole Sun trilogy

CHAPTER 0

Hell's Cross
Outpost Fisher Four
ANNOS MARTIS 239. 1. 12. 08:01

Ice forms on the lens of his scope as Fuse waves the red dot sight of his armalite above the soldier's ear. The blighter is a Sturmnacht scout, and he's no more welcome near the Hell's Cross mines than a chigger at an Orthocrat's garden party.

In the year or so since deserting his old soldiering life and coming to live among the miners, Fuse has seen more and more of Lyme's Sturmnacht deployed to Fisher Four. Where once you went months without seeing outsiders, now you couldn't hock a loogie without hitting one of those jack-booted thugs.

"C'mon now," Fuse says as the frigid air freeze-dries his breath.

With overgrown hair, thin sideburns, missing teeth, and ears too long for his pointed chin, Fuse rests against the iron-gated entrance to the mines.

The Sturmnacht soldier crests the hill. He scans the ridge with a pair of omnoculars.

"Stop moving about, see?" Fuse says. "I'm a fair din-kum shot in the right conditions." Especially if the conditions include a few kilos of C-42 explosives and a remote detonator.

When the soldier's gaze falls on the iron gate emblazoned with the words *No Work, No God*, he raises his rifle.

"Oy! The bugger's spotted me," Fuse says under his breath. "It's now or never."

He pulls the trigger. The crack of gunfire echoes across the Prometheus Basin, and the sound rises into the steel blue sky. The bullet hits the frozen tundra. It spits chunks of ice and snow into the scout's goggles. But except for gouging a large hole in the ground, it does no damage.

The scout turns to run.

"Carfargit, Fuse! You can't hit the broad side of a broadside!" He sights down the scope. He finds the target again.

Crack!

The next bullet hits nothing but air.

"I'll be stuffed," Fuse says. "I should've just blown the blaggard up."

He aims for a third shot, hands shaking.

Too late. The scout has reached the crest of the ridge. He's signaling his comrades. Fuse switches his scope to distance view. A few kilometers away, a company of armored turbo sleds turns toward the scout.

"Fuse! You call yourself a Regulator!" Swinging his rifle

over his shoulder, he tromps through a snowdrift to his bike, a hodgepodge of spare parts that can break a hundred forty kilometers per hour.

If he can get it started.

And if it doesn't explode.

Again.

He jumps on the seat, grabs the steering bar, and kicks the starter. The engine sputters to life, and he pats the gas tank. "That's my baby!"

As the sound of the Sturmnacht sleds grow louder, Fuse guns the engine and rips across the tundra, the studs on his tires chewing up chunks of ice. He plows past a steel tower lift mechanism and the tipple, then several small mounds of heavy guanite ore.

The bike skitters past a sign declaring DANGER! NO ADMITTANCE! His headlight shines on a small tunnel with smooth walls. He hunkers low, afraid to snag his noggin on the ceiling. Then with a squeal of brakes, he brings the bike to a stop. He grabs a signal box from a hidden nook. Types in the pass code. Then presses the dual ignition buttons.

Boom!

At the far end of the tunnel, the roof collapses, blocking the entrance to the east mines. If the Sturmnacht want to catch him, they'll have to haul butt to the west side, which he'd blow, too. If he had time.

But time's not on his side.

"Note to self." He taps his temple. "When the hurly-burly's done, get your carcass over here and open a wormhole in Tunnel B7."

Back on the bike, he zooms across the high-arched stone bridge that stretches across a mammoth gorge. Above is a sky of stone. Below is a dark abyss that some say reaches Mars's cold iron core.

Fuse reaches the far side and throttles down. He coasts into Hell's Cross, the former central complex of a subterranean mining town, now almost deserted. Faded flags hang from the arches. Rusted razor wire tops all the cracked stucco walls. Everything is coated in a fine coat of guanite dust. Home sweet home it ain't.

Fuse parks his bike in a flat-roofed corridor littered with empty crates. He runs up a flight of steps. Huffing for breath, he throws open the third door on the left and yells, "Áine! The Sturmnacht are coming!"

On a mattress in the corner, Áine rests with her back against the wall. Her moon-shaped face is puffy and covered in red blotches, and her pregnant belly strains against her threadbare overalls. She looks liable to pop in a nanosecond.

Áine's grandmother, Maeve, hovers nearby. Maeve's face is framed with silver hair and furrowed with wrinkles as deep as a canyon. As far as Fuse knows, she's the oldest person on the planet—he's never seen another mug so puckered and craggy.

"How d'you know they's the Sturmnacht?" Áine asks.

"I spotted a scout." Fuse frowns. "And he spotted me back."

"I told you to shoot anything that moved!" Áine says.

"I'm not like Jenkins was—shooting's not my thing, you know that," Fuse says. "Blowing stuff up is."

"Zip it!" Áine struggles to her feet. "There's no use in it now. We'll hole up in one of the survival vaults. Live on the emergency supplies. It's the only chance we've got."

Maeve clucks and shakes her head. "You're in no condition to run, Áine."

"She's in no condition to get press-ganged by the Sturmnacht, neither," Fuse says. "Those slavers need strong backs to reopen the guanite mines, and if you ain't fit for work, they'll find something else you're good at. Come on, you lot, let's get her moving."

Maeve gives a tight-lipped smile. "Since when do I take orders from you, Regulator?"

"Since right this minute." Fuse leads Áine down the stairs and through the courtyard, her head resting on his shoulder.

"There's a power sled 'round back," he says. "Step lively now. We've not got much time."

He lifts Áine into the ore loader. Maeve stuffs pillows behind her back and supports her head, then hauls herself into the driver's seat and starts the loader up.

Fuse kisses Áine and then scowls at Maeve. "Take care of my wife and little one."

"Who happen to be my granddaughter and great grandchild." Maeve tries to laser him with her eyes. "Don't you forget that."

Fuse's lip twitches as he turns to leave. The things he'd like to say. But now's not the time.

Áine grabs his jacket. "Where'd you think you're going?"

"To the surface," he says. "If you're to live, I've got to find help."

"I always knew you'd run out on me!" Áine says.

Fuse kisses her hand. "Ain't running out on you. Your grandmum's right here. Besides, I'm useless at this birthing business." He jumps to the ground as the loader starts to pull away. He blows her a kiss. "No child of mine is going to be born a slave. You've got to hide, before it's too late!"

"Nobody can help us!" Her bloated face turns into a sneer. "It's already too late!"

That's where you're wrong, Fuse thinks as he jogs toward a wormhole that will take him to the surface. *There's two somebodies that can help us. All I've got to do is find them before the Sturmnacht kill you.*